Pillow Talk

in the *Heat* of the *Night*

with

Elissa Gabrielle & Rory D. Sheriff
Lorraine Elzia & K. Roland Williams
Carla Pennington & Kenneth Alan Campbell
Niyah Moore & Stacey L. Moor
LaLaina Knowles & Marc Lacy
Ebonee Monique & Torrian Ferguson
Renee Daniel Flagler & Alvin L.A. Horn

Peace in the Storm Publishing
Giving Your Soul a Rise...One Page at a Time

Praise for Pillow Talk in the Heat of the Night

"Hiding in Plain Sight stirs up a medley of emotions and will have you swaying rhythmically in your seat as you read each line of this seductive literary pièce de résistance, written by the Dynamic Duo, Elissa Gabrielle and Rory Sheriff. Imagine warm, flowing chocolate, sweet and tempting as it can be...each chapter makes you want to stick your finger in and grab just a taste of what the characters are experiencing. Like the waters of two springs destined to meet, the words of these two writers come together to create a river of harmony that's sure to quench your literary thirst."

—SD Denny, Author and Freelance Editor

"From the moment I picked up 'If Only He Knew', I was drawn into the life of Taylor Middleton. This story made me laugh and cry as I rooted for the heroine to get her happily ever after. An erotic tale of how people can find love in the most unlikely places and circumstances. Love truly does conquer all. 'If Only He Knew' is a must read."

—Erotic Author Serenity King

"Triple Dribble is a real triple play for the reader, it's filled to the brim with love, desire and poetic flow, I could see the players and the plays in my mind's eye. I was also left unsure what love connection to root for and that's a good thing. You will have to run down the court and enjoy the game. Triple Double...A Tale of Lust and Basketball is that haute read that takes the reader there and satisfied. The poetic renderings are a very sexy addition. This story brings the fire."

—Angelia Vernon Menchan, Publisher-Author

"Heartache, pain, deception and passion! How rapidly Regina's most joyous occasion transformed into an unimaginable day of pain and strife. Leading her directly into a parallel dimension of unexpected deep sensual eroticism! Domenick's obvious commitment and unconditional love eventually led him to a pain that could never be reversed or overshadowed. That was until he was graced with Regina's true essence and unexpected night of nerve shattering passion. Carla & Kenneth really lit the reader's imaginations with this gut wrenching ride of illuminating excitement."

—Craig Pinckney Refour, author of *A King's Genetic Memory*

"Wow, the magic of love and attraction is the pulse of this story. I couldn't stop reading, couldn't take my eyes from the page, couldn't help imagining me in that place. Kudos to the authors for this wonderful love story that leaps off the pages and makes us all feel the heat of true passion."

—Diane Dorce', Author of *Loving Penny, Devil In the Mist, 52 Broad Street* and collaborator in **Bloggers Delight** with "Smoke." CEO and Publisher of Firefly Publishing & Entertainment LLC.

"Up, up and away in the clouds of lust, you won't need a parachute to break your fall as you land into the heat of this collaboration; Lorraine Elzia and K. Roland Williams. After its perusal you'll want another flight in passion. PHEW."

—William Fredrick Cooper,
ESSENCE® Bestselling Author of
There's Always a Reason

Table of Contents

If Only He Knew..7

Renee Daniel Flagler & Alvin L.A. Horn

No Competition 49

Niyah Moore & Stacey L. Moor

Triple Dribble 96

LaLaina Knowles & Marc Lacy

A Night to Forget 158

Carla Pennington & Kenneth Alan Campbell

Hedonism... 194

Lorraine Elzia & K. Roland Williams

Accidental Orgasm 257

Ebonee Monique & Torrian Ferguson

Hiding in Plain Sight.. 287

Elissa Gabrielle & Rory D. Sheriff

If Only He Knew

By Renee Daniel Flagler & Alvin L.A. Horn

Don't they know I can hear them?

"We're going to keep her sedated for a day or two longer. I don't want her moving around."

No! Please.

"Okay, doc, I'll make sure the nightshift knows to keep her on her sedation drip. I don't think she should move either. With a collapsed lung and multiple contusions, we need to keep her stabilized. I must say, even with the swelling, she's beautiful…and lucky to be alive. "

Lucky to be alive?

"Yes, she is. Her regular doctor came in to check on her. She said Ms. Middleton had been under her care for several years. She's a tough cookie and she's been through a lot. She even lost all of her hair at one point, but never her beauty or her will. This here is a minor setback. I fully expect her to recover."

"Looking at her now; it's almost hard to believe that at one time she didn't have any hair. Now she has a head full. She reminds me of my aunt with all that red hair against that brown skin." The doctor sighed and fell silent for a moment. "Would it be okay if I come in and keep an eye on her? I want to make sure we take extra care of her. It looks like she doesn't have anybody. On her chart there isn't anyone listed as an emergency contact."

"That would be nice."

I'm getting tired again. I feel so heavy. It must be that drip. It makes me feel…warm. Something is covering me. Can someone stop that damn beeping… go away. I can't open my eyes. Can't feel my tears. Wait…what are they saying now? Oh, Lord…am I being drugged…I feel a rush of, of, of…I feel myself breathing…I hear music…and…

I've always loved me some Prince and *Adore* has always been my favorite song. He sang that thing like he meant it. "I truly adore you." I love singing along with him. It sounded like he loved whomever deeply. I wished Emerson had kept on adoring me, but I've moved past him and all that hurt. "Right?" I ask myself aloud. "Yes, right!" I answered myself. Damn, he done drove me crazy, but as I look in my mental rearview mirror I see a new me– recovered! I'm whole again, moving forward and he is disappearing from my view. Good-bye Emerson; you were only a moment in my past.

The drive across the Golden Gate Bridge with my top down always makes me feel good. The feel of the soft, cool air caressing my skin soothes my soul. "Lord, thank you for this healing sun," I said out loud touching my…chest. I love when the tails of my head scarf blows behind me in the wind. It reminds me of a scene from one of those old school movies. It's going to be a wonderful sunset, and I can't wait to get to my favorite spot to take it all in.

The sun kisses me
And I kiss right back
I turn to the sun for embraces of heat
But come nighttime
I embrace the dark side of the moon and my lover and I do things that cast no shadows of doubt

But come the morning sun
I kiss my lover before I kiss the sun
Because I need the sun, but I want my lover when the sun goes down

That's good. I'll have to write that down after I park. "Oh no!" I pushed the wrong button again and now my song is stuck on repeat. I love my convertible BMW Z4 Roadster, but I have to learn which buttons are which. I always dreamed of owning this car and finally decided to get it as a present to myself for all I had gone through. It would have been nice to have had Emerson driving as I sit back, taking in the breeze with my pretty toes on the dash while the sun tans them. I wish I could reach over to his skin and push my finger into those deep wells he calls dimples and clefs. I hear Prince sing *Adore*, as we take in the lush hillside. But it's all over and I'm treating myself to living life without him. Shoot! It's his loss anyway. There's more to life than…well, anyway. I'm a good woman. He lost out.

Uh oh! I almost missed my turn. I can't wait to see the sun hitting the hillside park. And as usual, when I get to this point I have to deal with the teens blasting their loud stereos. Who told them everybody wanted to hear their music? I can't even hear myself think. And do they have to drive right behind me, assaulting my peace? It's a good thing they park on the higher level on the other side of the park, out of my way. Over there they can be loud, drink, and do God knows what else and I can enjoy my sunsets without their distractions.

❧

This kid is riding my bumper like we're connected by a tow hitch. Come on, now! Geez! He's so close I feel like I should ask him if he wants to get out of his car and jump in my backseat. These kids annoy me. I'm not driving any faster on these curves. So he'll have to wait. The roads are too narrow for him to go around my little car anyway! I mean, I love my music, but that's not music to me, and if they turn their radio up any louder they're going to shake something loose.

I narrow my eyes and zero in on the perfect parking spot and now I can say goodbye to those boisterous teens. They need to learn to take it easy on these hills…racing around these curves like they're crazy. One of these days they're going to have an accident. I'd hate to see them get stuck up on one of these embankments.

Ah, yeah! Overlooking the Golden Gate Bridge, the city, and the ocean from here calms me from the inside out. The caress of the winds whispering through the trees, lovebirds strolling around holding hands…seeing the windswept trees and people strolling down below on the trails…I wish I had someone to walk hand-in-hand with down there near the water.

Let me get out and stretch and let this sun drench my skin. Hmm. Oh, it feels so good.If I could, I would take off all my clothes and let the sun soak right through to my soul. I might have been daring enough when I had my double D's, but now… all I have are these scars snaking across my flat chest as a pathetic reminder. No amount of fake padding can hide what used to be there. I'm sure any man or woman can see I have no boobs, or maybe I'm just being self-conscious.

I see how men look at me. I can't help but think they discard me in search for women with bigger breasts, or simply bigger than mine, and that wouldn't take much. My boobs may be gone, but my behind is still in full play no matter what. Speaking of which, my damn thong is playing hide and seek again. I hope nobody is looking because I've got to move it out a little. Oooh, that feels better. Glad I wore this sundress…easy access, lift, get in, and get out.

I pull out my blanket and find a spot on the grass to lie down and let the sunset mesmerize me. I pull up my sundress a little so my legs can get sun, too. This feels so good.

Emerson. Here he goes again, popping into my mind. I can't stand that I still desire him. I need to focus on forgetting. I close my eyes and begin to enjoy the kisses of the sun's rays. This is peaceful; let me take a little nap.

"It's me, baby," he says as he strolls his long legs toward me in those damn perfect fitting jeans. "I was stupid, but you know how I feel about you. I do miss you."

"I don't know, Em. You hurt me pretty bad. You can't seem to make up your mind on whether you can handle me not having…I don't want to go through that again," I said what my brain told me to, but my body betrayed me. I could feel my womanhood beginning to swell and pulsate a little. "I don't think I can do this again."

"But, babe," he said with a husky rumble in his voice. My clit heard his voice and tried to answer him. I squeezed my legs and my eyes shut, but I felt wetness pooling in both places. "Can we talk about it? If nothing more, can I have you, baby? I want you. I miss your touch." His tone dropped to and even sexier octave.

My clit wanted to answer again. I turned my back so he couldn't see me struggle to keep it together. Why did I do that? Emerson walked up behind me and placed his hands on my hips. This is what he wanted —not to face me. His touch scorched my skin. I pretended his hands were paws, yet my desire continued to soar. He pleaded with me with hot, tender kisses along my neckline. I gnawed at my bottom lip. I want him to face what we can't seem to face.

I didn't want to be a fool again, but I needed to feel that sweet pain, though I knew my heart would feel like its tearing apart afterwards. I close my eyes again, trying to get my body and brain on the same page. He caressed my ass and then slid his hand toward my womanhood from behind. He avoids the rest of my body…my missing…removed breasts. My heart wanted him to stop, but my body lost the battle. His kissed my neck to seal the deal as my juices dripped past my thong. I need his hardness.

Emerson picked me up from behind and carried me to my dining room table. I reach forward, knocking things that don't break onto the floor and clearing space for my body. I spread my arms wide and hold onto the edge. As he'd always done so eloquently, from behind, he slid his tongue inside my fiery wetness.

"I've been dying to taste you."

He didn't even bother to take my thong off. Instead, he lapped my juices with his tongue. Sliding my thong aside, I reached back, spread, and then lifted my behind higher. Lightning quickened throughout my body and a groan caught in my throat. Emerson pressed his girth into me. I lost the battle with my heart at that moment. My body began to quiver under the pressure. I couldn't believe how quickly he'd driven me to the edge. On the brink of insanity, I whipped my head from side to side. My body began to quake. He pushed himself inside as far as he could go. With a slight burning, my body squeaked against the table from the friction we created. He slammed against me like an animal void of any kind of human passion. He dripped sweat into the small of my back. The roughness satisfied the urgency of my longing, but left me feeling raw...exposed.

It obviously felt good to him as he continued with ravenous strokes until he lost control of his own rhythm. Only the unadulterated lust remained. I didn't feel wanted. I was a means to an end. I could have panicked; I could have run to save my soul. Instead, I moved quickly, crawling away hands first, coming off the table and breaking my fall as best as I could. I scampered across the floor backwards, never taking my eyes off of him until my back hit the wall.

"Emerson!" I called out frantically; he peered at me. I looked under the table and the sight of his pants around his ankles added to my insulted being. "Emerson! You're acting like an animal. You can't even stand to face me. You don't want me as the woman that I am any more. You need to go! Go now!

"But, baby..."

"No!" I cried. "No breasts, no ass, no love. If you can't love all of me, you don't get to love me at all." I screamed, "I am still a woman! I am, I am! Now get out of here."

"Miss! Wake up." Someone started shaking me.

"Miss. Are you okay? He yelled.

"I'm not dead." I snap at the kid, embarrassed. It's a young man, probably freighted. I look around to get my bearings straight. I'm still in the park, lying down on my blanket with my sundress hiked up to the top of my thigh. The park had turned dark reds and browns with the last warm glow of the sun going over the horizon, casting soft glows and dim shadows from the lights of the Golden Gate Bridge.

"Ma'am. It's getting pretty late. I'll help you to your car."

Who the heck is he calling ma'am? I promptly thanked him as he helped me to my feet. Without another word, I gathered my blanket and other belongings and quickly escaped to my car.

I couldn't leave yet. I sat behind the wheel trying to get a hold of what happened. I buried my face in my hands and took a deep breath. Then I felt for my breasts. They still weren't there and the pain of no love lingered along with the end of a bad lover affair.

Chapter Two

"This is Niles Groove, your main man on your favorite Bay Area radio station. For all the lovers who gladly escaped the rush hour traffic and are now heading to the beach or their favorite park or you're sitting on your deck relaxing…I have a few words for you."

I faced the sun looking across the Golden Gate Bridge
Will love be there?
I walk in a rhythm
The breeze of the harbor helps to guide me
I never kissed my love
I never held my lover's hand
I've only seen pictures in my soul of my lover
I imagine my lover's voice
I walk the footpath of the Golden Gate Bridge

I stop in the middle
I wait for my love to arrive from the other side
I'm earlier …by hours
I don't want to be late
I pace to the other side where love will enter the footpath
I devour the sun and wait for love
I absorb the harbor lights to replace the setting sun
I'm in the middle, waiting as other lovers stroll by
Car taillights and headlights wiz by
A car stops in the middle of traffic
A horn honks as love exits a taxi, and run and joins me
We watch the harbor lights in silence
We hear our love song
We hold hands
We kiss
We leave together

"This is your main man, Niles Groove on your favorite Bay Area radio station. I hope you love that poem sent in by one of our listeners."

I'm sitting here listening to the radio in the park again. You wouldn't think I would come back after my last nightmare on my blanket. But I'm okay. I've had my moments like anyone who has felt love. Occasional thoughts of the past creep up and can drive anyone crazy. I'm human and sometimes memories of the past can make old pains appear fresh. I remember the day Emerson made it crystal clear that he couldn't handle being with me, yet I had sex with him one more time after he walked out. I'll never forget how he left.

He knocked lightly on the door, as if he didn't want me to answer. I had been sitting for three days, stewing in my anger and wearing nothing more than a tank top and panties. I decided to look reality square in the face and accept the truth he'd been showing me for weeks. Emerson didn't want me!

I answered the door anyway.

"Emerson?" I almost screamed and narrowed my eyes at the target of my anger. "How dare you show up at my door unannounced after what you did to me?" My lip quivering, I willed my tears not to fall. I wanted to shut the door in his face, but something in me felt that I deserved an explanation.

"I need to grab a few things and I'll be out of your way." Emerson tried to step around me and I stopped him by pressing my hand in the center of his chest.

Emerson huffed as if I were the one who had done him wrong. Fire flashes in my eyes. "That's it? You stand me up, disappear for days—no calls, texts, emails or anything—and you...you show up here today to get your things without any kind of explanation?" He huffed again. I reared my head back. "Oh, I'm sorry. I must have gotten it twisted; I thought I was your woman."

"Look…I can't do this anymore." He held his hands up in surrender and then tried to step around me.

Before I could protest, the tears sprang from my eyes. Those words pierced me like daggers to the heart. Hurt replaced my anger and I wanted answers.

"Why are you doing this to me?" Subconsciously, I touched my chest where my 38 D's stood proud before my surgery and I felt my heart slam into my stomach.

Emerson's eyes followed the path of my hand, and then he stepped around me. I couldn't move. I didn't move as he went into the bedroom, bathroom and front closet to gather the few things he'd left at my house. Then I watched him walk out of my house.

Tears streamed down my face.

I pull myself from that awful memory and try to focus on the beautiful sunset in front of me. Although traces of the pain he caused me remain, I'm over him. I look at the people strolling around enjoying the fresh air, the setting sun and simply life in general. I love my life.

Today, I'm staying in my car. I'll sit here and listen to some music, do a little people watching, and read my new book, *Peace in the Storm*. I read over my favorite passage.

LOVE SHADOWS
Cast shadows from sunsets of dreams
Like a rising tide love hungers to expand into sunrises
Fresh breezes like kisses I await
If only arms around me were a part of my time and space
If only a blowing on my collarbone were more than wishes and
feelings drifting in and becoming true
Rocking slowly I fight to keep my balance between dreams and
reality
For now, fantasies come and go in waves
I see what my heart aches for when I close my eyes
She leans her head on his back and wraps tight
They slow dance to the rhythm of still waters runs deep
He turns
Him and those dreamy eyes
Searing passions reflect double vision
He and I sink to sea floor and make a bed
Make love
Ecstasy floats up like champagne bubbles
The water breaks in joyful sensual turbulences
We rock
The water is still
I open my eyes
I'm dreaming of sunrises
Its cravings and swimming in love shadows…casting desires

As I look up from the page, I catch a glimpse of a fine specimen. Wow and wow! Speaking of shadows! He is worth the price of admission if there's a VIP ticket. A man…no let me rephrase that, a *gorgeous* man strolled past my car. I can only see his profile and from behind both of them looked good. I smell fine from a distance. He is nice and tall. At five-nine, I know a tall man when I see one, even when I'm sitting. His stride covered the earth. I grab my iPod, get out of the car, and sit on the bench. "Where is he?" I say out loud. Dang, I lost him. I look down the path in the direction I saw him walking. There he is. "Shoot! He's with a woman," I said and then look around to make sure no one heard me. She looks like a young chick, too. Some men like 'em young.

Well, at least my eyes were sprinkled with the delightful confectionery of a good-looking man. I'll never get mad at a little eye candy.

She looks so secure walking down the trail wrapped in his arms. Yes, I'm hating! She gazes at him as if he is the light of her world. That will be me one day. 'Let me stop tripping." I laugh to myself.

Let me go back to my car and sit back and enjoy the sunset as I listen to my music. *Damn, that man is fine.* Or at least what I could see of him is. The good ones are always taken. Some women don't care, but I do. I'm not interested in sharing. I want my man all to myself. The thought of having the warmth of a man causes small flames to ignite in my center. I swear, I need to find a man that can appreciate a woman like me, so I can get some…I mean, so I can have some companionship. As much as I love watching the sunset, it would be so much better to take in the beauty of it with someone significant.

I hope that happened sooner rather than later. It would be great to have more satisfaction than my fingers or my toys can bring. Like when I get that feeling in the pit of my core. I didn't want to always be the one to put out my own fire.

I look around, happy about my little corner of the park, as if it's carved out with me in mind. I lean back and lay my head on the headrest, hypnotized by the orange glow as the sun gave way to the night. I sit here thinking about the eye candy that passed by and all the things he could do to my body if he wasn't with another woman.

I look around one last time before I slide further down into the seat and lift my sundress in an attempt to rub out the heat rising between my legs. Warm moisture dampened my panties, causing me to breathe deeper. I tried to resist the urge, but…no…the need to satisfy myself once again is here.

The sun is dipping lower into the midnight blue sea as it cast deeper hues of orange across the horizon. A groan rose in my throat. My body has a mind of its own and a wanting that can't be dashed, leaving me no choice but to give in. I slip one finger inside me and my juices respond quickly. I angle my pelvis for better access and dip my fingers until the edges of my skin are liquid boiling hot.

I rub more vigorously, imagining that my hands were the hands of that fine man. In my mind I fill in the parts of his face that were blocked by the sun. I make him as gorgeous as I knew he had to be. I roll my lips in and slide my tongue across them. His face flashes before me and my whole center throbs so much that it almost hurts.

My head whips back and I grind my hips against the rhythm of my fingers hard until it feels like my pores are going to burst. Then it begins. First, it feels like a flame and it grows into an all-consuming fire and then an explosion. I feel myself rise out of my own presence and float back down to reconnect. The aftermath is rippling through me several times, causing the muscles all over my body to tighten. After the last wave has surged through me, I relax my shoulders and take a deep breath. Between my legs, the car seat is wet and the remnant of my essence covers my fingers.

I lean over and pull wet wipes from the glove compartment to clean off my hands and thighs. Needing a few more moments of stillness, I sit enjoying the cool crisp whisper of the night air as it caresses my skin. The dense darkness enveloped me like a smooth blanket, until my breathing returned to normal. I look around to make sure I don't have an audience, crank up my car and drive back over the Golden Gate Bridge with a smile.

Chapter Three

Those kids and their loud music were in front of me again, even though I arrived earlier than usual to avoid them. I know it is a large truck, but how legal is it to have all those people in the back? In my little BMW I can't see around it. They have the nerve to drive slowly when any other time they were behind me they were riding my bumper.

One of the girls is looking at me crazy. I'm sure she can't figure out why I'm smiling like a Cheshire cat. Despite these wild, crazy kids, I'm still smiling on the inside at the vision of that man I saw in the park. I don't care that he has a woman! Well, I do, but there is no harm in looking.

I'm glad my sexuality is finally coming back, and it is coming on strong. My doctor said my sexual desire will raise after all the chemo and other drugs were out of my system. I feel better about myself. My body is on fire and oh boy, the day before, my fingers went for a walk in the park between my thighs. Lately, my clit seems like a magnet for my fingers and toys. Even after yesterday in the park, I had to go home and get off again.

It still stings my soul looking up at all those young girls. They all have breasts pointing to the sky, and I don't have anything to point anywhere. On the other hand, despite that I'm lacking in that department, I still have my soul and I am still a beautiful woman.

Ah, finally that truck is speeding off and I see a nice place to park right next to my favorite bench. I look over to where I sat alone pleasuring myself yesterday, and laugh out loud. I hope someone don't think I'm crazy.

It's hotter than yesterday, and the sun is warming my arms and face. I feel sweat running down my back and I'm glad I didn't wear any undies—free and breezy. I want to go back to my car to get sun block, but I don't want to leave my things here on the bench. I can see my car from where I am and figure no one is going to run off with my book and my water, so I take only my phone. I don't worry about my car because I have an alarm that works even when I leave my top down. If anyone reaches into my car the alarm horn will start to blare. I click my alarm off and lean over and I spot my sun block on the floor.

"Excuse me, Miss."

Oh, Lord, a man is talking to me and I have my big butt bent over the door—all up in the air.

"Sorry to bother you, Miss, but my cell phone battery died. I always forget to plug it in."

I look out the corner of my eye as I start to stand up straight and see him! The man I'd been spotting walking through the park. He is standing right in front of my car. The same man starring in my fantasy love life. His voice sounds like Larry Graham's in the song, *One in a Million*. I drop the sun screen on the seat and some spills on the leather. I turn toward him and try to speak, but my throat is dry. I swallow hard and shade my eyes from the sun, buying time so I can look at him a little longer.

"I'm sorry…what did you say? I smile to appear friendly, but I'm smiling because I'm embarrassed.

"I'm sorry to bother you; I guess I should have waited until you were done. My problem is that my phone is dead and I need to make two quick, but important calls. If you want you can hold my wallet for security if need be. Can I please use your phone?"

Still a bit speechless, I walk to the front of my car, but keep some space between him and me. I'm sure I'm in no danger; I feel a sense of shyness is controlling my ability to speak. He holds out his wallet. I shrug my shoulders, and shake my head no, and then hand him my phone. I feel self-conscious of my non-existent boobs and step back.

"Thank you." He nods and smiles. "I have the same phone." His voice feels like it's coming through the ground. My toes stir in my sandals.

"Yes. They don't hold a charge for long. I have to keep it plugged in all the time." I'm happy I'm finally able to put a sentence together.

He starts to dial. I watch his long, thick finger. Why does the air feel so hot? He turns to the side a bit and starts to talk, giving me a nice view of his body. He is built like one of those guys who ride in the Tour de France, only he is dipped in blackberry juice. I'm barely able to hear his conversation. He is letting someone know he will cover the late shift if he has to. He hangs up and glances toward me. "One more quick call and I'll be out of your hair," he says and flashes another sexy smile.

I nod and swallow, trying to lessen the dryness in my throat. If he only knew I want his hands to run through my hair. My eyes are stuck on his handsome face, which is not a bad place to gaze. Now I wish I'd worn panties. I'm melting between my thighs looking at his body.

Whoever is on the other end of the phone made him smile and placed happiness on his face. I can't help but listen as best as I can, and I hear him say, "Hey sweetheart, where are you? I've been waiting to see you all day. I have some good news for us."

This man has called his woman on my phone. Is he crazy?

"Oh, you're here? You're down by the trail head? I'll see you in a few." He hands my phone back with a too-damn-happy smile.

"Are you done?" I ask, holding my hand out.

"I appreciate you letting me use your phone. Thank you so much." He turned to walk away, but stops. "Oh, by the way, with your beautiful golden-brown skin, you should put on some sun block to protect yourself from the sun's rays." Despite my annoyance, his comment and smile made me melt a little more.

He grins at me as if he is an expert on what I need. What I need is for him to go away. And he does. Damn, why does his butt have to be so perfect…ugh! I walk back to my bench and sit down too hard. "Ouch!" Then I realize I left my sun block in the car… double burn.

I'm tripping. That man hasn't done anything wrong. I even saw him with *her*. I want to be wanted—to have a love of my own.

I thought Emerson would have been the one. Maybe I should have given Emerson more time to adjust to me not having breasts. I wish our relationship hadn't ended so harshly.

When Emerson met me and while we dated before the cancer, I used to show off my girls proudly, and he loved when they were on display. Whenever we took pictures—and we took a lot—my voluptuous girls were pressed up against him. I haven't been able to look at pictures of us in a long time. Our mutual friend, Gina, whom I initially met through Emerson, loved taking pictures. She always tagged us on Facebook. After the breakup I hated seeing them, so I untagged myself in most of them, but I'm sure he left his up. He didn't know how to navigate Facebook too well and didn't log on much.

I don't know why, but I feel the urge to check his Facebook page. "What…who…oh, no!" There is some woman all over his page? Picture after picture, they are all hugged up and she has… large breasts. "No…oh, no!" Some of the pictures date back to when we were still together. I lost my breasts and he found them on another woman, and it seems that Gina took most of the pictures. So much for a good friend! I shared personal things with her. I guess that's why I haven't heard from her. Well, good riddance, sister!

Based on the dates of the posts, the last time we had sex he already had another woman hooked in his web of deceit. "Oh, shit!" I'm sitting here sniffling. I can't believe I'm sitting in the park crying. It's time to go. That bastard!

Chapter Four

"That's Brian McKnight doing an oldie, *One Last Cry*, coming through your radio with a tale of bereaved love. It is another beautiful day in the Bay Area, and this is Niles Groove, your main man on your favorite Bay Area radio station. To go along with the flow of the breeze blowing over and under the Golden Gate Bridge, let us listen to our hearts and teach our minds that we need love. No matter the past or what the future looks like at this time, we should all live for love. Hear my words and let them beat in your heart,

> *living once*
> *we all should try*
> *to have love*
> *to have that once in a lifetime chance*
> *you have to keep trying until*
> *you hold*
> *to embrace love as you say, Lord, thank you*
> *bow your head*
> *admit you don't have control*
> *to smile inside*
> *shows outside*
> *smiles return in kind*
> *if not*
> *life happens*
> *in steps*
> *living going around in circles*
> *until you win the prize*
> *but you must play*

to be a winner
love don't come easy
people come and go
but love don't come easy
tremble and shake fears away
open your soul
let windows open
let doves fly
let them fly away and carry away, tears, hurts
the purple rain
didn't mean to hurt you
dream the seemly impossible dream
then live that dream
say to love
I need you

"This is Niles Groove, your main man on your favorite Bay Area radio station. Enjoy your day leading into the night."

"He's right," I say to myself. I have to keep my head up when it comes to love. I'm driving to the park after sitting at home for three days in a row. I realized that I can't let things that are beyond my control influence my happiness. It's nice to drive through the park and not run into those kids with their loud music and crazy driving. It's a perfect day, the breeze is nice and calming, and it's helping me to commit and renew my attitude about all the things I want and wish for.

I park where I can look down over the park and water. The barrier is shorter, so I can see over it. I hope to see my fantasy man. I'm no longer mad at him. How petty of me to let something so sweet bother me. He wanted to call his woman so bad—to the point that he asked a stranger to use their phone. That's what I would want if someone loved me.

Even though initially upset, I still have a crush on that deep timbre in his voice, his smile, his arms, and his fine behind. Days ago when he jogged away from me, I wouldn't have admitted then, but after watching his ass move, he had me wanting to know exactly how he would make love to me.

Watching him move had me thinking in animalistic lust. I thought about how he could touch a place in me and drive me to do things some might call nasty. The thought of him having his way with me is making me smile. I could lose all my inhibitions by merely watching him move.

I wish he'd walk by. I'd strip him down naked with my eyes. The thought of him makes me smile so hard my cheeks hurt. I look down the trail and see the ocean flow into the Bay, hoping to see him *and* his woman. I close my eyes and the let the sun turn everything red, then I paint a sunset with him by my side. On the inside of my eyelids I dream of him and me.

I feel his hands in the middle of my back, guiding me down the trail to the water as he kisses me on both shoulders. We wander along the beach and the warm sand seeps between my toes. He kisses me as the sun paints us shades of red and brown. Then he sits me down on a rock and brushes the sand from my feet, fondling and massaging them as if he never wants to let them go. Our noses nudge, our cheeks touch, and we take in each other's scent as the waves rush in singing our song, *If This World Were Mine.* Nighttime creeps in and we join the stars and the city lights from afar. We find a private place behind rocks and damp sand and I let him do what he desires.

He's behind me, holding me against a big rock, biting and kissing my neck. His fingers comb through my hair. I feel his breath and his voice in my ear.

"I got you, baby. I'm gonna do things to you to let you know I will do anything for you. I'm gonna touch you as if I'll never have a chance to love again, but I hope it brings you to me over and over again."

I felt his body firmly against mine, pinning me as his huge hands roamed my body. Even without my breasts, he rubbed my scars as he licked my nipples. His hands made it down to the bottom of my dress and he pulled it over my head.

I stand naked in the night on the beach. At first it feels strange, but I know he wants me and I trust him. Before I know what is totally happening, I feel his naked body pressed against mine. His scent mixes with mine. He slides his manhood inside me and we smell like sex in the ocean air. He puts his hands on my hips and I push my ass back grinding against his hardness. His large hand already gave me a clue as to how wide and long he is. He feels so strong with every part of his body that touches mine.

He groans and whispers my name in my ear. "Taylor…Taylor, I want to kiss you all over. Can I do that? I need to taste you everywhere."

I manage to say, "Yeah." I think I answer him. My body responds. His lips start down my spine and my skin tingles. I feel the night time air, but I still feel like I'm overheating. I start sweating. It drips down my legs. I'm breathing fast and faint. He takes his time going down my back with his tongue…licking, sucking and kissing me. He lowers his body, squatting down to his knees and I start to miss the full body contact we had until his lips suck on the small of my back. I feel his tongue push out firmly. He starts to part the crease of my ass. Wanting and willing to go all out, I feel adventurous. I reach back and pull my cheeks apart and he wastes no time. I feel his tongue circling and inserting inside my tight puckering. I let go of one cheek and bend over a little, spreading my legs. I slide a finger into my own heated opening and place my thumb on my clit. I'm throbbing and can't help myself. I pump my finger almost violently in and out of my slippery hotness. I eased my wetness up to my clit and rub with almost the same rhythm of his tongue going in and out and around. He is so intense with his tongue; it's driving me crazy.

His tongue slows and then stops and he holds it in place while I rubbed my clit faster. My ass starts to tremble and I cinch tight with his tongue inside me. I come so damn hard I think I squirted on the rock in front of me. I try to say something that makes sense after being so caught up in what he's done to my body. I want him to know how good I feel.

My body is calming down as he kisses me all the way back up my spine in slow motion until he is sucking on my collarbone. I reach over my shoulder with fingers dipped in my juices. He sniffs them and sucks on them. Then in one quick motion he turns me around forcibly. His eyes peer through the darkness of the night sky and right into me. He smiles and I want to be nowhere else but with him.

I tell him, "I want to please you. What do you want? Tell me."

In that voice of his that seems to come from under my feet and soothes, he strokes my soul. "I'm receiving everything I want and that is to make you feel good all over and I'm not going to stop."

Once again he places his hands on my hips to help him squat down, but he stops where my nipples used to be. He sucks and licks me as if I had my 38 double D's. He makes his way down to the roundness of my belly and lets his tongue talk to my body. He's working his way to my clit and lightly circles ever so slowly. Two of his thick fingers probed into my heated opening. I tensed up a bit, feeling pressure. He holds his fingers, still allowing me to adjust. I push down and take in the joy and pain. I put my hands behind his head and hold him tight, grinding his face. His tongue dances and we slow drag in passionate lust.

We both notice someone walking along the water's edge, but it doesn't stop. We were kind of hidden away—lovers doing nothing lovers should ever hide. We are a moment in time and space. We embrace this chance to feel free, being on this beach with the black universe smiling down on us.

I become aggressive and take the lead, putting both my hands on the side of his head to lay him down on his back. I spin around and dig my toes into the sand and squat backwards over his face. I let his tongue continue to probe and lick me from hole to hole. In front of me his thick hardness is standing at full attention… raging…dripping. The ocean and the moon give off lighted reflections and I can see clear wetness seeping down his shaft.

I have one hand on his chest and with my other hand I take my thumb and forefinger and squeeze the head of his hardness while he keeps licking me. The wide mushroom shaped firmness of the head of his hardness is so slippery. I stroke it and his body reacts with jerks and humps as he moans in between my thighs and he keeps licking me, but now he loses his rhythm.

I rise off his face and move down, lifting my hips over his hardness and helping him zero in on my throbbing desire. I want to ride him…let him deep inside me repeatedly. I use his thighs as hand rails to support myself. I let the wide mushroom head go in about an inch and ride it right there. It feels so good hitting my G-spot. I want more in my inner throbbing so I ease down and take all of him. The night breeze is in my face and I can't get enough air. He fills me up…so much that I try to stop myself from being greedy. My insides open up to loving him and I pogo on his hardness. My ass teases his eyes and he is grunting louder and louder. So manly. "Oh. Oh. I'm cummin' again. Ooooh…Fssss."

Then I feel a pressurized warmer than warm release from him filling me.

Damn, I'm daydreaming to the point I've wet the seat of my car. I'm forced to look up, wondering why people are pointing and yelling.

"Hey lady, watch out; there's a truck coming down the hill. It's lost its brakes. Watch out!" someone is yelling.

"Huh? What's going on? I look around, hearing screams.

Chapter Five

"This is Niles Groove, your main man on your favorite Bay Area radio station. I'm gonna take a break from the music and try to make us be more aware. Hey folks we need to always be careful in life because often we have no control of what others do or don't do. I say this because of sad news I received from yesterday. A group of youngsters who were apparently speeding down a hill in the Bay Cliff Park lost their brakes. They hit a car and rammed it over an embankment. Unfortunately a lady was sitting inside of it.

"She's in critical condition, but it looks like a doctor and a nurse who happened to be in the park saved her life. The speedy medical attention she received after her car tumbled down hill for over fifty yards has made the doctor and nurse heroes. This story comes to us because it's reported the accident victim's car radio blared loudly with our station playing while being pulled from her mangled vehicle.

"We send prayers out to her and we ask everyone to be a lighthouse to bring her back to full health. Here's a poem for her, hoping for a speedy recovery.

"*LIGHTHOUSE*
A place on the bluff of my soul
A coastline made of a physical man
Is where I live in, and as a lighthouse
Inside me I glow
Guiding vessels of life ashore
I shine the brightness of ten thousand candle lights
In hope that the journey of lost will find their way home
The power of my light comes from my heart
Searching
Helping

Beaming over the vast emptiness of love needing a home
Dark nights when stars disappear and leave souls lonely
Fog laden days of no hope of the right direction
I send a beacon
Reaching
I wait for that one vessel
The fair maiden of the seas
I want her, the mightiest of all...to come to my port of call
I want her to dock underneath me
The lighthouse within me calls out
As tides, rise and swells drown hopes sending whole bodies to drift out of
   control
I spin within as a compass around the clock
Shining
Aging
Yet needed
Storms erode my fertile grounds
Solid rock of the man I am
I will not fall into turmoil of the sea
I will always keep a light on
For that one vessel to drop her sails and have no fear of running aground
I vow to keep sending and searching, and blowing a signal into the distance
   wind
From where I live in, and as a lighthouse I am
Never stopping until, she, my fair maiden is home

Get well, Ms. Taylor Middleton."

Chapter Six

"How long have I been here?" I ask the nurse who is staring at the beeping machines and writing notes on her chart. My throat feels raw and my voice doesn't sound like it belongs to me.

She jerks and looks at me with wide eyes like she's looking at a ghost. Then she smiles from ear to ear. I'm wondering why she's reacting that way and figure that I must look a royal mess. Assuming she didn't hear me, I ask again. "How long have I been here?" This time, I sound a little more like myself, but still scratchy.

"I'm sorry. I'm so glad to hear you speak. We've all been rooting for you," she said. I assume she is referring the hospital staff because I couldn't imagine who else would be rooting for me since I don't know too many people here. "Let me get a check of your vitals and I will call the doctor." She took my pulse, checked my temperature and blood pressure before hurrying out of the room.

I roll my eyes because she didn't answer my question and the gesture actually hurt. It feels like my sockets are swollen. My mouth feel like it has fur inside and my breath tastes like I've been eating steamed garbage. It's like fatigue is lying on top me and it takes so much effort to move my hand from my side to my face. Now I notice that I'm connected to wires and I begin to hear the cacophony of beeps and swishing sounds emanating from the machinery that I'm hooked up to. I snap my head back and forth, trying to take it all in, but that motion is sending shock waves of pain all through my body.

Whatever happened to me must have been bad. A single tear rolls down the side of my cheek. I think I'm about to experience my first panic attack. I pull my lips in and try to keep my composure. I'm sore and I can't begin to pinpoint what part of my face that pain is coming from. I close my eyes and begin to pray immediately to keep from losing my cool.

His voice rushed in to my conscious and I'm confused. I know I don't pray as often as I should, but I never remembered hearing the voice of God in a rich, velvety tone.

"Thanks, Nurse Rodgers," the voices said.

Ok, so that is not God, but it did sound familiar. I open my eyes and several people dressed in white coats and scrubs enter the room and stand around my bed, looking down at me with huge smiles on their faces. I blink several times before I zero in on one face in particular. I may not have been exactly sure about my whereabouts, how I got here or why I am here, but the one thing I did know is that the fine specimen of a man standing over me to my right looks familiar. From his mouth a smooth velvety voice arises. I want to reach out and touch him, but don't have the strength to lift my hand, so I let my eyes focus on him.

"Good morning, Ms. Middleton. It's great to see you awake. I'm Dr. Rielle Do you know where you are?"

I blink a few times to focus. I nod my head, "Yes," summing up the fact that I'm obviously in the hospital.

Everyone's smiles expand. "That's great," the fine doctor says. "Do you know why you are here?"

The question stumps me and I lower my eyes, jogging my memory to try and figure it out. I don't know why I'm here and that scares me. My eyes well up with tears and they stream down the sides of my face.

He and another nurse touch my hand in the same place, look up at each other and adjust their hands. The nurse rubs my arm on her side while the doctor rests his hand on mine.

"Don't worry; you've been well taken care of and you will continue to do fine." His eyes express such sincerity. "You were in an accident a few days ago and you were banged up pretty bad." My eyes widen when he says accident and he squeezes my hand as he continues talking. "But you're coming along nicely and you will do absolutely fine. Initially, you were in a lot of pain, so we kept you sedated. As the sedative leaves your system you'll gain more clarity. In the meantime, our staff is here to make sure you have everything you need until you are able to go home and we are all keeping a close watch on you…especially me."

The tears are still flowing, but somehow I feel as though everything will be okay. The warmth of the staff seems to surround me.

"Ms. Middleton," the nurse rubs my arm as she speaks.

I look toward her and turn my head slightly, trying to avoid any potential pain.

"Do you have anyone you'd like for us to call?"

I think about it for a moment. I don't have anyone here. I thought about my mother, but I don't want to worry her. I'd rather speak to her myself. Sadly, I shake my head no. The nurse gave me an understanding smile and nod.

"Okay, Ms. Middleton," the doctor says. "You're making great progress. We will keep you under our observation and as long as you continue to do well we will be able to get you home within a few short days." He shifts his focus to the nurse. "Let's get her a meal up here and see how she takes to food."

"No problem, Dr. We'll get her started on clear liquids."

Everyone leaves, but the doctor hangs back. He searches my eyes while I search his. I can't figure out why he looks so familiar to me. I never forget a handsome face.

He smiles and tilts his head. "Do you remember me?"

I take a deep breath and I'm racking my brain, but nothing comes up. I guess the bang up has shook some of my memory loose.

"You let me use your cell phone in the park the day before your accident. Luckily I had just arrived at the park when everything happened that next day. I tended to you while we waited for the ambulance to get there."

My eyes grew as big as a flying saucer as memories of this guy is coming back. I'm in awe of him for saving my life. I remember admiring him in the park. I want to crawl under the covers. I know I look a mess. Did he see me naked? If so, surely he's seen my... chest.

He smiles and pats my arm. "I've instructed everyone to take extra special care of you." Something in his smile is caring yet sensual, sparking a tiny fire inside of me. As tired as I feel, I begin to feel alive until I realize that he'd been exposed to my entire body and knows my truth.

Chapter Seven

"Yes, Mom. I've been taking all my medication and I do feel much better. I still have quite a bit of soreness and swelling, like with this knee," I say as I touch it. "But I'm able to get around. The cleaning lady came by yesterday, so the house is in order, too. I don't need you to fly all the way out here to take care of me. You've got enough on your hands with Dad."

"If you insist, but I want proof or I'm on the next thing smoking!"

My mother cracks me up. She's always been very protective and after my bout with the big 'C' it has become worse. She hates the fact that I don't live closer. That makes her more likely to panic, which is why I waited until I got home from the hospital before calling her.

"How about I text you a picture of me sitting here in the living room on my recliner, eating a pint of ice cream and watching old movies?"

"All that tells me is that you'll be good and fat by the time you get back on your feet!"

That woman made me holler. "I'm fine, Ma!" While I'm cracking up with laughter, the doorbell rings. I look up at the clock and its past 10 p.m. It can only be one person. "Hold on a second, Ma," I said, holding the phone at my side.

I look through the peephole and standing there is the good ole doctor. He's been coming by every day since I'd gotten home. I know he is only trying to be nice, but it makes me feel pitiful and uncomfortable. Exactly like my mother, he's making sure I'm eating, taking my meds, and asking if I'm in any pain.

Don't get me wrong, any woman would love the fact that a fine ass man keeps showing up at her door, but under the circumstances I'm not completely happy with it. Besides the fact that I remember him in the park with his woman, he knows that I don't have breasts and I'm sure it will only be a matter of time before he removes himself from my life. He is checking on me like I'm some kind of science project. I appreciate the kind gesture, but I don't want to set myself up for failure.

"Ma, somebody's at my door. I'll call you tomorrow, okay?"

"Alright, dah-lin.' Wait! Is it a man or a woman?"

"Ma!"

"Hey, I wanna have grands while I'm still in the land of the living."

"MA!"

My mother laughs and hangs up on me. I look down. I'm only wearing a tank top and panties.

"Hold on, please." I yell through the door. Limping to my room, I put on some comfortable cotton lounge pants over this huge contraption they call a booty. As big as my booty is, nothing can hide it, but I can't let the good ole doctor in with it on display. The thought of it makes me laugh. Imagine if I open the door and invite him in while wearing my pretty little lace panties.

I finally make it to the door and open it with what I hope is an appreciative smile. I try to be as cordial as possible because his visits don't usually last too long.

"Hey, Dr. Rielle. It's kind of late, isn't it?" I'm looking back at the digital time on my cable box.

He steps in around me. "Please. Call me Evan. Dr. Rielle sounds too formal."

"Okay, Evan." I can feel my brows rising, wondering why he insists on leaving the formal level and moving to the familiar one.

How would his woman like his patients acting all friendly? I wonder if he checks in on his other patients like this.

"Yeah, sorry. I'm leaving the hospital right now. It's been a long day. I brought some goodies," he said lifting the bags in his hands.

I raise my brows again. "Really!"

"You like movies?" he asked, moving further into the house. "I love some of the older black films like *Coming to America, Best Man, and Brown Sugar.*"

Wow, he said my favorite movie, Brown Sugar? A man after my own heart. I'm not sure about this, but when I look at his tight ass in those jeans I figure why not let him stay for a moment. I'll send him back home to his woman. What's the harm? Okay. I know this is wrong. I need to get this man out of my house fast.

"That is so nice of you. Actually, I'm watching Boomerang now and I have some of those same movies in my collection." I'm waiting for him to act like he is leaving, but instead he's sitting down on the love seat. "I appreciate you stopping by, but I don't want to keep you. I'm doing much better today. I don't have as much pain and I have a follow up appointment with my regular doctor at the end of the week."

"That's great! Good to hear!"

"Well, I'm about ready for bed," I say, hoping he'll take the hint because if this gorgeous man stays in my house any longer there will be a problem. I take pride in the fact that I'm not a home wrecker. Partly because as they say, "what goes around comes around," and I don't want to put anything out there that I don't want coming back on me. Therefore, I make it my business not to mess with other women's men—especially husbands. Secondly, I deserve to be number one in my man's life…when I find him. I guess he got the hint because he stood.

"Oh. Sorry…I thought…ah…well, it is late. Here are your movies and your goodies."

"Thanks." Our hands touch as I take the bag from him and again I felt that charge.

I pull my hand back and the bag falls to the ground. I lean over the best I can, brace my injured knee and at the same time he leans forward to pick up the bag. We bump heads and look up into each other's eyes. I can't seem to look away and he won't either. I break the gaze and he picks up the bag. We stand face-to-face and it feels like lightning flashing through me; I connect with him. I want to run my fingers across his full lips and slide my tongue across his perfect teeth. My heart is beating faster. I can almost hear it. He is still staring. I break the trance were in.

"Hey, Listen. Thanks for the movie and snacks. Um…"

He's leaning in and stops, then continues slowly until his mouth is on mine. I'm frozen. It feels so good. The soft moisture of his lips…the feel of his strong hands caressing my arms is enough the send me over the edge. What am I doing? I wonder, but I keep doing it until an image of him and his woman walking hand-in-hand in the park flashes before my eyes. I pull back and wipe his wetness from my mouth with the back of my hand.

"You have to go." I open the door and push him out on my one good leg.

Before he can protest I slam the door, lock it and fall against it. That kiss did things to me, stirring feelings that I hadn't felt for years, and gave me a satisfaction that my fingers and all the toys in pleasure land wouldn't be able to match!

Chapter Eight

The doorbell is ringing. I'm being awakened from my dream. I've fallen asleep on the couch again, catching up on some of my favorite movies and trying not to think about Evan's kiss from last night. After he left, or should I say, after I pushed him out of the door, I pulled out the big girl toys. I tried my best to quench the fire he started, but found that my fingers and toys weren't cutting it.

The bell is ringing. I check the time as I balance myself on the good leg, and see that it is after four in the afternoon. I haven't heard from Evan all day. He must have realized what a terrible mistake he's made kissing me the evening before.

"Coming," I yell to let the person know I'm my way. I assume it is probably Evan. He always waits patiently for me to make my way to the door. I'm almost hesitant to answer because I don't know what to say to him.

I finally get to the door and peek out. "Is that who I think it is?" I ask myself out loud. I look again to confirm my skeptical eyes. Yep, it is her—the woman that I saw with Evan in the park. Why in the world is she at my door? My first thought is to leave her standing there, but she already knows I'm home. What is this about? Did he kiss and tell?

I check my reflection in the mirror above my console. I don't look too bad. Then again, I'm not in a position to care about the competition. I can't believe I'm thinking about that. This woman is not my competition. I don't want her man. I don't care how fine he is or how wonderful his lips felt when he kissed me! I take a deep breath and pull the door open. "Can I help you?"

"Ms. Middleton?" the young woman asks, tilting her head to see me through the crack in the door.

"Yes. How can I help you?" I ask again, confused. She doesn't seem upset, but that doesn't mean anything. Women can be tricky.

"I'm Tiffany Rielle."

"As in Dr. Evan Rielle?" How did she find me? What the heck happened last night after Evan left here? Did she come to confront me? I can't even defend myself in my condition. This is the worst.

"Yes."

This woman is smiling at me. She doesn't look the least bit upset. Those are the ones you have to watch.

"Your husband…"

"My husband?" She fell into a fit of laughter. I open the door wider and stare at her. I raise my brows and watch while she laughs. "Dr. Rielle is not my husband; he's my father. I'm the nurse that helped him that day in the park."

"Oh." That is the only thing that I can bring myself to say.

"Ms. Middleton, my dad is in conferences all day today and tomorrow and asked that I come by and check up on you.

Her words are finally registering. I feel my mouth open, so I shut it. "Your dad?"

"Yes, Ma'am. Can I come in? This is getting heavy." Tiffany steps in carrying an old-fashioned cast iron pot and a bag of groceries.

Finally, my words were coming together. "Oh, I'm sorry. Follow me." I lead her to the kitchen and show her where to place the pot and bags.

"Thank you. I appreciate what you and your father have done for me, but I will be fine. I don't want to burden you by having you worrying about taking care of me."

"It's no problem." Tiffany is looking around my condo, taking in all of my décor. "This is beautiful," she said, pointing to an abstract painting I purchased on a trip to Grand Cayman.

"Thanks! I got that in the Cayman Islands. Please tell your father thanks and I'll make it up to him one of these days."

"I'm sure he'll love that!" Still walking, she continues taking in my eclectic collection of art.

I drag my way to the door to let her out. Instead, she finished surveying my house and sits on the loveseat—the same one her father sat on the day before. Like father like daughter.

I stop walking and think about what she said. "What do you mean, he'll love that?"

"I don't know what you've done to him, but he's smitten. I haven't seen him this giddy since before my mother passed away. He says there's something about you. You have a quality that he can't put his finger on."

I hop over to my recliner, sit down and process everything she's saying. "Your mother?"

"Yeah. She passed away three years ago." She looks down and traces the arm of the loveseat with her finger. "Cancer…but a different kind."

I winced and cover my chest without even realizing it.

"It's nothing to be ashamed of," she said, smiling. You're beautiful, like my mother, you are beautiful. I see why he adores you." She pressed her hands into the seat of the sofa and pushed herself up. "I guess I'll be going now. He's coming to check in on you as soon as he can."

I follow her to the door, walking slower than I did even with a busted knee. She turned back when she reached the threshold. "Give him a chance. He's a little rusty and this is not easy for him. And believe me; he can take good care of you. Trust me. I know."

I want to close the door, but instead I stand there and watch her walk to her car. I'm dumbfounded. "He adores me?" With my flaws and he barely even knows me.

Chapter Nine

"No, Emerson, I don't need help from you. I'm fine as I said when you first called. You found out through the newspaper weeks ago and now you're calling to check on me? This rings of bad timing. As a matter of fact, our whole relationship was a matter of bad timing. I do need one thing from you and that is for you to lose my number, and I mean it. Goodbye, Emerson. I wish you all the luck in life. And, oh, your new woman has real nice breasts."

It is too bad I can't slam a cell phone. Maybe I shouldn't have let on that I knew about his knew woman, or should I say, the woman he already had when he played with my heart, but it's too late. I wonder how I can I put a block on my phone. I want to make sure I never hear from him again. Talking to Emerson makes me feel a bit lonely, but not for him...I'm simply lonely. I need to take a nap. I don't need to get so agitated over a lost cause.

It has been one whole day since I'd seen or heard from the good ole doctor, and two days since he kissed me and I sent him out the door as if he was on fire. The funny thing is that he had me on fire, and I'd been smoldering ever since.

According to his daughter, he adores me. When she said that, my stomach flip-flopped. Nonetheless, I still don't know what to do with that information. Maybe he feels sorry for me, and I can do that all by myself. I hate to work myself up for nothing. I could be his rebound from the love he lost. A doctor that fine can have any single woman he wants, and some not-so-single. Then again, he seems like a grounded individual. I can tell by how he carries himself.

Before I consider having him in my life, I should fully recover and be able to come and go as I please when it comes to me being physically healed. I need to go at it alone for a while. I know one thing for sure…I can't kiss myself like that.

I can barely stand the idea of that man kissing me with those warm, moist, sponge cake lips down my spine. Dr. Evan Rielle has the touch. His hands send shock waves through me when he changes my bandages. I admit I want his hands to cup my ass when he kissed me and then I wanted to feel him slide inside of me. I wanted him to lift my legs wide apart and force them back until my knees were lined up with my ears and my feet dangling in the air. Oh, I can feel him grinding inside as I take all of him in. I think about his tongue parting my mouth and going so deep I'd be forced to push the back of my head deep into my pillow as I'm doing now.

"Oh, my goodness." I threw my head back reveling in my imagination. Where are my big girl toys? I need to quench my fire? Damn…the phone is ringing. "It better not be Emerson calling back and messing up my groove," I say aloud. I see Dr. Rielle's name come up and a quickening sensation arises in my belly. I have to remember to call him Evan.

"Hello." I try to keep my cool and answer as if I'm a grown woman in control of her senses.

"Good Morning. How are you feeling today?"

"Pretty good. Thanks."

"Would it be okay if I come by and check in on you after my shift later this evening? I need to talk to you."

"Of course. I look forward to seeing you."

"Most likely it will be late…possibly after ten. Please wait up if you can. I can't predict with all that can happen at the hospital. A beautiful woman might come in needing help."

"Oh, funny!" I hear his little chuckle. *I want some of your help.* "Okay, so, I'll see you later."

For a few moments, neither of us says anything. We sit on the phone listening to each other breathe.

Out of the silence, his rich, deep, velvet voice pours through the line in what sounds like an octave lower than before. "I guess I'll see you later…"

"Yes." I can hardly get a response out, needing a breath. I look at the clock and can't wait for night fall.

"I'd better be going," he said, breaking the silence again. "Have a great day."

"You, too!"

"Good bye."

"Evan?"

"What is it Taylor?"

"I'll see you later."

"Yes you will."

Chapter Ten

"This is Niles Groove, your main man on your favorite Bay Area radio station and that is Kem's, *Love Calls.* I want everyone who can hear my voice to know as the sun is setting over the Bay Area, the sun is never setting on opportunities for love, peace, and happiness in your life. And now by special request, Maxi Priest, *Won't Let It Slip Away.*

I'm glad my request went through. I'm listening to what I want to happen as I sit on my back deck. It's not the park at sunset, but I have a nice little view. There are rows of burning candles along my deck rail and the luminosity matched the reddish-yellow setting sun. My place sits high on a hill overlooking a valley of homes that the sun sets over. I look at the roofs of so many colors and I imagine all the different kinds of love that exist between the walls. I want love to glow under my roof as much as I wanted it to blaze in my body.

I'm little nervous about what might happen when Evan arrives, so I'm having my first glass of wine since my accident. I try to relax, but my mind is running faster than the current under the Golden Gate Bridge and butterflies are taking flight in my stomach. That call this morning left so many options open. I can feel him getting inside of me and me in him. It all makes me nervous.

I start reading my book, *Peace in the Storm*, to keep my mind off of him and the time. Watching the clock will not make him get to my house any sooner.

If you could
If you could feel my emotion
If you could
If only you could see the effects of you on me
If you could
You would not wonder if I care about you
You would know I'm for real
You would know
Feel the warm breath of my exhale, as my heart pounds
Look into my eyes, my eyes will not lie to you
Get lost in my embrace as I pull your life into me
Hear the sounds I cannot hold back
Let my voice enter into your soul, I sing euphoric joy to you
Gaze upon me, all you see is yours
You will know I do care about you
If you could feel my emotion
If you could
You could see the effects of you on me
You would know I'm for real

Reading isn't helping; I still can't stop thinking about him. I wonder if he could see the effect he had on me…those effects have been in place since I first set eyes on him. Lying back in my deck chair, chill bumps cover me all over even though I'm warm. I know he has seen my body, but in a professional sense. He will see my flaws and my…breasts. I shake off the reservations about him seeing all of me and tried to relax and enjoy the beauty of the sunset.

I hear a chirp and realize it's my cell phone. I jump up and look out into the darkness. My phone falls out of my lap. "Oh, my goodness," I yell. I've been asleep for hours right on my lawn chair. I pick up my phone to check the time. It's almost 10:30 at night. Oh, my! He texted twenty minutes before, and I'm now seeing it late. He is scheduled to arrive any minute. I better get to the bathroom quick to brush my teeth and fluff my flattened hair back into place. I'm going to light a few candles, put my iPod touch on my speaker system and let Pandora fill the space with soft soulful sounds of some R&B through the Musiq Soulchild station. I'm looking around to make sure nothing is out of place. Oh my…he's knocking at the door.

"Evan!" I'm practically singing his name. I invite him in with a sweep of my hand.

As he passes, I can't help but to stare him up and down. The black t-shirt he's wearing shows the tightness of his upper body. His jeans fit perfectly. His bright brown eyes, high cheek bones, juicy lips and chocolate drop skin comes together to sculpt the most handsome face I've ever seen set on a strong jaw. I almost feel like I'm seeing this man for the first time.

"How are you doing?" He leans over and kisses my cheek.

"Can I get you something to drink? Have you eaten yet?" I ask questions and before he can answer I pull myself away and create some distance. The heat emanating between us is enough to spark a spontaneous combustion. The energy that he's given off makes me feel sexy. That hadn't happened in a very long time.

I grab two bottles of water and fill two glasses with ice, place them on a tray and stop to take a deep breath before going back into the living room.

He stands when I re-enter the room.

"It's hot in here. Let's go sit out on the deck." I take the tray and head outside.

He followed close behind and I'm imagining his chest on my back. As soon as I put the tray down, Evan picked up his water and drank it down, straight from the bottle. He takes a deep breath and stares into my eyes.

"Remember I said I wanted to talk to you?"

"Yes." I said with more air than I intended.

"There's no other way to say it, so here it is. You had me from the first day I saw you in the park. I used to watch you—watch you read, sit in your car, sunbathe…all of that. I asked to use your phone as an excuse to get closer to you."

I cover my mouth.

He laughs. Then we enjoy a moment of silence and realization.

"When that accident happened, I realized that I wished I had gotten to know you sooner."

"Evan, I wished we had met before, too."

"Are you willing to let me get close to you now?"

"I want to, but I don't know how." I crossed my arms to hold myself, but from what?

Evan gently uncrosses my arms and takes my hands. He's looking into my eyes.

"Let me show you." He flashed a reassuring smile.

He moved closer, pulling me to him and he starts kissing me so deep. I'm feeling it in my soul. He wraps me in his strong, masculine arms. He pulls his magical lips away. I'm out of breath.

He's staring into my eyes again. "I can love you right."

My mouth is open, but no words come.

He starts lifting me up, cradling me like baby and carrying me to the chaise lounge on the deck. He lays me down and moves in covering every inch of my space.

Slowly, he's pulling the straps of my sundress down, kissing my arms along the way. I hold the fabric over my chest so that it won't be exposed. Evan moves my hand, looks into my eyes once again and then kisses my breasts one by one. My lungs fill with air and I quiver. A tear is rolling down the side of my face as he continues to give my breast attention like never before. His tongue licks and flicks over my scars and where my nipples used to be. His hands caress my hair, and down my entire body.

Giving special attention to every single inch of me, he's covering my heated body with soft tender kisses until I ache for his touch. He is my cure. My center throbs in anticipation. As if sensing my call, Evan moves down to feed my needs. He pulled my legs up, giving himself wider access. He starts playing with me using his fingers, rubbing, caressing, and then sopping at the juices he created. Then he teases the plumpness of the lips between my inner thighs with his tongue, pushing it in and out fast and then slow.

Evan dove in, sucking gently. Flashes of hot white lights seemed to flutter through me. With one hand, he pulls aside my lips and goes deeper. With the other hand he tweaks my nipples. Gently, he pushing his thumb inside of me, and my walls clench, wrapping his thumb in its warm embrace.

Suddenly my skin is hot and tingling even more. Evan pulls me closer. He bathes his face deeper into my wetness and sucks faster until the muscles in the middle of my center seize and spasms ripple through me. I'm moaning long and hungry, wanting him to stop because it's so intense, but I need him to go on and take me to heights in pleasure. I feel myself coming hard and fast. It clamors through me until I can no longer stand his touch.

Evan slid his body over me. I can feel his hardness wanting to break through his pants. I fumbled with his belt, hurrying to get his pants down. Urgently, we fuss over the rest of our clothes, tossing them piece by piece until we are both completely naked. I take a moment to adore his beautiful brown body before taking his long, rigid shaft into my hands. His manhood is searing and I can't wait to feel the hotness glide into me.

Evan is making me feel like a complete woman. In return, I want to give him my best asset I want to treat him to the vision of my ass and let him ride. I turn over slowly and while looking back over my shoulder I give him a teasing expression. He lifts my hair and kisses me along my neckline. He nibbles and bites lightly. Then his lips kiss down my spine until he gets to the small of my back. He places his hands on my waist as he moves in behind me. I feel his hardness searching for my heated opening. I move my hips to help him find me, and slowly, a little at a time, he pushes inside me. I hold still and I feel myself adjusting to his size. For a moment he lies lightly on my back. His hardness is throbbing inside me or maybe it's me contracting. Slowly we both began to grind. He is moaning in my ear. He mumbles, but it doesn't seem to make any sense.

He's moving faster, teasing the edges of my walls with his expanse. The friction is stirring me into a frenzy of pleasure. His grunts grow deeper.

"Ah, ah, ah," I chant with every plunge until our voices harmonize with the smacking of our flesh, filling the room with a sensual chorus.

"Oh …Ta …Taylor …" is all he can manage to say before his words give into a moan so primal it sounded inhuman.

"Evan!" I scream as waves of painful pleasure shoot through me.

His body is convulsing as mine shudders. He pulls out. I turn over and reach for his shaft squeezing and milking his explosion.

His back tightens and he lets out one last groan. Together we reach euphoric peaks then slowly float back down.

I'm curling my behind into his pelvis. I want to feel his heart beat on my back. I feel safe in his arms. We resume natural breathing, allowing the coolness of the night air to fan the smolder from the fire we've ignited.

"I know this may sound crazy, but I imagined…I hoped that making love to you would be precisely like this?" Evan said.

I kiss his arms that are holding all my fear awayand tell him, "If you only knew."

No Competition

By Niyah Moore & Stacey L. Moor

Joaquim

The objective is to conquer…

The smell of rain sifted through the room as steam arose from the floor. In the coolness provided by the storm outside, compounded with the heat from the fire pit on the other side of the room, and somewhere in the middle, magic happened. Separated from the world and enclosed in a hazy wonderland encamped by condensation, lust and satisfaction with *want* as the main attraction; two became one in more ways than one.

She, head flung back, hair dangling behind her, ached for more than just the teasing her lover insisted upon giving. His glinted laughs highlighted his intentions and when lightning struck, he held her tighter. When he counted the seconds until thunder came, the time ever shortening, he knew the eye of the storm would soon be upon them and then there would be no need to hold back what was to be.

Kisses were planted on dark skin in the dark while moans for more echoed throughout. It had been nearly two hours since the storm had come in and turned the day into night as the rain poured vigorously outside.

Since his guest had not wanted to leave in fear that her shoes would be ruined, Joaquim offered her to stay as long as she liked. He had offered her the use of his shower, a pair of sweatpants, and a t-shirt, but she had chosen to wear his robe instead after she lathered down and lotioned up.

By the time he heard the bathroom door open, the soufflés had been whipped up, the salad prepared, and the Veuve had been poured.

He chuckled when he saw her. The robe had overly draped her and nearly touched the floor as she walked on the balls of her feet toward him in the kitchen. What caught him off guard more so than the way her sepia skin shone like warm brass under the black sheen of his robe was the fact that her hair lay flat against her head. That was her *real* hair. Not that it would've been a problem if it wasn't her real hair, but to Joaquim, the aspect that her beauty was God-given added beaucoup points to her stock. However, when he saw the over-sized robe rise and fall in some places, in his mind, he couldn't stop her stock from rising.

The smell of the soufflés he had started to bake wafted through the air deliciously.

Nyenaire was happy to be in his company…

Ny, as she liked to be called, sauntered around the center island to where a small plate and a champagne glass waited for her. "I didn't know you could cook." Her smile spread as she turned her head from her colorful dish.

"You never asked," he gave slyly in return. "I'm not sure if you're allergic to anything, but this is just a basic nectarine and prosciutto salad with honey, shallots, arugula, and parmesan cheese. The soufflé has Asiago cheese, artichokes, and spinach in it."

"I'm not allergic to any of those yummy things. So, do you do this for all of your company?"

He laughed at her way of prying, "Only for the ones that get stuck here during storms."

His smile was infectious, and to her, it seemed more honest than not.

"So how'd you learn how to cook?"

"My mom was a chef. She always said that women weren't raised to know how to cook anymore more than men and some women choose not to cook at all. So, she taught all of us how to cook when we were little."

"Smart woman." Her eyes gazed out of his massive windows. "I'm glad we're in here instead of out there. That rain is nasty today."

Earlier, the two had gone on a fairly interesting product run looking for designs that would fit the aesthetics that their client had inquired about when the clouds rolled in. They had spent nearly four hours together, shared five cabs, and she had brushed against him in passing nearly as much as he had her.

The chemistry was undeniable and the pressure that surrounded them while they stood with bags by their sides, a box by his feet, and only inches holding them back from each other, could not be *completely* blamed on the weather.

It was inevitable.

It was coming.

Joaquim had suggested that since his place was closer, that they should drop everything off at his place instead of heading back to the office to go their separate ways until the next day.

"It would make more sense because if we go to the office now, you know Bergen will only question us about what we didn't bring back. This way, we can give our minds a rest and pick back up fresh when I lug all this into the office later. Cool? Cool."

He didn't wait for her to answer because his was the only answer he wanted to hear. Confidence exuded from his pores like the scent of sandalwood, bergamot, cypress, and something she couldn't quite put her finger on. Intuitively, she surmised while she turned away from his eyes as he threw up a hand to hail a cab, that she would soon enough taste the difference.

She found it odd that even when she wore her favorite outfits to work, he barely responded the way she was used to men reacting. He never looked at her breasts, even if she wore something *risqué,* and she *knew* the girls were pretty. He didn't turn around when she walked past, either. She only knew because she turned to look for him to do so. She assumed he would fawn over a request or offer what she wanted when she pouted, but he seemed to not be interested in her and something about that intrigued her.

Ny smiled to herself as a cab came to a slow roll at the corner where they stood while Joaquim picked up nearly all of the bags at once, sliding the large box with his foot toward the trunk. Before he loaded the bags, Joaquim opened the door for her, just as he had always done.

While he and cabbie loaded the bags, Ny checked her makeup and wondered if everything else she'd dreamed up would go exactly as planned. What she didn't realize was that things were going exactly as planned…just not *her* plans.

The plan had worked way too well for him and he knew that this would be another night of stories that the guys wouldn't believe. But then of course, they would believe it because he was who he was.

It was a short ride to his building and an even shorter walk through the lobby toward the elevator. When they exited onto his floor, Joaquim told Ny to reach into his right pocket and grab his key. She tried not to smirk as she slid her hand into his pocket and found what she wanted. When she withdrew, the fob was in her hand with two golden keys and one silver one. He told her as they walked to his door which key to use as he carried their purchases. When the lock clicked, Ny slid the door open slowly and she cooed, "Your place is beautiful! I knew you had good taste from all of the projects we've worked on, but this…I would've never imagined! How'd you find this?"

"Thanks. A friend of mine got married a year ago and his wife wanted a yard to start her garden and she made him sell it."

"*Made* him?"

"When you love someone, you want to keep them happy. You try to give them what they want and he wanted her. So, I got this for dirt cheap, practically."

Every woman that stepped through the doors to his not-so-humble abode on the penthouse floor showed no signs of wanting to leave, and in fact, found ways to stay in order to indulge in the amenities that were as abundant as they were unique. On most occasions, they proliferated their loose inhibitions with a few liberties that could not be had anywhere else. There was the 19th century Victorian chair with plush, purple velvet and gold trim that had a foot basin before it with a detachable faucet, the infrared sauna in the corner of his foyer, the Eversoak tub facing the window, the ambiance lights that changed depending on the rhythm of the music playing through the intercom system, and a floor to ceiling glass wine cabinet stocked fully except for two empty spaces. The amazing attributes to the place he called home were more numerous than a glance could uncover.

Joaquim's penthouse condo was a split-level loft with twelve-foot glass panels lined from wall to wall on the upper level where his bedroom was. There were numerous plants on the ground floor, which was a den of comfort with a covey of columns in the larger room and the simplicity of white marble adorning a small library that faced the other room. Several paintings hung from the walls—none that she recognized—while swatches of color, textures, and metal rested in the work area. The kitchen had a center island with a rack full of pots, pans, and other cooking utensils strung from it and every appliance was a consistent shade of brushed aluminum.

As Ny walked around his apartment, Joaquim decided that she would be his company for the remainder of the evening. He would nonchalantly offer her possibilities and watch her get caught in his wonderland. He imagined which wine would pair best with her. The taste of her lips, the aroma of her bare skin…Joaquim wanted her to take full advantage of everything he was prepared to offer her as he hoped she would do in return. Joaquim placed all of the products they would worry about in the morning and closed the door as he took off his jacket.

"Here, let me take your coat."

She gave it to him and he took it to the closet along with his while she thoroughly inspected what her eyes could see down to the tiniest details. Maybe she was dissecting his style, or attempting to recognize some pattern or layout, or maybe…she was looking for a hint that there had been another woman there the night before. Lucky for him, he was meticulous.

Ny didn't know Joaquim had walked up behind her…not until he spoke, "Are you hungry? I am…" She was startled by the amount of bass in his voice…almost like humming in her ear.

The vibrations did something to her and she turned to look up at him as the glare on her glasses covered what he would have otherwise instantly noticed in her eyes. She wondered if her blush had given her away…He noticed and she quickly turned away from him.

It was too fast…too soon to feel the way she did!

Seduction was part of her plan, yet she felt like she was the one being seduced. As her heartbeat sped, her thoughts raced of doing what she had dreamed about so many times since first seeing him. She wanted to tell him, but knowing that he may have not felt the same way halted her. She didn't want their relationship to get all 'weird', but something inside urged her to tell him, even warn him about her being in love with who he was and who he would be… brief him on choices she made about what underwear made his butt look the best every time she caught a glimpse of him when he walked away. *Definitely boxer-briefs.*

Ny felt that after so long, the moment for her to introduce a little more intimacy rather than honesty concerning her desires of him was finally perfect, but he did not need to know all of her secrets just yet.

Suddenly, the power went out with a dull hum as devices shut off abruptly.

"Uh oh…" she said.

"Damn, that seemed to have perfect timing…I have something better." He started toward the hall closet, opened the door, reached in, and handed her a small box of foot long matches. "Mind if I give you the tour? We'll just have to do it by candle light." He didn't wait for a reply. "This is the living room." He ushered her down three hardwood steps. "You have to take your shoes off if you're going to walk around, though."

"Oh." She did as he did before they stepped down into the rich white carpet, beyond the rounded backrest tufted leather sofa, away from the Classicon end table, and settled by the window for a view of the rain dancing on the patio.

Joaquim had shown Ny the things he had negotiated from former jobs that clients had paid to have customized, but then no longer wanted.He showed her things that she had only seen in the latest interior design magazines from the common space of the office, which a few of those things she couldn't imagine in real life. Truly, she was amazed by what he had amassed since he never bragged or boasted about them.

As she watched him move about his space, clearing a few things from here and there, Ny found herself smiling, knowing the exact reason why she allowed him to lure her there. The sky grew darker, yet still, the candles he lit worked wonders. The sounds of the rain helped her to realize she wasn't completely ready if things escalated in another direction.

"Would you mind if I freshen up? I feel icky. The city has been on me all afternoon."

"Sure, the shower is a little difficult. I'll turn it on for you."

They walked to his bathroom and Joaquim ran the water for her as she marveled at the sixteen jets. The steam started to build almost immediately.

"You have a Swiss shower?"

"You don't?" he guffawed. "Just kidding. This lever is for the hot water, this one is for the cold. You lift the bar to raise the pressure and push it down to lower the pressure. I only have one kind of body wash, so I hope your man won't be mad at you for coming home smelling like me," he said with a straight face and low eyes.

"I'm single." She smiled as the thought of smelling like him pleased her. "I hope your woman won't mind if I stay for a bit until the rain slows up."

"Even if I had one," he answered nonchalantly, "she would be cooler than that. I'm sure she would understand the need for shelter." He offered her a fresh loofah and a large cotton towel as he turned on the Bose Soundock and walked out of the interior room. Joaquim lit several more candles for her before arranging them amicably and pulling the door up behind him to exit the bathroom.

He closed the door and left her alone to bathe that beautiful body of hers and that even lovelier smile. He wondered for weeks how long it would take to get her to come over. It was just his luck that a thunderstorm would bring her his way for as long as he needed. His cell rang. It was a call from Arrica, a woman who tended to pique the most curious part of his desire because she was art in motion. He recalled she was going to be in town only for the weekend doing a Suicide Girl photo shoot downtown. Though he had plans to see her before she caught her flight back to LA, he put the phone on silent and placed it face down on the counter. He decided he would talk to her after his company left. She wasn't the type to hound him for not answering, so he didn't feel bad about not answering, but he knew once at work he was going to be forced to give her an answer. By then, he would know just what to say to excuse missing her call.

Joaquim made his way to the kitchen, lighting fifty various scented tea lights as he went, trailing a glow. He pulled out what he needed by the handfuls to put together something delicious for the two of them while the sound of the rain became the backdrop and his imaginings of her became his score. After he surveyed his refrigerator and freezer, he was convinced he had enough ingredients to make it work.

That was twenty minutes ago.

Now, she was sitting at his kitchen island, eating his food, licking her spoon ostentatiously and asking for more.

"This is wonderful," she said, swirling it about the glass where the soufflé had been.

"I'm glad you liked it. Sorry, there isn't more. I haven't had the chance to go shopping this week."

"No, it's fine. I'm in the mood for something else."

"What can I get you?"

"Something sweet...what do you have?"

He turned, opened the freezer door, and looked inside. "Let's see what I have here..."

Ny eased off the stool gracefully and walked to where he was, drawn to him, almost by some unseen force that made her want to bare her all and offer him the compass that would forever point him in the right direction if he promised not to lose the map. She wanted him for more reasons than one.

"I have a few ice creams, a tiramisu gelato, and a few sorbets... What are you in the mood for, Nyenaire?"

Before he could turn to hear her reply, she was pressing against him with her hands on the sides of his body as he rested his back against the freezer. She bit her bottom lip and looked up into his dark mysterious eyes. "I have something else in mind." Her fingers found the ways in and out of his shirt as she found his skin. Delight spread like a wave over her. The feel of him excited her even more and though this was what he was waiting for, he played hard to get, just to make her even more aggressive.

"What would you dooo-ooo for a Klondike bar?" he sang with a smile.

She smiled, but didn't answer with words. Her nails raked across his skin before she licked his chest.

He loved it when they thought they were in control.

Londyn

Step into the ring of fire...

One single, prompt text from him and she was on her way to his house. Within minutes, she was standing on his porch, ringing the doorbell in the middle of the stormy night. Harper opened the door dressed in a black satin robe to swathe his nude body, prepared for the night's promising episode. The anxiousness he revealed as soon as he opened the door was no surprise because he had become too predictable and she hated that.

"Hello there," he said as a slight unprecedented smile appeared on his mocha-colored face before placing a warm kiss to the side of her face.

"Hello."

Not only was Harper one of the few men that Londyn chose to keep her company, he had also been the preferred feature flavor of the month, having rightfully earned it with his persistence and tenacity. Even though he worked for her company's top rival, what they shared was best kept secret in order to keep their business relationship professional.

"Glad to see you could make it, Londyn."

She entered quickly to escape the night's cold, damp air. A fresh aroma satisfied her nostrils. His place always tended to smell so sweet like vanilla, honeysuckle, and lavender—a custom aroma combined with his own fragrance. Soft jazz played throughout and candles illuminated the path straight to his dining room. He more than likely had hors d'oeuvres as a midnight snack, but she wasn't going to eat. There was no need to pretend as if she wasn't there to be purely sexed —no love, just sex. He seemed real big on the romance. That was his thing. Sometimes she went along with it. If that suited him to maximize his own pleasure, then so be it; she would get something extra out of the night besides a great lay, but she wasn't in the mood.

Turning her feet in the direction of his bedroom, he followed behind her.

Two wine glasses filled with the 2009 Dominique Piron Brouilly Domaine Combiaty, a light red wine awarded the best during a connoisseur convention in San Francisco, rested on the nightstand, ready for them to savor. It was the same bottle he bought when he took her wine tasting. He was prepared in case she wasn't going to fall for the dining room trick. She smiled to herself because he was starting to learn her.

"How was dinner with the girls?" he asked.

"You know, detrimentally necessary male bashing and extremely freaky tales from women we live vicariously through…the usual." She laughed and smiled that smile of hers that made him wonder if he could get fired for sexual harassment from another firm.She was dangerous. She was beautiful. She smelled like they should be having sex. "Other than that, the food was good. How were drinks with the fellas?"

"Well, it wasn't like your night! It was cool, though…played catch-up over a few drinks about gripes, gringos and groupies. It was more shit-talking than anything else and lots of booze."

"Groupies, hunh?" she asked, watching him with an ever widening smile.

Harper was cute and she didn't doubt he had groupies, but she wished sometimes he would fall in love with someone else to stop him for falling so hard for her.

She sat on the edge of his bed with the wine glass in her hand as she wiggled off her turquoise five-inch stilettos and dug her pink frosted toes into his rug.

Before he sat down beside her, he offered, "Let me…" but it was too late because her shoes were already off. Bringing her feet to his lap, he massaged them. His eyes couldn't help but bathe in how incredible her long legs looked in that classic all-black, short dress. Her body was noteworthy, and even though she was thick, she was toned and fit.

She sipped the wine, "I can taste the raspberries and cranberries in this. I should've bought some, but I love the Shiraz I have." She licked her lips seductively before sipping some more. With a naughty expression coming back to her face, she began to feel a crazy sensation that ran up and down her spine. She could feel it every time his hands moved up to her toes. The spark started in her back and shot through her in waves. She shivered a little. "Mmmmm…Why do I feel a breeze in here?"

He lowered her feet and picked up his glass to catch up to her. "The window is open."

Londyn went over to his bedroom window and closed it. Her glass was nearly emptied before placing it back on the onyx table. She began to feel sleepy, but quickly shook it off.

"Are you warm now?" he questioned, searching her eyes for a sign that would tell him tonight would be different.

She nodded and sat on his bed again. "Yeah, thanks. I really love this wine. I need to get some bottles for myself…"

He stood in front of her with a sly, handsome smile appearing on his lips as if she placed a spell on him. Harper had one of the sexiest smiles she had ever seen on a man…straight and white. That's what attracted her to him when they first met at a networking event for single professionals last autumn. She'd found it ironic that he would be the *only* attractive black man in the building and also in the same exact position as she was with her company's direct competitor. His smile was the first thing she admired and just like she thought on their previous encounters, she loved that he had so much to offer.

But, she wasn't ready for love, or maybe she just wasn't ready for love with *him*.

"Get naked and lay down," she demanded in her own sexy way.

Harper did what she commanded without hesitation. As soon as he was laying flat on his stomach, she straddled him and massaged his shoulders, letting her soft hands slip down to his lower back. He let out all of his anxiousness, stress, and anxiety as he lowly hummed and moaned softly, a gratitude for her therapy. He loved it when she massaged him. He loved it even more after they'd been drinking.

"This wine has me feeling nice," he whispered into the thick air.

"You sure it's just the wine?"

"Your hands might have something to do with it."

"I tend to believe I have magical powers in these soft hands."

"I think so, too," he replied. "I can get used to this."

She kept massaging, hoping he wouldn't want to get too used to it. Anything sounding too much like a commitment was a sure way to send her running like a track star at the London Olympics. There were too many fish in the sea to settle. If she let him have her the way he wanted, she would definitely be settling for a man who wasn't quite the man for the job.

Her hands continued to knead into his muscles. She worked out the knots in his shoulders. With closed eyes and his face sinking into the pillow, his breathing became heavier, and she listened intently for hints of arousal.

When he turned around to face her, he lifted up her dress. Before she could tell him what she wanted him to do, he went down to please her with his warm lips as soon as he had her panties off.

She moaned as he sucked her thirstily. He always tried to maneuver that tongue in a way that left her panting. He was trying to make her more than just his love slave. He wanted to be the reigning king over her pussy.

Never…never…*never*…would he be able to wear that crown.

The way his tongue swirled as he sucked her clit, she could tell that he was trying to get her to cum in record breaking time, but that was where she had to draw the line and prove just how resistant of a lover she truly was.

"That's enough," she growled, curling her lips up, feeling her superiority rise like a tigress prepared to pounce on her prey while squirming from underneath him.

With a slight frown, he complained, "I was just about to make you come."

"No…you weren't…"

They stared at one another for a little while. In his eyes lay determination and enough resilience to challenge her. In her eyes lay a war of silent words and enough strength to triumph. He smiled because he knew she was more powerful than him. The only thing left to do was accept his fate peacefully.

She softened up a little bit by removing the rest of her clothing. "You know what I want you to do, Harper?"

Getting sexed from the back was her ultimate favorite position and she was ready to get straight to business. He knew exactly what she wanted and didn't deny her request because he didn't want to fight with her. He put a condom on that he kept in a little nightstand besides his bed. Melodiously, he played with her clit with the tip of himself once he was ready.

As soon as he penetrated her profound perforation, she turned to look at him with a look of gratification all over her face as she backed her ass up into him. "*Yesssssss*…just like that," she cooed.

Her muted moan began to rise as she buried her head into the pillow. In and out of her, he picked up his slow pace, feeling her juices trickle down between her thighs. She had both fists full of his comforter as she spread her own legs as wide as they could go before bucking back to get him to the place she wanted him to be.

"I want to ride you." She scooted away from him and pushed him on his back aggressively.

Breathless, he replied, "Come on."

Londyn climbed on top of him. She bounced in a rigid grind. As hard as he tried to fight the orgasm stemming from within, he came and that was fine because she did as well. Her almost damp body slid off and away from him. She didn't cuddle up next to him or whisper sweet nothings as if she loved him for giving her one hell of an orgasm. Instead, she put her clothes back on. "I'll hit you up later."

He watched her with the same puzzled look he always gave her when she left him too soon. Why was he so surprised? She came when she wanted, she saw what she wanted, and she most definitely conquered whomever she wanted.

Brushing off the awkward silence, he played his feelings cool as if he weren't looking forward to spending at least one night with her sleeping peacefully in his arms. Just as he dreaded, that night was no different than any other night they'd shared. "Alright… Drive safely. Text me or something to let me know you made it home, okay."

"Will do." She eased into her heels.

He threw on his robe to walk her to the door, feeling frustrated with her. Even if he offered for her to stay, she would've politely declined.

A long passion-filled kiss to his lips before she left was how they parted ways, the way he wished they parted the morning after. Harper wanted to endure as much as he could whenever she was in his kingdom, but she managed to dethrone him. He wanted the gratification of knowing that he would be the man to tame her, but each time she left, he realized that task had been one of the toughest he ever faced.

Truth of the matter is…*no* man could tame her.

Joaquim vs. Londyn

The night is the only competition...

It was a Friday night and after a long day at work, she and two of her friends couldn't wait to unwind at Burgers and Beers, a small, neighborhood friendly brewery with excellent service. They drank Blue Moons garnished with orange slices and ate turkey burgers at a table in the middle of the room. They talked and laughed at how cold Londyn had been to Harper.

"I still can't believe how you treat him," Yuri said with a frown. "Two long years of nothing but booty-calling and you won't even sleep at his house? He has to be tired of you by now."

"Harpers not tired of me. Spending the night is exactly what he wants me to do. Can you imagine how lovesick he would act if I slept over?" She threw her head back and laughed at the mere thought of waking up in Harper's bed. "I don't have time for that bullshit."

"You're a cold piece of work," Tavia said. "If I was him I would break up with your ass."

"We aren't in a relationship."

"But he tries everything to get you into a relationship."

"That's against company rules, Tavia."

"He doesn't even work for your company," Yuri reminded Londyn.

"I know! Even worse—he's my company's biggest competitor. It's a conflict of interest and I just don't want to get too deep."

"That's an excuse if I ever heard one. You don't let anyone get too deep with you, Londyn.Regardless! It's like your coochie is on a time-out from falling in love."

"If I didn't know any better, I would say she was born a man." Tavia laughed.

"What are you afraid of, girl?" Yuri sipped her beer.

"I'm not afraid of anything," she lied. "I just haven't met the right one. When I meet the right one, then just maybe I'll put the g-string on ice."

Tavia put down her glass and gave her best friend the side eye before they laughed together. "I don't think you know how to put them hot things on ice."

"The damned ice would melt," Yuri spat.

They laughed some more.

While the girls cackled like hens, Joaquim and his friends were at the bar discussing his rotation of females.

"How did you manage to not handle shorty while you had muthafuckin' *khaleesi* in your bed? Tell me how you did that! I want to hear that! Because I *know* she fine!" Claudio joked.

"Seriously? You're talking to me. You think I can't read these women? You give them what you want them to have. You tell them what they want. And Arrica needs to know I'm not a dial-a-dick. I'll hit her back when I hit her back. But, khaleesi? Maaaaaaaan, khaleesi is bad as hell for no damn reason," Joaquim said, shaking his head slightly while carving out Ny's figure in the air.

Ibin chimed in, "That bad, hunh?"

"And you know this!" Joaquim replied.

They all said in perfect pitch, "*Maaaaaaaaaaaaaaaaaaaaan!*"

"Yo, let's go find some Mrs. Parkers," Claudio said standing, scoping out the cuties across from the bar.

"What does 'khaleesi' mean?"

"Means 'wild queen.' *Game of Thrones*, homie."

"*Game of what?*" Ibin asked over the light blare of the music.

All three of his friends looked at him incredulously before they all stood up and walked away from the bar with their drinks in their hands to head to a table.

Claudio pulled Joaquim to the side and whispered through tight-teeth, "You aren't worried about them finding out about one another?"

"No…not at all. I'm not in a relationship with Arrica. It is what it is. We have an understanding, and it was clear from the gate. We all work together, but it isn't obvious, and Ny wants to be down with the same program— *my* program. I should have both of them over and make one cook dinner in lingerie while the other cleans in a French maid's outfit."

"This guy! It's not obvious *yet*. Just wait until they start getting jealous when they realize you're spreading yourself too thin. What if you come up in a confessional at lunch in the break room? With my experience, women always want others to know what they had. It's like marking their territory."

"True, but trust me. I got this and I'm not in the heartbreaking business…although I should buy stock," he said, raising his beer to his lips again.

"Someone is bound to get mad and have their feelings crushed."

"They're big girls. They know what they're doing. Besides, I won't let that happen. Right now I'm enjoying their company."

"Yeah, go ahead and keep cooking and pampering them and see if you don't wake up to four flat tires in the morning or cupcakes spelling out your doom on the front lawn! These broads are crazy nowadays, especially if you treat them like hoes!"

They laughed together before they toasted and gulped their beers.

"That has never happened to me…knock on wood." He knocked on the top of the wooden table. "As long as a man is up front and honest at all times, no one can possibly get hurt. You aren't supposed to fill a woman's head up with pipe dreams. You have to constantly remind her of the reality."

"Would you ever try to be in a relationship with one of them?"

Now that he had been seeing Ny, he thought about it honestly for a second before he responded, "I doubt it. When I meet the woman that can truly handle me, and I mean truly handle me, I will know it from the moment I lay eyes on her."

"You mean to tell me that you're looking for Mrs. Right?"

"I'm not saying that at all, *but* I will know if she's the one as soon as we lock eyes."

Joaquim's eyes drifted to where Londyn was sitting. It was at that very moment that she turned her head in mid-laugh and their eyes met.

He felt like he had inhaled cement powder by the pound. She was stunning.

She felt the connection as well. He dressed just the way she liked her men to dress, and was fine as hell. She licked her lips and couldn't focus on what the ladies were talking about. His laughter with his friends caught her attention from across the room.

"Hello…Earth to Londyn. Girl, who just made you stop all conversation?" Yuri asked, moving her head into the direction in which Londyn was gawking.

"I have to pee," Londyn said, scooting back from the table, not asking either to go with her.

Though beer always ran through her too quickly, she knew she was going across the pub to do more than just relieve her bladder. She had to pass his table to get to the bathroom and she was going to use that to see him up close. No thoughts of being nervous were present until she was upon passing his table. First glimpse of his eyes meeting hers, not only made her heart skip a few beats, it also threatened to stop all together. Saying that man was fine was an understatement. He was the epitome of what her ideal man looked like down to the scars and presumable tattoos.

His eyes said everything she wanted to hear from the way he didn't blink while she approached to the way he dared her to stare back at him while she walked his way. His eyes watched her until she disappeared into the bathroom. *The Law of Attraction* compounded an instant attraction that left her to fantasize the unknown with a man she did not even know.

A similar feeling rode Joaquim's imagination to the point where he decided that the best way to know her was to kiss her. Then he could tell.

While Londyn emptied her bladder, washed her hands, dried them, and then fixed her long hair to make sure she looked just as good as she did when she left the house for the night, Joaquim straightened his lapel, refolded is handkerchief and sprayed the cologne he had in his inner pocket while telling his friends he would be right back. Londyn fussed over her hair and would've touched up her lip gloss if only it wasn't at the table in her purse.

After taking a deep breath, she walked briskly up until she reached his table, where he seemed to be poised and waiting for her. Instead of passing him up completely, she took a chance and stopped. She couldn't think of a reason as to why she stopped so abruptly, but her nerves jumping confirmed that she was really standing in front of him. Joaquim knew why she was standing there. With a slight smile, he was glad she was.

She thought quickly on her feet and asked smoothly, "Don't I know you?"

With his smile widening, he replied, "I don't think so."

She thought she felt the heaven's gates open up just for her because the sound of his baritone voice was heavenly.

"Are you sure? I feel like I know you from somewhere."

"I'm positive. I never forget a face."

Feeling her nerves get the best of her, she suddenly felt like she made a mistake for stopping and for even making up something so crazy when she knew it wasn't the truth. Now, his eyes were on hers and his friends were also looking at her. She felt silly and for some reason she couldn't think of anything else to say other than, "I'm sorry."

She tried to walk away, but he stood up to stop her. "Wait… maybe you do look familiar."

Standing in front of six feet and four inches of sexiness, she stared up into his eyes and shook her head slowly. Her heart plummeted into her stomach and started beating there. "No, I don't think so. I thought you were someone else I knew. I'm sorry. Have a nice night."

He blocked her path a little bit, not invading, but subtly. "Wait a minute. Since, there has been a mistake in identity, and that's been established, can I get to know you? My name is Joaquim. What's yours?"

Finally finding her voice, she replied, "My name is Londyn."

He extended his hand to her. "It's very nice to meet you."

"It's nice to meet you as well." Shaking his hand, she could feel the chemistry coming from his palm, so she casually let go.

"Can I give you a call sometime?"

She twisted her lips into a smile. "How about I call you?"

"A man is always supposed to check in with a woman to see if she needs anything and that she is safe. Not the other way around. So, how about I call you sometime?"

Astonished, Londyn could only imagine how the color filling her cheeks had betrayed her attempt to seem reserved. There was no secret that the attraction was palpable. Londyn knew by the way he did not smile and held her gaze, that she would not be able to simply add his number to her collection of conquests. If she wanted him, and she did, she would have to play the game another way—*his* way.

Joaquim pulled out his phone and handed it to her. She timidly punched in her number and saved her contact. As she handed it to him, his hand covered hers.

Slick bastard, she thought to herself as she smiled knowingly. "Call me after seven tomorrow."

"I will," he smirked softly. "Have a lovely evening, Londyn."

She sauntered away, and peered back at him with a smile only to see his dazzling smile given in return.

As he watched her join her friends, he signaled the waiter before making his assumptions about her.

"That's what you call fine," Ibin said to Joaquim.

"I swear you are luckiest, dirtiest rat-bastard that I know. That kind of shit never happens to me," Claudio added. "She even did the whole *thinking you were someone she knew* bit! Did you fall for that?"

"Not for a second, but if she hadn't stopped, I would've followed her back to her table anyway. I saw her when she first walked in. She is amazing."

Londyn couldn't help but smile, because he was still staring at her. She dropped her eyes bashfully.

"Are you going to call him, girl?" Yuri asked.

"I didn't get his number...I gave him mine."

Yuri and Tavia stared at each other before resetting their dumbfounded gazes back to their friend. Londyn *never* gave out her number.

"You're going to pick up when he calls, right?" Yuri asked. "You're not going to play that phone-tag crap that you do, are you?"

"I don't know. It's like I can see it in his eyes. He would make me fall in love with him."

Tavia gasped while Yuri gave Londyn a wide-eyed look.

"Why are you two looking at me like that?"

"Because if that man can make you fall in love, then he would have accomplished the impossible," Tavia said.

"The impossible? You're too funny," Londyn laughed.

"It's not like you fall in love easily. Londyn, you avoid love like it's the black plague. I wouldn't be surprised if he ended up being just another number in your cell phone...that's if he even makes it that far."

Londyn thought of what her friends were saying. They weren't lying and the drumming of her heart confirmed that it would be best not to answer any number that wasn't already programmed into her iPhone.

The unpredicted possibilities lain before them were too numerous to count. However, he knew exactly where to start as soon as their clothes left their bodies. Her hair was swept away from her collarbone and settled along her back in one clean motion. He leaned in as his grip tightened around a tuft of her hair before he pulled her down on him. Her neck met the sky, chin found the North Star, and her vulnerability became too delicious for him not to indulge in. With his nose grazing her skin from her clavicle to the side of her left ear, he inhaled her slowly while her moans and soft breathing intensified by the second.

There was no need to rush. No need to let the moment slip between his fingers because she was the one he wanted since the moment he laid eyes on her. She felt the same way. Although she usually liked to get to the point, the way he tantalized her intrigued her beyond her wildest control.

Like déjà vu, Londyn had walked out of that bar, invaded his dreams and was now naked in his bedroom. The way she moved made him dare to follow. The way she looked at him made him want to be the only one she ever looked at that way again. She was stunning to the point of absurdity—a woman so beautiful it would be easy to understand how a thousand ships could have been sailed to regain her three thousand years before that day.

The smell of her was intoxicating as the combination of *verbena & rose* arose from her warm skin underneath him. Her soft breath darted in and out as her chest rose and fell in a heightened fashion. Her desire was blatant. Londyn bit her bottom lip before she huffed as she felt the man before her thoroughly. Although Londyn wanted to satiate the dripping desire that pooled at the end of her, Joaquim had contemplated this moment so much that he dared not rush the feeling for the sake of feeling her. Satisfaction lay in the choices of his actions and by the way she was acting, her power over him had abruptly shifted to his power over her.

Joaquim had wanted to walk up to her when she first walked into the pub, sweep her off of her feet and pin her up against the bar. Something about her made him want to risk everything for the moment and take the opportunity to discover what beautiful felt like without even knowing her name, yet he did not even approach her, even though he *felt* like he had known more about her than he could explain…like how her favorite colors were chartreuse and cerulean blue or how he knew she would appreciate lilies more than any other flower or how she wanted to be kissed.

Londyn combated her own mind as to whether she should answer his call or ignore him. After careful consideration, she decided to explore her new option. She expected only dinner… nothing else. *How did she end up going to his house for coffee afterwards?* In the back of her mind, immediate thoughts of leaving right after sex came to mind, but there was something in the way he touched her that whispered for her to come over and stay. The superior décor of his place wasn't the solitary cause. There was something about his hallowed out soul that crept over her in a reassuring way. He wasn't the average man.

Maybe it was simply his imagination, but there was something about her that was more than magnetic and he couldn't put his finger on it. Animalistic and depraved, the urges he had to subdue would rise like a leviathan out of her ocean of calm, roaring louder than any thunderstorm could ever dare to exhibit. The way she eyed him at the bar had placated that desire. And after several weeks of waiting for her to pick up or even return his calls, he was forced to wait for her.

However, there was no evading him any longer.

She was underneath him…naked—a mission that seemed to be unattainable at first.

If she hadn't suggested a dinner date, Joaquim would've stuttered out something he would have possibly regretted, so he was glad he let her take the lead and express what she wanted to do on their first date. He didn't think that offering her coffee would hold her attention since she seemed to be more headstrong than any other woman that he came across, but somehow she accepted. She didn't even hesitate and that made him want to solve her Rubik's Cube.

Her beauty clouded his mind unlike any of the other women he had dated and dismissed afterward. Yet, as he stood in front of her earlier that night, he realized there was nothing to be nervous about. Regardless of what was going to happen that night, he had already won by conquering his fear of her by making her laugh at dinner and tasting the wine that soaked her thick lips.

With his body so close to hers, defying her wishes to take her all from the inside out, she tried to resist him. "You're not allowed to kiss me that way." She feathered away from him.

Ignoring her statement, Joaquim kissed Londyn the way he had told himself she liked to be kissed. Both of their eyes closed, it was longer than what she would have liked and that was what he wanted. His lips covered hers and as he sucked on her bottom lip, his tongue ran across it slowly.

Moaning too loudly, she bit on his bottom lip hard to get him to quit trying to woo her with his mounting brief kisses.

"Ouch," he said with a slight frown while holding onto his throbbing lip, "I can't believe you just bit me."

She giggled. "I told you to stop." Once again, she pulled back, leaving him yearning to give her another long kiss on the lips.

He stepped back and watched her as she moved amongst the shadows as if she was not really there. Hidden amongst his wants, she fondled herself before she opened her eyes and light beamed from her fingertips. Though it was the sparse moonlight reflecting off of the dew that had coated them, Joaquim saw what he wanted to see and convinced himself that she was nothing short of amazing.

"You want me to chase you?" he asked.

"Don't you want to chase me?"

He smirked. "I won't chase you. I don't have to. We're already naked."

Londyn simply uttered, slow and coolly, "C'mere."

"Only if you promise not to bite me again…"

"I can't promise you anything."

Bare, unguarded, and prepared for a battle much like *The Battle of Gettysburg*, their worlds were beginning to collide. Unmasked and unafraid of the future, nothing was on either one of their minds except the way the other felt underneath their touches—desire… fire that set their action aflame as their sense of longing became excited by the pure enjoyment of one another. They began to take actions to obtain their individual goals.

He pulled her roughly to him and sucked her lips, not giving her the opportunity to bite him again, but to suck his tongue, matching his intensity. A soft moan escaped her while his passion was one that she had never experienced. His kisses and tongue moved down to her chin, neck and décolleté. He kept going until his tongue reached her belly button, but his trail ended right there.

Why was he stopping? She wanted to feel his tongue between her thighs.

He knew she didn't want him to stop, but he had to get her back for biting him. He teased her belly button, imitating the way he would maneuver and manipulate her clit. Her breathing became intense as sweat formed above her top lip from the feverish feeling that was amongst her. To drive her wild, as punishment for her thinking she was going to run away, gave him ultimate pleasure.

She tried to squirm her way up to trap him in a current of the deepest part of her sea, yet he refused to go for a swim. When she growled, he couldn't help but laugh. "Are you okay up there?"

Taking a deep breath to calm herself, she replied, "Why don't you move that tongue down farther and stop trying so hard to tease me?"

"How am I trying to tease you, Londyn?"

As much as she wanted to sink her nails into his skin, her violent matter was only because he was truly driving her crazy. Just when she was losing control over her own thoughts, she put up a good fight and he let her get away. She gently pushed him on his back to straddle him, looked into his eyes, and said in a bantering manner, "You know that thing you do with your tongue is very clever…tricky almost…but, you're trying to cross over into a place you don't belong. Are you sure you want to embark on a path of treacherous waters?"

He smiled up at her and said, "You are crazy; you know that?"

"I just want to make sure you don't drown."

"How can I drown when I'm treading water?"

She kissed him, this time controlling their kiss, and he let her. He wasn't one to lose control over anything unless he wanted to be controlled. His tongue followed her lead as she inhaled him. The fact that she knew he was letting her, just for a split second, be the captain of their ship, made him that much sexier. It didn't last long at all before he flipped her back over to lie on her back. Taking her feet into the palms of his hands, he kissed her ankles slowly.

Yet, again, he was teasing her…

She really wanted to feel the part of him that was hard and thick as she wiggled in anticipation of feeling him fill her up to capacity.

"Relax, Londyn."

She tried to take her mind off what he was doing and focus on his choice of music, which was compiled of artists such as Raheem DeVaughn, Usher, R. Kelly, and the Isley Brothers, but that was only adding gasoline to her fire.

"I can't…not when you're doing that. You need to stop playing and give it to me."

"What's that? What you want me to do to you?"

She whined, whimpered almost, as his tongue moved along her calf to the sensitive spot behind her knee. As small tremors began, he knew his job had only just begun. Although she declared at dinner that she wasn't one of those women who got hypnotized by a man in the bedroom, he knew he was showing her what it felt like to be mind fucked.

"GIVE IT TO ME!"

He did just that, but he took his time when he did, and only after his extensive foreplay was over. Inaudible words, hard slapping sounds, and soft cries of pleasure were the only things to break the sound of the night, besides the rhythmic tapping of his headboard against his bedroom wall.

Early the next morning, Joaquim woke silently and tried not to wake Londyn as he watched her stir before settling back into his pillow. Covered in the light of dawn under the iridescent, satin sheets, it made her look like she was a mermaid washed upon the shore with the foaming waves covering most of her body. The toasted brown parts of her that were laid bare were magnificent to behold. Still a bit groggy, Joaquim shook off the feeling to crawl back into bed with her because now that sobriety had started to resume, indecision about what last night meant for the both of them twisted his wants into anxiousness.

On one hand, he wanted to wake her with a kiss on the cheek and spoon with her until she woke and they could revisit what it was they shared until they both would be late for work. However, on the other hand, while he watched her lightly snore face down, he would have so very much liked to kiss her ass and then lift her leg over his shoulder and wake her with his mouth on her lips… the other ones.

The taste of her still on his lips reminded him that there was still so much to do. The possibilities were endless. Joaquim walked softly to the bathroom and pushed the door up, but did not close it. He talked to himself while the faucet ran and there was so much to discuss. Like, *would he think about her while at work? Would he tell his boys everything? Would she tell her girls everything? Would he see her again? Did she even want to see him again? Did they use condoms after the second time he came?*

The things that he couldn't recall were ghosts in the mirror. Steam rose from the basin and floated up into the dimness before him and what seemed unreal came to life when he saw his reflection. He smiled as he washed his face and relieved himself before washing his hands again. The bite marks she left were the proof he needed to reassure himself that he once again, like always, he was thinking too much about the wrong things. He shook it off and eased down to the kitchen to make coffee.

When he re-entered with two cups, one in each hand, she was awake and facing the window with the sheets draped around her waist. Her back, straight and taught, stood against the rising sun light like a lone tree sprouting in front of a rainbow. Her long, black hair jostled when she turned to face him. Her eyes found his and her smile grew when she saw him walking toward her with coffee.

In her mind lay disbelief. Had she really pulled an all-nighter? *So, he had gotten lucky…just don't let it happen again,* she told herself. This was the first sleepover in a man's bed in almost three years. Hit 'em and quit 'em had always been her motto, but she had to admit that his warm body next to hers reminded her of just how tired she was becoming of sleeping alone. To have great sex without any sort of an emotional bond, to run before getting hurt again, and to never look back once her pilot became unlit, were the things she did to protect her heart. What made Joaquim so different? Could she trust him? That was like an unsolved mystery.

While they sat on the edge of his bed in tranquil silence, sipping their wake-up calls, Londyn reached down and made him a new day. Still feeling how good he felt when he rocked back and forth inside, her kegel muscles pulsated in remembrance. He rose quickly with her hand gliding over his underwear.

She asked politely, "One more, please?"

"It would be my pleasure," Joaquim said with a wink as he sat his cup down and took hers as well.

Londyn pulled away and turned before they both laughed at how addictive their sex had become in the course of one night together. His laugh turned into an honest smile as he stalked her on the bed. Her eyes locked into his and while the sun rose even higher, the two fell into the bed for longer than they expected to. They were late for work, but it was worth every minute.

Joaquim and Londyn

The Big Bang...

Weeks later, while they continued to placate their urges in the day, they relieved themselves of their daily stress together and in the night, taking turns at one another's places. The two shared everything from cooking dinner together to taking long walks afterwards. From working out together to sharing showers to conserve water, they had become inseparable. These things were foreign to Londyn, but she enjoyed them.

One evening, they lay on her sleek and stylish Haute House sofa, massaging one another's aches from the intense workout at the gym while cracking jokes. Both of their senses of humor propelled plenty of laughter to leave both of their tummies sore. She hadn't spent that much time with a man in so long, she forgot how nice it was to have good company. It didn't hurt that he was such an excellent cook either.

Suddenly, Londyn asked, "What are you doing this Saturday?"

He thought about it while rubbing a small bag of ice over her right foot. "Nothing I can think of that's concrete right now. Why? What's up?"

"There's this award dinner that I have to attend for work and I need plus one."

"Why do you need only one?"

She smiled. "If you don't want to roll with me, you don't have to pretend like you're all interested, punk."

He returned her smile with his own while throwing a couch pillow at her. "No, for real…"

She sighed, looking away in the process, rubbing Joaquim's left calf and slowly found his gaze again when she answered, "Because this guy I was seeing…is the guest speaker…and I kind of want to show you off."

Joaquim stared at her while moving the ice bag up to her knee, contemplating the ramifications of them being seen together in front of one of her *conquests* as she called them, and how he would love to meet someone of her past to compare himself to.

"Sure, I'll go. What should I wear?"

She stretched forward and kissed his lips before she replied, "I know you know how to dress to impress."

"You know that."

"Indeed, I do."

Little did he know that when they arrived, arm in arm, with her looking absolutely stunning, he would feel a familiar pain in his stomach. For the first time since he initially saw Londyn walk into the bar, he felt tigers playing with butterflies.

This woman held onto his arm liberally. He heard someone call her name reverently before they stopped walking abruptly. The other man calling her name looked at Joaquim and Londyn as if he had seen a ghost.

"Londyn?"

"Harper…"

Joaquim thought, *here we go.* Though he didn't know at the moment that Harper wasn't the guest speaker she wanted to show him off to, his mood didn't seem to be affected with Harper's sudden presence. She, on the other hand, immediately began to fidget with her hands. As she cleared her throat, she only hoped drama wouldn't arise with her new interest being in the very same room with two other conquests.

A bit of hurt appeared behind Harper's eyes, though his voice didn't waver as he said, "I thought you weren't going to make it tonight."

Again, she cleared her throat, "I changed my mind, clearly…I thought you had some work you had to finish."

"I decided to take a break…Are you going to introduce me to your *friend?*"

Joaquim extended his hand and brandished that classic smile of his and spoke to the shorter, less muscular man that stood before them. "Joaquim Gerrend," he said coolly. As Harper reached for his hand, Joaquim gripped his firmly and added, "I'm the man she's been waiting for," without the smile.

Harper, speechless, couldn't say a word. The woman he worked so hard to get hadn't given him the indication that she had moved on…a reality that was too dry to grasp, but the indicator was now shoved in front of him.

When Joaquim felt Harper try to show his strength in their handshake, he immediately tightened his grip until he saw the twitch in Harper's face as he tried to fight off a grimace. Londyn had watched the two interact, but she did not see what the two men were actually doing. With that out of the way, Joaquim turned to Londyn, taking one of her nervous hands into his and asked her, "Are we ready?"

She nodded slowly, though feeling Harper's confused anger darting her way through his stare.

While Harper had attempted to throw his weight around because of the fact that he had accumulated so much wealth from the position he was in, and the fact that he had been sleeping with a woman he wanted off-and-on for too long now, he expected her to show him enough respect to not have him see her out with someone else. Londyn had no idea that Joaquim was not only going to be the best escort for the evening; he was also not going to play fair with *anyone* that thought to keep her from him.

Londyn made it a point to avoid the guest speaker after his speech because there was no need to put Joaquim through another cross fire. She had made enough men jealous for one night. With Joaquim's charm and charismatic smile in tow, she introduced him to her coworkers. The mere mirage of him actually being her man cascaded down like an unexpected fog. He was quite the eye candy to every woman in the room and she paraded him around proudly like an awarded prize medallion.

After a lovely evening with great dinner and music, the two walked out of the venue, hand in hand, toward the valet. While they waited for his car, Londyn wrapped her arms around his and smiled. She not only had more fun than she anticipated, but now they were free to do whatever they wanted to do for the rest of the night.

"What you want to do next?" she asked.

Joaquim saw them driving down to the water and walking along the beach. But the look on her face when she smirked and turned her face away from his gave him the answer he had hoped to hear. Mesmerized by the smoky eye shadow that blended into the copper that highlighted her eyes, Joaquim whispered the words before he realized he had even thought them, "How about we go back to my place?"

The car arrived before she could answer and Joaquim kissed her slowly with his eyes closed while the valet held open the passenger door. Again, he whispered his wants to her. "You've been outvoted. You don't have a choice."

"I don't?" she whispered back. "How am I outvoted anyway?"

Joaquim chuckled a bit, "Because your pussy is screaming *yes*... Can't you hear her? I can...Let's go." And with that, Joaquim led the way for Londyn to the passenger side, made sure she buckled her seatbelt, and softly closed the door to his A7 before tipping the valet.

She throbbed, even soaked through her panties as if he hadn't already made her dampen them throughout their evening together. Biting on her lower lip, she contained her instant excitement. This man, this man, this man…was moving his way into her life and without delay. He made it so hard for her to breathe half of the time.

When he strolled to the driver's seat, he saw Harper emerge with a semi-snide look on his face. Joaquim simply raised one eyebrow and tilted his head before he got in, and knew without a shadow of doubt that he would fight for her if it came to it, and he would enjoy it.

As Londyn took off her heels and stretched out her legs, her dress shimmered underneath the passing streetlamps. "The most beautiful shoes always hurt the worst…seems like it anyway."

"You women have it tough, but I really do love those shoes on you."

While he drove, she reached over, smiled at him, and rubbed his head lightly. The back of her fingers of her left hand followed the freshly trimmed beard until she reached his chin and they stopped at a red light.

He took his eyes off the road for a brief moment to observe her hint of arousal.

Londyn licked her candy painted lips slowly before she muttered, "Come closer."

When he started in, she pulled her right hand, the one she had been using to play with herself, from under her dress and placed them to his lips. The warmth of her dew turned cool almost instantly, but the aroma of things to come lit a fire underneath his already burning desires for her and she was given the choice of how she wanted to come before they had even arrived.

"I want to be on top," she said, reading his mind.

Her selection noted, Joaquim didn't say another word about it as he proceeded through the intersection once the light was green, which made Londyn even more anxious for them to arrive. The drive to his home was a mix of inebriated thoughts, subtle laughs, and pleasurable aches with a lead foot leading the way.

When they entered his home, Joaquim took off his jacket and tossed it onto the couch. Londyn strutted to him and undid his bowtie while looking deeply into his eyes. She had loved the way that he looked at her…like he wasn't afraid of what was to come… like he would always protect her…like she would always be his.

Joaquim slid his hands to the sides of her beautiful gown and squeezed at her waist before he pulled her closer and picked her up. While she giggled infectiously, he spoke as he lifted her higher. "I gave you a silent choice in the car. I didn't say how I would make you cum; I only let you choose where you would be when you did…on top, right?"

Joaquim carried Londyn over to the wall and pressed her against it while he bent down and spread her legs apart. Londyn, in the rush for the insertion, lifted her dress up by the fistfuls until the gown that had swept the floor was gathered above her waist. Joaquim had other plans, though. With her dress up and her lust exposed, Joaquim stood back to his feet with Londyn still in the air, repositioned her legs on his shoulders, and left his kiss on her second set of lips. Soft licks and pecks were given sporadically, but Joaquim was a *really* good kisser. His moans sent vibrations into her that made her lose her new fear of falling for anyone…

She felt herself falling…falling in love again.

His lips draped over his teeth and when he turned his head sideways, each lip was sucked slowly, pulled softly into his mouth and held in place with his tongue. Joaquim salivated at the thought of the next lick…the next flavor she would provide…the next ounce of her that he could revel upon. He ate her just like how he kissed—intensely.His tongue worked into the motions seamlessly and before he could get into his rhythm, Londyn was screaming, "Put me down!"

She hated to come so quick because it made her feel powerless, weak and defeated. Any time she let a man hold that kind of power over her, she always ended up feeling indignant. She felt violated that he could have such jurisdiction over her body, and the fear she felt in the power of the orgasm that was on the rise was like a wave drawn unseen out to sea.

There was no way he was going to put her down on her command. This was his time to show her just how much dominance he had with his tongue alone.

Her voice died in her throat as she held her breath and exhaled, "No…"

He whispered against her clit, "Yes," and other things to her no one had thought to say before him. His muscles flexed and as he took her from the wall to the middle of the hallway, Londyn gripped his head tightly, clenching as she exploded rainbow after rainbow, and saw only colors with her eyes closed due to the rush of pleasure.

She called his name fervently, amidst curses and unintelligible sounds, "…Joaquim."

A guttural burst found the air and echoed off of his walls as he walked with her blindly toward the living room. Though his conversation with her lovely little lady never ceased or interrupted, he made his way down the two steps and sunk his toes into the plush carpet. As he reached up for her, his right arm extended high as his left hand remained near the base of her spine. Slowly, Joaquim brought her parallel to the floor, and Londyn, in a throw of passion, pleasure, and champagne soaked perfection, found herself bucking toward the ceiling until her screams hit pitch and she shook so hard that she scared herself. All the while, Joaquim held her in the air, poised for *his* pleasure. As her twitching slowed, he laid her on the carpet and used his hands to remove what separated them. Her dress was subdued in one hand and her flesh was set free with the other.

And there, lying on his six-thousand dollar carpet, Londyn felt herself become herself, though she seemed like a stranger. Her nakedness felt right to her, and where the leaves of his numerous plants blocked the ceiling above them, she imagined that they were outside lying in a field of flowers with the stars out because she was truly seeing stars.

Again and again, Joaquim loosed his intentions for the woman in his arms in a way that only a man that had options could. It was not simply the fact that he *could* turn her out that excited him; it was the fact that he was willing to do it without anticipating the reciprocation of such a feat.

Then all of a sudden he stopped.

Londyn opened her eyes, inquiring about the end of her next journey overboard and stared into his eyes with a puzzled look. "What's the matter?" Her hands went to his face.

Nothing was the matter.

Not a word needed to be said as he rolled onto his back with her in his arms, placing her on top of him. His length begged to be put to use, but didn't send him into action. Instead, he ran his finger over her ear and pushed the hair back from her face. She stared at him briefly before the heat caught her face again and she felt herself blush. No one had *ever* looked at her like that, but it no longer scared her.

Love was waiting…

"Why must you stare at me like that?" she thought aloud.

"Because you deserve to be gazed upon."

His way, in pleasurable mounds, was unbelievable. A match he had been from the start, and her trepidation was replaced with a thrilling sensation throughout her whole body. Londyn leaned down and kissed the side of Joaquim's neck before she ran her hand down his side, over his hip, down his thigh and over to his center. She felt his size harden even more in her hand and his anticipation striped her wrist.

Lowering her kisses along his god-like body, she tongue massaged him over to the very tip of his hardened flesh until he was nice and wet. Once she had him all the way in her mouth, he groaned and clutched her hair with both hands. As her mouth formed an O, her tongue slivered along the sides of him. She sucked him so deep, tears formed underneath her closed eyelids and as she pushed him to the very back of her throat, she sensually took every inch with little difficulty. His length and girth more than aroused her as it shot an exhilarating feeling from the tip of her toes on up. Sucking and slurping sounds made him look down at her to make sure it was truly just her mouth that was making him feel so good.

When his hands left her hair to caress her nipples, he intensified that feeling even more. She moaned while still sucking, producing a humming sound, pulsating him. Right when she heard his toes pop from curling, she aimed him up, planted the balls of her feet on the floor, lifted her hips and invited him inside of her while reconnecting with his gaze.

Her eyes couldn't help but close as soon as he thrust up toward her. Squeezing her muscles as she moved to the top, she relaxed while sinking into him, coming back down. That caused him to grab her round plumpness with both hands with a sense of urgency that wasn't denied. She got on her hind legs and rode him while both of her hands held onto his shoulders for support.

"Damn," he exasperated breathlessly. "What are you made of?"

The look in his eyes wasn't the only thing that told her he was falling for her. She could feel him with each and every stroke. Flipping her to rest her back on his plush carpet, he placed her legs on his shoulder and stirred inside the very deepest of her deep. Keeping her eyes on his, she took note of his sex face in the purest form of ecstasy and tried to memorize it. Up to the heavens, her moan spilled out above them. Rigid grinds and resilient pumps had her thinking she was climbing up his walls. Though he would dig into the pursuit of her to give her every bit she deserved, she didn't flee.

There was no need to try to run away from him as she became submissive, the way a wrestler had when pinned to the mat. A grin filled her face as he pushed his pleasure so far inside of her, she could feel him in her chest. His slow pace accelerated and his rhythm, the one she had grown so fond of, set in. She could feel every muscle inside of her tighten up, yet she moved her hips to glide into him. Together, their chemistry created sex in the rawest form and inhibitions were shut down. Sweat beads formed on the both of their bodies as they climaxed and climaxed and climaxed again. He never pulled out. With every stroke, Londyn's pussy overflowed with his remnants.

The condom had broken and fear did not creep into his mind after he came a third time.

He had already made up in his mind to make her *his* and he was just waiting for her to make up her wavering mind, only her mind had been made up awhile ago. Once he managed to swing her body around, placing her on all fours, her favorite position, he gave it to her from behind in a new way. His stroke was unfamiliar. The way she thought she liked it from the back was no more. His way was better. His way was the only way and after moments turned to minutes, and minutes into memories, she gave in and loved every painful, pleasurable feeling he slid into her system. Her elbows started to shake, her back, which was once rigid, began to cave under the pleasure and her moan found the air like it had never before.

She called his name as he pulled her hair.

Each stroke was like a punch to her experience proving that she wasn't up to par with his. Every time her body tensed he found a way to make her weak. Every time she thought of a way to fight through the ripples of ecstasy and regain a bit of her composure, he pushed himself deeper into her while bellowing her name and clawing at her skin. She came a dozen more times off of that feeling alone. Shudders ran through her as she dropped her head and finally opened her eyes to see his balls slapping against her clit, sweat dripping from between them.

"What are you doing to me?" she cried as she buried her face into his carpet while sinking.

He hoisted her up with one arm and kept her there, leaving that question for her to answer on her own. *He* had conquered inside her ring of fire and she was more than happy to give him the title. She wasn't sure if it was the feeling, or the moment, or if she was delirious, but sentiments were echoed in the silence that surrounded them as slow motions carried into the early morning hours of the next day. Tomorrow had came sooner than he, and she was not sure if she thought it or actually said it to him, but she knew that *if* she had, she would not be afraid to say it again. There was no denying it any longer.

She loved him.

She had no choice.

Resting in his arms, she rubbed his chest while his hands were in her hair that had been dampened by her own sweat. Felt *too good*. Suddenly, envious thoughts of all the possible types of women whom lay underneath him bombarded her. *How many beautiful women had been given the queen treatment? Did that even matter?* She closed her eyes tightly and hoped she wasn't making a mistake by letting him move the boulder she had secured over her heart.

She wasn't completely oblivious to his ignored vibrating phone either. Whoever she was wasn't important enough to interrupt their time together, but for some reason, at that moment, she wondered aloud, "I can't believe this." Londyn traced her own name over his heart with her fingertips.

"What can't you believe?"

She rested on her elbow and stared into his bottomless eyes. "Out of all the lucky women you could be with tonight, I'm here with you."

He hummed while rubbing her back, leaning in and biting her softly on the curve of her neck, knowing why she was saying what she was saying. Londyn wanted an explanation or maybe even for him to tell her that she wasn't inferior, but superior…better than those that stayed at his place before her, but that was something he was never going to say because his actions would show that no one could compare to her and wasn't even worth mentioning. *She* was going to have all of him.

"I'm sure there are so many women trying to beat down your door."

"I only want one woman to ring my bell. Kiss me, beautiful," he uttered, pulling her down on top of him.

Their adoration for one another had blossomed, though in a very short amount of time, he surpassed her expectations of him. As her soft lips met his, her worries of other women trying to steal what was now hers disappeared.

She sighed and though his tasty lips were no longer on hers, but they lingered.

"Go 'head and say it," he said.

"Go ahead and say what?"

"Tell me what you want to tell me."

"And what is that, Mr. Cocky?"

He laughed a little at her humor. "You're the cocky one."

She hit him playfully on his chest. "Babe, I'm not as cocky as you are."

His eyebrow lifted. "Are you calling me *babe* now?"

"Um, I didn't…Did I?" She smiled down at him.

"You did…I like the sound of it." His eyes scanned hers, waiting. "And so, you were saying…"She tried to scoot away from him quickly, but he wouldn't let her as he scooped her back into his arms. "No, you can't escape…not until you admit it."

"Admit what? I don't know what you're talking about."

"You just called me babe." He wasn't going to let up.

"It slipped."

"Oh really?" He tickled her.

She laughed and then squealed once his tickling fingers drove her nuts. "Okay, okay, okay…"

He stared into her eyes, daring her to say exactly what he already knew. He wanted to hear the sound of her voice when she said those beautiful three words.

She deserved him just as much as he did her. Now, all she had to do was follow through and say it.

Grazing his midsection with her dainty hands, she asked, "You want me to tell you right now?" She climbed back on top of him.

A scoff graced his handsome face. "Yes…right now."

Once he was hard enough to slip back inside of her perfect grotto, she moaned, "Oh…you make me so wet."

Taking hold of her hips, he moved with her, in and out. "Tell me…"

She bit on her lower lip while trying to bury her voice. His profound thrust became rougher. No matter how hard she tried to fight the urge to tell him what she was feeling, his dick was the driving force that made it ooze out as she mumbled under her breath, "I-I-"

"Uh uhn…I can't hear you." A more powerful thrust followed his words.

She tried to catch her breath, but his quickened pumps went deeper. Her voice became shrill as yet another orgasm returned. "I love you!"

His satisfied smile blessed her before he sat up and stared into her eyes, almost getting lost in them. Then he said slowly, against her lips, so she could feel and hear his own sincerity, "I love you, too. More than you can imagine."

His smile rose from within him and before he had time to stop it, before he could wipe it away before she saw, he thought of their connection and melted into her. He was *inside* of her! His body had joined with hers and by the way her flower blossomed with his tilling, he was sure that she could see the rainbow shining over her ass under the moonlight.

The way he said it, made her tremble. With each and every movement he made, more honey flowed from her beehive as she gasped, "Oh my God…"

❧

Londyn lifted her head from his down pillow as soon as the first ray of sunlight beamed on her face. She had been in such a deep slumber that she knew for certain she'd snored. Judging by the way Joaquim was sleeping soundlessly, she hadn't interrupted him at all. Smiling to herself, she recollected the whole evening in its entirety like a lightning bolt flashing before her eyes and she felt her heart sputter.

As she placed a loving kiss on the side of his face, she ran her fingers through her hair and something felt different. With a scowl, she brought her left hand down to set eyes on a sparkling diamond ring reflecting off the sun and it nearly blinded her. She whispered, "What the…?"

This was more serious than she thought. His love for her had been well thought out, yet he never let on that he was thinking marriage. Matter of fact, he casually talked as if being a bachelor was something he preferred at times.

Was it too soon to go there? If it was, why didn't she feel that way? It had only been a few weeks, but her mind and body were, at last, on one accord. Though she had never been engaged before, she didn't have a doubt in her mind. If he had been any other man, she would've left the ring on the pillow, dressed, and left his place in a dash, refusing to look back. Darting her eyes from the ring to his serene body, she realized that she could truly spend the rest of her life basking in the pure personification of him.

She crept out of his cozy bed vigilantly. Once she saw to it that he was still sleeping, she headed to his master bathroom. After washing her face and brushing her teeth, she slipped her naked body into one of his oversized white t-shirts and headed down the hall. It was time to get familiar with his state of the art kitchen. The plan was to wake him with breakfast in bed.

As soon as she had all of the ingredients and utensils she needed to make waffles from scratch with cheese omelets and apple sausage, he entered the kitchen, shirtless, with a small smile, greeting her as soon as their eyes met. He placed a kiss on her lips with fresh spearmint tasting breath.

"Good morning," he said.

"Good morning."

He removed the few loose strands that fell in front of her eye during her search for pots and pans. "What do you think you're doing in here?"

"I'm sorry. Did I wake you with all the rummaging I was doing? You have everything so organized, but some things are too hard to reach. I wanted to surprise you with breakfast in bed."

"With all the noise you making in here, how could I sleep? It's time for me to get up anyway." He lifted her ring finger. "What you think about this?"

"Oh…this thing…" She shrugged as if it was nothing.

His eyebrows furrowed deep, creating lines in his forehead, as he tried to read her. Worry was on the edge of filling him. Just when he thought she was going to snub him, she giggled playfully, stood on the very tips of her toes, and wrapped her arms around his neck. "I think it's the most beautiful thing any man has ever given me. With that being said, my answer is yes, I'll marry you." Before he could reply, she kissed him passionately.

The moment they parted, he swatted her bare ass with a loud smack. "You look quite sexy in my t-shirt."

"And no underwear…"

"I see." He shook his head and chuckled. "Let's cook breakfast together. I don't think I can trust you with making waffles from scratch on your own."

"Are you trying to clown on my waffles when you've never had them before?"

"I don't have to taste them to know that mine are better. No dis…but, trust me."

"What? Please…" She scowled before twisting her lips into the shape of a kiss.

"*My* waffles, man…When I say they're the best…" He whistled.

"Don't tell me that we have to have a waffle-off. You don't want it, son!"

"No, you don't want it! All I have to say is that I hope you're ready because it's going down! Right now…here in my kitchen!"

"Oh, it's on!"

He scrutinized the ingredients she had out on the counter with his eyes before going to the pantry. "You don't even have everything you need to get it popping up in here. That's how I know you don't know what you're doing. You want to battle with the king? No problem, baby."

"Well, baby, you do it your way and I'll do it mine. We will see who ends up on top."

"The king always winds up on top…always."

She threw her head back and laughed. "I'll let you go ahead and think that. You can't overrule the queen in this kingdom, sweetheart."

"I don't know what kingdom you're speaking of, but must I remind you of my powers?"

A sly grin covered her face as she wagged her finger at him. "You don't play fair."

"I never play fair, but I'll give you a chance to show me what you got."

She filled a bowl of measured flour, baking soda, salt, sugar, three eggs, butter, and buttermilk. After mixing, she turned on the waffle iron and sprayed it with vegetable spray.

"You're going to have to wait until I'm done with this iron."

He pulled out another waffle iron for Belgian waffles, and plugged it up on the counter across from her with a coy sneer, "I'm not waiting on you…" Working with ease, he didn't need to measure out his flour, baking powder, confectioner's sugar, butter, milk, eggs that were separated, vanilla, and just a pinch of salt. He beat the egg whites with a whisk.

Seeing how he was flexing his muscles around his kitchen, she tossed a few pecans from his pantry into the maple syrup she was warming on the stove. After he mixed his batter, he combined liquid honey, a half teaspoon of grated lemon rind, fresh lemon juice, and two cups of fresh strawberries, halved.

She poured the batter into the ready iron and waited. As she watched him from behind, she couldn't help but enjoy their fun little competition. When her waffle was done cooking, she removed it from the iron, added whipped butter and poured the hot pecan maple syrup on top.

When his Belgian waffle was done, he topped it with his infamous strawberry lemon honey syrup and a garnish of whipped cream. He took a fork, cut into his, and fed her the first taste.

She closed her eyes as she chewed. "Mmmmm, yours taste so light."

"The egg whites make it lighter."

Taking the same fork from his hand, she cut into hers and fed him. He nodded in delight. "Okay, okay. Yours taste like a buttery haven. I like the touch of the pecans." He rubbed her cheek, removing a smudge of flour before looking around his kitchen. "You're such a messy little cook."

She smiled widely. "Yeah…You're so neat."

He placed a kiss on her forehead. "I'll clean up while you finish cooking that breakfast you had your heart set on. Your waffles still aren't better than mine, but are worthy enough."

"Oh, I'm glad I have the master chef's approval."

"As the future Mrs. Gerrand, your waffles have to be worthy or else you'd have some more work to do."

She nodded with a sly smile at the thought of him sending her to Joaquim boot camp if needed. While he cleaned up, she cooked breakfast. When he was done, she served him in bed, but the breakfast grew cold on the counter.

Triple Dribble

A Tale of Lust and Basketball
by LaLaina Knowles & Marc Lacy

Chapter One

WNBA Draft

"His touch unfamiliar yet so indulgent and tender
The tone of his whisper, overflowing with desire
Two people…us…we inhale sweet surrender
While the appetite fuels the fire
The fire of the words unstated
The fire of the expectation of his stimulation
The stimulation of my mind…body…soul
Two souls who shall intertwine
Until death we do part"…..
— Gabrielle Renfro

My parents have always been my greatest support system. They understand that for me, basketball is not just a game—it is my life. Being an attorney was never my dream …just Plan B in case Plan A was an epic fail. Both of my parents were successful and everyone in the home was expected to follow suit. I watched my parents work diligently in both their marriage and professions, and as a result, they were my first coaches off the court. Their work ethic, which was imparted in my siblings and I, contributed to my hard work and fortitude on the court. My siblings traveled the path designated by my parents, but I took a different route. Finishing my degree was never questionable or debatable; however, I would use it only as an alternative to playing professional basketball in the event I was not drafted into the WNBA. In my parents' era, a woman playing professional basketball was unheard of, but ever since the WNBA was founded in 1996, opportunities have been given to women wanting to play ball and get paid a lucrative salary doing so, not to mention the possibility of endorsements. Sitting here ecstatic that my parents support my decision to go to the WNBA, I wait irascibly for the announcement to be made. Being here at the Radio City Music Hall, in the same room with some of the nation's top prospects and coaches, is intimidating yet exciting.

"Baby, we are so proud of you. You have worked hard and it has paid off."

"Thanks, Dad. It means so much to hear you say that."

"I just hope wherever you go, it's not too far away from home because…."

From this point my dad's words fell on deaf ears. If I'm drafted, this will be my first time away from home. I am ready to explore all of my options and take full advantage of every opportunity that presents itself. It's not every day that a girl from a small town such as Shalimar, California gets a break like this and since we only live once, I plan to live life to the fullest.

This is surreal! I cannot believe I have the opportunity to pursue my dream of being a professional basketball player, I thought to myself.

Glancing over at my parents, their demeanor seemed to be one of pride. However, I knew there was some apprehension, mostly by my father as to what team I would play for and where I would be living since he would rant about not wanting me to live in Los Angeles. With the high crime rate and gang activity, most parents would shun at the idea of their daughter moving into the city and justifiably so. Over the past few days I began questioning if I had made the right decision by refusing the scholarship offered to attend law school at Georgetown University. With my mind racing and my body full of apprehension, I began to plan my entire life within minutes.

"With the first pick in the 2012 WNBA Draft, the LA Sparks select Gabrielle Renfro from Stanford University."

"The LA Sparks has an amazing roster this year and by adding Gabrielle Renfro to the team, they are certainly going to be the team to beat this upcoming season. With Gabrielle taking Stanford to the Final Four, finishing her second year as Stanford's all-time leading scorer and PAC 12 Player of the Year, it's obvious that she is a good fit. She can run the floor! At Stanford she was always the first post down on the break and has been rewarded for that. She also has an awesome mid-range jumper! She's just an overall addition to the LA Sparks."

"Gabrielle! Gabrielle! How does it feel to be drafted by the LA Sparks and to have the chance to play with some of the best players in the league?"

"It feels great! It's an honor to be chosen. I am grateful to everyone who has supported me over the years, my parents, my coaches and teammates at Stanford and I am happy to be a part of the LA Sparks legacy. I am looking forward to contributing in any way I can and to having a great season."

…AT THE AIRPORT…

"Hi, Natalie…its Gabby. I really wish you could have been here today. Yes, can you believe it? I'm going to the LA Sparks. I'm close to home and will be playing for the one of top WNBA teams in the league. I can still visit and watch you practice. They are calling my flight, so I will call you as soon as I get back to Shalimar."

"Excuse me, I wasn't eavesdropping, but you are going to be playing for the LA Sparks? I love the LA Sparks! I just realized who you are; you are Gabrielle Renfro! I've seen you on television a few times. I am a huge fan! Excuse me for rambling; my name is Jessica…Jessica Bordeaux and it's nice to meet you, Gabrielle."

"Nice to meet you too, Jessica. Yes, I was just drafted to the LA Sparks."

"How exciting and congratulations! Meeting you has definitely been the highlight of my trip considering I have been here at LaGuardia for almost 3 hours…layover."

"So, where are you traveling to?"

"I am heading to Los Angeles to audition as a dancer for the LA Earthquakes, expansion NBA Franchise. I was supposed to audition for Julliard School of the Arts until I injured my ankle a week before my audition, so I opened up a dance studio for inner city youth last year and came to New York for a mini vaca before my audition with the Earthquakes. I'm sorry; there I go rambling again."

"Flight 2613 from New York to Los Angeles is now boarding at Gate D12. Flight 2613 is now boarding at Gate D12."

"It's no problem. You are actually a breath of fresh air, but they are calling my flight so…"

"Of course, and if I do well on my audition, I am certain our paths will cross again. It's been nice meeting you."

"It's been nice meeting you, too, and oh, good luck on your audition. Knock em' dead!"

Chapter Two
LA Spark's Press Confeence

"Heaven
in a five foot eleven frame
and it would be
a doggone and low down
and dirty shame
If Ms. Gabrielle did not
bear the last name...of LaFleur..."
— Blair LaFleur

Wow! So that's Gabrielle Renfro, huh? We would make some beautiful kids. You heard me? Tall, too! She's every bit of that 5'11" they list her as. Man, what I would do to part that redbone sea. Good Lawd. The bruhs wouldn't never believe me if I told them that I was right here at Gabby's press conference. It's perfect timing, too, because the Earthquakes don't even start training camp for another couple of months. With this first advance check that I received from my agent, I think I'm getting my locks treated and floss some bling that would reel the Gabster right on in.

"Ladies and gentlemen, Gabrielle Renfro."

"I am really proud to be a part of the LA Sparks. It's great to be back in Southern California and I look forward to my family being able to come see me play basketball. I never thought I would be at this point, but to come this far is great. I am ecstatic that my dreams are coming true. I want to contribute in whatever way I can to the team and pay my dues."

"Gabrielle, it's pretty obvious that you value family. Are you looking to start your own family?"

"Of course...after I establish my basketball career, I would love to get married and start a family." Hmmm. She wanna start a family huh? Well, I can help this thang practice. Man, she just don't know. Ya boy has no problem putting this Louisiana thang on her.

"Will there be any questions for Ms. Renfro?" asked the presser coordinator.

"Yes. This is Bill Hamilton of WAQQ TV 41. Ms. Renfro, how will you make the adjustment living the life of a professional athlete in Los Angeles, California? There's lots of temptation out here you know?"

"Well, when I was living in Palo Alto, there was lots of temptation on Stanford's campus as well. After all, I did achieve a lot on the basketball court. We played on national TV on several occasions, and we won an NCAA championship. So you don't think that drew groupies?"

The presser attendees began to laugh slowly.

"I understand, Ms. Renfro, but how will you transition to life in LA as a professional athlete?"

"Sir, I'm a very grounded young lady. My family loves me. I'm in church as often as I can attend. Plus, I'm a hard sell. I was going to go to Georgetown School of Law eventually. So you know I have my priorities together. Well, I at least try to have them together."

"Question in the back? Oh, it's Mr. Blair La Fleur, draftee of the expansion LA Earthquakes."

Haha, look at how she's peepin' me. Lemme stand up so she can see her new power forward and father of her children to be.

"Um, yes, Ms. Renfro, my name is Blair La Fleur. And I'mina be ballin' for the expansion LA Earthquakes like the coordinator said. And I too need to learn how to be a professional athlete in this part of the country. 'Cause you know, back down in the Bayou, things are totally different." Okay, she never took her eyes off of me. I'm impressed with this thang already.

"Well Mr. Grambling State University, being that I'm from in and around this area, I think I can make the adjustment," said Gabrielle while smiling.

"Um...do you need help making any adjustments?"

"You're so funny. I, um...um am sure I could use a hand every now and then."

"And I use my hands every now and then too! I mean, I could use your hands. Or I could give you any hand you needed."

Blair La Fleur is certainly a charmer and he is fine, but contrary to his belief, it's going to take a lot more than his weak game to capture and keep my attention off the court.

Chapter Three
LA Spark's Training Camp

"The allusion of his hands lingers
Across my frame provoking me
In his absence to allow my fingers
To roam freely and discover my juices
Bringing me to ecstasy
Wishing my hands were his..."
— Gabrielle Renfro

"First, welcome to all the rookies. We are glad to have you on the team and let's make this a good season. Let's do some drills. Let's go, ya'll. Let's keep the momentum. Sparks on three. 1...2...3...Sparks!"

"Come on, move the ball...move, move, move!"

"Handle the ball, Renfro; handle the ball!"

"There you go...way to handle the ball!"

"What are you doing, rookie? Pick up the pace."

"There you go...now move!"

"Rebound the ball."

"Alright, alright, line up players...layups. Let's go! Count em' out loud."

"Come on, Renfro; count em' out loud."

Practice in the WNBA makes practice at Stanford seem like a breeze and coach is really riding me. Thank God I am active and staying on the move or else I would be plastered all over this basketball court because I am past exhausted and we have another hour or so of practice. Coach Taylor told me there would be days like this, so I won't complain since practice makes perfect. I've already worked so hard to get here, so I have to do all I can to stay here. It's imperative that I keep the mindset of, *work hard, play hard* as the saying goes. Speaking of playing, Blair is looking rather fine in those stands.I cannot believe I agreed to go to lunch with him. He is not the type of guy that I am immediately attracted to. I typically go for the suited and booted type of guy, but there's something about him that is edgy and enigmatic. Besides, I was born with a competitive nature, so the competitiveness in me desires to see what Blair La Fleur is all about off the court. I'm sure every Quake-ette and groupie will more than likely be longing for him as soon as they see him on television and recognize him on the street. I will absolutely keep my calm andallow whatever happens between us to happen naturally, whether it is romance or friendship I will allow him to take the lead and take heed only if he plays his cards right. I have never been the female that starts planning the wedding before the first date…not Gabrielle Renfro.

"Ok, water break is over Sparks. Get back out there! Layups… let's go!"

"1…2…3…4…5."

"That's it…count em' out loud."

Coming from the stands was a lurid, unfamiliar, "Let's go Renfro". With my concentration being on the court, I kept practicing and I couldn't afford to have coach thinking that any slight distraction could possibly throw my game off. I would be riding the bench if so. Maybe it was a fan. Maybe it was Blair. What if it was Blair? My level of enthusiasm went from seven to ten as that second wind I needed went in effect and I handled the ball like back in my Stanford days.

"Renfro, nice shot!"

"Come on, let's get it. We are not going home until ya'll start making more layups. It's not the three-point shot, mid-range jump shot or free throws that players miss most…its layups…the easiest to perform, but the most difficult basket to make because it's underestimated!"

"There you go!"

"Alright, Sparks…great practice. All of you held your own on the court today. Hit the locker room, shower and we have a brief meeting in 20 minutes."

Yes…great practice, accolades from coach and lunch with Blair. I would say so far, today is a good day. I cannot wait to get home and call Dad to fill him in on today's practice. I am thrilled about our first game and it's a home game. I'm not sure if I will be playing, but I will definitely be on the bench cheering on my teammates if I don't play. Maybe coach will tell us in the meeting who will be starting. I am ready to get out of this uniform. Of all days to have lunch, he picks a day after Sparks practice. There is nothing glamorous about sneakers, jeans and a ponytail on a lunch date. Perhaps my not so glamorous side will change his mind about all he was saying at the press conference. He appears like the pompous type that cares more about what's in between a woman's thighs as opposed to what's in her mind.

"Hey, Renfro! what are you getting into when you leave here? Some of us Sparks are going to go grab a bite to eat."

"Hey, Leslie! Thanks for the invite, but I'mma hang out with a friend. Count me in next time."

"Okay, Rookie…cool! You did your thing out there today… made us proud to have you as a Spark."

"Thanks, Leslie! That means a lot coming from a veteran."

I am famished, so I hope Mr. La Fleur broke open the piggy

bank for the Cheesecake Factory because I could eat an appetizer, main course and a slice or two of Godiva Chocolate Cheesecake. I will save him the expense of wine because I will reserve drinking until date number two if there is one. There…a little face powder and lip gloss works wonders, Blair La Fleur and lettuce wraps are calling my name. It's game time!

"Hi, Blair! You look nice and thanks for coming out to the practice. Are you ready to eat?"

…AN EVENING OF LONLINESS IN THE BEDROOM OF GABRIELLE…

On my bed, undressed, I turn and glance at the mirror on the wall and subconsciously his reflection stared back at me with hunger in his eyes. They were begging to wander his tongue tenderly over my breasts while stroking the inside of my thighs. The thought of this man mesmerizes me. He is a walking dream…my walking dream. Closing my eyes, picturing his tongue entwined with mine, I received the euphoria my body was experiencing. As a slight smile touched my glossed lips, I slid my fingers over my nipples, lightly passing over them both. With my body in an overwhelming trance, while feeling their hardness with every touch, I belt out a soft moan, "Blair". The arousal of the exhilarating tingle finds its way to my clit which is long overdue for some maintenance. Without resisting the sensation, seductively, I moistened my finger and slowly loved myself to convulsions of bliss, leaving me wondering if I should have asked him to stay for dinner.

Chapter Four
LA Earthquakes Practice

"Gabrielle
is my angel
but my angle with Jessica
is nothing more than for
jump-off purposes...
No, I'm not perfect and that's why I pray
and God forgives
even one that lives...in a lie...
Jessica is a seed, but Gab is the apple...of my eye..."
— Blair LaFleur

Man, I can't wait 'til the season starts. I really can't wait for Gabrielle to see her man play. I think once she sees me running up and down the court, dunkin' on fools, that'll mean from then on, it'll be automatic pre-game and post-game sex...without her even thinking about it. Now, that's what's up. It's hard to think about all this pro-athlete image stuff out here in LA when you're a young buck with nothin' but testosterone running through your body and big ends flowing through your bank account. I tell you what, these pre-season workouts were kind of fun at first, but now this stuff is gettin' old. I believe in working out, but damn. A brotha has to rest sometimes. I love being a pro-baller, but some of this stuff they can have...I mean, everything from the interviews, community work, photo shoots, team activities, guest appearances. Dave didn't tell me it was gonna be this intense. Man, I'mma have to get another agent who's gonna tell me the real deal. Everywhere you go, folks are watchin'. Now a few paparazzi roll by my condo every other day. I guess they're tryin' to see if I'm gonna live up to my bad boy image. And when they found out me and Gabrielle were kickin' it, it got straight up ridiculous. Besides TMZ clockin' us all of the time, some group approached us to see if we'd be interested in doing a reality show. Gab didn't say anything about it and I didn't either, but if she brought it up, I'd say no. They're just doing this to expose me…while they make money. They would like nothin' more than to see this N'awlins bad boy do something stupid. But this is what I signed up for, so this is what I gotta get used to. I feel like I don't belong to myself, but belong to the public. Man, I don't want nobody in my biz, but I guess that don't exist when you're a pro athlete in the City of Angels. Damn, they didn't tell us that the cheerleaders would be up in this camp holding tryouts. That fine ass Jessica Bordeaux knows that she's just walking temptation. I remember her from back in the N.O. Yeah, I know I'm wrong for this, but she just makes me not even worry about keeping a secret between us and not telling Gab. I knew back in the day, just by the way she looked at me, she wanted me. Don't no woman undress you with her eyes and not want to immediately get with you. It's like she represents everything that Gab don't. I mean, she's a freak and is fighting it. Hell, when she sees me, she just does the splits because those legs automatically spring open. Hmmm…I wonder if she can talk now. We still have a few minutes before workouts begin and I see that the cheerleaders are taking a quick break. Aight Blair, whatcha gonna do big boy? And, I must say, the "Quake-ettes" are looking mighty nice today.

"Jess! Girl don't act like you don't see me. If I didn't know any better, I'd say you were Meagan Good, or Meagan Good's twin sister."

"Blair? Man, they told me you were coming out to L.A. I couldn't believe it, though. I said I'd have to see it first. I didn't know you guys were holding workouts today."

"And I didn't know that you all had workouts either. They put us at this old Forum like we're not good enough for the Staples Center. The Wood up to no good. Gang territory all day."

"Well, you know Staples is Laker and Clipper domain. Besides, us expansion franchises gotta earn our keep before we get the luxurious digs."

"Yeah, I guess you got a point there. And speaking of dig..."

"Um, look here Mr. 1st Round Draft Pick. I'm glad you said that because I wanted to congratulate you on landing Gabrielle. She's a beautiful woman with a beautiful spirit. And there's something in me that says that ya'll will be good for each other...with your roughneck behind."

"What? So you thought I wasn't gonna acknowledge my boo? That's my baby there. No doubt. But you know, sometimes..."

"Sometimes what?"

"I just don't..."

"You just don't what, Blair?"

"See woman! I knew it!"

"You knew what, fool? Will you complete a damn sentence?"

"You're sittin' up here complimenting me on my girl, but you're lookin' at me with the googly eyes."

"Boy, please. You are a blast from the past. Yeah, you still sexy and all. Plus you got a fat, fat contract, but you know me and Gabrielle are good friends. And I respect my friend. You know I wouldn't get down like that."

"See, who said anything about getting down?"

"You know what I mean, Blair. Quit side-steppin' the issue. And if you are going to be that weak minded, you need to let her go and not drag her into any mess."

"So, if I let her go, you'd be game?"

"I didn't say that, Blair."

"But sweetie, you've had that look in your eye the whole time we've been talkin'. What's up with that? It's the same you had back in the N'awlins days."

"Ain't nothin' up! You are not getting in my panties, Blair. So just stop it!"

"Baby you're gettin' mighty intense for someone who doesn't have any feelings for me."

"I'm intense because I respect my friend and I'm not about to let you put me in a bad position. The thongs are staying on!"

Damn, she wearin' thongs, too? Ouch!

"Well, I remember a few good positions that you enjoyed back in the day. So why don't I call you and let's get up later on?"

"Fool, I'm about to get back to these tryouts. I can't believe your horny butt."

"But you like it, don't you sexy? And you didn't say not to call you, so you know I'm gonna make it happen."

"Whatever."

Whew! Man, that doggone Jessica just got finer with age. Let me go ahead and send this text message right now so that we won't waste a minute of time when we get out of practice tonight. *"Jessica, you know you fine, so how 'bout tonight, we make 6 meet 9? #letmemakeyouscream"* Ain't no way in the world she's gonna forget about ya boy. I guess I better make my way to the side room so that I can stretch and get my focus back on the ball court. I hope we don't practice too long. I'm glad summer league is right around the corner so we can get some good hoopin' in. I keep forgettin' that's the main reason I'm out here on the west coast.

...LATER THAT DAY...

"Jess, you know you want this, but you just won't say. Come on. You know that's how you women operate. It's always all about how something looks and not what it actually is. You want me, don't you?"

"Blair, I can't believe you sent me that nasty text. You old dog! You're so disrespectful. And you're lucky that I don't show Gabrielle what you've been up to."

"You won't do that. Because then, you know the woman is gonna accuse you of trying to take me, and not me trying to get with you."

"You make me so sick!"

"And you love it. That's what attracted you to me back in the day. You got tired of all of those educated cornballs. You need some excitement in your life. Let your boy remove those cobwebs."

"I ain't got no man, but I can promise you there ain't no cobwebs."

"Well, with me you don't need to go to Toys R Us. You'll have the real thing."

"I ought to come over there and shoot you!"

"Or you can come over here and give me a reason to shoot."

"Blair, if you weren't so bronzy and sexy, I'd hang up on your no good ass."

"But you won't. What time are you coming over to taste the treat?"

"What's your address, clown? I can't believe I'm even entertaining this."

"My condo is in Pasadena. It's in the Power Height's community right off of the 710. I'm in unit #55."

"I hear ya, big timer. I heard don't nothing but celebrities live over there."

"True, and I'm 'bouta make you a star."

...LATER THAT EVENING...

"Come on in, Jess and have a seat in the great room. I'll be off of the phone in just a sec."

"Baby, I told you some people were coming over today to check out the condo. They may do a photo shoot or two here. Ha, I can't tell you all of that just yet, but when everything is set, I'll let you know all of the details. Sweetie, you know you'll find out everything soon enough. Aight, now get to practice before you get fined. Love you."

Damn. Man, Jess just had to wear the leopard print skirt with a red halter top. Stilettos soundin' off in rhythm with those cheek claps. It's gone be some trouble tonight. I know it. "Must be Gab, huh?"

"Well aren't you the know-it-all? Whatchu drinkin'?"

"So, I guess you're not gonna tell me if my girl, Gab, was on the phone, huh?"

"If I did want to, it wouldn't make a difference anyway. Now you want that Apple-tini or Henny and Coke?"

"Henny and Coke is fine. What? You tryin' to get me drunk or something?"

"Tryin' to get you right, so you can chill and relax. Ha…chillax! Right about now I'mma hit this old school Kenny G and let you relax to it while I order dinner."

"Kenny G, huh? You got that Silhouette joint?"

"You better know it. One Silhouette coming up."

This doggone iPod better work today or it's gone get tossed.

"Ahhh, I love that man's sax. I just love a sexy sax."

Okay, now why is she lookin' at my crouch?

"So, since you love a sexy sax, do you blow?"

"Do I blow? A sax?"

"How would you like to blow my horn?"

"You gotta horn?"

"Yes. And it has a flavor I'm sure you'd enjoy."

"Is that so?"

"You know it."

"You'd do anything to get back in my panties, huh Blair?"

"You want me to say yes so that you can say no and fake like you ain't tryin' to give me no cut tonight."

"Anyway, boy…come on. Do you think your crazy butt can rightfully tell what a woman is thinking?"

"I can tell what you're thinking. Come over a here for a minute. Sit right by me."

Damn. Those bronze thighs are tight and those quad muscles are gyratin' every time her slue-footed ass takes a step. Whew!

"Now just look at you."

"Look at me…"

"You look real sexy sippin' that gnac and sitting right by me, too."

"I bet that's what you tell all of your women, huh?"

"All of my women? Sweetie, those days are gone. I'm looking to settle down now."

"Settle down with one chick on the side?"

"Look girl, don't spoil the mood."

"Why you uh…keep lookin' at my skirt?"

"I ain't lookin' at your skirt. I'm tryin' to look through your skirt."

"You always tickle me, Blair."

Got that ass now!

"You mean, you want me to tickle you, right?"

"That, too."

THANK YOU, HENESSEY!

"Stand up for me."

"And do what, boy?"

"Walk three feet in front of me and back on back."

"You just want to check out my ass don't you?"

"I been checkin' it ever since you been here."

"Now how you just gonna start unzippin' me? Dude, you crazy."

And she ain't stoppin' me either.

"Step out of that skirt."

"Now what, nasty boy? You want me to touch my toes like this?"

"Dang, Jess…you ain't never tasted this good. What you do, sit in a tub of Boston

Crème Pie? "

"Fool, that ain't nothin' but some Bath N Body Works. Damn, Blair. You gone make me…Ooooh Blair!"

"Ah yeah, you ready now…good and ready."

"Pull 'em to the side or pull 'em off you dread head bastard!"

"No problem, shawty. I'm just gonna lay here on the couch and unbutton these boxers, let the Magnum massage the stick and let you sit."

"Blair, somebody's gonna fall in love with somebody tonight. You feel so good in me. I could take my hands and run them through your locks all night. "

"Run 'em, baby…as long as you keep ridin'."

"Blair! Why can't we, baby? We make love so good"

"Why can't we what?"

"You know can't no one do it like me. Not even Gabrielle."

"Look, now…just concentrate on this tonight, aight?"

"You know she's jealous of how I do it."

"Jess, I'm about ta…I'm about ta."

"You about ta what, daddy?"

"Give you what you got comin'."

"Well, let me have it then!"

"I…Damn!"

"What, baby?"

"I wanted to pull out, unstrap, and let you taste the flava."

"Why didn't you? I know, it was so good you couldn't help yourself. Hehehe."

"Yeah, he, he, he, is right. Whooo. I'm kinda sensitive right about now. Hold still, babe."

"I ain't goin' nowhere."

"Damn!"

"What is it, Blair?"

"You on the pill?"

"Not now. What's up? What happened?"

"Condom is gone."

"You mean it broke? Broke off inside me? And you mean you…you?"

"Okay, Jess, let's not dance around this and make believe it didn't happen. But, yes, the condom broke and I popped inside you."

"What the hell are we gonna do now, Blair? Damn. See, that's why I shouldn't had my butt over here."

"Relax, babe. Just go in the bathroom, take your time, and see if you can retrieve it."

"I guess I have no choice."

"It's gonna be alright. We'll take care of what we need to take care of."

"What do you mean? This is my body, Blair…not yours. Just in case you forgot."

"Look, the sooner you stop talking, sweetie, the sooner you can retrieve it."

…TEN MINUTES LATER…

"Okay, I got it."

"Good. Anything in it?"

"Full."

Whew. It must have come off when I pulled out. Oh, well. Not the first time that's happened. But I do hope it's the last.

"Good deal, sweetie. Well, I had fun. Didn't you?"

"I did have fun…despite the scare. I may take a home pregnancy test in a couple of days just to be sure."

"Yeah. Please do that and holla back at a brother."

"So what? You puttin' me out now?"

"Well, Gab may come over in the morning, so you know how that goes."

"Hmmm. Okay. I guess I'm supposed to understand and be drama free, huh?"

"Um, pretty much."

"Well I'm gonna leave you a present. Take these and remember me. Because you may not see me over here again. Bye."

"Dang, so you're leavin' me with your thongs, but I don't even get a kiss good-bye?"

"You kissed me where and when it counted. I'm outta here. I'll holla later."

Boy, that ass is still jigglin' in that mini-skirt. Mmm mmm mmm…I just don't know if it's worth the drama. Well, I always say that, time passes and back to my old ho-ish ways. Oh, well. Jess knows what she's gettin' into. But Gab don't.

Chapter Five
Date at Mr. Chow's

"Nothing compares to the love he renders
To the warmth stirring inside begging to surrender
Surrendering tonight to each fragrant kiss…each long thrust
Envisioning him sucking on my clit with ice in his mouth
I gather my equanimity and quickly adjust
My emotions…"
— Gabrielle Renfro

I opened the door and saw the package that was left from the courier and with the sender being Blair La Fleur, I became overwhelmed with anxiety. After our conversation a few nights ago, he explained that I should be receiving something via personal courier. Eagerly, I unwrapped the package and discovered a beautiful Tracy Reese cocktail dress with a card attached simply stating, "See you Friday night, Gabrielle. I'm looking forward to spending quality time with a quality woman." There's no way he could pick out a dress like this alone. He probably used the concierge service at Saks. Nevertheless, the effort was priceless, the dress was beautiful and I was going to be fly wearing it with my new Jimmy Choos. I'm glad that I finally get to get dressed up for a change. I cannot wait for him to see me out of uniform.

…IN BLAIR'S MERCEDES COUPE…

Man, I simply cannot screw this up. I mean, I know I'm from the Nolia…and no, I can't take the Nolia outta me. All I can do is suppress it.Maybe I'm in over my head and tryin' to be somethin' that I'm not.But in the end, I think Gabrielle is worth the sacrifice.I know I can do it.I know I can.Gramps raised me to understand how to get and keep a lady.She ain't a ho, freak, or jump-off...she's a lady.And she's gone be my lady.One day she will be Gabrielle La Fleur.Come on, Blair!Don't screw this up, dog.I can't afford to.I've been tellin' all the bruhs about my prize catch.They been readin' articles, Facebook, and what not.Okay, I know I got ice in my veins.I'm cool under pressure.Ain't nothing to this.And as my rearview says, "Fool, you Blair La Fleur—the gangsta hoopin' pretty boy!"Okay, I'm good now.Let me go in here and claim my prize.Um, but first I'mma change this music to some jazz.Forgot I'd been listening to NWA and Master P all day.Boney J it is!

The sound of the doorbell startled me. Anxiously, I made last minute adjustments to my hair, applied a thin coat of MAC Lip Glass over my lipstick and answered the door. Standing boldly in the foyer was a vision of exquisiteness. With his goatee tidily trimmed and his dreads brushing his shoulders, he bears resemblance to an African god. His scent was certain to linger for days. The combination of Usher cologne and his pheromones caused me to long for him in a way that I have never longed for any man in the past. I was utterly taken by his physical presence and barely noticed the Stargazer Lilies that he had shown up with. Immediately, I almost made the proposition of ordering takeout and enjoying dinner at my place, but the proper thing to do is to allow him to court me. On the other hand, my body wants to skip dinner and get straight to dessert. Struggling with my wicked and innocent internal conflicts, I chose to allow him to take me out for dinner.

"What's up, Ms. Renfro?Beautiful flowers for a beautiful woman and here's to a beautiful evening indeed.You are one reason my Friday has been mighty, mighty nice.And that's just from thought only.Now, I get to see the real deal."

"Good Evening, Mr. La Fleur. The flowers are absolutely breathtaking. I see someone has been doing their homework or paying attention in our conversations."

"On and off the court, I am dedicated to winning. So, tell me, Ms. Renfro, am I winning so far?"

"Give me one second, Blair. I need to place these flowers in water and a vase. I will be right back."

I deliberately disregarded his question. Of course he was winning, but there is no way I would enlighten him to the fact. Not yet, anyway. He needed more than a bomb body, attractive arrogance and a fifty dollar bunch of flowers to impress me and I am not entirely impressed.

"So, are you ready to go?" I asked, approaching the living room and reaching for my handbag.

"Sure thing shaw...I mean, um, beautiful.By the way, the dress works for your body and my eyes perfectly."

Walking down the driveway with our fingers intertwined, he unlocked and opened the car door, carefully closing it once I was settled comfortably inside his Mercedes coupe. Once inside, with Boney James playing, he drove nodding his head as the soothing sound of the soprano saxophone released from the speakers. Unclear if this was a player move on his behalf or if he, indeed, was a true fan of jazz, I sat comfortably, enjoyed the ride and basked in the moment, the quietness and serenity. We did not speak much. Words were an unnecessary evil because his eyes spoke volumes. I felt relaxed...safe even. There was something different about this Blair La Fleur; something in my soul spoke this.As I struggled to keep my composure in an attempt not to appear anxious or desperate in any way, I could not resist the urge of gazing into his eyes as if I was one of his groupies. I was captivated by the notion that he was here with me. He was undeniably attractive and I am smitten by his six-foot-seven frame, bronze complexion and intellect. In my mind, I have made love to him a million times over. Tonight I will seal the deal.

"Good Evening. We got reservations for La Fleur. Or should I say the La Fleur's...ha?"

"Yes, Mr. La Fleur, your table is ready. Please follow me."

The hostess sat us at a table tucked away from the other patrons and I am happy because I am getting tired of running from the paparazzi. Hopefully, Blair and I can have a nice, private moment that's ours tonight. After perusing over the menu and conferring about what we would be eating, I became aggravated by the points and stares from across the room and, of course, I was not shocked that the paparazzi were tipped off as to our whereabouts. Still, we were determined to have a nice evening. "Good Evening. My name is Marcella and I will be serving you tonight. May I start you off with a glass of our featured wine, Pierre Gimonnet, "1er Cru Fleuron", Blanc de Blanc, Brut, 2004?"

"Actually, Marcella, could I get a bottle of that um...what's that? Pier Gomment? We are also ready to order. I would like the first course with Sautéed Rice and she would like the second course with vegetables."

"Of course, sir. One bottle of Pierre Gimonnet, "1er Cru Fleuron", Blanc de Blanc, Brut, one first course with Sautéed Rice and one second course with vegetables. Can I get you anything else?"

"No, thank you; that ought to do it."

Mesmerized that he took the liberty of ordering my favorite champagne and dish, I quietly chuckled. It was obvious at this point that he had been paying attention to my desires. I could only hope, by the same token, that he had been paying attention to my needs. There is no need for the waitress to suggest dessert...I got that. "Dinner was fantastic, Blair. We must do this more often. But it's getting late, so I think we probably need to get the check and call it a night."

As subtle as I could possibly be without being demanding, I let him know that I was ready to leave, but not because it was getting late. With a slight grin, I felt the warmness of his hand on my knee as he modestly responded, "Okay" and leaned forward to kiss my cheek. Licking my lips to signal to him that a kiss on my cheek is fine, but he has full permission to kiss my lips. You know… everything about tonight has been perfect. I hate that it has to end.

…AFTER DINNER…AT BLAIR'S

Foreplay began when he rang my doorbell and continued throughout the night with gentle touches and intimate discussions over dinner. Nervously, yet willingly, I followed him up the stairway into his immaculate bedroom.I underestimated him in every way. He does have some class underneath that rough boy exterior and thug persona. There was no need for sidebar conversation as we undressed each other in unison.Every part of my mind, body and soul wanted him immeasurably. His physique was erogenous and the fading scent of cologne was tantalizing. Gently, he brushed my hair from my neckline and softly kissed me. It was at that moment that I felt whole, even if what I was feeling was temporary.In unyielding exaltation, I whimpered as he caressed my breasts with his hands and teased my nipples seductively with his tongue. Against one written rule in my own playbook, I wanted to see if he tasted as good as he looked. As my tongue served as the escort, I licked him from his navel to his inner thigh making my way upwards, circling the tip of what would be my greatest desire before allowing my mouth to make love to him.

"Gabrielle….da-damn girl...you...you got me.You got me!"

"Shhh...let me please you."

"Well, pretty please…will you continue pleasin' me?Just take me!"

Stroking him deeper, his hips began to rotate violently.

"I'm getting ready to explode.I'm...get-tin' r-ready...to…"

"Come for me baby. I want to taste every drop of you."

As he tried to push my head away at the peak of his ecstasy, I resisted with all my might and swallowed his juices, and as I imagined, he did in fact taste as good as he looked. Removing the pillows that neatly adorned the headboard of his king sized bed, together we slipped under the sheets and anxiously I waited to feel him inside of me as he kissed my elongated frame. I desired him and wanted to take him in ways that were unimaginable…sinful even. I craved every inch of him. My toes curled as the sheets became submerged from my nectar when he placed his strong hands between my thighs and his impenetrable finger glided inside of me and I exhaled in excitement while cooperating, rotating my hips in small, gentle circles. As he placed the palm of his hand on the hood of my clit, I found myself on the verge of climax. He wailed as he adjusted himself accordingly and suddenly his mouth was on my vagina. Moaning in rhapsody as did I, he slipped his tongue repeatedly in riveting motion over my clit and my back arched. I was becoming slightly inpatient with his intentional teasing.

"Blair, I need you. Make love to me and after you make love to me, I want you to fuck me."

Reaching over to his nightstand, he pulled out a Magnum and I did the honors of placing it on my man, then breathless as he entered me, I welcomed all of him.

"Gabrielle, I thought you would feel good, but I didn't know you would feel…like…Nolia good. And that's the good-est!"

"You are just as good as I imagined you would be. You feel so good! Don't stop…please don't stop and don't hold back."

My heart began racing and my body craved him more after each thrust. We had all night and tonight I was willing to give him whatever he desired because he has given me what my body has needed for over a year. I whispered in his ear, "I wanna ride you."

Submissive to my demand, he turned on his back and watched me, with decadence in his eyes, straddle his manhood and put in work. Firmly, he cupped my breasts. My nipples became erect and not disregarding their need to be stimulated, he placed them in his mouth.

"Yes! That's it baby…you found my spot. Blair, I'm coming."

The consistent rhythm of lovemaking was now an erratic tempo as I rode him until we both came. My lifeless body gathered enough strength to lay my head on his chest. As he pulled me closer and wrapped his arms around me, all reservations and doubts were extinct. This is where I want to be.

Chapter Six
Visit to Magnolia

"Since we're in the Nolia
I'm hopin' Jessica
will back that thang up
and let a brotha put
something in the holia…
And hopin' she'll extend the lease
as my jump-off/dime piece
Showin' her off in front of the bruhs
and lettin' them know
what a professional b-baller does…"
— Blair LaFleur

"What's wrong, Jess? Why the sad look?"

"What's wrong? I can't believe you talked me into coming home with you."

"What's wrong with that? I didn't force you."

"Yeah, I know. This whole thing has been bothering me. I'm worried about my friendship with Gabrielle. And, that's her texting me now. What am I going to tell her?

She didn't know I was going to be out of town. Heck, she probably didn't know *you* were gonna be out of town."

"Quit bein' silly, Jess. I told her I was coming back to the crib. Their season's cranking up and she's real busy, so she understood."

"Yeah, she understood you coming home, but I bet she won't understand one of her best friends gettin' banged out by her boyfriend, now will she?"

"Um, Jess, do we have to have this discussion now?"

"Yes we do, Blair! Your dumb butt is sleeping with me and you have the audacity to parade me around town like your dime piece or something. I'm not your damn bimbo. Furthermore, everyone knows you're dating Gabrielle. Heck, you guys were even in a magazine together. This is so wrong."

"Okay, at which point did you decide it was wrong...before or after you decided to participate? We're here now, so could you please try and at least enjoy it?"

"Okay, Blair. You're right. You didn't force me to do anything. But I'm not your jump-off chick. You're not going to make me out to be some slut."

"Jess, I can't make you out to be anything you are not. But at the same time, I can't control what people think either. So with that said, can we just enjoy?"

"I guess, man."

Now I'm having second thoughts about takin' her to the bruh's party tonight on Canal Street. I have a funny feeling that everything from here on out is going to be a guilt sermon. I'm hoping she snaps out of it and just plays along. After all, she already made the ultimate sacrifice; may as well play the role. Besides, although she's an NBA cheerleader, it's not like she can get this treatment from any other player because of the no fraternizing rule. I took her shopping, got her hair done, she's eatin' well, and ridin' in my rented Phantom, too? She's in a way better position than any of her friends.

I know she'll get off my back once she sees the old house in Magnolia. But right now, we're gonna hit this West New Orleans Hotel in the French Quarter, relax, hit the Nolia, then go to the bruh's party later on.

...LATER THAT AFTERNOON...

"Jess, you look so good when you're relaxing. I wish you could relax a little more around me."

"I'm trying, Blair."

"You like chillin' in your t-shirt and panties, huh?"

"Yes. You're so silly."

"You got that look in your eye."

"What look, boy?"

"This look..."

It feels like her soft ass is just melting between my fingers. I don't know what type of oil she applies to her body after she showers, but that mango-cocoa scent smells delicious. It smells so good that I'm about to make my tongue an oil applicator. And those emerald green satin panties are about to come off, or be ripped off.

"Damn, Jess. You get finer by the moment."

"Mmm hmm. And your boxers are getting bigger by the moment."

"It's your fault."

"How is it my fault, baby?"

Her warm breath has just taken the inside of my left ear hostage. Damn, I just love it when her eyes roll to the back of her head. That means I can do what I want at that point. Her tongue tastes like sweet potato pie. Those perfectly arched eyebrows over those closed eyes means that it's crackin'. I can hear Gabrielle calling my name right about now. But her words are like a foreign language as Jessica's creamy thighs have come apart. First I see her chin, then I see her chest, navel, panty line...well I saw her panty line when she had her panties on. Paradise never tasted so good and based on the rates of her moans, to her, it never felt so good, either.

"Baby, please marry me!"

"Don't worry, boo. We can get married for tonight. All I want to know is...is daddy treating you right?"

"Yes, daddy, you're treating me more than right."

Okay, now it's time for her to taste what she tastes like. Our tongues embrace like two lost lovers. I almost forgot how she tasted because she now consumed everything I tasted. And now I'm on my back, and she's slid to my mid. Damn, is that what the back of Jessica's throat feels like? If that's the case, I don't want to feel nothin' else. Damn, I feel like a man.

"You ready, baby?"

"The question is, are *you* ready? I can feed it to you or you can take it."

"I'm taking it!"

She mounted me like a gymnast on the pommel horse...and so far, I give her a score of ten. She's so warm. And her inner sweat is leakin' all over me. Doggone thighs wrapped around my waist like a Boa Constrictor. She's squeezin' me something nasty. I feel like a Hostess Twinkie whose filling is about to explode. Her mouth is the oil tank and my tongue is the dipstick and that tank is sucking the oil right off the stick, and then putting it back on. And damn, the kitty cat is so wet; I feel like I can slip all three of my legs into it and still have room to slide something else in.

"You damn skippy you takin' it shawty because I'm tryin' to kill it."

"Well kill the kitty, baby, because it has nine lives. Now harder, please?"

"You better hold on to those sheets because I'mma break a headboard with your ass."

"Bring it then, you greasy, black and dreaded beast! Break me in two!"

"You gone have a new walk when I finish with you tonight."

Okay, now I'm gonna drill for that oil. She got me goin'. She's gonna know how the Blair stick feels. Hell, her friends gone know too! I'm goin' for the gusto, tryin' to make juice with the juicy.

"That's it, baby...take me to paradise! I want to go tonight!"

"What's my name, mami?"

"Blair, baby! Blair!"

"Who owns the kitty?"

"You baby…you! It's all yours. And I want to be all yours too, boo. Please let me have you. I'm beggin', baby. Please don't stop. Keep makin' me feel good."

"I'm will, baby…I will."

"Please leave her for me! Please baby! Please!!! You feel so good."

"You so crazy, you freak...my freak."

"So, I am yours, huh?"

"In a way, yeah."

"Kiss me and don't stop thrusting!"

"I won't baby, 'til it's, 'til it's, time...for me..."

"Time for what, baby?"

"For me...to....Agggghhhhh!"

What? Man, I can't give this jump-off up. She gets me right all of the time. If I could marry two women, I would. Lawd have mercy. I don't see how I can walk away from this. And I know I got some hell to pay, too.

"Kiss me, Shaka Zulu. Make me feel like your queen."

"Muah. There ya go, boo. You were great."

"Oh, was I really? Or are you just tryin' to feed my ego?"

"Both. Now, let's go get a shower."

...LATER ON THAT DAY...

"So this is the Nolia, huh? You know, growing up, I never made it to any of these parts of the city. I was always in those doggone parishes. My mom and stepdad wouldn't let me come down here with my friends. They thought I was too fast and the area was too dangerous."

"Yeah, it was kinda dangerous, shawty. But it is home sweet home. Speakin' of homes, I wanna take you to my grandmother's old house. That place brings back so many memories."

"I bet. I know she'd be proud of you if she lived long enough to know you made it to the NBA."

"Yup. Gramps was my heart. She put up with me and my bull more than any other family member would dare."

"These are some old and small houses. This area needs a retouch."

"Those houses you see are what we call *trap houses*. Anything you want could be rolled up right there before your eyes."

"Wow. It was like that?"

"Yup, and still is like that to a point."

"Um, we're not going into to the trap are we?"

"Nah, shawty, I wouldn't do you like that. Just wanted to show you the old digs. As a matter of fact, we're about to pull up on the block now. And there it is, Gramps's old two bedroom mansion. Looks like the city put a lien on it. I think when I get settled, I'm gone buy it back, refurbish it, and either turn it into a museum, or just rent it out."

"Don't rent it out, babe. There's too much sentimental value in it for you to do that."

"You right, shawty. I need to rethink this. But I still got time. Not gone be able to do anything major 'til those game checks come in."

"I feel you."

Damn, I'm starting to feel tingles up and down my spine. I miss Gramps. I miss livin' in this house. I miss the Nolia. When I save up, I'm coming back home and give my community a facelift. I can't let it go down. Can't let this house go down, either. Shoot, I might ask Gab if she wants to get married in this house. Shoot, they wouldn't be ready for that.

"Wait here."

"Okay."

Damn, they let this place go to junk. I can see it now, the back yard set up for a private ceremony…white tents, chairs, the works. Forget getting married in Cali, we gone do it right here. Yeah, that's right. And if she don't agree, then we could do an engagement party or something here. Gotta do *something.*

"Whew! Almost brought tears to my eyes, babe."

"I hear ya. Has Gab seen this place yet?"

"Now, why would you ask me that? And for the record, no."

"Just askin'. Are you thinkin' about bringing her here, too?"

"Jess...what's with all the questions, shawty? And don't tell me you just askin'."

"No reason. And no reason to raise your voice. Again, just asking."

"Don't no woman ask a question like that and she just askin.'"

"No big deal, Blair."

"Why you sounding so sad?"

"I'm not sad, Blair, but damn...how would you feel if you were me and about to lose you?"

"Lose?"

"When you get married! I know you're gonna marry Gab. And by the way you looking at this house, hell it might be right here! Let's go. I'm tired of the Nolia already!"

Now, how the hell did she figure that out? That damn woman's intuition crap is hell.

"Jess, stop jumpin' to them damn conclusions. I told you about doin' that babe. You just creatin' drama. Just chill. We gettin' outta here."

"Can't believe you rubbing it in my face like this. This is the thanks I get for being Blair's little freak!"

"You keep that up, and you gone be Blair's left little freak. Now, chill. We here.

Just chill."

"Not that simple. If you were in my shoes, you'd understand."

"Well, I'm *not* in your shoes, and I *don't* understand. Now, can we be pleasant Again, please? Let's make the best outta this trip."

"I know. I know, I'm trippin'. And yes, you didn't have to twist my arm for me to want to come out."

...LATER THAT EVENING AT THE KAPPA PARTY...

"Blair, I just don't feel good about this."

"You don't feel good about what, Jess?"

"Being at this party with your frat brothers, knowing they know that you're dating Gabrielle."

"Jess, we just got here. So, chill, will you? Besides, you know I'm dating Gab and you came all the way down here from Cali with me. Like I said before, we here. So just try to enjoy it."

Man, I know that this has got to be the last trip I take this heffa on. If you gone be a jump-off, hell just be a damn jump-off. Don't try to add stress to it by making yourself out to be something that you ain't.

"What's up, frat? Been a minute. Things good witcha?"

"You better know it, B. Congrats on getting that pro contract. You know you makin' the bruhs proud."

"Prechate that, bruh."

"So, this starlet must be Gabrielle. Gab, I must admit, you look a little taller on TV, but no less sexy, though. Oh, and by the way, you know ya boy had to write a poem about Gabrielle. The bruhs asked if I would perform it tonight. Now, before I do, lemme make a quick disclaimer…all the elements in it are make-believe. Just wanted you to know that before I kicked it. Aight, here I go:

"She's all out
and all in…
Gabrielle who
looks like she
can be walking sin
…but really she ain't
'cause she's a saint
in bombshell clothing…
All married brothers' eyes
when they see her
are roaming
4 and 5Gs

and this amount
of Gs usually makes it rain...
But when Ms. Renfro
steps on the scene...
She brings the pain
like a free throw after
an and one...
by a foul committed by the other team...
I just wish Gabrielle
was on my team
I want her so bad, I could cuss
but I'm willing to keep it clean
outside the bedroom...
But inside our love
there's gotta be headroom...to grow...
Not a seamstress but
there's no secret that I need to sew
my wild oats...
But for now I'll just fantasize
that Gabrielle realizes
that she is a wanted woman
by masses of men...
Whoever lands her
to marry her
should be able to take her off
and carry her
wherever the holy matrimony leads them...
And she understands
that their admirers need them...
Need them to be that example
of a couple...most desirable...
I'm hopin' he loves her EXACTLY how I want to...
-Pretty Boy Flow"

"Um, frat, nice piece…but um, this ain't um Gabrielle. This is a good friend of mine. Her name is Jessica. She's actually a cheerleader for the Quakes."

"Oh, my bad. Well how do you do, Jessica? Sorry for jumping to conclusions. You look lovely. Um, you gotta man? I'm sure you get that a lot."

"Well, not exactly."

"Are you lookin' for one?"

"I'm not really sure."

"Well, when you become sure, let a brother know. Here's my card."

I know frat ain't tryin' to take my woman and my jump-off. How disrespectful is that? He gone make me raise up on his ass. And yeah, I know I need to chill. Because if I do raise up, Jess will think I'm thinkin' more about us than I let on.

"Dang, Frat, I knew you was a baller. You still tryin' to have 'em all, huh?"

"Hey, you know how we do."

"No doubt. I'm gonna check out the honeys in the salon room. Gotta get at least one or two numbers before the Wobble comes on."

"Do your thang, frat."

"Oh, by the way, is Gabrielle coming? Reason I ask is because many of the bruhs wanted to get her autograph and pic of you two to put on Facebook. Oh, and speaking of Facebook, we sent her an invite, too. So, I don't know if she's in town or not. But let us know if she's rollin' through. Aight frat, I'mma bounce over here. Nice meeting you, Jessica."

Well, damn. Did this fool not see me with my fling? Why is he all up in my grill talking about Gabrielle? Oh shit, they sent her a Facebook invite? She knows about this joint?

Absolutely no pictures tonight. If I see somebody with a camera, I'm punchin' 'em.

And I guess I can pretty much hang up getting any more from Jess during this trip. Damn! Just my luck.

"So, um, did you know that your frat brothers were expecting you to bring Gabrielle?"

"I honestly didn't know, Jess. I do apologize about all of the questions and hoopla."

"Now you see why I'm uncomfortable? Hell, it's bad enough we're doing what we're doing, and now your bruhs are rubbing all of this in my face? I just don't know what you want me to do, Blair."

"And I don't know what you want me to do, Jess. I can't help what them cats planned. I didn't know. I didn't know at all. Hell, I feel disrespected, too. I'm a pro ball player, too, and a former member of this doggone chapter, and they gone roll out the red carpet for Gabrielle and not me?"

"Well, from what it sounded like, they were rollin' it out for the both of you."

"Yeah, the both of us if she was here. She ain't here, so they not givin' me no love."

It don't even matter at this point. The less attention, the better. Now I'm the one who feels like leavin'.

"Well, you want to stay or go now?"

"We can stay for a little while, Jess, but suddenly I ain't feelin' this scene too tough."

"I understand."

Chapter Seven
Visit to Shalimar

"This daddy's little girl
has her own
little world...to think about...
I've got to be bold
and treat this issue
like daddy has a common cold
and basically tell him...
To get over it...
But I do love him so
and so the story goes...
I'm a big girl now
and I hope he knows..."
— Gabrielle Renfro

It's going to be great going back home since I hadn't been in months. With any luck, I will get to spend some time with my family, stop by Stanford to see my old coaches and teammates, hang out with my girls and do some shopping with my mom. There is something serene about going back to Shalimar and getting away from the hustle and bustle of LA...not to mention the paparazzi following my every move, so home will be a much needed break. Driving down the 110, the landmarks began to look familiar and I became anxious about the welcome that I would receive from my family. I was unsure if my parents have been watching the news or possibly heard some gossip about my relationship with Blair, but since they never asked, I will just continue to blow it off as casual dating until they do or perhaps when I'm on my way to the alter one day. They would not be happy if I told them that this is the guy that I am thinking of marrying. Then again, my father would not approve of me marrying any man that was not a carbon copy of a younger him.Pulling up into the driveway and seeing the balloons, welcome home signs and my sister's car made the road trip worthwhile. Since my sister is here, I can confide in her about my relationship with Blair and she can help build my nerve a little to break the news to my parents. It's always easier to deliver unwelcomed news with somebody in your amen corner.

"Gabby! Let me help you get your bags. I missed you so much and congratulations on making the cover of ESPN Magazine, the endorsements…just everything that you are doing, Gab. We are all proud of you."

"Hi, sis! I missed you, too! Thanks for the congrats, but the last thing I want to talk about is work. Let's talk about you. How have you been? You look fabulous. Married life looks good on you. So when are y'all going to give me some nieces or nephews."

"We are nowhere near ready for kids yet.The only thing I am birthing is my career, so children are not an option for at least five more years. Speaking of married life, what is going on with you and Blair LaFleur? Are the two of you victims of the rumor mill or do we have a wedding to plan?"

"Shhh…not so loud. Yes, it's true, but I have not told Mom and Dad yet, so please keep quiet until I figure out when would be the best time to do so."

"Don't worry, my lips are sealed because when they do find out, I do not want them to know that I was a willing participant in keeping this secret of yours. Dad is going to flip!"

"Shhh…let's talk about it later. They are coming now."

"How is my Gabby doing? Your jump shot is looking good, honey, and of course you are just as beautiful as you were before you left home."

"Thanks, Dad. Well, I was coached by one of the best. I can't thank you enough for spending all of those hours in the gym and on the court training me after working long hours at the firm."

"You never have to thank me; just keep winning on and off the court and your ole' pops will be alright. I am proud of you, baby."

"Mom, I missed you so much. I smelled the peach cobbler from the highway!"

"I made all your favorites, so let's get inside before dinner gets cold. There is a peach cobbler in there with your name on it and Blue Bell vanilla in the freezer."

Just like old times, however, while making our way inside, I became overwhelmed with guilt. My parents have always supported the decisions that I have made, but I have doubts about them supporting my relationship with Blair. On the other hand, there was no way that I could disappoint them by deceiving them. I have to tell them while I am here and Blair has been calling me all day since I've been gone. He is not happy with the fact that I have not told my parents about him and does not understand that I have to tell my parents about us at just the right time…if there is such a thing. Still, the more I ask him to be patient, the more impatient he becomes.

"Mom, everything looks and smells so good. There is nothing like home cooked meals after eating take out most of the season. Mom…Dad…there is something that I need to tell you guys."

"What is it, honey? You know, in this family we have an open communication policy and we can tell each other anything."

"Thanks, Mom…I know."

"Well…what is it Gabby? You are not pregnant are you, Gabrielle?"

"No, Dad…I am not pregnant, but I did meet someone since I have been gone and it has gotten pretty serious."

"Well, honey, you are not pregnant and you met a nice young man; that's ground for a toast."

"Not so fast. She said that she met someone and it has gotten pretty serious. I will determine if he is a nice young man or not."

Looking around the table at both my mom and my sister, with their sudden interest being the food on their plates, I knew that I was up against Dad, alone. So much for my amen corner.

"His name is Blair La Fleur and he plays for the LA Earthquakes."

"Blair La Fleur? I saw a piece about him on ESPN. He was raised by his grandmother, his mother was a drug addict, he has been locked up for selling drugs on more than one occasion and if it had not been for his ability to bounce a basketball, he would probably still be selling drugs or behind bars. Gabrielle, what could you possibly have in common with him other than basketball?"

"He is actually a nice person, Dad, and his past is just that… his past and I love him."

With my father at a loss for words, his silence was a clear indicator that he was livid. However, I made the right decision by coming clean and not have them find out secondhand information about Blair and me.My heart sank as my dad excused himself from the table. Only moments before, he was expressing how proud of me he was and in a split second, I have let him down. Tears formed in my eyes as I thought about the disappointment that I probably brought to my family.

"Gabrielle, your father will come around. You know that you are his baby and he only wants the best for you. I am sure that Blair is great and I cannot wait to meet him. Give your father a little time. I will talk to him tomorrow and everything will work itself out. It always does."

A mother's love always has a way of making a way out of no way and sense out of nonsense. My mother's faith and strength always amazes me and she has not let me down so far, so if she says that everything will be okay, I will take those words at face value, and trust and believe them to be true.

Chapter Eight

LA Sparks Vs. Washington Mystics

"Okay so me and my second lady
are watchin' my first lady
inaugurate the WNBA hoopsters
from the nation's capitol...
She's grabbin' boards
and shot blockin'...
I knew Jess was gonna try
and do some blockin' of her own...
But I got this, and either she
or I are gonna be gone...
What gives?
Even without a clock,
Jess knows what time it is..."
— Blair LaFleur

"Yeah, babe! That's the way to grab that rebound. They can't stop you, boo. They can't stop you."

"Well, shoot. You cheer harder for Gabrielle than we do for *you* guys."

"Come on, Jess. That's my girl. I mean what do you expect?"

"Your girl, huh? What do I expect? You really don't get it, do you?"

"Get what? And why do we have to discuss this now?"

"Because ,Blair, I'm in the middle of something I shouldn't have even been a part of."

"Well, I didn't hold you at gun point to make you join up."

"I know you didn't, but you really influenced me. Honestly, it's not about whose fault it is. Bottom line, both you *and* I betrayed Gabrielle."

"And she's gonna get betrayed a lot more if we don't help her beat the Mystics."

"Blair, I don't know how I let you talk me into this."

"Again, sweetie...we're here at the Staples Center, in the middle of a big game, you chose to come with me, and now you're getting all sensitive on me?

"I've been sensitive."

"But doggone. I mean, you're really letting it out now. What did you do, go to a strong black woman conference or something after we hooked up? You here, I'm here and we cheering for Gab. So can we please talk about this later?"

"Well, I don't mean to sound like a brat, but I've been uncomfortable all along. I just couldn't think of when to bring this forward."

"Obviously not. Because we're in the middle of the game."

"I'll stop on one condition."

"What's that?"

"That you take me to the next home game..."

Man, these women think they can just woo you and have their way. They got those big brown eyes battin' and ain't a thing I can do about it. She feels bad about all of this, but she's not complaining one bit about the sex. Hmmm...typical.

"No doubt, shawty."

"Oh, and Blair..."

"What?"

Damn, I can't believe this heffa tongue kissed me in front of all of these people!

"Well damn, Jess. I don't mind you kissin' me, but they got it all on the kiss cam."

"Ooooh. I'm sorry. I guess I got carried away."

"And not only did they show it live, they're showing it again. And only everybody is cheering for us."

"I guess that wasn't a good move, huh?"

"No, not if you tryin' to be discreet."

Damn, and Gab's on the bench, too? I wonder if she looked up at the jumbotron and saw it. Lord, I hope not. If she did, both me and Jess are dead for real.

"Dang, Blair…so do they put every kiss up there on the jumbotron?"

"No, but if you are with the new LA expansion team, they do. And if you're makin' out with a cheerleader, they eat stuff up like this. Watch, they may even have it in the LA Times tomorrow."

"Oh, no!"

"Oh, yes. Jess, just be more careful. You know we can't carry on like this. That violates our rules of engagement."

I know this heffa didn't just forget that she is a jump-off. I should have never let her come to the game with me. "Well, Blair, do you want to know why I kissed you for real?" "Um, not really. But I am curious. If I let you answer, will you promise to stop talking about this? Because I'm quite sure we both have it coming from Gab later on."

"I love you. There! Are you happy now? I love you. And it's all your fault. I love you."

"So, what the hell am I supposed to do now? Huh? We had a deal, and your ass fell in love. What the hell is that all about?"

"I'm sorry, Blair. That's just the way it goes when you fool around."

"Well, you know ain't nothing gonna happen. Gab is the girl I'm gonna marry and that's it."

"You can marry her, but there will be conditions."

"Who the hell are *you* to talk conditions?"

Damn, now she got me gettin' loud with her and everybody is staring. Let me see if I can calm this down a bit before it gets too much more out of hand.

"Well, you know. Jess…things do happen and I understand that I played a major part in this wrongdoing. So, just let me say that you'll be taken care of."

"You promise?"

"Yes, I promise."

"Okay, give me a hug baby."

"Aight."

Damn, they got us on that jumbotron again.

"Look, Jess…let's chill with this affection stuff for now. They keep puttin' that damn kiss cam on us. This is not good."

"Okay then."

Man, I don't know why I do this to myself. Back in the Nolia, they said I was the master of shootin' myself in the foot. I was the first person in my family to go to college. I had a basketball scholarship, but didn't really produce in the classroom. And on top of that, I was the biggest ho on the yard. Hard to suppress that demon when access to beautiful women increases by the day. Lord, if I come out of this one alive, I'm gonna make my grandma proud by straightenin' up and flyin' right. I've got to stop this. Lord, please help me stop this.

…AFTER THE GAME…

"Girlfriend, you did a great job. Come give ya girl, Jess, a hug!"

"Jess, you're so silly. I played alright. But thanks for the love."

"You know I gotta support my fav LA Spark."

"Hey Gab. Baby, you held the paint down tonight."

"I did what I could do, hun. I appreciate my own personal cheering section. Ha…I saw you clowns cuttin' up up there."

Damn, she saw us? Okay, Jess, um, don't be eying me like that. You know ya'll women pick up on that stuff. Hell, I got a relationship I'm tryin' to keep now.

"You know it, babe. Jess and I decided at the last minute that we'd come to the game, sit in your fav cheering section and make some things happen. Well, I see it worked because ya'll won."

"I guess it did, hun. Thank you guys for cheerin' me on. I needed all the cheerin' I could get tonight."

"Gab, you did well, sweetie."

"I agree with Jess, ma. You worked it out. Those Washington Mystics wish they never even ran into you."

Dang, I wonder why she acting all dejected now. Hmmm. Now I'm kinda scared. But I'mma do all I can to keep everything light.

"So, um, what's on the agenda tonight, ladies?"

"Well, Mr. La Fleur, I'll have you know that me and your girlfriend have been invited to a party later at the House of Blues."

"House of Blues? I heard that joint's gonna be poppin' tonight. I need to roll through there, myself."

Now, I know they gonna invite ya boy.

"Um, not so fast ball player. I said Gab and I were invited. So it's girl's night out for us. So what are you gonna do besides not go to House of Blues?"

"You so funny, Jess. You know a brotha like me has plenty to do. As a matter-of-fact, some of my teammates talkin' about hittin' Universal Studios just to get away for a minute."

"Sounds like fun, babe. I know you'll be on your best behavior."

"You better know it, mamacita."

There Jess goes with those *um hum* stares. I told her about that. Looks like I'mma have to remind her again. Quit makin' them damn faces and gestures in front of my woman because I don't wanna hear about 'em later on.

"Well, we gotta little time before we hit the spot. Blair, Gab, let's go get some wings. Ya'll down?"

"That's a good idea, Jess. Blair, are you cool with it?"

"You know I'm always down for the eats."

...AT THE WING PARADISE...

"I wonder why everybody is staring at us. Oh, I know why, I'm only having dinner with LA Sparks and Earthquake superstars. I love it. Plus you're both nice looking. You guys got that mass appeal. Shoot, you ought to let me be your manager. I will round everyone up tonight and charge them for autographs."

"Jess, you have lost your mind, girl. But I like that idea for chargin' for autographs. Now that's gangsta. The true NOLA is coming out of you after all."

"Charge for autographs, babe? Man, it's way too early for that."

"Sweetie, it ain't ever too early to make money."

"And being that this is SoCal, everybody always expects some liberal taboo stuff to go on. I betcha paparazzi is lurking somewhere nearby, wondering what's going on between us three."

"Yeah, them TMZ cats probably think we gotta *ménage à trois* goin' on or something."

And boy would that be nice. These two round-booty tens right here are enough to drive any man berserk.

"Right. They'll print something about a two basketball player and cheerleader threesome."

"Now Gab, that's not too far-fetched, girl. Because the media knows anything goes around these parts."

"Jess, you said something then, my friend. When it comes to ratings, media don't give a damn about integrity and credibility. They just wanna put it out there. Then ask for forgiveness."

Shoot, I'd be a great media person. Just go for what I know, then suffer the consequences.

"That's right, ya'll. Let's give them something to print about. I mean look at us, we're camera ready. They can snap all day. We'll benefit from it. too. Maybe we can talk about that ménage and let somebody hear it and put it in an article."

"You guys don't be ridiculous. Trust me, we get enough press. We definitely don't need any bad press. It'll just be something that our attorney's become more popular on. We're in L.A., and this is how it is."

"You right, sweetie. This is what we signed up for. But you gotta admit, it does make you wanna flex sometimes to see what type of impact you can have."

"I understand, baby. It's very tempting. But you'll get enough flextime when you get out there and start grabbing those rebounds at the Staples Center against the Lakers and Clippers."

That's why I like my woman. She knows how to keep it real with a brother.

"Waiter! We're ready to order now. 'Cause me and my girl Gab got some stuntin' to do tonight!"

Chapter Nine
After Party, House of Blues

"Do you believe
that I'm naive?
Is the thought plausible
that I'm gullible?
Colorful images of uncertainty
have painted
the walls of my paradigm...
and all I want
is for my little light to shine
but I'm just not so sure
things are gonna pan out
the way I thought they would...
I just don't know...
Maybe I should consort with the dime dropper
of the neighborhood...
Or maybe I should just stick to shooting a ball,
that way, I'd never have to leave the safety of the court...
AT ALL..."
— Gabrielle Renfro

It's been a long time since I have been to the House of Blues and not much has changed. The same old, tired atmosphere… just new music and faces. It was a packed house full of ballers wanting to be rappers, rappers wanting to be ballers, video vixens wanting to be actresses and then there are the groupies looking for any opportunity to land a NBA player, poke a few holes in some condoms and collect a child support check for 18 years if she doesn't get wifed. I really preferred to stay in with Blair, but since Jessica insisted on a Girl's Night Out, I will make the most of the evening. Regardless, I am out of here in two hours. Just enough time to listen to some music, have a few drinks, two step a little and kick it with my girls. I wish I hadn't let Jessica talk me into this…I really wanted to spend time with Blair before my flight in the morning.

"It is jumping up in here tonight, Gab. Anybody that's somebody is here. I so needed this night to unwind. Come on, let's go to the bar and get a drink."

"Ok, cool…let's go get drinks. I could really use a Hennessey and Coke."

"Hennessey and Coke? Gab you never drink brown liquor and you always order Cosmos."

"Jess, tonight was a big win for the Sparks against the Mystics and since I am here, I might as well have a good time and celebrate hard."

"Now, that is true. You played a good game tonight, so you deserve a few Hennessey and Cokes. Excuse me, Mr. Bartender, we need a Hennessey and Coke and an Apple-tini!"

"Girl, you are crazy. I swear every time you open your mouth, you are flirtatious. Shoot, maybe Mr. Bartender will add an extra shot of liquor in our drinks."

"And maybe he will give them to us free, too."

"Jess, you are a mess. He is a bartender! The likelihood of that happening is slim, especially with all of the money he can make up in here tonight. I highly doubt that he will comp our drinks, but that guy is staring at you over there. We might be getting free drinks tonight after all."

"Yes, he is something delicious, but I will pass."

"You will pass? Jess, that brother is fine! He looks familiar. I think he plays for the LA Earthquakes, too. Yep, that's Blair's teammate, Crocker. I'mma ask Blair about him and have him hook ya'll up."

"Come to think of it, Gab, that is a great idea. I'd like to get to know Mr. Crocker a little bit better."

"There you go…. Mr. Crocker!"

As we laughed in unison and waited for our drinks, I vibed to the music, thinking about all of the freaky stuff that I was going to do to Blair and how I was going to do it when I get back from Minneapolis.I have been thinking about that man endlessly since we made love the other evening. My alter ego will be in full effect. Who would have known? Gabrielle Renfro and Blair La Fleur… one of the hottest couples on the scene. We have come a long way from the Sparks press conference until now. Gabrielle La Fleur has a nice ring to it. I can see it now…a small intimate wedding with a few close friends and family, a wedding cake adorned with Stargazer Lilies, a string quartet, and the whole nine yards.I noticed my teammate, Dina, sitting over in the VIP section with a few other teammates, waving me down. Dina Perez played standout point guard at Prairie View A&M before coming to the LA Sparksa few years ago. Of all my teammates, I am closest to Dina.

"Come on, Jess. Let's go over here. My girl, Dina, and some of the other Sparks are here."

"Ok, cool…come on let's go."

Humbled by the congratulations I received, I high fived other teammates and NBA players. I signed a few autographs for a few fans while Jess and I made our way over to where Dina and the other Sparks were.

"Gabby, great game! What has gotten into you lately? Or shall I say who? I saw Blair La Fleur up there cheering for his girl."

"Dina, girl you so crazy! Yeah that's my boo. He's a great support system and he helps to keep me focused and my game tight."

"Yeah, you and Blair are everywhere these days. Television. Magazines. Ya'll have become quite the 'lil power couple. Just be careful and stay focused on the game."

"Did you not see me on the court? I am more than focused, baby!"

"Well, since Gabby did not introduce us, my name is Dina… and you are?"

"Oh, I'm sorry. My mind drifted in a different direction for a minute. Dina this is Jessica. Jess this is Dina. Jess is a cheerleader for the LA Earthquakes."

"So, you cheer for Blair's team, huh?"

"I cheer for the LA Earthquakes, not necessarily Blair's team."

"Hmph…either way nice to meet you, Jessica…I think."

"Likewise, I think."

I'm not sure what is going on with this Dina chick, but this is totally an epic fail. I do not like her and I am quite sure the feeling is mutual. Maybe she saw Blair and me kissing on the jumbotron. Even if so, what business is it of hers? I swear by the way she is acting, you would think that she is screwing Blair. I see right now I am going to have to keep both eyes on this heifer and watch my back because she has a hidden agenda. I just have not figured it out yet.

"Come on, ya'll! They are playing the Cupid Shuffle. Let's dance," I said to break the tension that was obviously building between Dina and Jess.

"Gabby, I just want to sit here, have some wings, drinks and chill. I am really not in the mood to have my ass groped tonight. But, I do need to talk to you about something. "

"Sure, Dina…what's up? Is everything alright? Do you want to go outside and talk where it's a little quieter?"

"Come on, Gab, we were invited to one of the hottest parties in LA tonight. Let's have a good time. I am sure that whatever Dina has to talk to you about can wait?"

"Jessica, you go do what you do best—dance. I promise not to keep her too long."

Tonight the shit is about to hit the fan. I knew it…she saw Blair and me kissing and if she saw, I wonder who else saw? I have to find a way to get Gab out of here. I told Blair that I was not cut out for this love triangle and he needed to choose and now we are about to be exposed, but it does not even matter at this point because this needs to end anyway. And it's better for it to end sooner than later before I get even more caught up emotionally with him.

"Jess, give me a second. I need to make sure that everything is cool with Dina and then we can hit the dance floor. "

"You know what, Gabby…it's cool. We can talk another time. I wouldn't want your friend, Jessica, to have a temper tantrum over there."

"Yes…come on, Gab…let's go dance. I think I need another drink, too."

Hey big baller…this is Dina. Your girl played a great game tonight and you and your jump-off put on a great show for the audience on the jumbotron. I see some things never change. The only reason why I did not tell Gabby about us tonight is because we are on a winning streak and I need for her to stay focused on the game, not to mention the fact that she's my friend and I don't want to hurt her. But, Blair, I am warning you…you either end this thing that you have going on with Jessica or I will tell Gabby everything and I mean everything! By the way, hope you have a great season. Dina.

Chapter Ten
Gabrielle's House

> "Sin is sin...
> And I ain't tryin' to run
> from what I've done...
> All I know is that I've come
> a mighty long way...
> and Gramps used to work many
> long days to pave a way
> for me...
> It's because of her, I know how to
> love Gabrielle,
> But it's because of me,
> my soul has just bought a one way
> ticket to hell...or a jail cell...
> With that, I ain't tryin' to bring Jess down
> I just want her to go down
> then get from 'round here...
> So my baby and I
> can steer our ship to the waters
> of Holy Matrimony...
> Because I would die for her
> ...and I know she would die for me..."
> — Blair LaFleur

Man, I really didn't plan for this to happen, but damn, I guess it kinda did. And since it did, I may as well make the best of it. I got my own keys, Gabby and 'nem are at Minneapolis this weekend, and Jessica is drippin' wet horny. I'm tryin' to do better, but I guess you can take a player out the Nolia, but you can't take the Nolia out of a player. I'm a man, so I'm gonna deal with this situation. God only knows what's gonna happen when I deal with this getback I know Karma's gone heap on a brother. With that, I ain't gone worry. I'm just gonna sit my ass up in these boxers, chug this Hendog and Coke, watch a movie in Gabby's home theater, and wait for this jimmy waxin' I got comin'.

"Blair, babe, where are you?"

"Jess, I told you I'd be in the theater. Now, bring your fine ass on in here."

Damn, I was kinda pissed at her earlier in the day for trippin' on me while we were at lunch and I was on the phone with Gabrielle. But she's coming up in here with a cut-off sweatshirt and a pair of red satin panties with the word *open* on the back of them. See, this is what I'm talkin' about. If you get in trouble, you gotta make sure you get your money's worth. Now, that's what's up.

"Hey, baby, you need your Hen and Coke topped off?"

"Na, mami, I'm good. But I can't wait for you to top me off."

"Boy, you silly. What movie we watchin'?"

"I got Fatal Attraction on right now. You wanna check out something else?"

"Negro, you ain't funny. But yeah we can watch it. I'm cool with it."

Man, watchin' that heffa put those thick lips on the rim of that glass is doin' something to me. Dayum. Man, if I could get Gabrielle to join us tonight with her t-shirt and panties on as well, this would be a good night.

"Hey, babe, you look like you ready to rock now...right now. How 'bout we pause this movie and you break me off right quick. I'll break you off afterwards. Whatcha say?"

"Break you off? You don't treat a queen like that. You still talk to me like I'm your convenient jump-off. I told you about that. You want me to do for you, you gotta do for me. I got a list of demands, babe, and I think you need to adhere to them."

"A list of demands? When did you show me your contract? Woman, I'm gonna show you a list of demands. Bring your round booty over here."

Yeah, that's right woman. You know who daddy is. Come on over here and make my toes curl. Yeah, that's it. "Blair, you're lucky I'm in love with you. Because if I wasn't, your ass would have been as good as left."

Man, women know they are a trip. When they're about to give it up, they have to make sure they throw a dig or two in there to make it seem as if we not gettin' the draws for free.

"I know, boo. Now, come over here and make daddy happy."

That warm breath on my mid-section makes junior want to jump like Kriss Kross. Damn! Junior is a sucker for tongues. Whew. Man, Jess is deep tonight. Oh, my God.

"You good, Jess?"

"Uhr huhr."

Dammit, that's what the hell I'm talkin' 'bout. Work it, baby... work...it!

"Damn, Jess, you keep this up, you gone make me fall in love with you. And you know we can't have that. I'd have to do a big love and take you *and* Gabby to the altar."

Ouch, damn! I know this heffa didn't just bite me. What the?

"Jess! Girl, what are you tryin' to do? Ruin a brother for life? What's up with that?"

"If you know what's good for you, you'll just acknowledge me and no one else, Blair. This is my time. Please respect it."

Can you imagine that? A ho wants respect? Okay, I guess I can give it up to her if she's givin' it up to me.

"You got it, babe. Now, don't keep junior waiting. Ahhh, there you go. Now let's get back to this love thing."

"Uhr huhr. Uhr baby. Huhr."

"That's it, mami. I just can't...I just can't...I...I...whew! Baby, you doin' it tonight. I need to give you Hen and Coke more often. This is how you treat your man."

"Just relax, baby. Let Jess go to work on you."

Damn. Man, I'm so hard, I could literally hang Jess by her mouth while standing on the edge of a cliff.

"Baby, if you're thirsty, I'm about to quench it. Get ready… get uhhhh…."

Oh, here it comes. This has got to be a good one 'cause I've got a tinglin' in my chest like I ain't had in ages. Plus, I can barely breathe.

"Blair, you nasty SOB…you could have told me."

"My bad, babe. You did it so good, I just, I just, I couldn't resist. Go ahead and go into the bathroom in the hall, and I'll bring you a towel and a rag."

Wow, that felt so good, I'm kinda nervous now. I may have gotten her pregnant through oral. Damn! Whew! This is the good part about being a bad boy.

"Here you go, babe."

"You better make me see paradise when it's my turn, you fool. The way I hooked you up, you owe me forever! Now pass me that mouth wash."

"Hey you got it, mami. We'll be tit for tat. I gotchu. Trust ya boy."

" Now let's finish watching this movie."

"After you…"

Man, that doggone Jessica still has the jingling baby thing going. The ways those cheeks just clap when she walks can just hurt a brother…hurt a brother bad. Even though I bought those red panties for Gabrielle, Jessica is makin' those joints work for real.

"You gonna let me sit in your lap this time while we watch the movie?"

"To be honest, Jess, you coulda sat in my lap the last time."

"You're so bad."

"But my badness is goodness to you, right?"

"You better know it!"

Damn, we've been sittin' back up here for about forty-five minutes watching this movie and I'll be damned if I hadn't reached my peak through Jess' silk draws. Women with creamy thighs and apple bottom booties don't have a clue as to what they do to us fellas. She's just sittin' up here drinking that Henny, sittin' on my lap and got me hard as a rock.

"Kiss me, Blair."

"Sure, babe."

"No, fool…stick your tongue down my throat."

"Now, that's a can do. No problem, mami."

"You ready?"

"Ready for what, Jess?"

"You ready to feed the kitty?"

"Always."

No, she didn't pull those panties to the side and didn't ask where my rubbers are? I guess it must be the Henny that makes her want me to raw dog it. I better not. I don't want to disrespect Gabrielle any more than I have. But then again, if I'm going to get in trouble, may as well do it big and not get the max punishment for a minor offense.

"You better give it to me good, Blair. I'm not playing."

"Well you just keep sippin', 'cause ya boy is 'bout to start dippin'."

"I'm gonna turn back around because I want to look you dead in your eyes and I want you to look me back in mine while I'm riding you."

"That's cool with me."

Damn, she's ridin' me like I'm a mechanical bull or something. I wonder what's gotten into Jess. This is unlike her. But I like it. Man, I hope she's on the pill, too!

"So, Blair. Huh…whew! What's up?"

"Huh. You baby."

"Is that a fact? Huh…"

"Do you see anyone else?"

"No. But there is someone else…and there should be no one else."

"Baby, you know the deal. You know who I love. This is a non-conversation thing. Now can we continue to have fun?"

"What do you mean? I thought you loved me, Blair."

What types of drugs is this ho taking? She knows that jump-offs are limited in their benefits. This should not be an issue at all. She just won't learn for some reason. After this, I'm gonna have to find me another jump-off…that is if I'm gone continue this.

"Look sweetie…are we gone bone or moan and groan about a lost cause?"

"What do you mean by lost cause?"

"I mean, let's finish what we started here."

"Exactly. That means you're gonna love me back and marry me."

"Look here, dammit! I told your dumb ass a while back. You are a chick on the side. That's it! You agreed to this. You willfully participated in all of the sex and everything. You agreed to chill with the crazy talk. So, why now?"

"Because I love you Blair…that's why? Do you think I'd let you blow my back out night in and night out?"

"You do it 'cause you want my magic stick…that's why. You're a horny freak who needs to be tightened up every now and then. And tonight, you're the same, but drunk on Henny."

"So what…I'm drunk. I still know what I want. So what's it gonna be? Me or her?"

"What? You talkin' you and Gabrielle? It's Gabrielle all day, baby. You know that. Now, let me go ahead and get this nut, so we can be through and you can leave."

Now, what the hell is she gonna do with that picture of me and Gabrielle?

"I'm gonna break this picture. And it's gonna symbolize the breakup of you and Gabrielle."

"Look here, ho. You 'bout to wear your welcome out. Don't you touch that picture."

"And what if I do? Oops! My bad. I didn't know it was gonna slip outta my hand like that."

"Get your dumb ass up off me. You 'bout to be toast. Now, you need to get your stuff and get the hell out."

"Make me. You're mine, Blair. If anybody should be put out, it's your other ho, Gabrielle."

"You called my woman a ho? "

"You called me a ho! Why not?"

"You know, you need to be cut with some of this broke glass from the picture you messed up."

"Well, you need to be cut before I do."

No this heffa did not pick up that big piece of sharp glass and is threatening to cut me?

"Put that glass down!"

"I will once you tell me you love me. If you don't, I'm gonna cut off your manhood with it and put it in your mouth."

"Okay, play time is over. Give me that piece of glass before I take it from you."

"Say you love me!"

"No!"

"You bastard! You just used me for sex! After I tell Gabrielle all of the details, I'm gonna kill you both! That is if I don't kill you now!"

What the hell? Is she charging me?

"Jess! Stop! Jess, you don't know what you doin'. Stop!"

"I'll kill you, you son of a bitch!"

"Jess! No! Jess! Jess! I...."

Oh, damn! I told her to stop. Now my career is over. How will I explain to my team and my woman that I tried to stop her from stabbing me, and in the struggle, she stabbed her damn self?

"Jess. Dammit! I told you to stop! Why didn't you listen to me? Now you're bleeding all over the place! Hold still."

"Baby…I'm…I'm sorry. I…I…I need h-help. C-call 911, baby, please."

"Damn, Jess! I didn't ask for this shit to happen. Now look at you. Ah, man…where's the damn phone?"

I am done! There is no explanation for this. Jump-off is lyin' on Gabrielle's Persian rug, wearing her shirt and panties, with a big piece of glass stuck in her gut, blood all over the floor, and I got blood on my hands. Great. I'm toast. Ain't no way I'm getting outta this. Let me call 911 so I can begin getting ready for my prison sentence. Where's that phone?

"You mean this phone?"

"Gabrielle? Where the hell did you come from?"

"I came from Mr. and Mrs. Renfro. And this *is* my house, so I have a right to be here."

"Yeah, that's it."

"So, did she try and kill you, or did you try and kill her? And why do you have your half-naked jump-off bleeding all over my cream Persian rug? At any rate, I think it's best you go ahead and dial 911, Blair."

Man, I ain't ever seen Gabrielle look like that before. Whew! She got a crazed glare like she's 'bout to kill something and I hope it ain't me.

"Okay, babe, I'm doing it now. 911? There has been an accidental stabbing at 225 Malibu Springs Drive in Encino. My name is Blair LaFleur, and the victim's name is Jessica Bourdeaux. I swear it was an accident. She picked up some broken glass, was horsin' around, and accidentally stabbed herself. No, I'm not the home owner. I'm a friend of hers. The homeowner's name is Gabrielle Renfro. Yes. Please send someone fast. Jessica is losing a lot of blood. Again, I swear it was an accident. Okay, we will be here. Thanks. Babe, I thought you were in Minneapolis."

"Obviously, you did. And we were, but the second game got postponed due to structure problems in the arena."

"Why didn't you call me and let me know? Ain't you gonna put your purse down? You're makin' me nervous."

"Because I wanted to surprise my man. But now it looks like I'm the one who's surprised. Then again, I'm really not. I am fine with my purse...thanks."

"What do you mean, babe?"

"Blair, do you know how dumb you sound now? Do you realize how dumb this whole scene looks? One of my best no-good friends is over there dying because you decided to screw around."

"What? Don't tell me you're just gonna jump on her side like that? She wanted this more than I did."

"Oh, so you did want it, huh? Shoulda known this was gonna happen. All of the evidence was right before my face."

"Babe, I know that sorry is not good enough, but I still want to say that I'm sorry."

"You know what, Blair? As bad as I want to hurt you now, I'll only be hurting myself. I can't say I forgive you yet. Heck, I don't even know if we can be friends after this."

Damn, why is she so calm? This almost feels like a setup or something...a scene from a movie. And her good friend is over there just about to bleed to death. This is not right. I don't know whether to run or take advantage of this.

"Jess, stay alive for me now. The ambulance will be here soon. Stay alive for me. Okay?"

"I-I'm s-sorry Blair. I-I'm s-sorry Gab."

"Jess, just don't talk. Save your strength. Like Blair said, the paramedics will be here soon, darlin'."

"Baby, what can we do to help before the ambulance gets here?"

"I mean, I don't know Blair. This situation is messed up all around. I don't know if anything can be fixed now...or ever for that matter. But I tell you what."

"What's that? I'm listening."

"You're looking mighty sexy in those silk boxers."

I know she didn't. What the hell? Man, this is more than scary.

"So whatchu sayin' babe?"

"I'm sayin', are you gonna come over here and let me tighten you up right quick before the ambulance gets here?"

I can't believe I'm not even wanting to take her up on this offer now. I guess my mind is kinda jacked up. We are goin' to hell for this one.

"Okay, babe. I'm here…now what's up?"

"What's up? You're about to be up when I unbutton those boxers."

"Okay, well here, let me…"

"No, Blair, I got this. Look, hands free."

What? Oh, my God. This is, this is…this is yikes…whew!

"Go right ahead, babe. Let me feed that appetite.

There you go…slip junior right on in there."

"Yeah, baby…you feel that?"

"Yes, mami…don't stop. Please don't. Oh baby…don't…baby! Dang, babe…you got a harmonica in your mouth or something? You went from warm to cold. Oh! Oh! Don't! Don't! Gabrielle, what are you doing! Please don't, babe! Please, I…"

Damn, so this is what it feels like when you're about to have your manhood shot off?

"You didn't think I saw you kissing her on the jumbotron? Embarrassed the hell out of me and I'm looking like a fool in front of the whole City of Los Angeles? And now you got her in my house, in my theater room half-naked? And you thought I wasn't going to say a word? I betcha you won't stick nothing else that doesn't belong to you. Oh, and don't worry, I won't kill you with the first one POP! Ohhhh!She did it.

"Babe, had I known. Had I known…I…"

"Shhhh. It's okay, Blair. It's okay…just rest a minute. Lay right here. I'll be right back."

"Gab. Uhhh...I'm, Gab, I'm so s-sorry."

"I know you are, baby. I'll be right back."

Damn, man. My blood is as warm as this shell on the floor. And it tastes nasty. God, I don't know whether I should swallow it down, or spit it out. Either way, I'm done.

"Jessica, you alright?"

"G-Gab, I don't think I'mma m-make it."

"Sure you will. I have something that'll make you breathe better."

No. Not Jessica too.

"Open up, Jess. There you go. This will go directly down your throat and you won't even know what hit you. Love you! It's not a penis but it shoots just the same, bitch! POP! Now see what you did? You gave my man head but now you giving me your brains! Nasty heffa, you! Now I gotta clean up blood *and* brains."

Oh, God...tell me this ain't so. I'm losing so much blood that I can't keep my eyes open, but I could see a damn bullet leaving the back of Jessica's head. Damn, this is some Nolia shit here. The crib has traveled to LA to take me out! Lord, just let me go ahead and die now. I don't care where I go when I die. Just let me die. End it!

"Blair honey! Blair. Looks like we've got a mess on our hands. We got blood and brains. Now who's gonna clean all of that up? And look at you...you've just about bled to death. Look at you, eyes rolling to the back of your head. Now I can't let you suffer like that. Open up!"

POP!

...Now that's a triple dribble violation.

"Ms. Renfro, we have you surrounded. Please put the weapon down slowly, and kick it over to us. Easy now. That's it. Keep those hands up. You have the right to remain silent..."

A Night to Forget

by Carla Pennington & Kenneth Alan Campbell

Regina——I sat at the bar and nursed my fourth glass of rum and Coke. I needed something stronger than my usual Chardonnay. I needed to kill the pain and deception that was flowing through my veins and eating through my skin like acid. I glanced at the time on my cell phone, which made me flush the overflow of tears from my eyes. An hour and a half ago, I should've been named Mrs. Maurice Roundtree. And four hours from now, he and I should have been boarding our eighteen-hour-long flight to Dubai. Unbeknownst to me, Maurice had other plans that didn't include a wedding or life with me.

I knew something wasn't right after seeing the slightly worried faces of my sister and my two bridesmaids as they helped me into my eggshell, strapless wedding dress. They tried to keep smiles on their faces, but I knew something was wrong. They kept eyeing each other as if they were waiting on the other to say something. Maurice's sister didn't help the situation any. She was in a corner whispering on her cell phone while cutting her eyes at me. She tried to mask her worry with a smile, but I saw right through it. I could've sworn I heard her say to the caller, "He's not here." What did that mean? Who wasn't here? Her boyfriend? When she spoke those words, it dawned on me why my sister and two best friends were acting so strange. I stopped my sister from zipping my dress and stepped away from her and my friends.

"What's wrong?" I asked. "This is supposed to be a wedding and no one seems to be happy. What in the hell is going on?" It was like pulling teeth between the three of them. They were starting to piss me off. "What?! Is it Maurice?!" I shouted. I could tell that I had frightened them, but the looks on their faces when I mentioned Maurice's name were death-defying. Before any of them had the opportunity to respond, which they probably wouldn't have, my mother walked inside clutching a Bible. She only did that when something was extremely wrong. Her eyes were filled with tears. I could tell that she was fighting to hold them back as if to protect me. "What is it, Mama?" My eyes were beginning to well up, also, because I didn't know what was going on and everyone seemed too afraid to tell me. I knew if I wanted answers, I was going to have to get them myself. I stepped out of the dress.

"What are you doing?" my mother asked while scrambling to pick the dress up from the floor.

"Everyone in here is freaking me out, so I need to see what's going on."

"Baby, don't go out there." My mother forced a fake smile. "I'm sure he's on his way."

What did she mean on his way? Was she referring to Maurice? Is that who his sister was talking about on the phone? On his way? He should already be here.

I raced out of the room in my white silk robe that I grabbed on the way out. I passed a few guests who looked as though they had received some devastating news. Once I made it to the church doors, I yanked them open. All eyes turned to me and the guests that were obviously leaving stopped in their tracks. The whispers started again. The shock and horror on their faces would forever be branded in my mind. I pushed through them and ran to the altar. I was confused. Maurice wasn't there. I couldn't understand because his limo and groomsmen were present, but there was no Maurice in sight. I rushed to his brother for answers that he couldn't give me. The only thing that he supplied was a sorrowful look. "Jason, where is he? Where is Maurice?" I panicked *while shaking him. He swallowed the lump that seemed to be lodged in his throat and shook his head.*

Embarrassed and confused, I hurried back into the changing room to call Maurice. Something had to be wrong. He must have been hurt or tied up somewhere. My numerous calls to his phone went straight to voicemail. After an hour of crying and swatting away my family and friends, he finally text me: I can't do this. I've fallen out of love with you. When you go back to the apartment, you will find that my things are gone. I'm sorry, Regina.I wanted to reply, but his words numbed me. My sister retrieved my phone after it fell from my paralyzed hand. After reading the message, she quickly wrapped her arms around me. I felt nothing. My world had collapsed on top of me. I couldn't move. I didn't want to move and I definitely didn't want to be comforted. The whispers grew louder and the curious eyes grew bigger. Everyone felt sorry for me. All of a sudden, I felt even more alone. The walls began to close in on me.

"Why didn't anyone tell me?!" I screamed after hopping to my feet. "You all knew and no one told me!" I stabbed them all with my words and my eyes. At the moment, they mean nothing to me. "I hate you! I hate all of you!" My sister tried to wrap her arms around me again, but I pushed her away. My mother rushed to me and I pushed her away as well. "Just leave me alone! Leave me alone!" I dashed out of the church.

I had no clue as to where I was going after diving into the limo and ordering the chauffer to drive. He kept glancing at me in the rearview mirror. He knew what had happened. It was even more embarrassing that a stranger knew that Maurice had stood me up at the altar.Every time I glanced at the empty seat next to me, I burst into tears. Maurice should've been sitting beside me, holding my hand, fondling me and kissing me as we drove to the airport for our week long honeymoon in Dubai. Thousands of non-refundable dollars were spent on a trip that neither of us would be taking.

"That bastard!" I screamed causing the chauffer to glance back at me for the hundredth or so time. I needed to numb my mind and riding around wasn't going to help me do so. The apartment was definitely out. "Driver, can you take me to the Renaissance on Carnegie?" He nodded in the mirror. Fifteen

minutes after arriving at my destination, I grabbed my bag out of the trunk and rolled it inside the hotel. People stared and whispered. They must have known that I had been dumped as well then it hit me...I was in a robe and four-inch heels. I looked like a prostitute.

"Ma'am, do you need any help?" the male receptionist asked when I made it to the desk. "Do I need to call the police or..." I must have looked like Tina Turner in What's Love Got To Do With It minus the bruises.

"No, I need a room for a few nights," I interrupted. After paying for three nights, I received my key and boarded the elevator. Once the doors closed on the onlookers, I broke down. I fell against the wall and released the tears that I'd been wrestling to conceal from everyone else. When the elevator stopped on the seventh floor, I hurried to my room where I dove into bed. I tortured myself, trying to figure out when and where everything went wrong. He had every opportunity in the world to tell me that he no longer wanted me, but he chose our wedding day to make a complete fool out of me. I cried myself to sleep.

I awoke nearly two hours later hoping that my experience was merely a dream, but it wasn't. I was still living a nightmare. I was still covered in the robe that I wore when I made a mad dash out of the church. I was still wearing the diamond, solitaire engagement ring. It was not accompanied by its mate... the wedding band. It was not a dream or nightmare. I was living a horrendous reality.

The nap didn't help ease the pain. It only made me wish that I was asleep longer because the thoughts and heartache disappeared. I needed something stronger to help me get through the ordeal or at least put me back to sleep.

I spent nearly thirty minutes in the shower bawling my eyes out before I noticed my skin had started to prune. I forced myself out of the shower and cried a little more as I rummaged through my luggage for something to throw on. Each item that I pulled out was new and contained store tags. They reminded me of the new life that Maurice and I were about to share. I eventually settled for a piece, dressed, and then headed to the bar where the horrid thoughts continued to take their toll on me.

I still couldn't believe that after six years together, Maurice decided to end things through a text on our wedding day. I should've picked up on the signs when he started staying out later than usual, coming home later than usual or leaving for work earlier than usual. He would cancel lunch dates with me and make up excuses as to why he didn't want to go catch a movie. Those were things that we did on a regular basis. The changes began a few months before our wedding day, so I figured it was wedding jitters and I left it alone. I knew when the big day came, they would all go away. I didn't think he'd go with them.

"Ma'am, the bar will be closing in about an hour. I can close out your tab here or charge it to your room," the waiter jarred me back to the present while trying to avoid eye contact with me. I glanced up at the wall clock and realized that I had been in the bar for nearly two hours. I couldn't blame him. I was a wreck. Every five or ten minutes, I would break down into a wail of tears at the thought of something memorable between me and Maurice.

"Just charge it to my room. I'm sure I'll be back tomorrow night." I sniffled. He nodded his head. I didn't want to be around any of my or Maurice's family or friends, so I left that scene at the church. I didn't need the sympathetic looks or to hear *I'm so sorry*. I was right where I needed to be…getting hammered.

"My man, can I get a shot of Cognac?" I turned to my new neighbor who looked as though he needed as much to drink as I did. He smiled at me when our eyes paused on one another.

Domenick—— "Make that a double shot," I addressed the bartender while recalling the one person that had changed my life. She was like water…free flowing, uncontrollable and hypnotic like Niagara's falls.She once possessed the calmness of a soothing, country, cold, transparent stream.As the years progressed, she became the destructive forces of a Tsunami.Now, at this time she was the thunder rattling the windows of my soul. She is Alleanna. "Thanks," I said to the bartender after retrieving my drink and effortlessly pouring it down my throat. I tapped the top of the bar for a refill. Drinking was not my cup of tea, so I could only imagine what it was going to be like waking up the next morning. There comes a time in every man's life when he does something wrong and regretful. This was my time. I gladly accepted this minor infraction.

It was only nineteen years earlier that Alleanna and I had promised that it would take death to separate us.It was nineteen years ago that she promised me happiness, even if it meant we would live in a one room shotgun house. All we needed was each other. At least that's how I perceived things.

The year was 2007 and the economy began its quest to do what no one else was supernatural enough to do. Like destructive waves beating on the banks of ocean front property, the economy started the erosion process of the impenetrable fortress that once protected our love.Alleanna was no longer my Queen.I, the one true King that reigned supreme in her castle, had been served eviction papers.I had to leave.Divorce had planted its white flag on our marriage.I was no longer enough to encourage her to keep our relationship alive.Love's tsunami had relocated us to a place that was no longer recognizable and we could not find our way back to the promise that had been broken.Love reneged and left me staggering to regain my poise.

Years passed and everything in me was longing to be with someone who could un-break my heart.Valiantly, I fought to ward off all who tried to pursue my affection; yet, my battle-worn and chiseled body was feeling the effects of being love starved. Having been born under the zodiac of cancer, I wore the desire for affection like a badge of honor. I was ready to have my fire-breathing dragon slain, dowsed by the moisture that could be produced by only an equally battle-tested woman.I was prepared to explore the deep dark caves of her body. It was at this moment that her mind didn't matter. It was time for me to live again. I downed my cognac.

After Alleanna, I never really gave women a chance. If the woman didn't look like Alleanna, smell like Alleanna, sound like

Alleanna or smile like Alleanna, she wasn't a keeper. My friends and family deemed me as borderline insane, but I wanted what I wanted. I needed what I needed. It took a few expensive therapy sessions to make me come to terms with the fact that *my* perfect Alleanna was gone. That beautiful smile that I awoke to every morning was gone. That long, chestnut brown hair that I constantly ran my fingers through was no more. Those light brown eyes that I would get lost inside of whenever she would look at me had disappeared.

The sniffles coming from my left began to blur visions of Alleanna and that slightly bothered me. I wasn't ready to let her vanish from my thoughts. My visions of her were all I had left. They were the only things that kept me going. Alleanna was my life. Although she was no longer with me physically, I still had a hard time of letting her go.

I turned to the seemingly helpless damsel sitting next to me. I watched her finish off the contents in her glass. Her eyes were swollen. She had been crying. Tears followed the path that the mascara had streaked down her cheek. Evidently, she was going through a rough patch as well. "Bartender, whatever the lady is having, freshen up her glass and double me again, please." The damsel turned and gave me a puzzling look.

"Oh, no. No, thank you. I've had enough for tonight?" Regina addressed Domenick with a warm smile as she used a napkin to wipe her eyes and nose.

"Are you sure? You seem a little empty over there." Domenick smiled back.

Regina did something she hadn't done all day. She giggled. "So, how about that drink?"

"Okay. If you insist." She surrendered. The bartender prepared their drinks.

"Forgive me if I'm too direct, but I must ask," Domenick spoke, "why are you crying?"

"That's not direct. That's plain ole nosey," Regina replied with a slight attitude.

"I'm not being nosey. I'm only wondering why you're here alone at a bar crying."

"So, you think since you bought me a drink that I'm going to spill all my business to you?"

"Look, ma'am, I am not asking you to sleep with me. It simply looks as if you could use a non-judgmental ear. I don't mean to intrude. You just…"

"I just what?" Regina snapped. "I just look like someone who didn't see the signs that her fiancé didn't want to marry her and left her standing at the damn altar?"

Domenick and the bartender locked eyes. "Keep 'em coming. She needs 'em as much as I do," Domenick said to him. The bartender laughed, but quickly stopped when Regina cut her eyes at him.

"And what is *that* supposed to mean?" Regina snapped again at Domenick.

"It doesn't mean anything, sweetie. I promise." Domenick hoped his words would soothe her.

"Keep your drink!" Regina hopped off the barstool, but Domenick gently grabbed her arm. Regina stopped in her tracks and turned to him.

"Please. Don't leave. I could really use the company as well." Domenick pleaded with his eyes. He was a little taken aback by his own actions. Any other time, he would be happy to see a woman walk away, but this time, that wasn't the case. He wanted her to stay. "Let's start over. Hi, my name is Domenick." He introduced himself, then extended his hand to her.

Regina stared at his hand. She had wanted to vent to someone all day. Little did Domenick know, he had become the guinea pig.

She placed her hand inside of his. "It's nice to meet you, Domenick. I'm Regina." She sat back down.

"So, I see you have something you need to get off your chest?" Domenick suggested.

Regina sipped her drink and replied, "Seems you do as well since you came barging in here ordering double shots of cognac."

Domenick laughed heartily. thinking back to Alleanna's snappy comebacks. "So you got me all figured out, huh? Yes, I do have a lot on my mind. I miss my wife." He didn't expect his words to shoot out in such a way, but they did and he couldn't take them back. "I'm sorry for that."

"No need to apologize. Your feelings are your feelings," Regina reassured. "Did she leave you? Seems like a lot of that is going around." She continued thinking back to Maurice's betrayal. The thought angered her, but she held her composure.

"She's dead," Domenick answered.

After hearing his words, Regina felt ashamed for what she had said. "I'm sorry, Domenick. I didn't mean to…"

"It's okay. Today is our anniversary. I take my vacation around this time every year. This is where I first told her that I loved her. It's a self-torture that I deal with."

Suddenly, Regina began feeling a little awkward. While she was crying over a man leaving her, Domenick was hurting due to his wife dying. There was no comparison with the two. "If you don't mind me asking, how did she die?" Domenick sighed deeply as if he didn't want to relive the pain all over again. "I'm sorry. I know that must be a touchy subject."

"Again, no need to apologize. She is not physically dead. Simply put…she's dead to me. She gave up on trying.Anytime a person gives up trying to make life work that to me constitutes a dead person walking. You know the old saying *it is not over until it is over*.Well let's just say that the pallbearer threw his shovel of shit…I mean sand on our marriage!"

Regina felt a slight sigh of relief that Domenick was going through something similar as she. Feeling himself near a breakdown, Domenick quickly changed the subject. "Now that you know why I'm drinking my pain away, tell me more about your farce of a wedding day." Before Regina could tell her story, the bartender interrupted.

"I'm sorry, folks, but the bar will be closing in about twenty minutes."

Domenick pulled his money clip from his back pocket and handed the bartender two hundred dollar bills. "Take care of her tab as well," he told the bartender.Regina opened her mouth to object, but Domenick stopped her. "If anything is going to part from those precious lips of yours, it had better be to answer my previous question." Regina blushed.

"Well, my story is somewhat similar to yours. I guess you can say that it's more embarrassing than anything. I was dumped at the altar." She laughed after speaking the words. "Maurice and I have been together for six years. He proposed to me after three. We've been planning the wedding for the past two years. What's even crazier is that we were in the process of purchasing a home. Oh… Oh…and let's not forget that he dumped me via text."

Domenick playfully choked after her last statement. "You're kidding me, right?" Regina powered up her cell phone. Once it was on, she pulled up Maurice's text message and showed it to Domenick. "If you ever see him again, will you slap him for me and all the other real men in the world because that was foul." Regina released a roar of uncontrollable laughter. "Laughter looks so much better on you than tears," Domenick spoke, causing Regina to slowly halt her laughter. For a brief moment, they locked eyes. The bartender interrupted their gaze when he handed Domenick his change and receipt.

"I guess that's our queue." Domenick smiled at Regina.

Not wanting to end their conversation because she wasn't ready to revisit the embarrassing thoughts of Maurice standing her up, she blurted, "Well, we can finish this conversation in my room if you'd like." Domenick turned to her and even the bartender cut his eyes at her. "I'm sorry. That was too much. I was way out of line," she apologized. She was slightly embarrassed, but Domenick made that feeling go away.

"I'd love to finish talking with you, Regina." It was the truth. In that brief meeting, he wanted to know more about her. It slightly stunned him that he was willing to open up to her as well. He pulled his money clip from his packet again. "Give me a bottle of cognac, a bottle of rum and a can of Coke." After placing his order with the bartender, he turned to Regina.

"Are you trying to get me drunk and take advantage of me or something?" she asked with evil eyes.

"No, I'm not. We're both drinking, so I thought we'd take it upstairs where we're about to finish *talking*," he stressed.

"If you say so," Regina replied. Just remember this…I've spent five years taking self defense classes." He laughed.

"I won't do anything that you don't want me to do." He winked at her and she smiled. "We can order room service when we get up to your room. We need something on our stomachs with all this alcohol, don't you think?" She nodded. The bartender reappeared from the back and rang up the items for Domenick then handed him the receipt. "Damn!" Domenick nearly choked after looking at the receipt while handing the bartender the money. "I should've gone to a liquor store." He chuckled while handing Regina the bottle of rum.

"Domenick, we don't have to have the alcohol. We…" Regina began. but was quickly interrupted.

"Regina, it's okay. I was simply joking around," Domenick assured.

"A-A-Are you sure?" she stammered.

"I'm positive." He stepped off his stool and reached out for her hand. She gladly placed it inside of his. He helped her off the stool. Feeling a little off balance due to the alcohol she had consumed, she locked her arm around his to keep from stumbling. She thought her move would make her feel uncomfortable, but it didn't. She hoped that Domenick wouldn't oppose to her actions. He didn't. Little did she know, she beat him to the punch. He saw her stumble a little as she climbed off the stool. He was prepared to do anything in his power to make sure that she didn't fall. Domenick was slightly ecstatic that she would lean on him for assistance. It brought back a brief memory of a night out with Alleanna. Alleanna wore a pair of heels that were uncomfortable on her feet. She needed Domenick's assistance to walk. Domenick chuckled at the reverie.

"Are you laughing at me?" Regina asked

"No, I'm not. I thought of something funny from my past. That's all." Regina lay her head on Domenick's shoulder. When she realized what she had done, she quickly lifted it. "You're okay. I don't mind." Domenick gave surety. She nestled her head back on his shoulder, then they started toward the elevators.

Regina——I began to have second thoughts as Domenick and I entered the elevator. When the doors closed, my body became a statue. Again, I began second guessing myself. Everything he told me at the bar could've been a lie to get me to where we were heading. He knew I was vulnerable and he knew I would possibly do anything to forget the previous horror and embarrassment that I endured. Well, if that were the case, he was right. I wanted to forget the three thousand dollarcustom made wedding dress, the sympathetic looks on the faces of my family and friends and most of all…Maurice. I wanted to forget everything about the day. If that meant sleeping with Domenick, then so be it.

Domenick turned to me when he noticed that I wasn't moving. "Are you okay?" he asked. I was mute. "Regina, if you're uncomfortable with this, it's okay." When I didn't move, he reached to reopen the doors. I wasn't ready to part ways with him.

"Seven," I uttered. He turned to me.

"Excuse me?" he questioned.

"M-My room is on the seventh floor."

"Are you sure about this, Regina?" I nodded. I took a deep breath when he pressed the button.

I still had time to renege on my decision, but the voice of reason was nowhere to be heard. The slight jerk upwards caused me to stumble a little although I was already leaning on the wall for balance. Domenick noticed. "Do you need to use my arm again?" He smiled while extending his arm to me. I gladly accepted it. I wanted to be closer to him and allow the scent of his manly cologne to hypnotize me again as it had done on our stroll to the elevator.

The way he allowed me to hold on to him reminded me of a time when Maurice had to grab hold of me after we exited a whirlwind carnival ride. He ended up having to carry me to our car. A small part of me was hoping that would be the case with Domenick and I. *Calm down, Regina*, I chastised myself. *This maybe the place, but it's definitely not the right time.*

As the elevator began its slow climb, I secretly stared at Domenick. At the bar, we were too engrossed in our conversation for me to grasp the full effect of how sexy he actually was. When he smiled at me a few times, I noticed a single dimple in his right cheek. I also noticed the small gap between his two front teeth that took nothing away from his handsomeness. In my opinion, the gap heightened it. He stood about six feet even with a slender build that formed a print in his shirt. I should've been ashamed of myself for pawning over this man when I was about to marry another just a few hours ago, but I couldn't help myself. Domenick was there and not Maurice.

Domenick——Regina was neither aware of my nervousness of being in her presence, nor was I going to reveal this to her just yet. We men are supposed to be rock solid.I was not sure if I was nervous of the fact that she reminded me so much of my dear Alleanna or nervous of the fact that something could possibly go down between us tonight.Never have I allowed myself to be alone with another woman since the first day that I met Alleanna.Well, let me correct that. Never have I allowed myself to feel such a way while in the presence of a woman. Never had I fallen under the control of the scent that a woman's body emits as it progresses through the stages of sexual arousal.Whatever it is, I was losing this fight.Although I have wanted to move forward, I have been petrified with the thought of being able to perform sexually when given an opportunity.Alleanna was the last woman that I'd slept with. She knew my body and I knew hers. She knew what turned me on and vice versa.

Whenever a woman touched me, I was afraid that the team would not rise to the occasion even though it got massively hard when I thought about women and pleasured myself. They say that it is hard being a woman, but I think that it is harder being a man. There is so much at stake if a brother cannot get his *man* to salute. He risks any future opportunities at getting that sweet nectar or any other because the word spreads like wildfire when you and your best man are nonfactors.

I glanced at Regina and chuckled internally when she swiftly turned away from me. Evidently, she and I were both going through the same thing. She was so beautiful and sexy standing there in her canary tube top dress and canary and brown open toe heels. I couldn't believe that I was admiring her in such a way. Oh God, I needed to feel her beautiful, soft, red glossed lips nibbling on my shaft.Damn! I bet she would use that tongue of hers to bathe my man like a kitty cat taking the time to clean herself. I wondered if she could read my mind.If not, I bet she knew something was materializing because this space was starting to feel awfully small. It was getting awfully hot. Damn! They should keep water on these elevators. That is funny as hell because the trip is not that long, but it sure felt like an eternity. My eyes became fixated on her ass. It was nice and round and sat up high. I bet I could set a glass atop of it and it wouldn't fall. Man, I wanted to rush that tight plump bottom and pin her up against the walls like Alleanna and I used to get down when she came to visit me on my lunch breaks. Yeah some rough sex would be what the doctor ordered. I would love to jack knife her, bend her over, cock my shot gun and see what I could shoot. It was hard for me to gather my thoughts on the elevator because my imagination was working overtime. Regina had done what other women had failed to accomplish. She turned me on. She aroused and tempted every fiber of my being. I was ready to pound her until her legs trembled uncontrollably. I smiled while thinking that there was such a disparity between what was taking place in my mind and what I was afraid would not happen in reality.

❦

The bell went off signaling that they had made it to the seventh floor, and then seconds later, the door slowly opened. Each waited for the other to take the first step out.

"Well, I'm not sure which room is yours," Domenick said, causing Regina's cheeks to flush with embarrassment. She didn't budge. "Regina, again, we don't…"

"My room is that way." Regina pointed down the hall and interrupted what she knew he was about to say. She was not turning back. Domenick was her temporary fix, her temporary savior and her temporary everything. She stepped off the elevator. Domenick tried to mask his eagerness to follow her, but she couldn't help but notice when he bumped into her. He silently cursed himself as he stared into her eyes when she turned around. The dark eyeliner and lightly brushed gold eye shadow made her eyes stand out even more. He didn't want her to look away from him. As they stared at each other, her lips slowly curled upward into a bashful yet flirty smile. The attraction was definitely there.

The short walk to her room seemed like a country mile to the both of them…much longer than expected. Their hearts beat fast and simultaneously with each step that they made. They were both eager and nervous at the same time. Regina felt more and more devilish knowing that Domenick was behind her. She knew that he was watching her every move so she swayed her hips from side to side a little harder than she usually would do. Little did she know, every sway of her hips enticed and aroused Domenick and for once, his feelings didn't bother him. Alleanna had moved on, so why hadn't he? He was being faithful and loyal to something that no longer existed.

"We're here?" Regina spoke when she stopped in front of her room door. They both swallowed imaginary lumps in their throats. As soon as she was about to slide the key into the door's slot, her cell phone rang. Without thinking, she looked at it and froze when she saw Maurice's name. "Is he serious?" she spoke softly hoping Domenick didn't hear her, but he did.

"Is that him?" Domenick asked. She nodded. "Maybe you should answer it," he suggested with a slight feel of anger coating over him. He knew the night was about to come to an end before it even began. He watched her stare at the phone. He could tell that she was going through the motions of whether or not to answer it. He was right. Regina couldn't believe that Maurice was calling her. As far as she was concerned, Maurice could join Domenick's ex-wife at the imaginary cemetery that he had buried her in. The phone stopped and then it rang again. "Answer it, Regina. You need to face this and maybe this is the time."

"Why should I? He had months, even years to tell me that he was no longer in love with me but he chose to embarrass me in front of my family and friends. As far as I'm concerned, he can go to hell with gasoline boxers." Domenick laughed causing her to laugh as well. "I know you, of all people, understand how I feel." She was right. He did know how she felt. It was hard for him to come to grips when, out of the blue, Alleanna asked him for a divorce. He knew exactly how she felt. He didn't want to see or talk to anyone.

He watched Regina helplessly stare at the phone as it rang over and over again. A lonely tear fell from the corner of her eye. She was helpless…torn between love and hate. That was a bad place to be. It was worse than purgatory. He felt that he needed to come to her aide and hoped she wouldn't slap him for what he was about to do.He reached for the phone. He wanted to snatch it from her tight grasp but a part of him wanted her blessings for his future actions. He knew that if the ex heard a male's voice, he would be extremely pissed and jealous and he knew Regina wanted him to feel just as shitty as she felt.

Regina looked at Domenick's hand. She knew there were two ways this would go if she handed him the phone. He would either turn it off or answer it. She wanted him to do the latter. Maurice needed to hurt, too.She placed the phone inside his hand.Her prayer was answered.

"Hello?" Domenick answered. "Yes, this is Regina's phone… She's here with me…She doesn't want to talk to you…You should know why she doesn't want to talk to you…Maybe you can try her again tomorrow because we're about to have a few drinks…" Regina could hear Maurice scream obscenities at Domenick and it warmed her heart to know that he was pissed. Maurice hung up and called right back. When Domenick answered it, Regina grabbed it from him, gave Maurice a piece of her mind then turned the phone off. "I think we ticked him off." Domenick chuckled.

"Who gives a damn? Now, where were we?" she asked as she slid the card back into the key slot again. The light glowed green.

With his eyes locked on her, Domenick reached in front of her and opened the door.

"Are you okay with what happened?" Domenick asked before removing his arm and allowing her to enter.

"It helped a little." she smiled weakly.

Once inside the room, Regina gasped at the mess she forgot that she made. As Domenick was about to enter the room, Regina quickly pushed him back out and closed the door. Feeling a little worried, Domenick jerked at the handle but it wouldn't budge. "Regina, what's wrong? Is everything okay?" The door flew open causing him to jump. Regina looked a little stirred. "Is there a problem?" he asked as he tried to look around her and into the room, but no such luck. The door was opened slightly enough for her to shove an ice bucket in his chest.

"We need ice…for the drinks," she stated, then quickly closed the door again. Domenick was still a little worried, but figured everything would be okay once he returned with the ice.

Regina——I leaned against the door and took a deep breath as I stared at my clothes and shoes that were scattered across the floor and beds. Knowing that it wouldn't be long before Domenick returned, I immediately began retrieving the items and shoving them back into the suitcase. I paused when I came across one of the silver and blue, silk, spaghetti strap gowns and robe that I had planned on adorning on one of the nights in Dubai. *No need to let it go to waste*, I thought. I finished repacking the other items then quickly slipped into the gown. If nothing transpired between Domenick and me, at least I would be comfortable while we drank and talked. I sat at the foot of one of the beds and forced back tears as the vacant altar crept inside my thoughts. My phone was sitting next to me and it took everything inside of me to not turn it on and call Maurice back. Being vindictive was not my cup of tea, but it did feel good to know that my and Domenick's actions angered him. He had cut me deep. There was no coming back from what he had done. It was bad enough that he left me at the altar, but what hurt worse was the fact that he had fallen out of love with me. There was no need for any apologies. Those were all the words I needed to hear. Domenick was doing a wonderful job of making me forget about the day.Although what we did in the hall was somewhat childish, Domenick knew what I wanted and needed him to do to make me feel a little better.I snickered as a smile molded on my face. I sat on my hands to keep them from fidgeting and eagerly awaited Domenick's return

Domenick——I stared at the closed door in disbelief and confusion and wondered what in the hell had I gotten myself involved in.I didn't play games.I must have been temporarily out of my mind as I thought about Regina using me to get back at her man.I bet she wished that it was Maurice who stood behind her at the door as she unlocked it, but it was me instead. I could smell her sweat as I breathed on her neck.I imagined the juices running down her legs in a trail to be wiped away by my tongue.I wondered if her room was probably the room that he reserved for them which meant that he knew exactly where we were. I was slightly nervous knowing that he could walk in on us at any given moment. I had to admit that the excitement was thrilling, but it was something different than what I was accustomed to.How could someone so damn fine let herself stoop to playing this type of game? There was a neurotic turn on in thinking that we could be caught.It had to be a turn on for her and could probably end up being the best lay that I have taken part in.I felt so out of control. There was a certain hypnosis to this.I had to pull this together and regain control.I shook with fear knowing that the worse result is that one or all of us could end up dead.Hormones make you stupid and brave. This rush was making me lose my mind and then it hit me. This had to be a new room that he knew nothing about since they were supposed to fly away later. That took a load off. He didn't know where we were. His actions demonstrated that he was still in love with her, but he could've just been pissed at the fact that the woman he was about to marry was now with another man. No man could stand a situation like that. Hopefully, his loss was about to be my gain.

❧

After retrieving the ice and then walking back to the room, Domenick stood at the room door and took a deep breath. He was nervous and the shaking of the ice bucket was proof of that. A few of the cubes fell from the bucket. He glanced at the cubes and then kicked them down the hall. "Get it together, Nick. She's only a woman." He scolded himself. After giving himself a ten second pep talk, he slowly raised his hand then tapped on the door. He clutched the bucket tightly so that no more ice cubes would fall.

On the other side of the door, Regina hesitantly lifted her body from the bed after hearing the knock. She took baby steps toward the door as she untied her robe. She wanted Domenick to know that she wanted him. She knew that sex with a stranger was only a temporary cure for her heartbreak, but it would have to do for the moment. After blowing a long wind through her lips, she opened the door.

Domenick's eyes widened with pure pleasure at Regina's unexpected wardrobe change. The canary, tube top dress was flattering against her form, but the blue and silver gown painted a better picture over her curves. She was even more stunning. "Wow! You look amazing." He gawked at the sight standing before him. She smiled and stepped back to allow him entrance into the room. "So, what was so important that you had to shut me out of here for a few minutes ago?" He chuckled as he scoped the room to find nothing out of sorts.

"I needed to straighten up a little. I didn't want you to think I was such a slob." She smiled before removing the ice bucket from his hands.

"I need to ask you something," Domenick said as he rubbed the back of his head to show a hint of concern. Regina set the bucket down on the table and walked to the kitchenette area to retrieve two paper cups.

"What is it?" she asked while preparing drinks for them both.

"Is this the room where you and Maurice were supposed to…"

"Ewwwwwww! No!" she cut his question. "Maurice knows nothing about this room. I came here to get away from everything. I couldn't go back to our apartment after his blow," she continued after handing him his drink. His suspicions were correct.

"I was only wondering because what we did on the phone was foul and I didn't want any surprises."

"You won't have any surprises from him and I apologize for dragging you into that."

"It's okay. It was kinda fun." They both laughed. "Has he called back?" he asked while taking a seat on one of the beds.

"I don't know. I turned the phone off when we were in the hall," she answered while taking a seat on the other bed. She crossed her left leg over her right. The leg lift caused her gown to slide up a little. Slightly embarrassed, she covered the exposed thigh skin with the robe.

"No need to be bashful now. You changed into that outfit for a reason." Domenick flirted heavily. His words shocked him and forced him to take a long sip from his cup. He was seconds away from flipping the robe back open, but she threw a loop in his plans when she stood up. She reached for his cup.

"Let me refresh your drink." She beamed with naughtiness. She made sure that she stroked his hand with her soft fingers when she retrieved his cup. Domenick watched attentively as she sashayed across the room. The way her French manicured toes glided across the carpet with every effortless step that she made turned him on. The way her black hair bounced as she walked excited him and the icing on the cake was the way she smiled at him. Her smile could brighten a homeless man's day. He couldn't contain himself any longer. He stood up and headed toward her.

As he began his ascent toward her, everything appeared so surreal. It was as if time stood still with every step he took in her direction. His six-foot frame appeared to dawn an S upon his chest for he seemed super human. His bald head was free from razor bumps and his hazel eyes had turned a shade of green. This forty-six year-old man did not look a day over twenty eight.

Damn, damn, damn, Regina thought as she felt Domenick near her. Her back was facing him, but she heard his stealthy footsteps. When they were on the elevator, his orange American Eagle brand shirt and Abercrombie & Fitch acid washed jeans revealed that there was nothing soft about him. He was hard from his head to the feet. As she stared down his body, she got stuck at his crotch. It appeared to be full of nothing but dynamite. She hoped that she'd be the match to light it. She yearned for that explosion. She could only imagine that she would be able to withstand his thighs and crotch pounding against her body. She stopped breathing when he stood behind her.

Regina——Oh my, God! Why is he this close to me? "Let me help you with that," he offered before removing the rum bottle from my trembling hand. His breath on the nape of my neck when he spoke caused my nipples to harden. I retrieved the cup when he handed it to me. He then filled his cup. I could only imagine what was going through his head as he stood behind me and drank his cognac. "Am I drinking alone?" he asked when he noticed that I hadn't touched my drink. I lifted the cup to my lips and took a small sip. I was a nervous wreck and when he placed his hand on my thigh, I damn near lost it. I took slow sips from my cup as he ran the tips of his fingers up and down my thigh. I breathed quietly. "You're so soft," he whispered in my ear. The sips turned into one long gulp. I dropped the cup on the table once I emptied it. He reached around me and prepared another drink. I figured he was trying to loosen me up, but I didn't need another drink for that.

To hell with that rum. I was ready for another type of intoxication. Once my second drink was prepared, he handed it to me. I declined it by shaking my head from side to side. It was an odd turn-on not being face-to-face with one another. There was no need for any more liquor. My previous mission of getting drunk to wash away the day was sidelined as soon as I allowed Domenick inside my room. After turning down the drink, he didn't bother to refill his own.

Domenick——When she didn't accept the drink, I knew what that meant. It was time and I was ready. I slipped my forefingers in the front of her robe and gently peeled it off her skin. I couldn't resist kissing her exposed shoulders as they were taunting me to taste. I noticed her body trembling. I shrugged it off as her having the chills, and then it dawned on me that she was probably just as, if not more, nervous than I was at the moment. I clasped her shoulders and tenderly stroked them. That seemed to calm her a bit.

"Domenick, this is so wrong," she spoke softly.

"I know this may sound corny, but it feels so right." I locked my fingers inside of hers. Her trembling picked back up again. "Are you afraid of me?" I asked boldly. She blew out a long breath.

"No, I'm afraid of me. A few hours ago, I was supposed to be married, but now, I'm here with you…a total stranger."

"Nothing has to happen, Regina. It's been a while for me, too. I know what it's like being with only one person for years."

"That's what I'm afraid of. I shouldn't want you, but I do."

I unlocked my left hand from hers and moved her hair to the side as if I was opening a curtain to let the sun shine in. I was a sucker for a woman's neck and hers reminded me of Alleanna's. I wanted to kiss it and latch my lips on to it until she purred. "I want you, too, Regina."She turned to face me. She raised her hand to a submissive posture and ran it through her hair. This movement raised her full breasts and exposed the print of her dime sized nipples. I couldn't restrain the pearly white smile that I know beamed from my face.At that moment, I knew what was really on her mind and was convinced once and for all that it was the season to rock this.She was so beautiful. It was easy to want her. I wanted to erase the pain in her heart. I wanted her to forget him and, for the moment, I wanted to forget Alleanna.

I gingerly kissed her forehead and repositioned myself behind her allowing my bulging, pulsating thickness to touch her perfectly formed cushion. Before she could speak, I was already massaging her temples with my finger tips and running my fingers through her hair.I decided to wait a moment before I unleashed the Kracken on her. This was a moment that I had waited years for and I wanted to savor every bit of it like one would do an aged wine.

Regina——His gentle caress sent chills from my scalp to the bottom of my feet.The surge was undeniable, yet explainable. I wanted him. He wanted me. I was like heated butter…ready to melt into his arms. "You're so tense," he said when his smooth hands reached my shoulders. I was so lost in the moment that I hadn't noticed that he had stopped massaging my temples.

"Well, you know why."

"Well, we need to do something about that."

The tension in my shoulders slowly eased up as he tenderly pecked them. I closed my eyes to take in the moment. My tremors stopped…a sure sign that there wasn't a damn thing wrong with what we were doing and about to do. My body wanted what it wanted and I was not going to deprive it.

Feeling extra naughty, I poured a small amount of Cognac in his cup, lifted it from the table and spilled a taste on my right shoulder.It trickled down my back. I hoped he would take the bait that I wanted his lips on my skin. "I'm not one to let a good brandy go to waste," he whispered in my ear. A second later, my shoulder belonged to him and his tongue traced the cognac trail down my back.I was happy that I was barefoot because if I was still in the four inch heels, I probably would have toppled over. The tremors started up again as he lowered the spaghetti strap. He didn't want to leave any space unattended.

He cupped my right breast that was now exposed and gently molded it inside his hand as he slowly removed the second spaghetti strap with his other. There was nothing for either strap to cling to, so the gown danced down my body and onto the floor. Shockingly, he followed it. He was now on his knees cleaning the cognac that had found its way to my butt. I clutched the table as his lips explored their new plush toy. I lowered my head and silently called out his name. While still on his knees, he turned me around, his face now nestled on my hot box. I felt his tongue on the outside of my thong as he traced a trail from it to my belly button, to my breasts, andthen finally landed on my lips, which happily parted to allow him entry. He was such a gracious tease. "I want you," he whispered hungrily as he lifted me off the floor.

Domenick——I tried to mask my eagerness as I carried her to the bed, measuring my steps closely so that I wouldn't miss a beat and stumble. Being the cause of her falling to the floor was not in my plan. The only falling I wanted her to do was into my arms. This was the furthest I had gone with any other woman after Alleanna's love betrayal. That betrayal weighed heavily on my heart and wouldn't let me allow anyone inside. A kiss here, a kiss there was where I drew the line, but there was something about Regina. I was very attracted and drawn to her. We were both dealing with issues of love, but we were ready to set them aside to indulge in a night of physical pleasure. I was pumped about being with her and shockingly, I wasn't afraid to show it.

I kissed her lips as I slowly lay her across the bed. I was anxious and desperate to have her. I lay on top of her and stared into her eyes. I could tell that she was afraid, but there was nothing for her to be afraid of. I had no intentions of harming her. I wanted to make love to her over and over and over again if my body permitted me to. Yet and still, I could tell something was bothering her.

"Having second thoughts?" I asked, crossing my fingers that that wasn't the case.

"No, I'm not. For the past six years, I've only been with one man." I brushed her hair out of her face as I listened to her talk. "A-A-And I've never had an orgasm with him." I held back my Kermit the Frog face. Was she serious? I couldn't fathom being with someone for six years and not having an orgasm. That only proved to me that he neither cared, nor was he attentive to her needs.

"You're joking, right? You two were about to be married."

"I wouldn't joke about something like that." I could tell that she was bothered by the situation and that it made her feel slightly embarrassed.

"Well, tonight, I promise you that you will have more than one orgasm," I promised as I pecked her forehead…then her nose… then her lips. She released a heavenly breath. When I placed my hand between her legs, she jumped. "Regina, relax." I hoped my words soothed her. I could feel her wetness through her thong. That excited me and made me want to stick my chest out in triumph. She moaned softly and gently bit the inside of her lip, making me want to taste it again. I slid my hand inside her thong as I savored her lips and tongue. She wrapped her hands around my neck when I slipped two fingers inside her wetness.

"Domenick…" she breathed inside my mouth. My third leg was throbbing to be released from captivity as it beat with excitement, but he had to be a little bit patient because she and I both were enjoying the foreplay. I enjoyed watching the faces that she made as I delved around inside of her. I intensified the moment for her when I massaged around the outside of her clit with my thumb. Her moans intensified as I stared into her eyes that were begging for more. She locked her fingers behind my hand and pulled my face to hers. "I think I'm about to cum," she spoke softly against my lips as she rolled her hips a little faster. She added thrust movements this time that made me finger her a little faster. Her pants and moans increased and I felt her thighs tremble. She squeezed my back and gently pressed her nails into it. "Oh, my! Oh, my! Domeniiiiiiiiick!" she howled before collapsing like every bone in her body had gone fluid. I placed my head up to her ear.

"That was one," I whispered before descending into her drenched abyss.

❧

Regina trembled with anticipation as Domenick's face made its way between her legs. Her thighs trembled even more when he planted wet kisses on the inside of them. She tried to control her breaths, but that was a battle that she couldn't win so she gave up. He pushed her legs up so that her feet would be planted on the bed. He gently pressed her feet to keep her from moving about. Her breaths became sporadic as she felt his breath near her creamy center. As soon as his tongue made contact, she tried to kick out of his hold, but he clutched her ankles a little tighter. He wasn't about to let her get away.

As he tasted her cherry pie, he couldn't help but think back to Alleanna being the only one he ever tasted in such a way. As with Alleanna, he was eager to have Regina in all kinds of ways. He couldn't control it when he was with Alleanna and he couldn't do it now that he was with Regina. He wanted her and he wanted her to know that. Her body twitched as he made his way inside and around her walls. His skills were more than she could stand. She did everything she could to break away from him, but her efforts were thwarted with each attempt.

Maurice had never made her feel such a way. In fact, he hardly ever provided her with oral pleasure and when he did, she wished he hadn't. He made her feel like she was forcing him to do it against his will and she didn't appreciate that. They had no real emotional connection when they had sex and she felt that was the reason she never had an orgasm. On the other hand, Domenick was extremely attentive as if he was where he wanted to be. This excited Regina. She couldn't contain her emotions and the electrifying feeling that soon pulsated throughout her body. She exploded.

Regina———"That was two," Domenick said, standing and smiling at me as my body jerked hysterically. I needed to catch my breath to allow my body to be jumpstarted. I knew he wasn't done with me. His eyes told that story, followed by his actions. He removed his shirt with his eyes still glued to mine. Maurice never looked at me with longing eyes. This made me want him even more and it also made me want to do something I hadn't done in a long time. I sat up, slipped my forefinger inside a loop of his jeans and pulled him to me, slowly unbuttoning his jeans then unzipping them. "You don't have to do this, Regina," he said. I smiled and glanced up at him.

"But I want to." I pulled his jeans and boxer briefs down below his ass. After seeing what he was packing, I wanted to change my mind. It was right in my face…hard and ready. I wrapped my hand partially around the thickness because that was as far as it would go and then I massaged it for a few seconds to get up the courage to put it inside my mouth. I was testing out my gag reflexes as well because I knew I'd be gagging if I allowed it all the way to the back of my throat. He seemed to be enjoying the massage because he was moaning and raking his fingers through my hair. I knew I couldn't go on with the massage forever, so I talked myself into going in for the landing. I gently pushed him back a little and slid out of the bed and onto my knees, never taking my eyes off of him.

Domenick—I blew a long wind when I felt her breath on my Johnson. That feeling, alone, made me want to erupt, but I had to hold back and make sure my feet were planted securely on the floor. She massaged my wholeness with her hands while her breath teased it. For some odd reason, Alleanna entered my mind. Although she and I were one and I loved her to the depths of my soul, she lacked one thing—she refused to perform oral sex on me. After one attempt that freaked her out, she never tried again and I didn't press the issue. It slightly bothered me that my wife wouldn't have me the way that I loved having her, but I let it go. She made up for it with kinky sex moves and allowing me to go inside the back door from time to time. She was my wife and I could only respect her wishes. Her decision not to perform the act didn't stop me from pleasing her. I wanted her to know that I was okay with her decision and that I wasn't a tit for tat type of guy.

Regina thumped Alleanna out of my head when the tip of her tongue traced up and down the veins of my member. It was difficult to mask my emotions. It had been years since I last had a woman show any attention to *him*. I glanced down at her and locked my eyes with hers when I saw that she was looking up at me. She swept her tongue across her lips. "Your turn." She winked her eye. I could've sworn I grew a few extra inches when she did that. Seconds later, my thickness was inside her mouth.

Domenick tried to maintain his composure as Regina's mouth danced up and down his pole. He nearly lost his footing as she pleasured him. It had been years since he last had a woman satisfy him in that way. He had almost forgotten how good it felt. Tingling sensations started from his toes and worked their way up to his eyes and they quickly flickered when Regina's lips latched tightly onto his muscle.

Regina enjoyed the fact that she was providing such pleasure to Domenick. She never felt comfortable performing the act on Maurice. Often times, he made her feel as if it was her obligation to do it and that took the satisfaction out of it for her. That wasn't the case with Domenick. She knew he wanted it, but she also knew that it was not something that she *had* to do. Every dip her mouth made onto Domenick's jolly erased a thought about the day's earlier events. She hoped her actions didn't make Domenick label her as a slut, but she desperately needed the distraction.

Domenick massaged her temples as she dipped and bobbed. He felt sorry for what happened to her earlier. He hoped she didn't feel that he was taking advantage of her because that was the furthest thing from his mind. He wanted to take her pain away just as she was making his disappear. All of a sudden, he felt his pipe bursting and he pulled away from Regina to allow the liquids to spill on the floor.

For a few seconds, they stared at each other before he helped her to her feet. He stepped out of his jeans and boxers. Their eyes told each other that there was no turning back. They had to finish what they started in order for their night to be complete. They would deal with the consequences later, but at that moment, it was about the two of them. Domenick passionately kissed her as he gently laid her across the bed. He noticed a tear roll out the side of her eye. He kissed it away as he steadily entered her.

Regina—— Maurice was no longer in the room. Domenick had taken his place. I gladly accepted the substitute. His eyes stayed glued to mine as he made his mark inside of me. Every slow stroke sent me into a parallel universe…into an unknown abyss that I never embarked upon. He planted heavenly, yet hungry kisses on my neck and chest. While doing so, he never missed a beat between my thighs that were now suctioned onto his hips. I couldn't pull them away. I didn't want to. "Domenick," I whispered in his ear. That seemed to set off a spark. He lunged deeper inside of me. "Oooooooo, Domeniiiiiiick!" He deserved that call. My nails found their way into his skin as I squeezed his shoulder blades. They flexed with each of his movements. My hips danced along with him. He unwrapped his arms from around my shoulders and pressed his hands firmly onto the bed then lifted his body. I bit the inside of my lip as I watched him observe his exploits down below.

"It's a beautiful sight, Regina," he spoke softly. I assumed he wanted me to see the show. I lifted my head and glanced down. I licked my lips when I saw that his machine was well lubricated from my fluids. I could tell that it had no intentions of giving out any time soon. After that visual, I lowered my head back onto the fluffy pillow. His right hand explored my body as it slowly made its way up to my neck. He gently squeezed. My eyes widened. "I'm not going to hurt you, Regina. Just relax." For some strange reason, I believed him. Our eyes locked once again. He squeezed a little tighter. Shockingly, my lower body rolled and thrust a little harder and faster. My breaths and pants were a little faint, but my honey dip never missed a beat. He soon matched my speed. "Just relax,

Regina, and let it come to you." Moments later, it did. He removed his hand from my neck and allowed my body to go through its convulsions. "Let me know when you're ready for another round."

Domenick—— I lay on the side of Regina and hungered for her once more. I could tell that her body had been deprived of what I had given her. Little did she know, I was feeling the same way. I wanted to make sure that we pleasantly drained each other before we were yanked back into our somber reality. Her body twitched and jerked for minutes before it finally calmed down. When she noticed me staring at her, she covered her face with a pillow. I assumed she was embarrassed. I removed the pillow. She quickly covered her eyes with her trembling hands. "No need to hide," I teased before kissing her nose. She giggled and then removed her hands. I attempted to climb back on top of her, but she stopped me. She pressed my shoulders onto the bed. I was like a kid in an arcade with a pocket full of quarters as I watched her mount me...reverse cowboy style. Just like her hands, my thighs began to tremble with excitement. I was happy that she couldn't see me because I could only imagine the goofy smile on my face.

"It's been a while since I last did this, Domenick," she said hesitantly.

"Take your time. I'm sure you can get the hang of it again," I coaxed. Indeed, she did. I squeezed the shits when she lowered herself onto me. She was extremely wet and that made the moment more joyful. I rolled inside of her as she bounced up and down on my pogo stick. I gently slapped and squeezed her hips. She reached between my legs and toyed with my sacks. "Damn, Regina!" I bellowed. She rode me like I was a fierce bull that she was trying to tame. I wanted to obey her, but I couldn't. With her still on top of me, I sat up. My face was now pressed against her back and my fingers tiptoed around her thigh and into her wet zone. I squeezed her tightly with my free arm so that she wouldn't topple over.

"Domenick! Yes! Ooooooo! Yes!" she bawled as she slowed her roll. I slowed mine as well. I took small nips at her back with my teeth. She grabbed my hand and we both kneaded her breasts. It was a magical connection that I wasn't ready to end, but my loins had other plans. I had to stop my eruption. I rocked us over and forward. She was now on all fours with me still positioned behind her.

"Arch your back for me, baby," I commanded. She spread her upper body across the bed with her back end tooted high in the air. "Ooooooo…Just like that," I said softly. Again, I was like a kid in an arcade with a pocket full of quarters.

Regina allowed Domenick to hit rock bottom as his tip drilled inside of her. In fact, she wanted him to go as far as he could. She made sure that he did by backing up on his strokes. She reached between her legs and tickled her middle while Domenick swam for pearls. She squeezed her walls to tighten them around his tool.

"You're not playing fair, Regina," he panted when she flexed her kegel muscles. He wasn't about to let her have all the fun. She glanced back at him with a displeasing look on her face when he pulled out of her. He teased her middle with the tip of his drill. Each time she tried to back up on it, he moved. "You see, I can play unfairly, too," he whispered in her ear when he lay across her back.

Seconds later, he climbed down off the bed and flipped her onto her back. He grabbed her legs and ravenously yanked her to him while lifting her legs onto his shoulders and leaning forward. He was amazed at her flexibility as she grabbed her thighs and assisted him. She was now folded over as far as she could go. Their faces met. Their breaths mixed. The moment was intense. Their hearts beat at the same rate. They were connecting on more than a sexual level.

He saw past her immediate need and she saw past his as well. She placed her hands on his smooth cheeks and pulled his face closer to hers. She had to have his lips on hers. He eased inside of her as their lips met. Her legs were blocking his desirable kiss so he spread them apart. She kept them raised high so that he could have all of her. The kiss and sex were beyond measure.

"Can I have you for the rest of the night?" Domenick asked with his lips still pressed against hers.

"Yes," she answered eagerly. Her silent prayers were answered. She wanted him all night as well.

Domenick rolled onto his right side and maneuvered her onto her side in front of him. He placed her left leg over his and re-entered her. She turned to him and they lip locked again. Surprisingly, both of their fingers fondled her clit. Regina's mind, body and spirit were meshed as one. Domenick had taken her to a place she knew nothing about, but wanted to stay for a while.

Domenick wiped away the misty sweat that had formed on Regina's back. Her moans sent him on edge. He rolled and thrust deeper inside of her. He placed his hand around her neck again and gently squeezed. Regina couldn't believe what she was permitting him to do. He was a complete stranger who turned her on to something she never knew she'd enjoy or submit to.

"Breathe, Regina," Domenick whispered as he listened to her faint breaths. She softly clawed at his arm hoping he wouldn't take her actions as her wanting him to stop because she didn't. His hands around her neck intensified the moment for her. While she rolled, he thrust. It was a rhythm made in orgasmic heaven. He squeezed her neck a little tighter and she clawed at his arm a little deeper. Their bodies began to jolt at the same time. Their thrusts and rolls hastened. He grabbed her chin and turned her face to his. He had to kiss her as their moment of ecstasy was about to make its debut. No words needed to be spoken. Their bodies told it all. Their dams ruptured.

He held her tightly in his arms as they patiently waited for their calm to kick in. She brushed the tip of her fingers over his skin. Neither knew what to say to the other. Their eyes wandered across the room since they were in a position where they couldn't look into each other's eyes. They were both happy that they couldn't. It was an awkward moment.

Regina eased from his hold and sat up on the side of the bed. Still, neither of them looked at the other. Regina forced herself to believe that she had done nothing wrong, but the weird feeling was overwhelming. Domenick could tell something was bothering her and that a little guilt may have started to set in with her. He sat up and wrapped his legs around her.

"We're supposed to be forgetting, remember?" he reminded while strumming his fingers through her tossed hair.

"It's not that, Domenick."

"Then what's the matter?" he asked inquisitively.

"I don't regret doing this and I should."

"If it helps any, I don't regret this either."

"Domenick, I was about to be married earlier and look where I am now," she sighed.

"If you don't regret this then maybe you shouldn't have been married to him. Things have a funny way of working out for the best." For some odd reason, she felt that he was right. She stood up and reached out her hand. "Where are we going?" he asked after placing his hand inside hers and standing up. She didn't answer. She led him into the bathroom where she turned on the water in the step-in shower.

"I worked up an appetite, but I think we should shower before we go out," she said as she laughed.

"What if we just order room service and stay in?" he suggested with a devilish smirk on his face. "We were supposed to do that before we started drinking anyway." They both laughed. He backed her into the glass shower doors that were quickly fogging up from the steam.

"That sounds like a good idea, too," she agreed before their lips fused. He lifted her off the floor and she wrapped her legs around his waist. He hardened. He reached around her to open the shower door then carried her inside. The water felt like hot, inviting rain as it poured onto them. A weird yet spontaneous feeling draped Regina. "Domenick?"

"Yes?"

"I may be living a lie or a fantasy at the moment, but I'm happy."

"So am I, Regina."

"I'm not ready for this to end."

"Neither am I." Regina took a deep breath before speaking her next words.

"Come to Dubai with me."

"I thought you'd never ask." They both smiled then engaged in a serious kiss. He pressed her body against the tiled wall and guided his missile inside her.

Hedonism

by Lorraine Elzia & K. Roland Williams

Hedonism

Pursuance of pleasure as the only intrinsic good.
It is the idea that all people have the right to do everything
in their power to achieve the greatest amount of
pleasure possible to them.
It is the maximization of net pleasure
that surpasses any amount of pain.

Chapter 1
Journey Divine

"Does that feel good?" The tenderness in his voice was evident. His slate grey eyes generously conveyed the same sincerity that rode on the warm currents escaping from behind his smile.

"Yes, very good," she responded with a sly tidal wave of her own.

"Good, because I don't want you to feel uncomfortable by any means." His Australian accent was sexy to her, just like the five o'clock shadow lining his strong jaw bone. Both gave her a warm sensation between her thighs that she enjoyed immensely, but tried to hide.

"I trust you. I trust you with my life," she purred. The throbbing in her sex box hit a harder speed and she moved willingly to its inner pace. It had been way too long since her sex had danced with the devil; and because of that fact, a man's words possessed a power that only a third leg should.

Everything in Kennedy's life had come down to this exact moment in time. This, possibly the most important day of her existence, was upon her…a day that would give new definition to her life and who she claimed to be. She fought to control the urge to give a eulogy to her past and say goodbye forever to the younger, slimmer version of herself that lingered relentlessly in the shadows—the Kennedy that could party all night with the best of them, and then get up and jog five miles the next morning like it was nothing. Those days were behind her now, but it didn't mean that days just as fulfilling, just as enjoyable, and just as memorable, weren't ahead of her. In fact, she had read somewhere that the latter half of one's life was the best half. She could only pray that was true.

Turning forty had been a rude damn awakening for Kennedy. It marked the half-way point in a life…give or take a year or two for good behavior. Her glorious day of birth had become both a blessing and a curse; and it was the reason she was where she was at this precise moment with the man that she was attached to—literally. Forty was old enough to know what you didn't want in life and wise enough to know how to make the right decisions. But here she was in a questionable position, participating in a life-altering indulgence that might be a wrong decision. Yet, the thrill of the experience overrode her thought process.

The harness that connected their bodies was as tight as a second skin. The nylon straps and stainless steel rings bound them together as one. Their breathing was in sync with one another and his body was pressed up tightly against her ample ass cheeks…just the way she liked it. A death-defying adventure had the intimacy of the beginnings of foreplay in her mind.

Cold air occupied the space that they were in and wrapped around them in a frigid cocoon. His body heat warmed her, making her fantasize—momentarily—of making love in the outback with him as her *down under* lover. His warm, intoxicating breath sent chills down her spine, comforting her while she prepared herself for the inevitable. Intense fear rippled through her veins and Kennedy could feel the goose bumps forming on her breast, enlarging her nipples with anticipation even through all the gear she had on. Slowly, she ran her hands down the front of her body trying to soothe her physical excitement while focusing on the moment before her—a moment she hoped would reignite something that had gone dormant inside her…a feeling she desperately needed to recapture for her own sanity.

A walk on the wild side with a stranger was just what the doctor ordered and would remind her that she was still alive and breathing. Or at least that was the plan. Growing old gracefully was for the birds as far as she was concerned; Kennedy wanted to inhale all that life had to offer. She still couldn't believe that she had the courage to follow through with the act.

The courage indeed.

Courage and tenacity were what coursed through Kennedy Styles's veins, even more so than blood or plasma; she was sure of it. She was known for doing things that scared the faint of heart; it was her trademark and was the stuff that made her the courageous woman that she had become. Just like all of the Styles women before her—Kennedy was a force to be reckoned with.

It was *her* show today and she was center stage—right where she belonged and right where she liked to be. Her girls were all in attendance, watching her interact with the handsome Australian stranger. They were all living vicariously through her. Secretly, she enjoyed the devotion. As if riding vapors of sisterly support, Kennedy could feel their love and admiration for her. She fed upon it. She needed it. She also sensed that her girls were fantasizing about having the guts to do what she was about to do, and to be doing it with such a fine morsel of a man as her current partner in crime. Kennedy got off on her girlfriends' envy. It fueled her with the courage she needed to do this and all that she dared to do in life.

Emory was the name of the tall, attractive Australian that pushed himself up close and tight to her rear end. He was the source of her sensual tensing and uncontrollable gyrating in rhythm to his movements. Protocol dictated Kennedy's dependence on him. Lust demanded she enjoy every minute of it. Emory made her obey his will without question. Giving up her power and control was a feeling that was foreign to Kennedy. As foreign as the country from which her stranger hailed. But she silently enjoyed taking direction from him. Shit, it wasn't like she had a choice. He called the shots. She followed his lead. He was a professional and knew exactly what he was doing, which gave Kennedy a sense of calm that eased her inner, suppressed fears. The vulnerability she felt turned her on. It was sexy even in the midst of a dangerous situation.

The small aircraft climbed higher and the temperature dropped away like the earth from the small window to her left. This event was something that her girls had set up and coordinated for Kennedy without her knowledge…a surprise.

Those bitches, she laughed to herself.

Winter, Salima and Allanda were all her girls from college. Career women like Kennedy, all were true blue friends to the end. She trusted them explicitly. When she opened the envelope a week ago while they sat at happy hour at Zapata's Bar & Grill, she questioned their friendship and their love for her, but only for a brief second. She knew immediately that their gift was genuine…a once-in-a-lifetime opportunity. One she couldn't easily say no to.

"Do y'all have an insurance policy on me that I don't know about?" Kennedy asked sarcastically as she looked each woman directly in the eye. That was the first thing that entered her mind. Understandable, given the clutter of empty martini glasses scattered across the white linen table.

Winter was the first to chime in, "Of course we do girl." It was more of a slur than Winter's usual clear pronunciation. Her Master's Degree in English was lost amidst an elevated blood alcohol level."Yes, and we gone cash in, too, so we can leave the rat race behind to enjoy early retirements, all on your dime babe."

Salima and Allanda laughed before Allanda raised her glass and stood up in their private booth—the same booth that they had been reserving once a month for the last three years.

"Raise your glasses for a toast," Allanda said, swaying side to side, trying desperately to act as though she were in control of her movements.

"To our girl Kennedy…today you're forty, fierce, and fabulous!You've made it to another year on this side of the dirt and we're happy that you did. You are epic…exactly what a woman should be! Strength, dignity, and brains all wrapped up in pure beauty! You got it going on, girl!"

"Yeah, girl," Salima added, "I'll second that and say this is *your* time—time to live life to the fullest as if each day is your last."

"Baby girl, we love you and although I have never had a sister, you've held that role for me since freshman year." Winter, being the most emotional in the group, gave her toast and fought back her tears. They all followed suit in fighting their own individual water works…to no avail. Warm hugs surrounded all; cocktail napkins wiped away tears.

"I love you all, too," Kennedy said."Thank you for being there for me, I couldn't ask for a better set of women to call my girls!"

As they composed themselves and Salima flirted with their waiter as she did once a month, Kennedy stared intently at the envelope in front of her - the gift her girls had given her. It was the spark to the fire of her indulgence high above the earth today…in the clouds, soaring like a bird.

Emory's breath was heavy in her ear bringing her out of her brief daydream.

"It's almost time…are you ready, Ms. Styles?"

"I am ready; let's do this!" Her words had a renegade confidence to them, almost as if she was daring herself to play a game of *chicken* with her own life.

The pilot's voice echoed over the plane's loud speaker; barely audible over the roar of the airplane's engine.

"We're now at thirteen thousand feet…it's time. You know what I want to see."

Kennedy obliged him with a gloved thumbs-up gesture into the air as he began to shuffle them closer to the open door of the small plane; not even an inch separated the bodies of her and the Australian.

My first, and probably my last tandem jump, she thought.

The sky was clear through her goggles. For a moment she thought she could see clear to heaven, but she shook off the vision.

"That parachute is packed properly, correct?" she asked with a half-smile.

"I packed it myself, Ms. Styles…no worries."

"Okay, let's do this then!"

A small light above the door turned from red to yellow. Emory stepped up to the opening that separated Kennedy from the safety of a perfectly good plane, revealing an open abyss below her. A sea of white clouds seemed to open themselves up to her, begging her to join in a game of horizontal foreplay in the skies. Fear engulfed her, but she took a deep breath, reminding herself that *fear* was a dirty word to Styles women. From the preflight instructions, Kennedy knew that she would be the first out of the plane, technically, even though she and the Australian were attached by the rig.

The fact that her girls had bought her this gift, yet decided not to engage in it themselves, bothered Kennedy at first; but she had always been the most adventurous of the group. Besides, she wanted to prove to herself that she could overcome her fears of the unknown and set an example of what was possible with a little Styles audacity and spirit.

The light above the door turned from yellow and flashed green. Her heart sank. She knew the moment to put on her big girl panties and do what she had come to do was at hand. There was no turning back.

"We are over the drop zone," the pilot said excitedly over the crackling intercom. Emery grabbed the doorway with both hands. His arms were spread eagle and so were his legs. Kennedy had to shake off images of him in that same position—naked and fully erect—lowering his dick into her mouth as she lay on her back—mouth wide open—allowing him to give her a true taste of the southern land.

"Go, go, go! Your friends will meet you on the ground!" Emery's instructions were loud and forceful, giving her a chill. Then, without another thought or word, they were both out the door and into the open void of free fall.

Kennedy gasped in appreciation of the feeling of weightlessness. A lump formed in the back of her throat; for a moment she swore it was her heart trying to escape.

What have I allowed these bitches to get me into, her mind inquired. Instinct to survive made her panic briefly, but after a few seconds her fear rushed away.

Once clenched teeth and tightly sealed eyes found a way to relax, going with the flow. Adrenaline guided the feeling flowing through her body. She summoned years of yoga and meditation to help guide her breathing, controlling her elevated heart rate. Kennedy opened her eyes and saw the plane pulling away from them into the distance, and growing smaller as she and her instructor hurtled toward mother earth. Gravity knew its job well.

Emory checked his altimeter and they did a few of the free fall maneuvers that they had practiced in the classroom.

"Exhilarating" was the only word that could come close to explaining the feeling of falling at terminal velocity. The feeling was indescribable; she hadn't felt anything like it before. Her body experienced every sensation known to man, but at a heightened intensity to each of her senses. Every inch of her body was covered with small, raised bumps of ecstasy. She felt satiated… almost orgasmic.

The man behind her made her feel safe. Strangely safer than any man who had been recently in her life…and yet she had only known him for a day.

The ground was stampeding closer and the harness straps between her inner thighs pulled tightly around her pussy. It hurt so good as she pushed her thighs harder against the straps, forcing the intensity deeper inside her as she fell faster and faster.

As they both plummeted, gravity tugged on them, summoning them to earth. The fields below were like a patchwork quilt rising closer and growing larger. The constant tug on her pussy from the straps added to the excitement of the sky dive, along with the bonus of the bulge of Emory's cock vibrating against her from behind. Kennedy wondered what sex would be like in free fall. A true mile-high club.

The light hovering on the horizon yielded a majestic beauty leaving Kennedy mesmerized. The Atlanta skyline was way off eastward in the distance. All she could hear was the rush of air around her and the feeling of invigoration and solitude. It was a spiritual moment unlike any that she had ever experienced. Her entire body sang a sensual *Halleluiah.*

The instant motion of their bodies in that moment must have taken Kennedy to the edge, because an orgasm enveloped deep inside her and she succumbed to its power. It was small, but served its purpose and finished the sky diving adventure with an unexpected ending that even her girls couldn't have predicted. *Talk about your happy ending!*

Kennedy and Emory came to a perfect landing just feet away from the large bull's eye painted in the green field. Cars were lined up in the open area. Her girlfriends were anxiously awaiting her arrival. They had their cell phones out filming every moment of the ninety-second trip from plane to earth. Her girls ran up to Kennedy all giddy and animated with excitement, waiting to hear the details of what has often been described as the most exciting thing a human being could ever do on the planet.

Emory gave Kennedy a high five and released her from the sky diving rig. It took her a second to get her feet under her; her body was still in shock from the experience and the orgasm.

"Was it everything the brochure said it would be?" Winter asked smiling."You the shit, girl! I can't believe you actually did it! We've got some great footage!" The comments of her girls came at her in rapid speed from each of them. Taking a breath, Kennedy pulled her safety helmet off, freeing her short, neat auburn twists. Her caramel complexion radiated under the midday sun. With a perfect smile she responded.

"That was the most unbelievable thing I have ever done! Words can't describe it. Now I can check that shit off my bucket list!"

Her eyes glanced down at the flyer that had been left under the wipers on the windshield of her car. *Hedonism—give your life and your libido a treat.* The cardboard advertisement screamed.

"Now it's on to the next big thing!" Kennedy snickered as her fingertips rubbed the postcard between her fingers.

"Life's too short to live in ifa, coulda, woulda and shouldas… I'm riding this bitch till the wheels fall off!"

Chapter 2
Intimate Revelations

There is an innate feeling deep inside every grown man that signals him when a time for change had arrived in his life. Just like the transition from boy to man was unconscious but consequential, so were other aspects of a man's existence which begged for a starring role etched on the grand marquee of his life.

The warning call came to Aiden; not as a whisper, but as a commanding echo from above which he could not silence any more than he could silence the beating of his own heart. It was a call for change from the norm. It was both desired and ordained. Implementation was merely coincidental in the scheme of things. Sometimes the charge for action took years to reveal itself; yet other times it overtook a man all at once, in one sudden and dramatic moment like the shattering impact of a head-on collision. No matter the form of delivery, a man must beckon to the call once he hears it.

Within this timeless, euphoric space, he realizes with unmistakable clarity, that the cosmos, exactly as it is within that moment, is absolutely perfect in speaking to him. Everything in his universe is at one in agreement. Aiden knew he was but a pawn in the chess game of his own life. Once the call was heard, he had no choice but to answer.

Aiden's call came through the blinds of the conference room window. His attention was drawn away from the meeting at hand and redirected to a point of light in the distance. It was a moment of intuitive revelation for Aiden a moment that he could only describe as an epiphany, or an awakening. In a timeless instant, his understanding and experience of life—his life—was completely and irreversibly transformed. The change was at a deep and fundamental level by a completely unexpected and enigmatic moment in time.

Aiden Lucas Cross could feel deep within his core that the time had finally come for him. If growth was the only evidence of change…then Aiden had slowly been losing the race. Like a bolt of lightning, he realized that now.

Refusing to keep allowing his yesterdays to continue to be his tomorrows, Aiden mentally vowed to do something about it. This *new* feeling was whole and integrated. Any sense of fundamental separateness was absent from him. Anxiety faded away, leaving peace in its wake, completely and utterly eliminating any doubt.

"Aiden. . . you were saying?"

Transfixed and looking skyward, Aiden snapped back from his revelation with a smile on his face. He took a deep breath; filling his lungs as if for the very first time. A light bulb went off in his head, showing him the glow of a future he longed for.

It's time for a change, he mumbled to himself, absorbed in his mental, life-altering decision.

He was a new-born babe in a room full of sharks in thousand-dollar tailored suits. A glass ceiling he was appreciative that he was able to break, but that accomplishment only satisfied a portion of his total being. Something he hadn't really given much thought to until the *call* from the window.

Aiden had been staring out over downtown Atlanta from the fifty-fifth floor of the *Bank of America* tower in the heart of the city—the highest man-made peak in Atlanta—one thousand feet above the busy streets below. A glorious view, one that spoke of financial corporate success, and yet he was momentarily oblivious to his surroundings. Nothing really mattered for the first time in his life—nothing career wise that is. The reflection of light that caught his eye was that of a small plane that dipped away in the distance over a Georgian suburb before careening off into the clouds.

"We're waiting for you, Mr. Cross." Malaya Jefferson's voice dripped with sarcasm as she greeted him. Malaya was the VP of Operations for one of the largest financial institutions in the country; as such, she wasn't used to having to wait for any man… even one as attractive, intelligent, and upwardly mobile as Aiden.

The boardroom was filled to capacity. A large, flat screen at the front of the conference room was scattered with faces of BOA execs being beamed into the corporate meeting via video conferencing. High-powered corporate diplomacy seeped in the air. The moment was extremely important. The participants meant business. The smell of money, and how to make more of it, lingered like a recently sprayed air freshener in the air around them all. Yet Aiden's mind was shamelessly elsewhere; somewhere just as important to him, but for a totally different reason.

Standing six feet tall, athletically framed, with strong cheek bones, a killer smile, and with the kind of profile that could easily grace an ancient coin, Aiden was definitely the product of a great gene pool. He was the kind of shit that businesses on the move *and* horny single women desired desperately, but for different reasons.

Aiden was not only a man gifted and deeply submerged in physical beauty, but he was also graced by God with a brain. One that landed him into an Ivy League college and eventually a high six-figure salary with a top-executive position in one of the highest-ranking banks in America. All of which were good things to most, but which for Aiden, felt like an anchor around his neck, dragging him into an abyss of a corporate dog-eat-dog world that was void of excitement and individuality.

Be careful what you ask for…you just might get it. Aiden uttered that phrase to himself often.

As he watched the plane in the distance, he was more and more aware that he had been fighting the wrong fight for the last ten years. *What good was an MBA and a so-called great career really worth if happiness and personal satisfaction did not accompany it?*

Strong words…an even deeper reality.

"Mr. Cross? Care to join us?" Malaya's irritation was escalating. The rolling of her eyes put an exclamation point on her curt words. Turning to face the assembled executives, Aiden couldn't help but notice Malaya tapping her pen on the large, oval mahogany conference table in front of her. Her narrow eyes and subtle grin hinting at the more devious thoughts lurking under her professional appearance.

She needs a good, long, hard fuck right about now, and I'd love to give it to her—AGAIN! Aiden thought to himself as he carefully chose his words before speaking.

"As you all are aware, as of one week ago we purchased all outstanding shares of MBNA Corporation. This acquisition represents liquid assets of three and a half million dollars. This merger did not have any negative material impact on the operations of the corporation. They are still intact."

He strolled toward the center of the room with a swagger of confidence that suggested he owned and controlled the moment…and in reality, he did. He always did just by virtue of him entering into any space.

"I would like to suggest that we transfer all shares of US and Asian futures business to that corporation. As a result of the transfers, it will make MBNA a futures commission merchant and thus save us millions of dollars in commodity trade taxes over a five-year term. It's simple math. Ladies and gentlemen, now is the time for us to swallow up the weak and spit out their carcasses while they are in the mind frame of cutting their losses. *Carpie Diem* people! It's time for us to seize the moment."

Aiden continued speaking as he lowered himself into a leather high-top chair next to Malaya. The associates flipped through their presentation packages page by page,scanning numbers and verifying facts. Everyone seemed to be highly impressed with Aiden's attention to detail and knowledge of the foreign market.

"The industry is scared right now because of the economy. Simple minds think simply. The *Bank of America* is anything but simple. We are stable. Our numbers don't lie. Now is the time for us to capitalize on our commanding position and strike while the irons are hot!"

A chill ran up his spine as he felt Malaya's silk stocking feet slowly and seductively slide up the bottom portion of his leg. Each toe caressing his calf muscle sensually as if on a mission to start a fire in the region higher than where her feet could reach from her seated position. *The girl gave good leg…*he'd give her that. He could feel himself slightly gyrating in his seat from the feeling coming from her foot action.

"Yes, the acquisition is a risky one as all are, but if the plan falls into place like we think it will, we will all be pushed into a new tax bracket and this institution will own foreign trade futures for the next decade or more."

Aiden rocked back and forth in his chair with his hands crossed in front of him as Malaya continued to stroke his leg under the table with her feet. Her simple attention was a source for his simple pleasure. Her face and body language gave no indication to the others in the room of her foreplay with Aiden under the table via manicured toes. He secretly enjoyed mixing business with pleasure at a moment when the big wigs had no clue what was happening right under their noses.

"Mr. Cross, can you guarantee that we won't get burned?I mean, this is a very risky venture that you're suggesting we undertake…and we are not using Monopoly money here to back it. This is real money that we're talking about. We can't lose sight of that."One of the characters on the big screen interrupted.

He was a cartoon character in Aiden's mind…but a good associate never lets that opinion be known, so Aiden just smiled and kept his opinion to himself as he contemplated his answer.

Malaya's strokes were slow, long and seductive…comforting to his mind and his body. Aiden's third leg can't help but remember the warm coziness between her thighs. It begged him to ignore the need to be a professional and to give in—instead—to the freak deep within him. His manhood wanted to bend Malaya over the expensive table in the middle of the room that hid their secret foreplay; ultimately giving her what she clearly craved and wanted to receive.

He enjoyed her attention, but stayed true to the team in being focused.

"As you are aware, I can't make you any promises when dealing with futures, sir. All I can give you are my recommendations based on the numbers and the history of our competitors to date. What I *can* say is, if we do not capitalize on this moment and don't reallocate the funds to support this move, we will lose capital and you will be sitting here in this very office wishing you had taken the risk. The moment is now. We need to live in the moment if we want to continue being on top."

Aiden's words, delivered as a selling point for a business deal, bitch slapped him concerning his life as well.

Live in the moment if you want to continue being on top.

That's what he said to the others in the room and it was also the advice he needed to take for himself. It was confirmation for him that the *call* he answered just minutes before was a red herring for all aspects of his own life, professional and personal. Everything in his life hung on risk and faith.

Malaya's feet continued to stroke him.

The up and down motion of the heads of everyone in the room continued to stroke him.

The nod of approval from both the devil and angel that sat on his shoulders stroked him.

Aiden was getting stroked…left and right.

Yet none of it gave him the feeling of satisfaction that he needed. He sucked his teeth and leaned back in his overstuffed, leather chair of importance. Then Aiden exhaled for the first time in a long time.

Satisfaction was bliss for him at that moment. Satiated by his performance before the associates and craving a taste of what Malaya's toes promised from under the table, Aiden made a mental note to pencil momentary gratification into his *Day Planner*. After all, one should never forget to smell the roses along the way… but the truly adventuresome make it a point to remember to pick the petals of those roses and throw them around the room for ambiance as well.

The meeting ended as all meetings do, with people grabbing brief cases, iPads, coffee cups and scampering away to offices in various corners of the building and branches in the city. Charisma, God-given talent, and a calling for what he did for a living had all prevailed. Vanilla-colored associates loved his mocha-chocolate ability to make shit happen. He would say to himself that he had them all fooled, but even he had to admit that he was good at his craft. His due diligence was done long before the assignment was ever issued and delivery of presentation was second nature for him, so closing the deal came with ease.

His chair in his office was far more comfortable than the one in the conference room. It was as if it was made, specifically by design, for his ass and his ass alone. A king needed a throne befitting his attributes, and Aiden had squeezed his ass every time he sat in it while whispering "Welcome home" as he relaxed in it.

Her office phone number was on his speed dial. He'd called it a million times. Mostly for business, but for the occasional mid-afternoon phone sex as well when she was in the mood. Her foot foreplay was good, but her phone sex skills were even better. In a weak moment, Malaya was always good for an orgasm via the ear…a long-distance fuck for *all* of the senses. She also knew how to ride a dick and looked very good on paper as well, as the saying goes. Brains, beauty and career minded…most definitely,

Malaya could make a man happy and she had made Aiden smile from time to time. However, she was not for him. There was no Yin/Yang match when it came to the two of them—no chemistry there beyond a decent conversation and equally decent fuck. Much like most of the women Aiden had met lately, the connection just wasn't there with him and her. You just can't force a square peg into a round slot. *If it don't fit…don't force it.* It *was* what it *was* when it came to Malaya, and what it wasn't…was love. As perfect as she was, she wasn't the right one for him. He knew it. She knew it. But they both let it be what it was along the journey in the pursuit of momentary gratification. They knew they would never be a "we"…but both were okay with doing "me."

Malaya's imperfection did not stop him from pushing the digits that would result in him spending the night between both her sheets and her thighs for the evening. He needed what she was offering, and she was a cool ally that didn't bring drama to the table after each orgasm—a desirable trait in a fuck buddy from his standpoint.

He was starving and she was the ready-made meal that he enjoyed. Cooked or raw, Malaya always served it up to his liking. A cracker, in the hands of a starving man, was more than sufficient to fill the needs of the famished, so Aiden picked up the phone and dialed her number knowing that if nothing else, his dick would be fed.

Chapter 3
Paradise Unveiled

"Will you be needing further service, ma'am?"

The slow, worry-free tempo of his voice made Kennedy want to sway in unison to his simple words. He—just like the clear blue waters mere feet away—possessed a laid back, relaxing spirit of a place barely tainted by modern civilization.

Switching her gaze back and forth between the beauty of the beach in front of her and the beauty that was waiting on her beck and call, Kennedy couldn't help but smile at the dichotomy of the delicious choices before her. *The beauty of choice.* She thought, before staring hungrily between the two, desiring them both.

Her dark, slanted chestnut-colored eyes darted downward at the name tag on his shirt. They lingered there longer than necessary, but she couldn't help herself. Bold letters introduced him as Jacques; a name that tempted her almost as much as the tight shirt which clung to his chiseled upper torso. She resisted temptation to tear his shirt off of him, releasing the sinewy muscles that almost begged for the attention of her lips and tongue.

Long, brown dreadlocks with golden highlights, touched to perfection by the sun, swung freely, side to side, as he picked up her bags with ease and deposited them next to the white wicker couch in her bungalow. His movements, effortless in production, forced her to unconsciously tighten the muscles in her pussy as if she were doing *Kegel* exercises just for the hell of it. She felt herself moving in slow motion, gyrating unnoticeably to anyone outside her skin…slight precise movements. Just the way she liked them. Tightening and releasing, tightening and releasing.

Enjoying the quick vaginal fuck she was having with herself, Kennedy hoped her actions were unnoticeable to him as she gave her pussy walls a quick tease at his expense. With each bend and flex of his muscle-toned arms she bit her bottom lip, wishing she had a bottle of hot massage oil nearby and the added nerve to ask him to sit back and let her have her way with him.

"No…Jacques. I don't need anything more. You have been more than kind." Her lips lied as her body thanked her for the secret treat she had given it.

"Enjoy your stay…waters can be addictive, mon," Jacques uttered while placing the bags, one by one on the plush carpet gently."Make you wantta' run into dem till your heart bursts wide open and dances with the sea. You are just like the rest of us when we cast a gaze upon the beautiful creation which is da sea. We become her slave. She is our queen. Not-ting' can stop us from giving her due praise. Welcome to Jamaica, mon, where everything is Irie. No worries…just happiness. That is my wish for you, ma'am, during dis here stay in the islands. No worries… just happiness."

Kennedy couldn't help but smile at Jacques' sexy, island-cultivated accent and charm—simple, yet instinctive to who he was. It was sexy to her, even though she knew it was merely natural to him and not something produced on demand for tips. He had also said one of the few pieces of Jamaican slang that Kennedy had managed to learn before her trip—"Irie," which meant, "Everything was cool and good," a reference to positive emotions or feelings. That simple line of thinking pleased Kennedy. It's what she needs…what she desires…what she came to the island beach in search of in the first place.

She watched as Jacques opened her balcony door across the room from the king-sized poster bed. The wooden, hand-carved bed was generously draped in a white, cotton net canopy. Her room looked just like it did in the brochure…no false advertising here. Everything in her view, including Jacques, was romantic, relaxing, and had a hint of, *If I have the chance to get into some freaky shit while I'm here…this is where I want it to go down.*

Sea gulls played on the warm air currents as the midday Jamaican sun was offset by a cool mist from the Caribbean Sea. It coated Aiden's face as he walked the shoreline in front of the lavish resort. Jet skis zipped across the waves in the distance as he dug his feet deeper into the sand with each step. He felt the tension in his shoulders breaking away piece by piece, almost disappearing on contact. His complete nakedness was a totally new feeling for him. But he had decided to go with the flow of the island as he waited patiently for his room to be prepared.

When in Rome, do as the Romans do.

Surprisingly, removing his clothing and his inhibitions at the threshold of the resort wasn't as foreign a feeling as he expected it would be. Maybe his bravery was due to the fact that he had the kind of dick that most men only dreamed of. Hanging midway down his long thigh, it was indeed a third leg. Being blessed in that regard brought with it a stronger sense of confidence. His flat, wash board abs and broad muscular shoulders only added to the total package. It was not a thing he typically even considered at home. Sure, he worked out and ate right, but until he had to reveal his junk for the world to see, it never really was that big a deal to him. Nevertheless, he was here and he was as nude as the day he came into the world, along with everyone else in eye shot.

Fuck it, he thought. This is what it was supposed to be about. This was what he came here to see and do—a challenge like no other. To do this, one needed balls and it was a good thing that his matched the size of his dick.

Hearing laughter, Aiden looked up the beach and saw a couple chasing one another through the sand. The voluptuous woman ran slowly in front of her pursuer—a well-built, tall, dark-skinned man in his twenties. Her large breasts—supple and promising—bounced freely and deliciously under a loosely tied, floral bikini top. Aiden mouthed a, "Goddamn!" as he watched her back field in motion as she ran. The hesitancy in her movements made her intentions clear…she wanted to be caught. She was a willing victim in a seductive game of *catch me if you can.* Aiden smiled at the romantic game of cat and mouse taking place in front of him. Black love always made him smile; and black lust—his own—moved him further up the beach in search of his own passion. Their laughter was silenced by a kiss as they fell to the ground, allowing the sand to be their only blanket as they kissed passionately, arms and fingers exploring every inch of the other's skin. The man's dick pressed up close to the woman's pussy without entering her—slowly grinding instead against her clit as they sucked each other's tongues.

Aiden felt his heart sink a little in his chest as he watched the lovers making out in full view—unashamed and uncaring of any witnesses to their public display of affection. Their actions were just another part of the game and excitement of the Jamaican resort.

This place is supposed to be all-inclusive. I wonder if that means I can get some of that given the price of this joint. Shit…I hope so! Aiden thought to himself as he licked his lips in anticipation of fulfillment of his own desires.

A romantic at heart, Aiden believed in love; he believed in the concept of two becoming one. He just hadn't been privy to being the victim of Cupid's selective arrow. The moment in the boardroom when he received *the call* had been his epiphany. He knew the time had come for him to change his status concerning love…or at least lust. After all, God helps those that help themselves, and he was a man of action with the tools to help himself.

The email advertisement had been a sign. The fact that it made its way into his inbox and not the spam folder of his work email was fate. He knew it the moment he saw it. He was supposed to see the advertisement and make his way here to obtain some of the action the island promised. No salesman was needed…only action on his part.

The email spoke of Hedonism…of leaving the mundane world behind and concentrating on the flesh…on lust and on sinful indulgence. It was the kind of email that normally would have fallen prey to his delete key, but for some strange reason—one that Aiden could only surmise as fate in hindsight—he gave it a bit of attention. More than a moment's morsel of his thought. The more he read, the more he was convinced that he should partake in a walk on the wild side. That email. That reading. That moment of thinking, *what if* had twisted his straight-laced thinking and opened his eyes to different possibilities than the *safe* ones he had previously entertained.

The light came on for him at the board meeting and the ad was the alarm for him to get up and take action. As Aiden slowly walked by the couple on the beach, feeling like a voyeur to their intense actions, he knew he had made the right decision in coming here. He could feel it deep in his core. She was here. The one for him. The one he desired. The one that would fulfill the void in his heart. He could feel it. All he needed to do now was find her.

Ain't nothing to it, but to do it. She's here somewhere. I can feel it. Aiden said to himself as he headed back toward the lobby of the resort, hoping he could finally check into his bungalow.

That's when he saw her. Yet off in the distance, she was there. Naked. Speaking to him in a language that did not require words. He watched as she stretch her torso into the sky. His mouth began to water. His manhood started to rise to attention as well. She walked around in unadulterated glory in a bungalow on the corner. A small amount of pre-cum made its way to the eye in the opening of the snake nestled between his thighs, ultimately escaping from his manhood without warning. As his eyes took in her beauty, his mind made note of how to find her as he put his clothes back on and headed toward the resort lobby.

She sat on the large, white chaise lounge on the deck overlooking the beach in front of her. She had made notes of all of the things in the brochure that she planned to attend. She was a woman on a mission, and that mission was to have as much fun as sinfully possible.

Fuck it! No one knew her here, she could be anyone she wanted to be, and what she wanted to be was *wicked.*

Her eyes looked curiously left and right surveying how close her neighbors were. She surmised they were close enough for ease of entry should either suit her fancy, yet far enough away for her to enjoy a little privacy. Kennedy did the unthinkable, at least in regards to her normal mindset. She stripped down to her birthday suit. *Befitting of the occasion, she* thought to herself as she removed layer after layer of not only her clothing, but her inhibitions as well. Each fell to the ground in a tidy little pile in front of her as she stepped away from them both. She raised her arms toward the sky and tilted her head back, closing her eyes and allowing the Jamaican sun to kiss every inch of her exposed skin.

She was alone.

Just like her soul wanted her to be at the moment.

She felt a freedom encompass her like a tidal wave against the beautiful shore within eyesight. Others saw that same freedom in her every time they looked at her, but Kennedy never felt it within herself before, although she was good at pretending that she did. She had always been a pro at putting up a good front. It came naturally to her. Living it was something altogether different.

But this vacation would be different.

She had prayed it would be.

Promised herself it would be.

And set her mind in determination that it would be.

Implementation was only coincidental in the scheme of things. Or at least that was what she kept telling herself.

After a deep inhale of sea air and an exhale of all pretenses that she carried with her day by day, Kennedy placed her sunglasses over her eyes, laid back naked on the padded chaise lounge and smiled.

She took the last sip of the exotic cocktail that had been given to her upon arrival. A long exhale of momentary satisfaction escaped from deep inside her as she grabbed the pile of her clothes from the bottom of her chair and stood up, invigorated by her first few moments in Jamaica. She walked back through her bungalow doors hoping destiny was just a notch away on her itinerary.

Chapter 4
Bumpin' & Grindin'

Aiden lost his Italian sandals at the door, as was his habit to do at home, and enjoyed the welcoming coolness of the ceramic tile against his bare feet. It was a small, simple means of relaxing that brought him joy. Dropping his bags, he immediately perused the contents of the mini bar that sat next to a relatively small desk in room 222. His favorites were stocked in abundance, just as he had requested prior to checking in. He was a man of certain tastes, certain luxuries; he liked what he liked, and asked for it in advance when possible. Cracking the seal of a travel-sized bottle of *Classic VSOP Cognac* and pouring it over a few cubes of ice already waiting for him in his room, Aiden thanked God for small favors of sinful indulgence. After the flight from hell, and the stroll along the beach witnessing a slice of passion that he longed for, he craved a stiff drink like a sinner needed to confess his sins.

Aiden's eyes surveyed the bungalow. The Jamaican resort was represented well. He was pleased by the subtleties provided to ensure mental and sensual relaxation. The room reeked of romance, sensuality and sexuality—an erotic cocktail he couldn't wait to taste. A Balinese bed sat in the middle of the room facing open glass French doors to a beachfront balcony. Tropical plants, flowers, scented candles and curious wooden artifacts filled each corner of the room. The leaf-shaped, bamboo ceiling fan circulated floral and musky fragrances throughout, giving a calming and euphoric aura to his temporary surroundings.

Yeah, this is exactly what the doctor ordered. Exactly what I need. Aiden thought to himself as he slowly allowed his surroundings to engulf him and erase the memories of the corporate world he had willingly left behind.

Andrea, a tropical depression that sat just one hundred miles out in the Caribbean Ocean, had tossed his small plane around like a helium balloon in a heavy breeze during his flight into the island, shredding his nerves in the process. The storm threatened to put a serious damper on the weekend's festivities; he only hoped it would stay at bay long enough for him to enjoy all that the island had to offer. Aiden needed a little self-indulgence in his life and he cursed Andrea for being the bitch that she was. He prayed that she was done raising her leg and pissing her wrath upon the island that promised him more than a few good reasons for a stiff boner.

Suddenly, a thumping sound caught his attention, shaking him from the serene tranquility of his thoughts. Slow and gentle at first, then picking up momentum and crescendoing like the music piping over the resort's speaker system. It didn't take long for Aiden to figure out what was causing the disruption. The bumping against his wall was his next door neighbors, seemingly engaged in a serious session of headboard-banging therapy. Moans and groans emanated through the saw grass paper on the wall shared between the two bungalows.

She was a screamer.

Aiden shook his head, hoping that his adventure on the island would bare similar fruit. The thumping next door began to arouse him. He knew that the purpose of coming to this resort, and not some other, was the draw of exploring one's sexuality. Testing the limits that made you who you were—and possibly, if you were lucky—transforming you into someone else. Someone bold and sexually free. Even if for a short time. The pace of the sound against his wall quickened. The mere knowledge of the source for the thumping teased at the confines of his underwear. His dick started to suffocate behind thoughts of what was transpiring on the other side of the wall.

Her screams got louder.

The tempo increased dramatically.

The pounding became more forceful as if it would smash the plaster that separated him from them. Aiden couldn't help but massage his third leg in hopes of calming it down a bit as he walked across the room trying, unsuccessfully, to be unfazed by the actions in room 224.

Something about spying on another couple during intercourse created a rush, and Aiden's dick began to swell, larger and larger, with the thought of what the couple next door was doing. His mind created images and situations concerning what positions they were engaging in.

Was she a freak? Were there toys and gadgets involved? Did she handcuff him? Did he spank her?

As if they were in the room with him, Aiden could see, in his mind, their bodies wet with sweat and beautifully contorted for the purpose of ecstasy. He could smell the unmistakable scent of sex and passion in the air. . . simply put, he visualized fucking in progress. He enjoyed the scenes frolicking through his thoughts and his mind indulged in the sin of envy. His body reacted in unison with his thoughts. Escalated blood pressure woke his libido, but he would stave off that feeling for now. He had to. No need to waste a good nutt on thoughts when the island promised actions on a higher level, and more intense than what his mind could visualize. He reminded himself of that fact as a quick shower and a nap prepared him for the night's activities.

A line of empty miniature *Grey Goose* bottles, his second favorite liquid guilty pleasure, led to a pile of clothing next to his king-sized bed. He lay there, butt ass naked, staring at the huge leaf blades of the ceiling fan above his head. He exhaled a piece of pretense that always seemed to normally surround him. Aiden grabbed a complementary resort robe, wrapped it around himself and began flipping through the channels of the flat screen TV. He watched as advertisements for the island's offerings ran on a continuous loop.

Fifty Shades of Hedonism was apparently the top activity for the weekend's itinerary. It was promoted as a chance for the resort's couples to unleash their inner Anastasia Steele and Christian Grey with a complimentary bondage kit, complete with restraints, a blindfold, a feather tickler and, of course, a gray tie. The cheesy manner in which the advertisements were portrayed reminded Aiden of cheaply made porn; the only difference was that promises took the place of the almighty money shot. He couldn't help but laugh. Even bad porn served its purpose; and so did the *Fifty Shades of Hedonism* advertisement. As poorly as it was done, the island's knock-off version of the popular book still piqued Aiden's interest. He wanted to be Christian for a hot minute and longed for an Anastasia at his beck and call. He knew of the novel—it was all over the internet and on every talk show on TV, but he hadn't had the time to read it for himself. If things went as planned, he could bypass the book altogether and simply live out its story line instead. For a moment in time, he needed life to imitate art. He had come prepared to give in to all of the things that had once been taboo…at least for him. The things he hadn't made time for because he thought they hampered his way up the career ladder. *What better way to forget the corporate grind and move on to the things in life that truly mattered?* A buffet was still a buffet; and he was starving.

Aiden was a man that wanted to explore his options, and it

seemed the resort had plenty of options, choices and possibilities for him to sample. While still in disbelief that he was actually in a place known for sexual corruption, Aiden felt a sense of guilty pride at showing the size of his balls just by being a part of the guest list.

In exploring his options, Aiden had chosen the *nude* side of the resort instead of the *prude* side. *Hell, if I am going to do it, might as well do it to the hilt! No need for half stepping*. He said to himself. He was ecstatic at the view his garden view room offered. A lush flower and palm-filled expanse of garden lay outside his window, wrapping around a large swimming pool. All of the people walking to and fro outside of his window were naked.

"Nude has its perks!" Aiden said out loud as he watched plump ass, after plump ass, walk by outside of his bungalow window. *There is a God!* He uttered in unison with the sway of each bootilicious stroke of ample buttocks dancing to a rhythm of its own under smooth, chocolate skin. He had seen a sample of the patrons of the island before checking into his room and smiled at the fact that watching naked people would never get old to him. He could do it all day, every day, and his dick would thank him for the show.

The lovers in room 224 were in their final laps it seemed, the banging now just a subtle and occasional bump. Their moans hushed into quietness. *Good for them*, he thought. *Hope the hard work was worth the orgasm*. Aiden gave up praise in the same manner that a thug would pour out a bit of intoxicant at the graveside of a fallen homeboy.

Aiden's mental display of affection was interrupted when his smoldering eyes narrowed at the sight of a woman walking, towel in hand, to find a comfortable chair to relax in. She stood out from the rest of the passersby. He remembered her well. She was the woman from the bungalow on the corner that he had seen before. Her movements not only asked that she be a distraction in his mind, she commanded and expected nothing less from him and others by her simple presence. The curves of an exotic goddess made him sit up involuntarily. A fusion of what appeared to be black and Hispanic descent, wrapped up in cinnamon skin against a sapphire blue sky, dictated he take notice.

Aiden couldn't help but reach for his manhood that sat hidden under the thin robe he had been frolicking around in. Blessed below the belt with no less than ten inches of dick that had profoundly changed many a woman's life over the years, Aiden had given his lovers the least religious reason to call upon God or whomever they chose to worship religiously. That same orgasm-induced tool begged for attention. He watched the stranger's ample ass jiggle as she sashayed toward the pool. The image of her backfield in motion enticed him. She had a way with words spoken from her butt checks that seduced easily. An indiscernible tattoo was etched into the small of her back. Her tramp stamp. He wanted to see it—up close and personal—marking it with HIS scent. Aiden reached next to him without taking his gaze off of the poetry in motion in eye's sight and located his bag. A small container of baby oil found his hand as he pulled it out and glazed his cock with a healthy portion. He continued to watch her as he stroked his manhood over and over from top to bottom, giving it the attention it asked for. An uncontrollable grunt escaped from his lips in the process.

As she lowered herself suggestively onto a lounge chair, she turned to reveal a perfect set of D cups that sat out at attention. Dark areolas looked at Aiden from afar, seemingly seeking him out. Short, auburn twists framed her lovely face. God had been specific in the details when creating this exotic creature. A small triangle of nicely trimmed hair pointed down to her sweet spot— her sex—an area that Aiden longed to claim ownership of by planting a flag of his seed, marking his territory. She was definitely a woman who paid attention to the details and watching her from a glance, he had to give her props and due respect for being who she was. He licked his lips in appreciation and fought the fire that was now throbbing below his belt line. He wanted to explode and release all of his inhibitions.

Priding himself as an open minded, passionate, and non-selfish lover—one that any woman would have loved to show gratitude to given his particular skill set—he was reminded that there had been women in his past. Even one that could have been his wife; but his desire to please his banker, more so than his woman, drove her out of his bed and ultimately out the door. Simply put, Aiden had never been a man to stay long enough for intimate pillow talk. He would give his all in the process of lovemaking, but once the act was done, there was always a report that needed reviewing. . . always a proposal to write. Lovers were always sloppy seconds to his desire to chase the Omni-potent allure of corporate, career-building tail. After several years of thinking about it, he realized that he had just been afraid to settle down and commit to a woman. A split tail, no matter how good, never enticed him as much as a phat bank account did. It was sad, but true. Sex was good to him; but dead presidents, and the pursuit of them, had always given him more intense orgasms.

A week in Jamaica would change that. At least he hoped and prayed it would.

Hungrily, he watched her. His mouth watering uncontrollably with her every move, he hoped that she, or someone like her on the island, could make him bust a nutt on the same level that cold hard cash did. He was tired of green, paper-induced orgasms and longed for physical ones instead.

Becoming an addict to all of the sexual stimulation around him, Aiden squeezed the slab of spongy meat growing and pulsing in his hand. Messaging it from its limp position into one that could do major damage on command. A smile bitch slapped him as he watched it grow. Oil drizzled onto the engorged, mushroom head, rolled down the shaft, and met his tight grip at the base of his healthy erection. Brown eyes, still firmly planted on the now sitting beauty, Aiden began to work his hand up and down, massaging the oil into his swelling cock. His hands slid across the flesh of the already thick veins that were second nature to the pipe he had been blessed with and often laid. A pussy pleaser that is what took up residency between his five fingers at the moment; and once it showed up, it begged Aiden to allow it to come out and do damage, or at least play nicely with a willing party. By nature, Aiden may have chased dollar bills, but his dick chased warm, tight cervices that longed for exploration.

There, admittedly, was hesitation in his stroke. If anyone were to walk by the window of his bungalow they would have fallen privy to a nice show. *Hard dick, mid stroke, money shot impending… yeah, a nice show in deed.* One that Aiden had never provided to any stranger before in his life. He had never experienced or provided anyone with a voyeuristic experience with him as the center attraction. But there was something inherently exciting about the possibility of someone walking by and stopping. Looking. Staring. Enjoying. Watching him stroke his hardness to the point of release and orgasm.

That was the point of the row of large windows with no blinds. There was nothing to hide behind on the island. No pretense. A lowering of inhibitions, spoon fed or forcefully injected by circumstance. The tenants of the resort for the week ahead of him had all sold their soul like he had. Their souls belonged to sin. There was no turning back. The pursuit of individual sexual freedom and satisfaction was all that was on the menu for the week. That hurt-so-good feeling would be intensified and showcased for all in attendance. Resistance was not an option. Hedonism is what was paid for and what would be given. An experiment in self-indulgence of individual pleasure was considered paramount. Feelings, or anything of that nature, were second to pleasuring the flesh.

Man, woman, black, white, fat or slim; it didn't matter. That was the point of Hedonism. A pursuit of sexual enlightenment.

. . *Nirvana.* A mental state where pleasure far exceeded any pain and no one got hurt in the process. Yes, after he stroked his dick, Aiden's eyes rolled back in his head uncontrollably as his thoughts, along with the rest of him, rode a wave of intense dick palpitations. He planned to clean up the aftermath, don nothing more than a fluffy resort towel, and find his way to the pool and the woman who now filled his mind with her sex.

Chapter 5
Introduction to Desire

Sultry calypso music led his footsteps. Island beats forced him to stop mid-step and sway side to side as he made his way out the frosted glass doors. He smelled sex in the air and couldn't wait to taste a bit of that ambrosia up close and personal. Armed only with the resort's towel that barely covered all of his endowment, and with the liquid courage that now pumped through his veins thanks to the mini bar in his bungalow, Aiden headed in the direction of the music and the spot the TV advertisement had suggested. Final destination—Hedonism's Meet and Greet—an introduction to maximum pleasure for those who were green to the island's wares.

A thumping in his heart pushed at his skin harder and harder with anticipation, allowing the lust of his body to be a catalyst of bravery that would relax his mind. He had come here for guidance. Mentally, he thanked himself for his choice to come alone. Hedonism was not a male bonding moment. He didn't need his buddies tagging along. This, just like other moments in his life, was something he needed to endure alone if it were to be a success.

Hurricane Andrea, while a bitch just by virtue of her existence, had only caused drive-by affects when pissing her threatened wrath on the region. Her bark had been much worse than her bite and Aiden thanked God for His token of goodwill. His weekend wouldn't be a wash after all. He would be able to taste the sexual fruit of the gods. Andrea had left debris in her path, but nothing that a few scantily-clad islanders couldn't clean up while visitors comingled sexually as usual. Her damage was minimal and the resort's promises were major by comparison. Aiden hoped that the removal of Andrea's threat would allow the resort to live up to expectations. His heart, soul and dick needed it to be true to its advertised word.

Temperatures, kissed by angels, and luke-warm rays from the sun saturated the spot where the introduction to the satisfaction of lust was supposed to take place. Lounge chairs, adorned with both naked and skimpy-clothed sexual specimens, took up every single available space as far as the eye could see. Sun glasses and body oil decorated both men and women alike, creating an appetizer of flesh. The small areas not big enough for lounge chairs were filled to capacity. It was standing room only in every direction with people holding small glasses with rainbow colored miniature bamboo umbrellas in them. The more adventurous were in the pool, playing a game of naked volleyball complete with its own set of naked cheerleaders. Bouncing breasts and ass entertained all who watched.

To the left of the pool was a small section of the beach with a waterfall that housed a wet bar behind it before dropping off into the Caribbean Sea. Coral blue water cascaded down the front of the bar, surrounding the man-made sanctuary like a velvet curtain hiding the sin inside. Nothing more than a comfortable wade in the water separated it from the crowded shore.

His dick led him.

Aiden was just being obedient in following.

Removing his towel before stepping into the water, and keeping it safe and dry above his waist line, Aiden started out on a seek-and-find mission in search of ecstasy. Reggae beats pulled him in and seemed to do the same to the current under his steps in the water as he waded toward his destination. Blood pulsated through his veins in rhythm while destiny whispered in his ears. Chants from the resort's announcer competed with the beats, reminding the occupants of the reason for the season—lust— and the pursuit of it.

The time had come for the seasons to change and Aiden was ready to say goodbye to the winter of his discontent and hello to a spring of self-renewal.

❧

"Another *Jamaican Smile* please," Kennedy said to the half-dressed waiter working the floor area of the wet bar. It was her third of the trademark drink and the effects were starting to caress her ever so gently. She was feeling no pain as she felt her body sway uncontrollably with the music playing in the background.

"You might want to take it easy pretty lady. This drink is not for the faint of heart," the waiter said, wiping up the residue of condensation that had accumulated on her table from the two drinks she had already consumed.

"Do us both a favor, handsome…do what you do best and bring me another one," she said before blowing him a kiss. Her eyes darted around the bar area before becoming fixated on the small dance floor in the corner. The gyration of the bodies on it made her envious. They moved to a rhythm all their own. Some couples were on beat with the song playing. Others moved to music only heard by the two bodies melting into one. Kennedy forced herself to stop looking. Their X-rated sexual tangos were too much for her to endure. Her envy was too great.

A gaze in the opposite direction spotted him. Droplets of tears from the sea sprinkled his chest. That was the second thing

227

she noticed as he emerged from the water. His pearly white smile was the first.

Umm, umm, umm," she thought upon first glance. Her initial reaction was intensified as the rest of his body shed the reminisce of the water. *Well, Goddamn!* was her second thought as the rest of his body fully emerged. Her eyes were in love. Or worse case… at least lust. *Now that's the kind of man a sista wants to leave an imprint on her spleen!*

Instinctively, she raised a finger to her mouth, sucking and biting it to calm the nerves of her desire. She readjusted herself in her seat and pulled down her sunglasses, looking over the top of them to get a better view. Like a voyeur, she watched as he stood at the brink of the bar's shore and dried himself. Meticulous and sexy were his actions. Kennedy felt a bit of jealousy toward his towel as it got the chance to touch his skin. Masculine and rugged were his strokes as he hit every crevice of a body sculpted for sin. He was a cunt tease even without trying.

Kennedy couldn't tell if it was the fire between her legs or the two rum-filled *Jamaican Smiles* that led her actions, but before she knew it she had grabbed her own towel and walked over to the handsome stranger.

"You look like you could use a little help; and even if you don't *need* help, indulge me in the spirit of circumstance." She taunted him, staring at his body with little, if any, eye-to-eye contact.

Kennedy couldn't believe the boldness of her actions, but loved the fact that they took charge in a situation she normally would have been shy in.

Aiden couldn't believe his eyes or his ears. He continued to pat himself down as he stared at the very same woman whose *sex* had lead him to the bar. He chose his words carefully, ensuring he wasn't a cock blocker to his own sexual destiny.

"It would be rude not to give in to a woman's wishes; and I have never been a man that anyone labeled as rude. My mother taught me better than that."

He lightly grabbed her hand, placing his seductively over hers and the towel she was holding to his chest. Guiding the strokes of her efforts to dry him, he stared deep into her eyes.

"Thank you for the hospitality, pretty lady. Maybe before the end of the event, I can return the favor." Aiden smiled as he covered his bottom half back up with his towel.

"Don't do that on my behalf. I was enjoying the view." Kennedy chuckled as she playfully stopped rubbing him and walked back to her table.

Corruption can smell corruption and the decay of moral principle lingered in both their thoughts. Aiden followed her. Just like she knew he would. He couldn't help himself. Her tramp stamp called him to engage her further. The eternal sign of peace with rays emanating from it. Inner peace. He liked it and licked his lips as a sign of applause as he watched her cheeks in motion.

Kennedy paused, midstride, looking over her shoulder…

"I'm sorry, I didn't catch your name."

Chapter 6
Swinger's Tango

"My name is Aiden," he said as he walked up behind Kennedy, soaking up all of the thickness and feminine attributes she had to offer.

So thick…I'd love to catch that thrust and give it back to her, he thought. Instead he said, "How are you just going to start something and stop mid-stroke like that? Besides…you missed a few spots."

"Is that right? That's funny; I thought I was pretty thorough. You look dry to me. What did I miss? Most men like a little bit of moisture—or so I'm told—it keeps all the vital parts moving like they should," she said with a wink.

"Really now?" a raised eyebrow preceded Aiden's words.

Kennedy had spent a lifetime perfecting the art of flirting—the tilting of her head, biting of her lower lip, and the subtle movements of her body. She had learned at an early age that a woman's power was not just in her pussy, but in allowing a man to feel as if he were in total control and leading him down the path of her own choosing.

"Well, you've given me the pleasure of keeping things nice and moist; now it would be nice to know the name of the benefactor of my treat."

"My name is Kennedy; it's a pleasure to meet you." She let her name roll off of her lips in a sinful manner she knew he would enjoy.

He extended a powerful hand that swallowed hers completely. Kennedy's softness against his strength was a tantalizing and potent mixture. They sized one another up and they both were pleased with what they saw and felt. His shoulders were wide, arms muscular and abs sculpted as if from dark brown granite. Kennedy assessed him as a man that gave a shit about his health, appearance and his body—all of which turned her on that much more.

"Well, Kennedy, can I buy you a drink or two?"

"I don't see why not, Aiden. Nice name by the way...it suits you. It speaks of heaven and hell rolled in one."

Aiden felt an uncontrollable chuckle escape his lips.

The water feature behind the bar added to the ambiance. Pastel fluorescent lights faded in and out bathing the area in color and flooded the senses. Reggae pumped through the sound system, moving the crowd to the rectangular dance floor. The breeze flowing effortlessly throughout the bar brought forth the salt-laced aroma of the sea. Kennedy thought, *if ever there were a place where Hedonistic philosophy would thrive, this would be it.*

"You down to do a shot with me," he asked while summoning the bartender in one fluid gesture of his hands.

"Seems you already know my answer." She smiled.

Kennedy knew that most women knew within moments of meeting a man if she would ever fuck him. So far, Aiden was totally on point. She crossed her fingers and prayed that he would not say or do something to turn her off.

"You know…I have a confession," Aiden playfully diverted his eyes away from Kennedy.

"A confession…hmmm, that's interesting. We already making confessions, are we?"

"This one is not a bad thing; or at least I don't think it is."

"Well, let's have it."

"Okay, but only after our first shot." The dark-skinned bartender dropped off two large shots of *Silver Patron*. After they threw them back, Aiden grabbed Kennedy's hand and they found a tight spot on the now packed dance floor.

❦

Some say that Reggae music is the perfect baby making music—music that the devil could sing to. In the midst of other partygoers seeking sexual bliss, Reggae provided the perfect backdrop. The most conservative person could free their inner freak and become whoever they wanted to be. The sliding of sweaty flesh on flesh, gritting of teeth and the sheer enjoyment of sin in action freed those in the crowd; Kennedy and Aiden were no exception.

Their bodies found the perfect rhythm that pulled them in as one. The only things separating their nether regions were the towels that barely clung there between them. Others in the crowd danced totally naked. Tongues slithered together and hands groped without concern for prying eyes. Aiden's hands were warm on the small of Kennedy's back. They eventually found their way to her plump ass. She wished that he would free the large pin that held her towel in place. But she wasn't sure he was ready for all of that. Their eyes locked as they lowered themselves side to side on the dance floor to the slow dance hall beat, smiling silently, bodies talking and introducing themselves to one another organically.

"I'm ready for that confession now." Kennedy smiled.

Aiden thoughtfully rubbed away the sweat from her brow. Her auburn twists glistened in the dance floor's spectacular light show.

"I saw you earlier. I noticed you at your bungalow and watched you walk to the pool. I couldn't take my eyes off of you."

"Stalking me, huh?" She laughed.

"No, never that babe…just admiring from afar."

"So, what did you think?" Kennedy spun around with her back to him, allowing her ass to speak and wait for the answer. "The same thing I think now…I want you bad as hell."

"You know it's funny because I wouldn't think I would be your type."

"Really? What type of woman do you see me with?" Aiden was curious as to her opinion of his selection.

Kennedy scanned the crowded dance floor and dropped her gaze on an attractive, slim, fare-skinned woman. She was tall with flowing, black, naturally curly hair.

"Ha! Really? Not even close, babe. I like my women thick with meat on their bones." He eyed Kennedy and winked. He held on to her hips as they continued to sway to a Calypso beat.

"I see you with a guy like that." Aiden nudged his chin in the direction of a tall, muscular, white man who danced with a black woman on the far side of the floor. The man he referred to challenged the stereotype that all white men had small cocks and no rhythm. He moved well and had a cock that boasted both length and girth.

"Nawh, not my thang. I love my chocolate *way* too much!" Kennedy laughed and shook her head."But there's no shame in his game, I see."

"None!" Aiden responded as they both cracked up. "You wanna get out of here?" Aiden's eyes smoldered with passion, triggering Kennedy's punnani to pulse.

"Sure. I was wondering how long it was going to take you to ask."

They exited the club and walked along a grove of swaying palms. The sunset lit the sky in royal blue, burnt orange, and crimson, framing the horizon like a vintage painting. Aiden grabbed Kennedy's hand and stopped her in her sand-filled tracks.

"What's up…" she began to ask, but before she could utter another word, Aiden pulled her into him and seized the moment by kissing her. She had no desire to fight him and submitted to his will.

"Damn," she said, "you don't waste any time, do you?"

"We don't have a lot of time Kennedy. And I want to spend every moment with you, enjoying this island and all that it has to offer."

She admired his aggression and take-charge attitude. "Well, okay then." She moved in and returned his affection with her own. Her warm tongue trailed a path into his sweet mouth to meet his tongue half way.

"Excuse me." A voice summoned them from a few feet down the beach. "Good…we thought we had lost you." A slight Spanish accent accompanied the woman's warm, sultry voice. Aiden and Kennedy breathed deeply, calmed themselves, and turned to see who was calling them.

"Hi, how can we help you?" Kennedy was just starting to get into the groove of this man and now this interruption. *Shit, not now!* she thought as she acknowledged the woman.

"Well, hi…my husband Orlando and I saw you two inside the club and you looked so cute together that we wanted to introduce ourselves."

The woman was wrapped in a sheer, black fabric in the style of a toga. Her nipples poked through and her curves strained against the material, accentuating her ass and small waist. She had the kind of lips and eyes that exuded sex.

"My name is Octavia. We just got here today and wanted to introduce ourselves…maybe have someone to hang out with a little bit while we're here."

"Excuse my wife…she is the people person in this relationship. Sorry to just walk up on you like this," the man who was with her spoke up. He shook Aiden's hand and smiled at Kennedy. Tall and athletic was his build and his Spanish accent was slightly heavier than his wife's—reminiscent of the male actors on popular Telenovellas. He wore fabric around his waist as well and an imprint of his dick pushed through, catching Kennedy's attention immediately. His eyes lingered on her exposed breasts and he licked his lips.

"Nice to meet the two of you," Aiden said."Where are you from?"

"Miami…South Beach to be specific, by way of Havana. How long you been married?"

Before Aiden could respond, Kennedy spoke up, "Five years…five happy years." Aiden played along with Kennedy's ruse and smiled at her.

"Nice…we've been married three."

"We were wondering if you wanted to hang out a bit and have a drink with us." Orlando and Octavia looked and sounded Cuban. Both had black, curly hair and strong Hispanic features. Both were highly attractive and seemed fun loving and innocent enough.

"Sure," Aiden said, "Why not? Let's go."

"Great!" Octavia giggled, "Let's go back to our suite. We have a large bar set up there. You will not be disappointed. We promise."

❦

White sandy beaches guided the path of four to a spacious luxury bungalow. Orlando and Octavia had an upgrade as far as the resort rooms were concerned. Nestled smack dab in the heart of the *nude* side of the island, their bungalow seemed to be center stage for a view of all things hedonistic. The inside of their room was draped in silks and filled with high-end furniture. Three bedrooms went in different directions, each with its own bath.

"Nice digs," Aiden said as he walked in and kicked off his sandals. A multitude of bottles lined the bar area, with every mixer imaginable to start a party off right. A fruit basket sat partially raided, with cheeses and crackers set up on a long dish.

"Make yourselves at home. What can I get you two to drink?" Orlando played the courteous host.

"We've been drinking *Patron*, if you have it," Aiden answered as his eyes took in all of the sights around him.

"I got you; no problemo."

Orlando pulled four small crystal glasses from the bar area and began putting ice cubes in each glass before filling them to the rim with the *Patron*. The sounds of ice clicking against each other teased Aiden's senses as he admired the art work of Jamaican heritage on the walls.

Octavia walked up to Kennedy and whispered into her ear. Aiden noticed Kennedy respond with a laugh as she shook her head up and down, answering yes to whatever question she had been asked. Aiden made small talk with his male host, all the while keeping an eye on all that was happening around them. The ladies continued to sit off on their own, chatting in hushed tones.

"Honey, may I speak with you for a moment?" Kennedy motioned for Aiden to walk with her down the hallway.

"What's up?"

"Well…it would appear that our hosts are into some kinky type shit. Chica told me that back in South Beach they're into the swinging scene. Now, they're not going to do anything that might make us feel uncomfortable, but Octavia has made it quite clear that they are interested in the four of us taking things to the next level together if we are interested."

"Are we?" Aiden chuckled as he raised his eyebrows, feeling out her intentions.

"I figured since we were here, in this place, that maybe we could indulge into something beyond the norm," Kennedy answered, searching his eyes with her own to size up his nerve."We both paid a lot of money to come here Aiden, and in doing so we were looking for something. We won't find it if we are scared to try something new."

"Hmmm, and you're cool with that? Have you done this kind of thing before?" His eyebrows rose even higher than before.

"Never!" She laughed."But I'm the kind of girl that will try anything once…twice if I like it." Kennedy winked at him.

"For the record, I've never done anything like this, either, but I'm not opposed to trying. Shit, let's see where it goes! Trying and tasting is what we came here for. What better way to sample Hedonism than to jump right into it, right?"

"Okay, if you're cool…I'm cool. What we do in Jamaica stays in Jamaica, bet?" Kennedy extended her pinky finger and Aiden extended his in a vow of silence—their first secret.

❦

Octavia started the party off properly. She dropped her toga to the floor and exposed her coke bottle shaped body. She stepped to Kennedy who was not quite prepared for her first female-on-female encounter. Kennedy had never indulged before, although she had been hit on by women off and on over the years. Octavia could tell Kennedy had never been with a woman. She could smell it all over her; the thought of being the first to bust Kennedy's same-sex cherry turned Octavia on.

As she ran her tongue playfully down Kennedy's neck, Octavia could feel Kennedy's heart beat quicken with every kiss that trailed her collarbone. The warmth of her mouth and tongue moved with a purpose down to Kennedy's breasts. All feelings of apprehension quickly escaped Kennedy through every pore in her body, motivating Octavia to continue on her mission. Slowly, Octavia ran her tongue in circles around Kennedy's titties, chasing her nipples before aggressively sucking them delicately as if she were famished for the taste of another woman's breast.

The role of pillow princess was played well by Kennedy as she lay still, allowing Octavia to have her way with her. In the distance, Kennedy heard a soul soothing moan. It was her own. She noticed her body dancing in motion with Octavia's tongue taking lead. Kennedy's body enjoyed it and reciprocated without asking her mental permission. The small residue of resistance that Kennedy possessed let go and went with the flow, releasing all her fears and tension. Before she knew what was happening, she relaxed and fell gently back on the bed, allowing Octavia to fall on top of her. Aiden and Orlando stood quietly behind the women, watching in awe and sipping *Silver Patron* from their glasses.

Hedonism put a spell over the room.

Sensual eye contact danced between the women as Octavia slid the towel down past Kennedy's thick hips, revealing her now throbbing, damp pussy. Kennedy's nipples had swollen and stuck out at least an inch making her excitement clear for all to see.

"You have a beautiful wife, my friend." Orlando spoke to Aiden, keeping his eyes glued to the scene playing out before the two men.

"Thank you. So do you."

"Then this should be easy for both of us. This is why she chose you two. Octavia has an eye for such things," Orlando added, taking another sip of his drink.

Kennedy continued to relax. *Shit, if I'm going to do this, then damn it let's do it,* she thought. Octavia kissed Kennedy slowly at first. It felt like her first kiss, and in reality, it was since it was the first one she had experienced with a woman. Kennedy received her passion and returned her own in kind. She reached for Octavia's nipples and pinched them gently, yet firmly, the same way she liked her own nipples pinched—just hard enough to cause Octavia to bite her bottom lip with the sweetness of the pain. Kennedy knew she was doing it right because Octavia kissed her more deeply, more erotically, and more passionately. Kennedy could feel the woman's hot pussy on her thigh…her wetness leaving its own kisses below.

Kennedy's pussy was on fire now. Her sex was throbbing uncontrollably. She could feel her lips swelling and engorging with excitement. Lust was taking control and she loved it. She looked at Aiden through a sexual haze that pushed any remaining inhibitions that she might be feeling away. Both men watching began to stroke their cocks. They couldn't help themselves and they longed to be part of the action, but waited patiently for an invitation.

Kennedy couldn't help but notice the approval of the men shown from the initiation of self-gratification on both of their parts. She became even more aroused with the sight of two big, hard dicks being stroked. Her fantasies of having multiple dicks in all of her holes quickly descended upon her. Just the thought of a cock in her mouth and pussy, entering and exiting at the same time was enough to almost make her cum.

Octavia had done this many times before. She knew exactly what spots to kiss and lick…and how long to stay there before moving on to the next spot. Her mouth hovered mere inches away from Kennedy's pussy and her own pussy lips were slick with her own juices. Octavia grabbed both of Kennedy's thighs and raised them up in the air as she fell to her knees and spread Kennedy's pussy wide open.

An eagle's eye view of tasty, sweet pussy…just the way Octavia liked it.

Kennedy couldn't believe she was doing this. Logic and good sense assured her that it was just a dream, but Octavia's hot tongue sliding across Kennedy's clit brought her back to reality.

This bitch is eating my pussy and it's good!

Octavia continued to lap at Kennedy's love fountain. It churned up a sweet juice that the Latina was happy and eager to drink. Her skillful tongue danced across Kennedy's clit, dropped down to her opening and back up again. She flicked her tongue gently, and then sucked on her clit harder. Kennedy panted and grabbed Octavia's long, black mane, pushing her pussy into her mouth and moving in a selfish hungry rhythm.

Aiden's dick was swollen to capacity. He had always loved the sight of two women together at once, and his fantasy was coming true. And it wasn't a porn on his DVD player, but happening at his very feet. They were beautiful together. He jacked his dick, trying not to pay much attention to Orlando who watched his wife go to work on Kennedy. Orlando didn't pay Aiden any attention either; instead, he smiled and shook his head speaking to Octavia in Spanish…egging her on.

As if prompted by a foursome movie script, Orlando moved in to the rear of his wife and gently rubbed her back. Then he smacked her ass hard and that action just pushed her to lick Kennedy with more passion. As the sound of his hands hitting Octavia's ass echoed throughout the room, Kennedy's eyes rolled uncontrollably to the back of her head; she was lost somewhere in the outer realm of ecstasy. Aiden expected her to speak in tongues any moment as she squeezed her own breasts and pinched her nipples, rolling her hips to Octavia's oral dance.

Orlando raised his wife's ass up in the air and slid the head of his dick inside of her. She gasped in approval without looking back. She never stopped her oral attack on the feast in front of her. Not to be outdone, Aiden moved in on the bed. Ten inches of stiffness preceded him. The purplish hue of his cock, along with its swollen mushroom head, was ready to go to work. He leaned in and kissed Kennedy's lips gently and she grabbed his face with both hands assuring him that his presence was welcomed. Aiden sucked her nipples and squeezed her tits. Her upper torso arched in acceptance of his touch.

Orlando continued his role…shoving his cock into Octavia inch by inch. He grabbed her hips and began to pump into her furiously, making his presence known to the deepest crevices of her inner walls. A foreign language seductively accompanied each stroke. The dirty Spanish talk between husband and wife was sexy, even though Aiden didn't recognize a word of it.

Once again, *Hedonism put a spell over the room*…its occupants mere zombies to the deep sexual trance they were in.

Octavia reached up and grabbed Aiden's cock stroking it. He closed his eyes and moved with the beat of the entire bed. Kennedy licked her lips as Aiden's dick was being jacked just a few inches away from her empty mouth. Every inch of her body yearned for the feelings she was feeling to never end.

Octavia was now taking her husband's trusts full steam ahead. She tooted her ass upward into him and arched her back happily receiving his pounding.

"Fuck it like you own it!" she managed to say between sucking Kennedy's clit.

Octavia slipped a finger into Kennedy, bringing her G spot to life. Kennedy's pussy swallowed Octavia's finger whole and coated it with her thick, sticky, orgasm-induced juice. Octavia rubbed her own clit as Orlando beat the pussy up from the back and reached around and squeezed her nipples to ripeness. Kennedy licked her lips and grabbed Aiden's dick, guiding it into her hot, awaiting mouth. She was going crazy with the insanity and lust of the moment. Every fantasy, every sick thought, every nasty sinful moment materialized, dissolved away and materialized again…all in a matter of seconds.

Aiden slid his dick in and out of Kennedy's mouth lovingly. The warmth of her lips and tongue welcomed him home where he belonged. She took him in completely, her deep throat game on point with no gag response as a chaser.

She's a keeper, Aiden thought to himself.

"Oh shit...fuck me Papi...fuck me...harder!" Octavia screamed and Orlando fulfilled her desire, slamming into her harder, spreading her ass cheeks further apart in the process. He pulled his dick out of her and lay her on the bed next to Kennedy. Both women's thighs were spread eagle and on top of one another. Orlando slid in between Octavia's legs and started eating her pussy while rubbing Kennedy's clit into submission.

Moans of acceptance exited Kennedy's mouth as she worked on Aiden's cock, licking the head and the shaft. Her eyes were glued to Aiden's—his ecstasy etched into his expression like it had been sculpted into clay. The passion between them while sharing the experience was a stronger scent in the air than the smell of sex produced by the foursome.

Aiden moved between Kennedy's thighs and lined up the head of his dick with the dampness of her pussy. He rubbed his dick up and down her clit, teasing her. She smiled at him and panted.

"Don't tease me baby...FUCK ME! Fuck this pussy like it's yours!"

"Like it's mine?! Damn!" Aiden pressed into her, gently at first. Her pussy gulped him in with very little resistance. Her tightness made him want to explode.

"Damn!" They grunted in unison at the introduction of his sex to hers.

Octavia reached over to guide Aiden's dick even deeper into Kennedy's love hole and he tweaked Octavia's nipples with his left hand and Kennedy's with his right. His strokes were long and deep into Kennedy and he did not miss a beat while multi-tasking between the two women.

"You want this pussy fucked? Now take this dick!" Aiden deep stroked Kennedy and she threw her pussy right back at him, accepting his length and girth eagerly.

Orlando and Octavia panted, moaned and groaned inches away.

The aroma of sweet sex was heavy in the air. The humidity caused all four participants to sweat heavily, yet they continued fucking furiously as if their lives, or at least their orgasms, depended on it.

The bed bounced with two women getting fucked simultaneously.

Two dicks slamming into two hungry pussies.

Excited breasts and sweaty balls bounced while the bed rocked like they were in the midst of an earthquake. Moans created echoes, while backs arched to the ceiling. Asses pumped and thighs and knees dug into the bed for more leverage. Hardness slamming against softness created a beautiful ballet of lust.

Their lamentations provided the sound track to their dance.

They were not alone.

Shadows loomed outside of the window.

People eager to watch and critique, gathered outside of the lavish bungalow to watch the show through the un-curtained windows. Couples, hungry to fulfill their own desires, used the show in front of them as momentum and fuel to create their own excitement outside the windowsill. Breathing increased in the spectators, along with blood flow. Lips licked hungrily outside as the foursome fucked on their side of the glass.

Aiden and Kennedy were oblivious to the voyeurs beyond the glass. Aiden's dick was hitting her spot in a way that she had not experienced in a long time. She was totally filled to capacity and loving every second of it.

"Oh, shit," Kennedy screamed out…I'm cumming baby… I'm cumming…don't stop!" Aiden let his deep stroke continue as he reached his own point of release.

Octavia and Orlando came first. Orlando released all over his wife's breasts and she rubbed his love into her skin as if it held the secret to eternal youth.

Kennedy came harder than she had ever cum before and Aiden pulled out and dropped his hot, sticky load on Kennedy's stomach. They all collapsed. Chests heaving and the sounds of heavy breathing filled the room.

Moments later the foursome was surprised and honored with the sound of clapping. As was the tradition in Hedonism, the onlookers gave their review of the lovemaking they had witnessed. The voyeurs beyond the glass gave their approval with a round of applause, accompanied by sinful smiles.

Chapter 7
More than Bargained For

Slight snores and sweet morning breath entered his nostrils, ushering Aiden gently from a state of broken slumber. The flame of the evening moonlight brought a wicked smile to his face as he watched her sleep mere inches, face-to-face away. Each breath taken pulled them closer to one another. Each exhalation formed a space that Aiden desperately needed to fill. He pushed in closer to her even if only by mere millimeters. He wanted her as close as a second skin.

Damn, she's perfect. Even as she sleeps. My sinful little angel. He thought to himself as he stared at the beauty beside him.

He couldn't help but question the veracity of her beauty—had God constructed this beautiful specimen just for his selfish benefit? *He must have. How else can she look this good and fit me this well?* Instincts of a cynic made Aiden want to believe that his reality had been altered, but her natural presence suggested to him that it had not. She was who she was, and he was just appreciative for the opportunity to be able to witness and taste her in all her glory.

He was learning to love every inch of her world…retouched or untouched as it was.

An urge to push one of her small, burgundy twists of hair away from her eyes over took him and he gave way to impulse. As he did, Kennedy turned her back to him. The softness of her ass against his flaccidity immediately demanded a carnal response. It forced him to spoon with her. As she settled in with a comfort that normally only familiarity could dictate, he tightened his grip around her waist. She wanted him closer to her and he was happy to oblige.

He could smell it in the air; the pursuit of their self-satisfaction was narrowed by the brevity of their days. The final hours of Hedonism silently, but forcefully, shouted their inevitable arrival. Aiden unwillingly accepted that reality as he witnessed the rise and fall of her chest, the slow, soothing release of her exhalations and her steady calming heartbeat against his body.

All *good things* end; and Kennedy, at least for him, was a good thing.

Lustful eyes surveyed every inch of her skin. She was just right in every way possible…at least to him. Right height, right weight, right hair, right smile, right mentally and the right tightness of her pussy muscles. Check, check, check and check on all the things that were important to him. She was all that and more…a splendid fortune that he had only dreamed of until right now. Not to mention, she considered and treated him like a king. Down to her core, Kennedy was a piece of sexual spoilage that had always been a plus to him when it came to mate possibilities.

A mate?

Was he really considering that? After such a short period of time?

Wasn't Hedonism about flesh and pursuit thereof? Flesh and flesh alone. Fuck the heart! His head spoke the words, but they fell on deaf ears.

Aiden's heart recognized his internal need to categorize things into their neat and tidy compartmentalized boxes. It's what he did for a living. The only thing he knew. He fought his instinct to define things and to over analyze, running his nose up and down the nape of her neck instead, inhaling all of her and the essence of who she was. The scent was pleasurable.

Aftermath sex sure smells good on her, he thought to himself.

Being in the spotlight for all eyes to see their actions with the Spanish couple had sent a thrill through both his spine and Kennedy's. They had tasted the fruit of a sexually liberating place and enjoyed the nectar that lay therein. Engaging in sex with another couple was not native to either of them, yet they had enjoyed it immensely. But that act had only been a tease…an appetizer of hunger and thirst of wanting one-on-one kissing, fucking and tasting of each other again…this time *alone*.

A good nutt had demanded they rest. Their bodies had commanded it and they had obediently given in to orders. Retiring to one of the rooms in the Spanish couple's bungalow, Aiden and Kennedy had fallen asleep on top of the bed, covered only in each other's arms, a light sheet and the heat of recent sex to keep them warm.

That was after the foursome act…this was now.

Now Aiden was ready for round two.

He hoped his lover was up for it as well.

Lascivious hands caressed Kennedy's thighs gently in the midst of his thoughts. Slowly, he rubbed her body, applying pressure where needed to produce desired results. Unconsciously, she stirred slightly, inching her body closer into him, turning around briefly to make momentary eye contact before her tired eyelids did what they did best —close.

"Ummm, babe. That feels good. Imma need you to do that again and again and again. Don't neglect a spot; I wouldn't want any part of me to get jealous of your touch somewhere else. Keep doing what you're doing." Kennedy's body seemed to hum along with her words as she pushed her ass closer and closer into Aiden's dick, grinding slowly and rhythmically into his body.

"My body's calling for you," she said in a tone half controlled by sleep.

"Your wish is my command, beautiful," he stated as he continued to rub her body. An action that seemed to bring him just as much pleasure as it brought to her. She reminded him of a kitten the way her words and her body purred against his naked skin. Her ass was the next recipient of his touch. The small of her back and her shoulder blades got in line for his attention before he left a trail of kisses along the route his hands had taken.

"I hear your mouth talking, but it's only you and me now; think you can handle that?" he whispered in her ear, but not before biting her lobe gently.

Without opening her eyes, Kennedy's body answered for her in the form of an arch that pressed deeper into his body as if it were trying to reach down to his very soul. She pumped her ass into him while grinding on the air in front of her. His hands roamed her strategically like an explored move across a map.

"I don't remember saying the word, *stop*, so your hands should still be in motion!" Kennedy gave orders while letting it be known that she, too, was up for round two.

The spot above her ears was caressed by her fingertips as she moved one or two of her twists from the place they dangled, guiding them to a resting place behind her ears. She tried to play coy, but she wanted Aiden; she wanted him so badly that she thought her heart would stop beating if she couldn't taste him again…at least once.

His touch had awakened her inner slut and her sex begged for his attention.

She knew he was watching and she didn't care. Actually, it turned her on that he was. Normally, toys that required AA batteries sufficed, but in mixed company her hands would have to do the trick.

Elegant fingertips fanned down the side of her face and upper torso before flirting with her breasts with a squeeze, then making their way down to the cleanly shaven spot above her pussy. As she touched herself physically, she danced with thoughts of Aiden mentally. One finger, then two, was used as she began to finger fuck herself while continuing to push her ass into Aiden. Savagely, she worked her front side, while letting Aiden know she wanted him to work the back.

His mouth watered as he watched her and felt the soft, yet firmness of her ass as it grinded into his dick. Partial erectness became instant wood. He already knew she was a woman that he could never deny. Sampling her made him long for the full course meal. In the game of cat and mouse, he recognized his role was the latter. She had put a spell on him from the moment he saw her on the beach, and truth be told, he didn't mind being her zombie. But not before putting a spell on her of his own.

Two can play this game. And I can play it well! Aiden smirked as he watched Kennedy's body squirm around in the bed, feigning for more of his touch.

"Are you sure you can handle me? I've been known to be quite addictive?" Aiden asked as he kissed her shoulder blades before grabbing her ass tightly. He felt the fullness of his cue take control.

"We're all addicted to something, handsome. My addiction might as well be you," she answered in a voice that indicated she was already riding a self-induced sexual high.

He slapped her ass. A deep, slow moan escaped her lips, indicating approval of his slight infliction of pain and that she wanted him to do it again. Always a fast learner at reading a woman's unspoken commands, Aiden knew when a woman wanted it rough. When circumstances asked for it, that's how he gave it. Sexually, he knew when to follow a woman's lead. A good lover knew how to give in to a woman's needs while inserting leads of his own.

Harder slaps were applied to Kennedy's ass. Not enough to bruise, but hard enough to give her a pleasurable sting. She moaned louder as her ass jiggled from his touch. The sting made Kennedy wince. A sense of embarrassment covered her face as she acknowledged that she was enjoying her sexual ass whooping—something she had not engaged in before. Between slaps, she grabbed his thighs, pulling him closer.

"I couldn't help but notice that you have strong legs," she moaned while riding the hurt-so-good feeling she was receiving.

"I take it you approve and that's a good thing?" he uttered, rubbing each of her butt cheeks while tapping them again.

"Strong legs and stamina are signs of a good philly." The tracing of her fingertips ended with a firm squeeze.

"Oh, so I am nothing more than a horse in your stable, am I?"

"Are you objecting to my desire to take you for a ride?"

"Hell, if that is where this conversation is going, then saddle up, baby."

"I can tell you are a man that is used to being in charge; let me take charge of you for a change."

"Go for what you know!" He smiled as he rolled over on his back, dick rock hard and sticking into the air like a tower.

"This is going to take a bit of trust on your part. Do you trust me, Aiden?" Kennedy seductively questioned him while positioning herself over his waist, her pussy aching to receive penetration.

Aiden…even the sound of his name spoken from her own lips made her wet. As she stared at him waiting for an answer, she couldn't help but notice that his eyes and his body screamed sin; she just prayed for the opportunity to join him in a sexual hell.

"Trust you? I barely know you." He laughed as he placed his arms behind his head with an air of arrogance.

A smile crept over Kennedy's face and she asked the question again."Do you trust me?"

He let his guard lower and his heart peak for him."Yes, I do."

Kennedy kissed him deeply, reaching past his shoulders and slowly removing the cases from two pillows under his head. No words were spoken as she used each one to tie his hands to the bedposts.

Adrenaline pumped through his veins as he fought the urge to set himself free.

"Trust me, Aiden," she whispered as her mouth continued to kiss down his neck and chest."Give in to the feeling; quit trying to fight me—give me what I want."

He closed his eyes, loving the way she made him feel. Apprehension begged him to free himself; pursuance of something different made him submit to her will—Hedonism took control.

"What's your dirty little secret, handsome? I know you have one…we all do. What's yours?" Kennedy wrapped her lips around his dick, moving slowly at first in an up and downward motion, the warmth of her tongue dancing wickedly against his pulsating flesh.

"Shit!" he uttered, not giving her more than that.

"You're here to let go, Aiden. Let it all go with me." She moved her tongue in small circles before deep-throating him."I promise not to bite unless you ask me to. Trust me, Aiden. Tell me a secret so dirty it turns you on just to admit it."

He smiled at her, and with only the pillows as witnesses to the words spoken between lovers, he did…sharing not only his secret and his sins, but also the ugliest lustful desires of his heart.

Kennedy smiled in satisfaction of his confessions. Then she puckered her lips and blew gently on the edge of his dick.

The eye in the middle enjoyed the gentle breeze she applied. His whole body shook on command.

She was good at giving head. Aiden would give her that much. He was receiving the best he had ever had…but sex was still just sex…*wasn't it?*

Her hands worked in unison with her mouth. No area was left alone to catch cold. Each part received the warmth of her mouth and hands. Aiden's balls exhaled at the attention given to them personally. She took them in whole…two at a time…licking and sucking them as if they held the cure for cancer.

Hallelujah, his balls tapped approval upside the confines of his mind.

"Damn girl, what is it that you want from me?" he asked as his head pressed further into the pillow behind it.

"I want all of you!Is that too much to ask? We may never have this moment again, so right now…I want it all. All of you, Aiden…no holds barred. Do you trust me?" she repeated her words between a grip of her lips that was so fierce it promised to suck him dry.

"Trust is a two-way street, Kennedy. Do you trust me?Do you trust me enough to allow me to leave a bit of myself within you?"

His orgasm was approaching. He fought it with all his might.

Kennedy sensed his impending eruption. The sinner in her worked harder to help it along. Her movements of both hand and mouth picked up pace. Her jaws felt like they would collapse from exhaustion due to the sucking force she was applying.

"Give it to me, baby." Her eyes closed knowing the real question and demand at hand behind his question.

"Will you?" Aiden sighed as his load made its way to the top of his dick, threatening to erupt at any moment.

"Yes. For you…I will," she said before releasing the grip of her mouth and the pillow case from his right hand so that it could finish off the job.

He heard her words. The ones he wanted to hear. The ones that signified a connection that most lovers refuse to intimately share.

He came.

She swallowed.

Lust erased all shame and trust traveled between them as Hedonism put a spell on the room.

❧

"Your turn. Be specific. Tell me *exactly* what you want, Kennedy."

"Tonight, handsome, I just want you to make love to me until my energy drains and you feel the yearning inside me."

"Consider it done, Kennedy. Your orgasms belong to me," he whispered in her ear as he pulled her closer to him underneath the showerhead—place they had retreated to say their final goodbyes.

Their tongues danced a tango that signified it was last call. Within hours they would be separated, heading back to worlds that did not have the other in it. Urgency and desire dictated they make the moment last for as long as it could.

Water ran down the small space between their bodies and he kissed her as her hands slowly lathered his chest. She lingered with each caress. Aiden swore he saw a tear in her eye, but dismissed the thought, convincing himself that the steam was playing tricks on his eyes.

At first, their movements seemed synchronized, like an R-rated, choreographed dance on a Broadway stage. No real action. Just an illusion. But quickly, following Nature's cue, Aiden picked up the pace. Entering Kennedy from behind, he made sure to let his hands and his lips make love to her in the same manner his dick was…gently…sensually. Soon it was hard to tell if the steam in the bathroom was produced by water or by lust.

"Thank you," Kennedy said as her arms rose behind her, wrapping themselves around Aiden's neck, pulling him closer and deeper inside her.

"You're welcome," he said before leaning her slightly forward for a better angle for insertion.

They both knew what was happening between them and what their roles were respectively. He knew he was to be her chocolate treat without noticing the emotional tie that was building between them.

He could do that. *If* that was what she truly wanted.

Her hands grasped the sides of the enclosed glass shower for traction and a silhouette of serious fucking took form. For the better part of eternity, Aiden banged the hell out of Kennedy's back, pretending not to see her emotional tears in the process. He knew what she was feeling in her heart because he felt it as well. Neither of them gave it a voice. Instead, they went with the moment. Aiden stopped his sexual rampage only long enough to change positions, picking her up and using the wall to brace them both as he drove his dick into her while they stared at each other face to face…heart to heart.

Two minds let go of pretense and definitions, allowing pleasure of the flesh to take the lead. The Hedonistic way.

With each thrust, Aiden went deeper and harder…more passionately. He took her body through Winter, Spring, Summer and Fall and Kennedy loved every minute of the change of seasons of her life.

Fuck walking straight, Kennedy wanted her pussy to be paralyzed and in a lust-filled coma.

Aiden continued on his mission to make that a reality to the point that moonlight turned into sunlight's glow in ushering in sexual freedom. Kennedy's libido bore witness to a new day.

He gave her his all.

She willing accepted it again and again.

Aiden was home.
The place they both knew he belonged.

❦

His white boarding pass seemed to mock him, teasing him in a manner that said, *I hope you enjoyed yourself because that's all behind you now.* Indulgent fruit had been tasted and Aiden had savored the moment. But it was still just a moment; even though it had lasted a couple of days. That's the problem with appetizers… they give you a bit of variety and soothe the palate, but in the end, they are still just a sample of a bigger, more satisfying meal that you have to pay more for in order to enjoy.

Aiden had gotten to the airport early and paid extra to board the plane with the preferred passengers. Although he was at the back of the plane, he hated standing in lines and eased his stress by making sure he was one of the first people on the plane no matter where his seat was. He prayed that the person next to him on the flight would have the common decency to respect his need for them to shut up and allow him to be lost in his thoughts. The gods were compliant by leaving an empty seat between him and the next passenger.

"It's a long flight, sir. Do you need anything to make you more comfortable?" the thin, blonde flight attendant asked from behind a smile that was clearly forced.

She was sexy, but Aiden liked dark meat.

"No, thank you. I have all I need." Aiden stated as he put his headphones on his ears, catching an old blues song mid chorus. . .

Just the thought of you, turns my whole world a misty blue.

Fuck!!! he said under his breath at the reality that his heart was being twisted in a knot by fate. He closed his eyes and let the words, his memories, and the blue skies outside his window, rock him to sleep.

❦

Why the hell did I pack so much luggage? Kennedy asked herself as she tried to push the overstuffed carryon in the bin above her head. *I didn't even unpack this bitch in the first place, let alone wear half of the shit inside.* She chastised herself while giving one last shove to the bag before taking her seat next to the window. She was running late. Her norm. She was one of the last people on the plane and she could feel the cold stares of others as they watched her behind glances that suggested she was getting on their last nerve with her tardiness. Lucky for her, she was seated near the front of the plane and didn't have to be a spectacle for too many passengers to gawk at. Bitchiness and irritation engulfed every part of her mood and she couldn't figure out why.

Whoosa, heffa…Whoosa! she shouted in her head, trying to calm herself. After all, she had just had one of the most relaxing weekends in her life. There was no need for the anxiety that she was feeling.

"Aiden…get back here!"

Kennedy heard the words and her head did a double take around her, only to see a middle-aged, white woman wrestling with a blond haired, blue-eyed, seven-year-old menace to society.

Suddenly, Kennedy's mind felt at ease as she hummed the lyrics of one of her favorite old blues songs. A sense of calm engulfed her as Etta James sang, "Just the mention of your name…turns the flicker into a flame."

"Can I get you something to relax?" the thin, blond flight attendant asked as she was paid to do.

Barbies and their fakeness! Kennedy thought to herself as she shook her head in further annoyance.

"I wish you could bottle up some of the stuff I had back on that island, but I know you can't, so I'll take a Bloody Mary, instead."

❧

"Ladies and Gentlemen, we are approaching our final descent. It's a lovely seventy degrees in Atlanta and we will be arriving on time. For those of you for whom this is your final destination, you can retrieve your bags at baggage claim area number four. For the rest of you, please check the monitors in the terminal for the gate areas for your connecting flights. It has been a pleasure, and thank you for flying *American Airlines*."

The pilot's announcement was scripted and mechanical, Aiden thought to himself as he gathered his belongings and waited his turn at the end of a long line to exit the plane. He was one of the first on, but unfortunately, one of the last off.

Damn, I should have left my car here, he thought to himself once he was off the plane and downstairs trying to pick up his bags as he looked out the airport glass doors at the line for taxies forming in front of the baggage claim area.

The turnstile seemed to move in extra slow motion, but he swore he saw his bag coming just behind a large piece made by *Louis Vuitton*.

Finally, he thought to himself as he reached for his suitcase.

His arm hit hers and he could feel a warmth shoot through his body that was eerily familiar—a warmth that he would never forget as long as there was blood in his veins. He knew the owner…even before connecting with her face to face.

"If I didn't know any better I would swear you were stalking me," Kennedy said to Aiden with a smile on her face and a sparkle in her eyes.

"Please, girl…you're the one that gets off tying people up. Stalker tendencies seem to run in your blood, not mine," Aiden said as he pulled his luggage from the belt."Is this one yours?" he asked, removing the *Louis* next to his.

"How did you know?"Kennedy said as she helped him.

"It fits you. You seem to like *big* things. A woman like you likes a big, but comfy fit for ALL her attributes." His sinister grin teased her.

"You never said you were from Atlanta, Mr. Cross," Kennedy stated while heading toward the mechanical doors, pulling her bags behind her.

"And you never shared that bit of information about yourself either, Ms. Styles. I guess you have more secrets than I was able to uncover in our short time together." He shifted his bag on his shoulder.

"You never asked, handsome. And as far as uncovering secrets goes…well, there's always tomorrow." Kennedy blew a kiss in Aiden's direction and winked at him."Would you like a ride, handsome?" Kennedy asked as she pointed in the direction of a car waiting for her right outside of the baggage claim area.

"I'm always open for a ride from you, beautiful. And you can take that any way you want to take it," he said as they both began to put their luggage in the trunk.

Aiden opened the back door of the car for her and once they were inside, their lips immediately began to lock like two magnets with no choice but to give in to the force drawing them to one another. Passionately, they took up where they had left off on the island. The heat of their moment was interrupted, momentarily, by the driver's voice.

"Kennedy, you have a lot of explaining to do. I guess you had a good time given the fact that you brought home a physical souvenir instead of your usual shot glass or vacation T-shirt. But that shit aside…my only question to you is, where am I taking you? Your place or his? I don't care where y'all go, I just want y'all out my car before you leave a mess on my back seat," Allanda joked before putting the car in gear.

Accidental Orgasm

by Ebonee Monique & Torrian Ferguson

Chapter 1

After a long day at work all I wanted to do was go home, grab a beer, sit in front of the TV and fall asleep. I hate my job and the people I work with. Lately my life has become rather boring and mundane, consisting of nothing more than obligation and routine. I just roll with the flow instead of changing circumstance. I walked into my apartment, staring with eyes filled with disgust at the walls that have become tormenting guards in the prison that is my life. I toss my keys up on the table next to the door and flop down on the couch while reaching for the remote. The answering machine on the table calls me. The persistent blinking, red light indicates that I have three messages. A sound escapes my lips before I even realize that I am making it. It is a sigh of indifference to the world around me and its need to connect with me on some level or another. I could care less of its need; I'm oblivious to its desire.

I pressed the play button and walked into the kitchen to grab that beer I had been dreaming about. I'll admit it, I'm a little out of date and behind the times on a few things, but I figure if it's working why bother it? No need to rock a boat that is sailing from point A to B without a hitch.

"*You have three new messages. Message one…*" the machine said as I walked back past it on my way to the sofa.

Hello, this is a courtesy call from¼" I turned the TV up and didn't listen to the rest of the message.

Fucking bill collectors, my mind says.

"*Message two…*" I heard the machine say as I walked to the bathroom to clean up a little.

"Hey, wuz up, man?" I knew it was my best friend asking me to take his broke ass somewhere. My eyes roll to the back of my head as I flopped back down on the sofa, legs propped up on the arm rest.

"*Message three…*" the phone announced.

I reached for the remote to look for something to watch on TV.

"Hey, baby," a sexy voice said. I jumped up and ran back to the machine.

"I missed you today. All I could think about was the last time you and I were together. You fucked the shit out of me and I loved every second of it. The way you just took the pussy was… oh, damn…I'm about to cum just thinking about it. Call me back, baby. A repeat performance is in order."

I stood there with my mouth wide open. I didn't know who the hell the message was from, but she sounded so fucking sexy! I reached for the phone to dial *69 when I realized that I had deactivated that feature from my phone because I wanted to save a few bucks.

"Damn!Ain't that about a bitch! Just when I need that shit, I don't have it." As the words escape my lips I also realize that I forgot to change the battery in my caller ID box, so that was out as well. So not only do I not have the capability of calling her back, but I have no way of knowing who the hell she was.

I need to move into this decade and upgrade my shit!

I beat myself up all night trying to figure out who the hell my mystery caller was. I even called a few exflings to see if one of them may have made the call. That was not a good idea at all. One called me a "fucking pervert" for trying to fuck her in the ass. The other told me never to call her again. She's the one that said she was down for whatever, but it seems that *her* whatever and mine didn't follow the same definition...but that's another story. Needless to say, it quickly became clear to me that none of the women in my recent past had made the seductive call that held an orgasm for me at bay.

The next day was just like every other day.I hate my job and the people I work with. The only thing that was different was that my mind couldn't let go of the call from the night before. It encompassed my every waking thought.I daydreamed about that sexy voice on my machine all day. I made love to it at least a thousand times before a.m. turned to p.m. and it took everything in me not to go home during lunch to see if*she* had called again. I couldn't get her voice out of my head...nor did I want to.

I watched the clock on the wall as the seconds ticked away loudly. Each stroke of significance vibrated in my ears as if a sexual tease. Finally, the hands hit the destination that I had been waiting all day for—5:00 p.m.—quitting time.I was out of that place, on the road and home faster than I had ever been before. It's funny how a potential lay can motivate you when nothing else does.

For the first time in a long time, my tiny apartment no longer seemed like the same prison it had been. The living room seemed brighter as I opened the door and raced immediately to the answering machine. My fingers traced the black machine as I wondered to myself if I was crazy for expecting to hear the voice of a person I didn't know.

"Hell, I don't care how crazy I seem," I said aloud as I pressed the play button. "You have two new messages," the electronic tease announced.

I stood there waiting to hear if it was her again. I was like a kid waiting to see if Santa was coming around the corner. My stomach was in knots, but I couldn't move. I needed her to be on the other end of the line whispering a desire for me and only me.

"*Message one¼*" the machine said in what felt like slow-motion or a deliberate infliction of pain.

"Hey, baby," the voice cooed effortlessly. I wanted to jump out of my fucking skin. I had never been so happy in my life based solely upon listening to a phone message.

"You didn't call me back last night, baby. I waited up for you. Why do you tease me so? I lay in the bed and pulled out my little vibrating friend and massaged my pussy to a frothy mess. It was a sloppy second to you, but I had to make do with what I had. A wet pussy should never go to waste, so I put mine to use. Baby, I had cum everywhere. It was so thck and creamy. Too bad you weren't there to see it or enjoy it.But I gave it a stroke on your behalf. I ran my fingers through my pussy lips and then stuck them into my mouth, sucking them dry, imagining that they were your dick. I tasted so good, baby.Exquisite chocolates have nothing on my sweetness. Do you remember how I taste? I bet you do!Damn shame I had to waste all of that on a sex toy. Care to change that? Mmm…why don't you come over tonight? Come and taste me, baby. Feast on me while I feast on you. Imagine me wearing a black lace bra and thong set—my 40Ds barely being contained within the confines of the lace bra. Imagine them staring at you… begging you to touch them…begging you to caress and suck them. Can you see my nipples, baby? See how hard they are? Imagine me walking over to you and lowering my head into your lap, grabbing your dick, and¼."

"*End of message,*" The answering machine announced as it cut into my mystery girl's message.

Got damn it! That shit was getting good. I have to change the setting on the machine to record until the other person hangs up.

I didn't even pay attention to the second message. My mind was consumed with the first. I had to know who the mystery woman was. Her voice alone made my dick hard. The seductive way she whispered her message raised my body temperature. The dirty little things she suggested made my heart beat faster in anticipation. *Who was she? Where was she? And how could I taste her?*

The whole situation was starting to drive me insane. I had pussy—her pussy—on the brain. Release was the only option, at least for my sanity. I couldn't help myself; I jacked my dick over and over again thinking about the sexy ass woman in the black lace bra and thing set. I had no clue what she looked like, but that had no bearing on my need to have her. From her bra size I can only hope she was a big girl. Voluptuous equals satisfaction in my eyes. The bigger the better. The more curves a woman has, the more gratification she delivers. I love plus size women. There is nothing sexier to me than a big girl in a thong. Seeing that string disappear into the middle of a huge round ass is intoxicating. Damn, that shit drives me wild. A big woman with a big amount of confidence to go along with all that God gave her will have me whipped every time.

The next day I wanted to call in sick at work and tell my job I wasn't coming in. Nothing would have given me more pleasure than to sit around the house and wait for the phone to ring so I could finally find out who the owner of the sexy voice on the other end of my phone line was. She had me pussy whipped and I hadn't even had a chance to smell it or her yet. Everything in my core wanted to play slave to her phone call, waiting on it hand and foot; but reality dictated that I go to work instead.

The day was less mundane. The voices of my coworkers and my boss all seemed to be muted as I looked at them and smiled through their foolish gibbering. Nothing fazed me. Nothing could remove the smile that she had placed upon my lips by the simple, yet seductive trinkets she had placed in my mind. Unachievable deadlines, insurmountable paperwork, and unrealistic expectations, which all normally wore heavy around my neck during my nine to five, no longer had any effect on me. The trivial antics of the work place were invisible. All I could see was the light at the end of the tunnel waiting for me when I got home and could hear *her* voice again.

Work hours—the time of day that often felt like a ball and a chain on my body and on my life—suddenly took on the realm of being a means of passing time until she and I could meet again, if only via electronic message. As I walked the halls of corporate life my senses were awakened to every woman I encountered. Animalistic desires began to overtake me. Suddenly, I was a kid in a candy store noticing all of the tasty flavors around me. Womanly gestures that normally would have gone unnoticed by me grabbed my attention.I could smell every woman in the building.I could hear the rubbing of their thighs as they walked by.And for some strange reason, almost every woman in the building seemed to have big tits…or at least bigger than I had ever noticed before. I smiled at all of them, hoping that someone would fess up and admit that she was my mystery caller.

That never happened.

But I didn't let the disappointment linger. Even if none of the women in the office was the one that had awakened something that I had been missing, I was still having fun noticing all of the huge breasts that called my workplace their second home.

Note to self: Make friends with all my big -tittied coworkers.

Tick Tock, Tick Tock…the minute hand on the wall moves slowly, yet purposefully to the position that brings me joy—5:00 p.m. hits and I was out the door like a bat out of hell. I ran to my car and shot through every red light on the way to my apartment. I ran to my door like a small child that had to pee. I couldn't get the key in the door fast enough. When the door finally opened I pressed play on the answering machine and heard the automated voice say, "*You have one new message.*"

Please be her, please be her, please be her. I silently prayed as the machine got ready to play back the message that had been left for me.

"Hey, love," she purred like only *she* could. I pulled my dick out, slathered it with Vaseline and got ready to enjoy myself. I had changed the setting on the machine, so I knew it was not going to cut her off this time.

"You didn't call me again last night, baby," the soft, sexy voice said.

"I waited up for you last night. I lay in my bed and imagined you behind me again, fucking me as hard as you could. Mmmm…I could almost feel your hands under my stomach grabbing my waist, pulling me in every time you dove deeper and deeper inside of me. You know how Mama likes it when you pull all of me close to you."

"Yes! She's a big girl! I love it!" I hear myself scream to an empty room. Her reference to *all of me* lets me know that there is more of her to love than just sticks and bones. *Just the way I like it!*

"Oh, baby, you feel so good inside of me. Can you see me, baby? I'm still lying in my own pool of cum. Thick and sticky… can you see it, baby?It's that way because of you. I came thinking about you licking my pussy today. How your face was engulfed in my fat, wet pussy. I have a surprise for you, baby. I went to the salon today and got all of my kitty hair waxed off just for you.My clit is no longer hidden. Can you see it, baby? Lick my pearl, baby. Suck on it for me, please, baby. You want to hear me beg for it? Is that what you want? Please baby, stick your tongue deep into my pussy. Yeah…just like that.Deeper, baby. Deeper. Squeeze my ass while you eat me, baby. Oh, yes! I'm loving this!Make me cum again, baby.Make my pussy your own."

I stood there and stroked my dick like crazy. Her words, the sound of her voice, and the erotic phone sex she was delivering made as hard as a man that had not had any pussy in years. I swear I could smell her heat even though she was not there.

"Baby, can I turn around so you can eat my ass? Let me show it to you before you answer. There now…can you see it? Mind if I give it a slap just for you? Look at it, Daddy. Do you like how it jiggles each time I slap it? You like what you see, don't you? Yeah, I know you do. That big smile and hard dick let me know you're pleased and I like pleasing you. I bet you could make it pop, baby. Touch it. Don't be afraid…it doesn't bite; it only begs for your touch. A kiss would be nice; a lick would be even better. Did you notice the peek-a-boo effect of my thong? Yeah, I KNOW you did; how couldn't you help but see the way the top of my thong winks at you as it disappears into this big ass of mine? You love that shit, don't you, Daddy? We both know you do. Big, fat asses get you hard, don't they, baby? Are you touching yourself yet? Yeah, I know you are. Stroke it one good, long time for me. "

I was ready to cum just from the description of her ass and the thought of seeing it in motion.

"Yeah, you like that way I shake my ass, don't you, baby? Want me to shake it all over your face? You like that, huh? Slide your tongue into my ass baby. Slow and steady at first, then pick up speed. Yeah, baby, suck my ass hole. Make it sloppy wet like only you can. You know the way I like it. Eat it like you owe me rent!"

I was just about ready to cum when she said, "You feel me shaking, baby? Can you feel the tremors you cause deep within me? You know what that means? I'm ready to cum, baby. I want you to eat my pussy while I cum all over your face. Can you do that for me? Will you allow me to cum all over your face?"

I stood there and screamed yes to my sexy-voiced friend.

"Ok…here it cums. Oh shit, baby! I'm cumming all over your face. Taste it! It's sweet isn't it? You like the flavor, don't you, baby? Ummm can you feel that? My nectar is flowing heavy now, just for you. Eat my fat, wet pussy baby. Eat that shit! Awh damn!!! Put your face in it!"

I rubbed my face imagining that I had it deep in her pussy, drinking her sweet cum. I shot my load all over myself. I loved the feeling of my own cum spraying all over my legs.

"Oh, baby, you have to come see me tonight. I need you, baby. Please come see me tonight. I love you, Greg."

Greg?

Hold up my name is Darren! Who the fuck is Greg? Damn! I realize that my mystery woman has been dialing the wrong fucking number.

Chapter 2

My life has always consisted of accidental orgasms. The nut I got or helped someone get was always for someone else, except for my first night as a college freshman.

I was in Daytona Beach, Florida on a Saturday night. It was the beginning of a new life for me…the start of being an adult.I walked the campus taking in all the sights, sounds and ambiance that college life had to offer. And the women…damn there is nothing as satisfying to the eyes as a rainbow of beautiful women with beautiful, curvaceous bodies. I was in heaven thinking about all the sin I would get into for the next four years.

The Omegas were having a back to school party and it looked like the entire campus was invited. New to the campus and even more green to college life, I couldn't wait to experience a frat party and the Omega kick off sounded like the perfect opportunity to get my feet wet in how to party college style.After very little coaxing on my part, my college roommate, Rod, decided to go to the party with me. I was happy to have a partner in crime.

"I met this fine ass mami at the mall last week," Rod said in his thick New York accent as we got ready for the party. I hadn't met anyone in Florida yet, but I didn't care. All I wanted was to party, meet some fine women and see what the big deal was with Omega parties.

"You've only been in college for a few months Rod; you're not supposed to be trying to chase a woman around yet, man. You have to do a little sampling before you buy anything," I said with a chuckle.

Rod waved me off and continued applying his cologne.

"She was so damn fine, yo. I don't even mind chasing that one."

I shrugged my shoulders and headed to the door.

During the entire ride over to the party, all Rod could talk about was the woman he'd met at the mall in the food court. Apparently, she was built like an Amazon and had stolen the big city guy's mind.

"She gave you her number; right? Why are you chasing her down to a party?" I asked as we walked toward the door and out the dorm.

"First off," Rod said with a smirk on his face, "I'm not chasing anyone."

I sucked my teeth in disbelief as we got in the car.

"Second off, I just want to see what she looks like taking all of this dick," Rod said with a straight face as he pointed down toward his jimmy over and over until we both couldn't control our laughter at his corny ass joke. "By the end of the night you just watch and take notes—I'll have Trina wrapped around both my finger and my dick!" Rod said as we pulled in front of the frat house.

The outside of the house was just like the others I had walked past as I toured the campus. It was quite ordinary looking, with nothing of significance to catch your eye except the Omega logo promptly displayed from the roof. But the outside appearance was deceptive in terms of what was going on inside. From the moment we walked in I felt like I was in a mad house. There were wall to wall people and each one of them had a drink in their hand. Most were dancing ass to groin in the middle of the room and each corner had a woman pinned up against the wall by a jock hoping to get lucky. I had never in my life been to a party with so many people before. I saw women there that looked like models. Their hair was tight, jeans were hugging the round asses that black women are known for and the music was banging. The vibe in the house was off the hook and everyone was having a great time. I tried to remove the look of shock off my face, but I am sure it was clear that I was out of my normal element. If you know anything about the Omegas, you know that they have some of the craziest parties on the planet and this one was no exception.

Squeezing myself in between humping bodies that used loud, thumping beats as an excuse to move their hips in sexually suggestive ways, I made my way to the back of the open area being used for dancing and found the source of alcoholic deliverance. The view from the bar area gave me a bird's eye view of the party and I decided to stay in place for a while so that I could fully absorb all that college party life had to offer. I watched a little and indulged a little and after a few hours of drinking and dancing, a young dark-skinned girl jumped up on the kitchen table and started dancing as if she was on a stripper stage. She was tore the hell up from all the drinking she had done, but I guess she was feeling the music and feeling a little slutty at the same time. Her spontaneous striptease caught the eye of every guy in the room like flies flock to shit, and all the fellas ran into the kitchen while reaching into their pockets for one dollar bills. She took off her shirt and revealed a small mouth full of chocolate titties. I guess from the small top she was wearing, it looked as if she had more tits than she actually had. My dick went soft at the sight of them. They were perky, but I'm more turned on by a mouthful than a Tic Tac.

I turned away and pushed myself through the growing crowed and headed outside to look for Rod. The party was so big, we'd seemed to have lost each other from the moment we walked in the door hours earlier, but we didn't mind. Neither Rod nor I needed a babysitter when it came to partying. As I searched for him to see if he was having any luck with the girl from the mall, I noticed the most beautiful woman at the party standing by herself, drinking and dancing to the music. My eyes lit up as I noticed her large, beautiful, redbone cleavage spilling out the top of the shirt she was wearing. Mentally, I could hear her breasts screaming to be released from their bondage. The night air was blowing and her nipples stood straight up every time Mother Nature touched them. I stood back and watched as the Goddess danced and swayed her ample ass back and forth to the beat of the music. My dick began to run down my leg and gain girth as it stood in awe of the magnificent woman within my view. She turned and looked directly in my eyes. I wanted to say something, but my mouth wouldn't move. She smiled and motioned me over with her finger. I took the last sip of my drink and walked over to her.

"Hey, wuz up? You like standing over there, watching me dance?"

"Yes, I must admit I was enjoying watching the way you moved."

With that she shot me a beautiful smile and got closer to me. I could feel her breasts start to press against my chest. I wanted to reach up and grab two handfuls of her titties.

"You want to feel them, don't you?" A wicked grin spread across her face. She slowly looked down at her cleavage and looked back up at me with a very seductive look in her eyes. "You can feel them if you want to. They don't bite."

I reached up and slid my hands across her huge, round breast. If my fingertips could have gotten a hard on, they would have. Without thinking, I lowered my head directly into her cleavage, licking my lips in the process. The warmth of her contained breasts was warm and inviting.I had to taste them. My tongue danced across her tits while my hand squeezed and pushed her breast even closer together. I tried to smother myself in her titties. I wanted to become one with them. Savagely, I ran my lips across the exposed surface of her top, kissing every inch of her bountiful bosom.

"Damn, boo, you move fast as hell! We went from you touching them to you damn near sucking on my nipples!" Her eyebrows were raised as she stated the obvious.

"My bad, baby; it's just that you're some damn fine I couldn't help myself. It was like your titties were calling me." I chuckled a little at my aggressive actions and the horny display of my hunger to have her breasts in my mouth.

She laughed a little and leaned into me again and said, "Let's take this inside. It's getting colder out here by the second." She grabbed my hand and led me back into the house. We walked through the rear door, unnoticed because now there were three small chested women dancing on the kitchen table, so no one even looked in our direction. They were more concerned with the show in front of them than two parties starting a sexual walk of shame. We strolled past a few rooms and I heard the sounds of women getting the shit fucked out of them. I could feel my dick jump, hoping that it would get some of the same thing going on behind those walls. The goddess continued to lead me and I followed like a love sick puppy waiting for a treat. We continued down a small hall lined with sports memorabilia and I noticed a room with a partially open door. I couldn't help but look inside as we walked by and I saw the president of the chapter hitting some girl from the back while she was eating another girl's pussy at the same time. Threesome heaven—every man's fantasy. I knew right then and there what frat I wanted to pledge.

My new friend led me to a small room in the back of the house, but she might as well have been leading me to ecstasy because that is what I was anticipating. The whole dorm house smelled of indulgence and lust and I wanted a taste; the rhythm of her stride told me she could deliver. I watched her back field in motion as we entered the room. My tongue moistened my lips as she turned around and looked me in the face while her hand grabbed my bulging dick. Instinctively, I, again, went right for her titties. I took her shirt off and finally got to see her gorgeous mounds in all of their glory. She started to unzip my pants as I unzipped hers at the same time. Shit was about to go down proper and me and my dick were both ready for any and everything she had in store.

I was her puppet as she had my dick in her hands, rubbing it and massaging it, trying to get it as hard as she could. I stood still and let her have her way. *Who was I to not allow her to take the lead?* I sucked her nipples while I played with her pussy. She was wet as hell…just the way I like it. I don't know what happened, but it seemed like someone else was coming out of me. I felt like I was another person. I pushed her on the bed and she fell with a soft bounce while smiling up at me. Her eyes displayed an amazement and pleasure at my actions. I guess I startled her with the push, but I didn't care. She wanted it and so did I…so why take it slow? She fell back on the bed with her legs wide open. The gateway to gratification called me and I answered on the first ring. Before she could gather herself, my face was buried nose deep into her meaty pussy. I felt myself exhale as the smell of her sweet spot engulfed me. I love the smell of pussy and I tried my best to suck her clit as hard as I could so that I didn't miss a drop of the juices she released. I was famished and her pussy was the delicacy my mouth desired. The harder I sucked the more she got into it.

"That's it, nigga; eat this pussy. Eat all Mama's pussy!" Her thighs began to shake with each flicker of my tongue and the suction of my lips. Whenever her body tried to instinctively pull away, I grabbed her thighs tighter, making escape impossible.

I did what I was told and began to lick her wet slit until I could feel her coating my upper lip with cum. I love it when I'm eating a pussy so good it gets white froth on it after a while. She grabbed the back of my head and demanded that I continue to eat her out.

"Yeah, nigga; you ain't never had a pussy this good before! You know it and I know it. But I got something else for you. Eat my ass, muthafucka!"

I instantly stopped eating her tasty pussy and directed all of my attention to her pretty tight ass hole. I pushed her legs as far back as they would go and went face first into her ass.

"Oh, hell yeah! That's what I'm talkin about. Lick my asshole, nigga. Lick it!"

I had never known an ass to taste so good.

"Turn your big ass over and let me eat it from the back!" My demands upon her shocked me as much as they shocked her, but we both obliged.

Without hesitation, she got on all fours and tooted her ass high in the air. I grabbed her high yellow, plump ass cheeks with both hands and spread them wide open to make sure I saw her beautiful brown eye. It stared back at me and winked that it was okay for me to enter. I stretched my tongue out as far as I could and began to slowly slide it into her ass. She wiggled at first at the intrusion, but the rest of her shaking body told me to press forward and come on in.

She began to moan very soft, almost as if she was chanting or speaking in tongues and I allowed the sounds of her soul to play as the soundtrack in the background of my actions. I could tell I was pleasing her beyond anything she had experienced before. I fucked her ass with my tongue for a few minutes. Suddenly, I felt her legs start to shake more violently than they had before. I knew what was next, but I wanted to hear her say it.

"What you shakin' for? It's that good to you?"

"I'm 'bout to cum!"

"You want me to stop eating your ass to let you?"

"Hell no! Don't take your tongue out of my asshole! Keep doing what ya doing!" The tone of her voice indicated that I had no choice but to do as I was told; and quiet as kept, I was happy to oblige.

I continued to fuck her ass until she started to scream.

"Oh shit! Oh shit! I'm 'bout to…God damn!"

I knew what she was doing, but I still wanted to hear it. "What you doin' baby? Tell Daddy what you doin'?"

"I'm cummin'. Put your face in it."

I took my tongue out of her ass hole and quickly placed my face into her exploding pussy. I opened my mouth and allowed her to coat my face and tongue with her sweet pussy juice. My dick was hard enough to cut a diamond.

"Stay right in this position I've got something else for you." I said as I rubbed my hands across my lips, removing her residue.

She stayed in the doggie style position as I applied a condom and slid my thick dick into her pussy.

"That's it, baby; put that big ass dick in my wet fuckin pussy." She moved side to side helping me ease myself in.

I would normally start out slow and work up a good speed, but she was so fine that all I wanted to do was beat the hell out of her pussy. Once my dick was all the way into her I began to fuck the shit out of her. I tried to pound that pussy into the ground. Something took over me and I fucked as if I were in some sort of seductive trance. All I could hear was the splat sound of my dick digging into her wet pussy. Other than simultaneous moans, neither of us said a word as we moved back and forth, allowing our bodies to scream for us. I grabbed a handful of her hair and pulled back. That really got her going. She arched her neck and back upwards as a sign of approval. "I love having my hair pulled. Pull it, baby! Tame me… tame me now!" She began to make sounds that I had not heard before…not quite a growl, but more like a loud purr.I couldn't quite place the sound, but I must admit that my ego got something of a boost at being the source of causing it.

I guess with all the noise we were making, neither one of us noticed the small crowd of people that had gathered at the door watching us. We finally noticed they were there when someone said, "That nigga fuckin the shit outta ole girl!"

We both looked up without missing a beat and saw a small crowd gathered, standing there cheering us on, but we were too wrapped up in the moment to stop. I figured I might as well put on a show for those in attendance. She must've been thinking the same thing, because she kicked it into another gear and started throwing her round ass back at me with a fierceness that I knew would give me back pains in the morning.

With one hand still pulling her hair, I took the other hand and smacked her on the ass. The velocity of the quick spanking left a huge print on the left side of her red bone ass.

"Damn! You doin' all the shit I like. Smack my ass again!" she said loudly as if she were trying to be heard at the back of a theater.

I didn't need any coaching from that point. I spanked the shit out of her while I drilled her like a miner looking for coal. I watched as her big ass wobbled back and forth with every one of my thrusts into her.

"Lay on your fuckin side!" I yelled as I was ready to move to another position. The animal in me was coming out. I felt like the king of the jungle and I was going to conquer that pussy at will.I was center stage and destined to put on a show. I was in search of not only a good nut, but a standing ovation for the onlookers as well.

She quickly lay down and threw one of her legs high into the air. I got behind her and continued beating that pussy up. I could feel a pain running down my aching legs and generating from the middle of my back from all the harsh thrusting I was doing, but I could care less.It was show time and my aim was to please. This time we are facing all the spectators at the door. More people had come to view the show and we didn't mind one bit. I squeezed her big titties hard as I fucked her.

"Pinch my nipples, Daddy!" She winced as she threw her backside deeper and deeper into me. I pinched her nipples harder while I plowed into her.

"Is that what you call a pinch? I said pinch them!" She chastised me, begging for me to inflict more pain.

I started to pinch her fat nipples as hard as I could. I could see on her face she was in a pleasure-pain state of mind. She wanted all that I was giving to her to be given harder, and I made sure I delivered.

"That's it, Daddy. Pinch them muthafuckas!"

I pinched them as hard as I could. She was in pure ecstasy at that point and I was having the time of my life.

"I want you to taste your own pussy on my dick. I said in a tone louder than I usually speak during sex."

"Bring it here," she said, pointing to her lips.

I took my dick out of her pussy and went up to her face, careful not to land on her as we both changed positions. I shoved my dick into her mouth as she had instructed me to do. I wanted to see how much of my dick I could shove down her throat before she'd gag. My balls were damn near on her chin before she started making gaging sounds. I snatched my dick from her mouth and a long thick trail of spit was all over my dick. I loved the sight of it.

"Gag me, Daddy. Do it again; gag me!"

I shoved my dick in a second time, this time trying to push my dick through her skull. She loved every moment of it and I got off watching her reflexes in full affect.

"You making me feel like a slut. I love it!"

I looked around at all the people that were watching us. A few of the fellas had their dicks in their hands jacking off and a few ladies had started rubbing one another as they watched the show. The scene at the door way was almost as erotic as the one in our room.

"I want you to get on top, sexy!" I whispered as I leaned down to nibble her ear. I eased down on the bed and laid down on the mattress as she stood over me. The image hovering over me sent a rush of blood back to my dick, inflating any limpness that might have wanted to emerge.

"Now that you have gagged me with your dick, what you think I'm about to do to you?" she asked as she wiped her mouth.

Before I could answer, she dropped her big ass right on my face. I could hardly breathe. She put me in the very submissive state that I longed to be in. She was smothering me and I loved every second of it. I tried to stick my tongue all the way up her pussy as she rode my face. I had to literally push her off my face in order for me to be able take another breath. She was killing me softly with her creamy thighs and I couldn't think of a better way to go.

"You like that shit, don't you. You like being smothered by all this pussy, huh?" Her words rode the tide of her upward and downward strokes.

All I could do was look up at her in total submission. She slid off my face and left a trail of pussy nectar from my face to my dick. She put my dick inside of her and began to bounce up and down. Just as I imagined, she was a big girl that knew how to work what she had. I was in heaven. I cupped her huge tits as she continued to work me as if she was riding a horse.

Then it happened.

"Oh shit, baby. I'm 'bout to cum."

Upon hearing my words, as if on cue, she grabbed my throat and began to choke me with both hands. I felt my air beginning to shut off with every passing second. The lightness of air in my lungs intensified my impending orgasm. My dick felt harder than it had ever felt before. She continued to bounce on my dick and strangle me at the same time. I was in so much pain and so much ecstasy at the same time that I didn't know if I was coming or going; and yet, my threshold of pleasure made it all worthwhile.

I couldn't say a word. My eyes seemed like they were going to pop out of my head. Just then I felt my dick shoot a wad of cum right into her pussy. I was on the verge of passing out when I felt another shot fire out of my dick. *Two for the price of one.*She had done what no other woman had done in such a short amount of time—she had made me come back to back.My balls emptied themselves once and then gave an encore performance. All I could do was lay still, enjoy the ride and let it happen. That's when she let my throat go. I just laid there motionless…gasping for air…finally able to breathe normally again.

That was the best nut I ever got! I thought as the colors in the room began to take on a normal hue. My passion was color blind, but seeing things for what they really are is a luxury that, unless you are void of breath, you take for granted.

I loved being choked to the point of almost passing out while busting a nut. That shit was unreal.

She walked over to my face and lowered her messy, wet pussy onto my mouth. I slurped all of her cum out of her. The people at the door went wild. People were slapping hands and a few of the guys actually came while watching us. It was awesome. Once everyone left the room, she began to get dressed. I sat up on the edge of the bed and watched her.An unusual neediness enveloped me.I needed her.I wanted her.I had an urge for what we had just shared to never end.

"So do you have a name, beautiful?" I figured since we both had just had mind-blowing sex, it might be good to have a name to go with the memory.

"Trina," she whispered, out of breath.

My eyes widened as I searched the crowd to make sure Rod wasn't among them since I had unknowingly just beat up the pussy that he was hoping to call his own.

Chapter 3

Ever since my girl, Trina, started working at that new job a few years back, shit ain't been the same. She never takes me around her friends, nor does she talk about them at all with me. It's as if she makes sure that the two worlds never meet and especially don't collide. I don't know anybody personally that she associates with anymore. We used to have the same circle of friends, but now that shit's over and done. It was a slow, but steady placement of me into a different category in her life. This morning Trina broke up with me. The lame ass reason she gave for the breakup was that whenever we have sex, she feels that I always want some crazy, outrageous shit.

"You always want to fuck me in the ass. You are constantly asking me to suck your dick. You want to disrespect me by bringing another bitch up in here! I can't take it anymore!"

She ended her rant by stating that in our relationship, she always wanted to make love and that I, on the other hand, always wanted to fuck. Maybe I'm missing something, but in both cases doesn't a dick go in a pussy? Isn't the end result the same?

Even with that question lingering in my thoughts, I was hurting like hell at the fact that our union as a couple was over. I'm not a man that likes to be alone and sex is always on my mind, so I decided to call my local telephone chat line for a distraction from my failed relationship. Within a few minutes I met a woman named Carla. She said that she had a caramel complexion, huge tits, a round ass and a short haircut. She sounded like my type of woman. I let her know that I was not looking for a wife or a girlfriend at the moment and that I was only in the mood for getting mine tonight.

Now let me explain the chat line. There is no reason to try and give a girl your best game on the chat line. If you're on there, everyone knows what you're on there for. The only reason I went into my *I'm not looking for anyone* speech was because I met this one bitch, fucked her, and she went crazy; she started calling and texting and wanting a serious relationship. It was as if she forgot where and how we had met or the unspoken rules of the chat line. Because of her, I always issue a disclaimer when I begin chatting.

Carla told me that she and her boyfriend had just broken up and she was looking to get over him really fast. The whole conversation was working out better than I had hoped. After getting all the preliminary bullshit talk out the way, it was time to get down to why we both were on the line.

"So, Carla, are you down for some nasty, freaky shit tonight?" I asked, trying to make sure I was not going to end up being dumped by one prude and then end up picking up another prude on the rebound…all in one day.

"I'm down for whatever," she responded with a huff in her voice like I had insulted her with my question. Then shit got interesting.

"But the real question is…are YOU down for some real, nasty, freaky shit tonight?" she asked, trying to pull my punk card.

"Hell yeah! I'm down for whatever you want to get into."

"Cool. My girl just came over and she wants to get into a threesome tonight. I figured if you were down, then you could come over and we all can get up."

Now that's my type of girl! I wonder why more women don't look out for their friends like that. She was putting her friend first. That shit made me almost tear up thinking about how good of a friend she was. I jumped around the room trying not to make a lot of noise while still holding the phone. I was going to have my first threesome, but I had to act like it was no big deal.

After several seconds of trying to catch my breath, I answered, "Yeah, I'll come over and we can make it happen. But tell me what your girl looks like."

"Oh, she sexy as hell. She's about 5'6" and she's got some big ass titties and a fat ass. She and I both wear the same size clothes, so I know she's a size 22 or 24 in some things."

Oh lawd! That's perfect for me. I love BBW's. Two big girls fucking me tonight. Damn, I'm gonna love this.

"Your girl sounds sexy as hell. Have the two of you *been* together before?"

"All the time. She and I have been friends for about two years now and we like to have threesomes as often as possible. Most of the time they've been with my boyfriend or his friends, but tonight we want to branch out a little. We're tired of fucking the same four niggas all the time. I want to feel a new dick up in me."

I could hear her friend talking in the background, "Yeah, I wanna suck a new dick tonight!"

Where are these kinds of women during the day? Why do I only get stuck with bitches that don't suck dick, don't want me to smack them on the ass, and don't take it in the ass? Damn, these women sound like the type you take home to Mama. Well, on second thought….

Our conversation continued for about another five minutes before Carla added, "Can you hold on a second? My girl wants me to take off my pants so she can eat my pussy before you come over She always likes to have me to herself before we get with other people." I could hear both women giggling at Carla's confession.

I didn't know what to say. I just sat there and held the phone.

"Shit might get a little noisy while she's eating me, so don't trip."

I was like a kid in a candy store—I was so happy. There was no way that this was happening to me. Shit like this never happens to me. I guess Carla's girl was licking her, because the next thing I heard was, "Yeah, baby, lick my pussy. Mmm…suck on my clit a little. You know I like that shit."Carla was talking to her girlfriend and the way her voice lowered let me know that she was enjoying being a meal for her friend.Then she turned her attention back to me on the other end of the line, "Damn, baby, you listening to us?"

Again, I didn't say a word. All I could get out of my mouth was, "Uh huh."

Carla giggled a little then started talking again.

"Mmmm…stick your finger in my ass while you eat me. I want you to get my ass nice and open for our friend later tonight."

OH SHIT! Not only am I going to have a threesome, but I'm finally going to fuck a bitch in the ass. That's always been a fantasy of mine. Damn, as far as I'm concerned Trina should have broken up with me months ago if shit was going to turn out like this. Any pain I was feeling about her dumping me was quickly leaving me as I listened to the women on the other end of the chat line. I wanted to pull my dick out and rub it till the skin came off; but I wanted to wait and save that first blast of cum for the two of them.

Carla continued, "Hold up, baby; let me get on my knees on the sofa. I want to feel your face in my ass."

This shit is wild! I'm loving it. These two are off the hook and I'm lucky as hell to be the one to have caught them tonight. I could hear them playfully laughing and then I heard what sounded like a vibrator.

"Oh, shit,,, that's it, girl. Shove that vibrator in my ass!"

I heard several hard smacks and light screaming. Jealousy took control of my mind as I tried to visualize what was happening on the other end of the line. Thoughts of the two curvaceous women rolling around placing a vibrator where my dick should be filled me with envy.

"I'm cumming, baby! Lick my pussy while I cum. Oh damn… you eat pussy good!" Carla was practically yelling now.

My dick was rock hard like it was going to bust out of the skin that contained it.I felt like I was going to faint if I didn't cum and cum soon.

"Hey, we need to get off the phone." I commanded. "I have to have both of you right now!"

I knew Carla could hear me, but for a few seconds longer her only response was deep moaning followed by a few grunts before momentary silence. I shifted in my seat trying to wait for her orgasm to subside long enough for her to return to talking to me.

"You want some of this, don't you?"

"You damn right I do.And I promise to give it to both of you harder than that vibrator ever could." I tried to sound cocky, yet desirable.There was no way I was letting an opportunity like this slip by me.

"That's a tall order to fill and you can best believe I plan to hold you to that promise," Carla said before giving me the address to where the two of them were.I hung up the phone and jumped in the shower. I wanted to make sure every inch of me was clean and lickable. I felt like I was ten years old and it was midnight on Christmas Eve. I was excited. Sexual anticipation consumed the air that I breathed. I couldn't stop smiling. I put on a nice pair of jeans and a black wife beater. I sprayed on my Sean John cologne and was out the door in no time flat. I didn't even worry about putting on my boxer briefs. I figured why put them on when the goal was for me to just kick them off anyway.

I pulled up to the apartment that Carla had given me directions to and my stomach was in knots because I was so nervous. I rubbed my hands on my jeans to make sure they weren't sweaty and I put a mint in my mouth to make sure that my breath was fresh before it was tainted with the smell of pussy. As I turned off the car engine, I tried to hype myself up to keep from looking like a bitch, given the sexual delights that were steps away from me indulging in.

You got this, nigga! Own this night. Own both of them. They are there for the taking.

All I could think about was going deep into the folds of both women tonight. You could cut glass with my dick as I got out the car. I was ready to join the party that the two of them had already started. I walked up and knocked on the door. It only took one knock before I heard the turning of the locks on the other side. Slowly the door opened and there stood Carla. She was just as fine and sexy as she had described on the phone. No false advertising there. She answered the door dressed in a black and red bra and thong set, both of which left very little for the imagination.

I didn't know if I was supposed to shake her hand or how I was supposed to handle our initial greeting, but it didn't seem to matter because Carla pulled me close, gave me a slow but seductive hug and bit my earlobe before pushing me back and staring at me from head to toe.

"You'll definitely do," she said as she closed the door behind me and began walking away. I took her actions to mean that I was supposed to follow her.

"So, where's your girl?" I asked looking around the room, trying to see if I could see her before she saw me.

"She's in the bed room waiting on us. When I walked out to answer the door she was playing with her pussy."

That's what I'm talking about. They doing the damn thang. Damn, I wish I had a female like this, I thought to myself as I continued to follow her lead.

We turned the corner and went into the room. My mouth fell open. I couldn't believe my eyes. It was like I forgot how to speak.

"This is my girl, Trina."

"Oh, shit!" I screamed as I saw my ex-girlfriend lying there with a look on her face that screamed surprise and excitement.

I wanted to be pissed about it, but in all honesty, I had two nearly naked, fine ass women wanting my dick in them; I'd be mad later.

"Y'all know each other?" Carla asked as she rubbed my back and led me closer to the bed. She grabbed my crotch before pushing me down in front of Trina who was sprawled out near the headboard, dressed in a pink negligee. Trina and I avoided direct eye contact and shook our heads.

"Nawh, she just looks familiar." I lied as I sat on the bed.

Carla wasted no time getting things started. She began lighting candles and soon I heard the soft sounds of R. Kelly playing in the room as I tried my best not to think about the fact that my ex-girlfriend was sitting right behind me.

"Yo, y'all got some liquor?" I asked, standing up from the bed.

Carla excused herself from the room to get us something to drink and I took her exit as a good time to face Trina for an explanation.

"Well...." I said as I looked at my fine ass ex-girlfriend.

"Well what, Darren? Don't even trip.Before you start questioning me, remember that we are both here for a good time. And you can always leave if you're going to bitch about this," she said as she sucked her teeth and adjusted her bra.

My dick jumped at the sight of Trina's big ass titties. They had always been my weak spot with her. The caramel mounds sat perfectly with an oven-toasted, brown nipple right in the center.

"Nawh, I'm not trippin," I said with a raised eyebrow, "but I am about to fuck the shit out of both of y'all."

Trina squinted her eyes and finally began to giggle. I couldn't tell if she was nervous or happy; either way, I didn't care. I just wanted to nut.

"Is that right?" Trina asked as she stood up just as Carla was entering the bedroom with a bottle of Grey Goose and three shot glasses.

"Let the party begin," Carla said as she put the Goose and the glasses on the night stand.I made myself comfortable on the bed, ready to get a taste of what I had come for. I reached over and started to squeeze Trina's nipples as Carla crawled on the bed toward me. Watching her move seductively on all fours made my dick hard as a brick. My wildest dreams were about to come true. I had waited damn near all of my life for this moment and it was finally going to happen. I was having a hard time containing myself and my dick.

Carla ran her blood red nails down my chest as Trina sucked on my neck. I could feel the hair standing up on the back of my neck. I reached around and grabbed a handful of Trina's perfectly round ass. My hands felt like they were at home again. I had forgotten how smooth her skin was. Flawless. Carla pulled my pants down and with one swift motion she had my entire hard-on almost down her throat. The air in the room seemed to have been instantly sucked out with the intensity of her head skills. Trina worked her way around to face me.

"Lay yo ass down!" she demanded. The tone of her voice was one I had not heard from her in a long time. Without really knowing why, I instantly obliged without hesitation.

"Yeah girl, we bout to have fun with his ass tonight. I see already he's obedient," Carla said as she sucked on Trina's diamond hard nipples.

"Stick your tongue out."

Again, I did as I was told. Trina crawled up my body and found the perfect seat directly on my face. I tried my best to shove my tongue as deep into her as I possibly could. The smell of her sex made my dick jump and both women smiled wickedly at each other.

"Here, girl…drink this while that nigga eats your pussy."

From underneath Trina I saw Carla hand her a shot glass with the Goose in it. Both of them laughed as I was being smothered in pussy and ass while they took shot after shot. All of a sudden I felt a warm sensation engulf my dick. Since Trina was still on my face I knew it had to be Carla sucking my dick again. Her head bobbed up and down. I could fill her spit running down my balls as she sucked me.

"You want to cum, don't you?" Trina asked.

I couldn't answer because my mouth was full of her swollen pussy lips.

"Keep going, girl; get him right to the edge," Trina said to Carla before finally getting off my tongue. Then she looked me in the eye and asked, "You want to fuck me, don't you?"

Why the hell was she asking dumb questions at a time like this? She obviously knew the answer.

"Yes!"

"Well, you're not going to"

Hold the fuck up a second. Did she just tell me that I was not going to get the ass? I was confused as hell. Normally, at a time like this I would have been intrigued, but now I'm damn near pissed and I'm gonna fuck something tonight. I guess the look on my face told her exactly what I was thinking.

"You're not going to fuck me, but you can have your way with her. I just want to sit back and watch."

For a second I had the *dumb as hell* look on my face. Then it hit me. She was still bothering me, like she did when we were together. When she and I dated she would never do anything I really wanted to do. It didn't matter if she wanted to do it as well. If it was something that I mentioned or showed interest in, she was dead set against it. This was another one of those times.

"Fine, I'll play your game." I grabbed Carla and tossed her on her stomach on the bed. I snatched her thong down and grabbed her hips and pulled her into the doggy position and plunged my dick as deep into her as I possibly could. I plowed into her again and again while Trina sat and watched us. With each thrust I delivered, I made sure it was harder than the one before it. Carla was grabbing at the sheets and biting her lip between screaming. It was clear she could care less about the mind game Trina and I were playing with one another.She was just enjoying the banging and I was enjoying giving it to her.

"You like the show?" I asked as I smacked Carla on the ass while my dick dove deeper into her. Trina nodded her head then began rubbing her still soaking wet pussy. I grabbed a handful of Carla's hair and pulled back as I fucked her. I wanted Trina to know that she was missing the dick of a lifetime. I leaned forward and gently bit Carla's neck as I fucked her. That sent her over the edge. I felt her pussy tighten, then a sudden release. What happened next surprised me. I felt water splash against my pelvis and run down my leg.

"Goddamn, she's a squirter!" I yelled with excitement. I looked over at Trina and even she looked a bit shook at the sight of Carla pumping what seemed like gallon after gallon of female cum all over me and the bed. I knew it wouldn't be long before I shot my load. I spread her ass cheeks apart to make sure she was getting every inch of my dick. Trina had what looked like four fingers going in and out of herself as she watched me pound her friend. I felt my balls tighten a little. I managed to get a few more strokes in before I exploded.

I pulled my shiny dick from Carla's pussy and aimed the head of my dick at her ample butt cheeks. I stroked my dick a few times when....

THIS IS HOW WE DO IT!! Montel Jordan's hit from the 90's rang out. My eyes popped open. I sat up and looked around the room. My cell phone alarm was going off. I snatched the sheets back, hoping that Carla and Trina were hiding underneath them.

"It seemed so real. All of it seemed so real" I said to myself as I lay in the middle of the bed alone. "The party, the phone messages, the threesome…they all seemed so real." I guess that's what I get for reading Elissa Gabrielle's, *The Heat of the Night* and drinking Ciroc before going to bed. Well, I guess I'll read another chapter and take another shot and see if I can catch that elusive nut I've was just about to get.

Hiding in Plain Sight

By Elissa Gabrielle & Rory D. Sheriff

Alana Carrington
Thirsty for His Power

I adore him.

Rhyme and absolute reason fled from my grasp the very moment our souls collided. Clearly, he is crafted from the depths of divine artistry, yet, I don't merely love him with my eyes alone; I love him with my soul. I adore him with every breath I take. He is the measure of strength. Vivacity. Sanctity. Hope. All variations of him sought me and I happily opened the door for every part of him this morning. Every morning. He is my heart-racer. My pleasure releaser. The very reason this smile that I'm ashamed to wear sweeps across my face. My spirit-lifter in a world that takes hearts and leaves them out in the cold to be devoured by those who have no right to them. My soul-catcher; making me completely whole. I have fallen in love with a man who doesn't even know me.

Weekday mornings have become a focal point of pure excitement for me for what seems like an eternity. Penn Station in Newark—my Utopia. Peripheral vision—my playground. Staring at the floor of this century-old train station is commonplace for me. It serves as part of the daily ritual…the hustle…the moneymaker. The floor is dismal beige—most likely a reflection of the souls who've crossed it over decades. The floor, when waxed and shining aglow, that too, is reminiscent of some of the spirits who've floated across it. That's life. Circumstances dictate who we are at the time and place of where we are. I was once dismal and beige and now I'm shining, glowing, and experiencing life in all of its splendor. Today the floor is as dirty as my thoughts and the only thing I can stare at while the red flushes from my face, the sheer embarrassment my mind houses when I think about him.

I adore him.

I close my old leather bound journal that I have opened and closed since I was a teenager. Now, as a woman earning my way through life, and as a respected woman in society with some notoriety, I replace the paper I have written my poems and thoughts on with fresh paper to continue to give my pen a place to venture where my life has not. Indelible ink claims residence to my inner-sanctum.

My journal fiddles in my hand as I reopen and pen more of my weekday morning's points of joy that touch my soul. Coffee in hand, hot like I imagine his lips to be, I sit and wait for my train amidst daydreams and hopes.

My peripheral vision is my playground of swinging high, looking up at him from a distance. My eyes can't stand the teasing of the vision of his fineness. I then stare at the floor of this century-old train station. It is commonplace for me. It serves as part of the daily ritual to undertaking to own my hustle…to control my moneymaker.

The floor, dirt, grime, and passing life stories I read like tea leaves trying to find my way back. The drab, beige floor is the earth tone of the dirt that covers my love gone away. No matter how dirty, reflections of the souls crossed over for decades have grounded in memories.

I need to write. For the third time this morning, I am reopening my journal while waiting for the train…knowing damn well I come here an hour earlier than I need to just to see him. My love. The words.

Rhyme and absolute reason fled from our grasp the very moment our souls collided.

Five days a week.

Our devotion failed to lack in vitality; enthusiasm unwavering.

The soul-tie vibrant; intensity clear as autumn leaves

on once dead bushes that exhaled new life for the season.

Vanquished our fears of a love unfathomed to embrace the dawn.

Pleasantly rested in your willing arms as we drifted to sleep

only to be awakened by the light of the sun and

the sound of the

living waters running deep.

Forever mine.

Five days a week.

A gun-metal gray sky overlooks the streets of this city. Gloomy in its appearance, I peek through the floor-to-ceiling glass doors and see the overcast. Then, I sneak a look at him—my passion-trainer. Supremely good, beautiful, and magnificent, he carries the nature and the presence of being a deity. Over time, my heart has somehow managed to worship him like he is my god. He is divine in all forms of the word. Perhaps divinity and purgatory at the same time. Hot, searing, yet, sharp and cold as ice.

I call him my passion-trainer because I often feel I'm running out of breath when he enters my vision. I sweat and need water, and I turn hungry for his beautiful, chocolate, sweet skin.

Now, I'm not that far gone, I'm merely enjoying my wish list in a man, in how I see him every day for just a moment in time. I know he could be like any man I have met who is hot and searing in appearance, but could be inattentive and dark, cold as ice, or mean with ego gone wild. If possible, I want to know the conflicting sides of him without my heart being caughtup in the rapture of love.

If my estimation is correct, by what I see, the pleasure of the journey would be all mine. Like that one wine you serve and everyone admires—the age, the strength, that body, the taste, but you never take anyone to the cellar.

I look over my glasses and sneak a look at him. I'm like many early morning train station survivors; I have sunglasses on and peek over the top. The voyeur in me resumes to watching the players, the deal makers, the hustlers, the entrepreneurs, students and teachers and all who pass through these halls daily to get a bite of the Big Apple—the city that never, ever sleeps, and where there's room for everyone at the economic table.

It's 8:03 a.m., and the magic begins.

Most likely, he, like me, is a voyeur—careful in his movements like he's being watched. Only a voyeur moves the way he does. Someone who watches and knows he's being watched. After he's been standing for some time, I assume scanning the station, he sits. He crosses his legs to where I can witness the slight bulge between his thighs. In my wildest dreams, I picture …Mandingo dick.

My cheeks hurt from trying to keep from spreading to the widest smile one can produce. I'm dropping all of my friends for this dick; it's that kind of dick I visualize. Glory, glory, hallelujah dick…it's that kind of dick that will force me to speak in tongues.

Following his neck, my eyes peer up to his jaw line. Chiseled in manly perfection. He was born of blessed seed. Like if Isis and Zeus somehow met and their souls communed, then made universal love on a beach of jet black sand. The goatee is groomed graciously and deliciously around his mouth. Makes me wanna holler.

8:04 a.m.—He unfolds his newspaper and places the top right under his eyes. He stares at me. I pretend not to notice. The newspaper covers his face. He stares. I feel it. I feel the heat he emotes over to me. His energy is palpable. It's intense. I cross my legs, trying to hush the purring.

8:05 a.m.—Brother to the night is scoping. If his eyes have laser technology, I wonder where the red light would be on me. His thoughts and intentions are hidden under tiny letters and behind the daily news. Walls on fire…set ablaze by the nasty vibes he's sending my way. My right leg twitches. Trying to sit still, I'm having trouble. We're playing the game once again. I'm a willing, yet unwilling partner in his mental seduction.

I glance in his direction. He stares at me. Doesn't blink. Doesn't flinch. A heavenly smirk crosses his lips. Teeth, white, the windows to his soul tell me everything I need to know. He's fucking with me. I turn away. Exhale.

There's no one in this train station but the two of us. Thousands move through and bypass us to their individual destinations, yet together, like two spirits aiming for the chance to greet, we are alone.

Lord, have mercy; I'm so thirsty for his power.

8:10 a.m.—He folds his paper and gets up. Our train is called. I hear the conductor over loud speakers, chaos, shuffling feet, dragging suitcases, and voices on cell phone conversations disconnect. "Track one non-stop to New York City, boarding now." It's déjà vu all over again.

Getting up, my hands spread across my skirt to remove any wrinkles. Standing up straight like my mother taught me, I arch my back and run my fingers through brown and honey-kissed long ringlets of natural hair. Fixing my blazer, I toss my hair to one side and flirtatiously, I look in his direction.

Bending over, he grabs his attaché and on his way to standing upright, he glances in my direction. I return the glance, but don't acknowledge him in any form. I simply grab my briefcase, throw my shawl over my arm and make my way toward track number one.

Perfect day for these two-inch pumps. They're high enough to accentuate my long but thick calves, yet my heels are low enough to enable me to walk with confidence. An extra swing in my hips accompanies me down the hall.

We walk together, yet apart, to the platform, number one, heading to New York City. And as the crowd of people fill the platform, awaiting their ride to their day's destiny, he enters the train on the south side of the corridor and me, the north.

I scan through the throngs of passengers. I see him as if the others are his subjects. The man is supremely good at how he carries the nature of being a deity over my heart. He has somehow managed to make me worship him. We have a twenty-minute train ride, so here I go again; I pull out my journal.

he found me as the petals of april's flowers
and the rain from may's showers
dropped lilac scented drops of love rain
onto my bottom lip
our souls crashed like waves
upon a shore after high tides
spirits made love over galaxies
hearts intertwined
over lifetimes
joy danced over an orange moon as the sun
shone bright
over 365 days of paradise
he entered my psyche long before I knew he existed
see-through secrets
slow and steady

made an appearance into my daily existence
came with a pure heart
eternal as a dove
I am remembering love…

I love watching him every morning, holding the pole with his chest budding like a plate of armor, and he has no clue I'm tripping all over him…I like that. My eyes follow the curvature of his lips as he sips on whatever is in that cup. He moves in precision…even in the way he places the lid to his mouth.

The train hums along tracks and vibrates, and shakes and jostles my body. I place my earplugs in and Coltrane is kissing my inner ear while Mr. Handsome-Black-Man standing over there treats my eyes.

I hear the sultry sounds of his horn, Coltrane that is, and try to imagine what sounds might whisper from that beautiful black man when he parts his delicious lips.

His hands are so large and so immensely strong. I know he can handle this woman. He likes all my curves. He loves my good and plenty. His large hands touch my thigh, and my panties can't absorb my wetness enough. My sweet scent floats in the air and I can see the arousal in him. My fingertips trace his nipples. I taste one. He grabs my bottom; I slightly pull back and he forcefully pulls me in and embraces me like there is nothing in the world he wants more.

I open my eyes. Exhale. Walls, wet, warm…needing attention. I cross my legs. I squirm in my seat. Coltrane is still playing. I picture his erection, so strong and so long and my nipples harden. I want to put my name on his hardness while I'm inhaling. I open my eyes and his body is twenty feet away standing, holding the passenger pole and his body shakes and jostles with the train. I close my eyes and picture him inside of me. He's in so deep, I'm breathing for him.

The conductor pulls me out of my trance. "Ladies and gentleman, we have now reached New York City. Enjoy your day."

My panties say I have already enjoyed a good part of my day. My heart agrees. My mind won't move past it all.

I exit the train along with teachers, students, hustlers, deal makers, and deal breakers, and they scatter. I see him, he sees me, and within the blink of an eye, he's gone.

Alphonso Ibari
Infiltrated Soul

Every piece of me belongs to her.

I'm anticipating walking through the doors of the train station, and immediately putting my eyes on my angel. I'll be lifted and gifted the moment I see her. As I lift my head off my pillow, my morning hard-on might be from dreaming of her all night long. I have never been moved in a way that this beautiful angel moves me.

When it comes to her smile, her eyes, that walk…my ego and my soul unite in agreement that she is the one. The one. The crazy thing is—I don't even know her name. I haven't heard her speak. I don't know the tone of what must be a sweet voice, yet in my daydreams, I'm having joyous conversations with her. Her sweet lips part in a way that makes me lose my mind, I imagine. Something as innocent as a smile would force me into psychosis. In those same daydreams, her flirtatious smile is so powerful it weakens me. She is ruling my heart. She owns me. Every piece of me belongs to her.

I wake with excitement every weekday morning. I laugh and think about the title and line in a song, *How Long Has This Been Going On*. She invaded my soul some time ago, yet we have not met.

My job—I love it; it's one of best jobs in the world, and on top of that, five days a week a perfect stranger evokes such passion in me. I live to walk through the train station doors and ride the rails for twenty minutes of mental stimulation.

My attitude is way out of character; those who know me, including me knowing myself, recognize that my inner cool has vanished when it comes to this beautiful woman. I almost feel like a young lion, ready to become the alpha male of the pride, and she's my prize. Like all things worth fighting for, I must work out and practice my moves to strike with maximum impact, to disarm her, and capture her. This is a game of kill or be killed. I have to make the right move, and more importantly, I have to wait for the perfect time to strike. What's weird or should I say different, is that I'm so comfortable in this zone.

Come back to reality AL. Shake it off. You cannot possibly be this damn weak. Get your head back in the game. You're the man! Chicks drop their panties at your feet. How are you going to allow a chick you don't even know to infiltrate your soul like this! You are THE freaking Assistant District Attorney of New York City…Brooklyn-born, baby, so act like it. Let's go!

Analyzing my desires with my first cup of coffee to get my bearings, I jump in the shower. The hot water streaming, my sweetly scented, but manly body wash runs over my finely tuned body. I work at keeping my skin soft, but my body hard.

Closing my eyes, I imagine the soap and pulsating rain setting from my showerhead are her fingers, finger-painting my chest, abs, and thighs. Our lips on each other, we moisturize each other's face. I can see myself turning her around forcibly and washing her back, but how quickly I bend her forward and slide my slick hardness into her slippery tightness. Holding her hips as the hot water pours between our skin as I pound against her ample ass.

Whew, she's got an ass on her. The kind of ass that will make a man lose his religion. Thick, sweet, soft, round ass. My ass. One day. All of her will be mine. And, rightfully so.

The water is turning cold, and I'm rinsing the soap from my hand and hard-on. I'm alone with my fantasy of her. Tempted to release what she has built up inside of me, my right hand caresses my long, hard shaft. My left finds stability in leaning on the shower door. I picture her lips. I see the bounce in her stride and those hips swaying from side to side on her voluptuous frame. She has the type of body that men want, yet are careful to desire. Intimidating, yet utterly inviting. Seeing her pretty, golden thighs wrapped around my neck, I look down to get a clear visual of a pretty, pulsating pussy. I don't know whether to eat it or stroke it or take turns doing both.

"Ha," I chuckle out loud. I can't do this. *Get your head back in the game.*

After my long shower, and while drying and adding lotion, I find myself singing all kinds of love songs. *You Give Good Love to Me* by Whitney or *The Best You Ever Had* by John Legend. I know my neighbors must wonder what in the hell is wrong with me. This girl has obviously infiltrated my emotional gene.

My queen has infiltrated my soul. The core of my being has been taken hostage by a woman who doesn't even know my name.

After brushing and rinsing my teeth, I continue my singing. I break out the Murray's hair grease. It's a must that the waves in my hair are looking good. I dance my way to my closet. It is now time for me to dawn my shiny knight's armor, in this case it's a tailor made Armani suit.

I reflect on how coordinated she is every day, so I know I have to come correct. I pick out a dark blue pinstriped suit, coordinated my tie and socks, and the most important of the entire look—the shoes. One can never go wrong with Italian leather. I believe that you can tell a lot about a man by looking at his shoes. I have caught her looking down and then eyeing me up.

Yeah, I'm feeling and looking like success. I need a good woman to help complete my success. Maybe she is the one.

They say a man is as he thinks. The man I am is a well-groomed, intelligent, grown ass man, but there is no hiding my hardness or street awareness. It is advised to step-off if someone chooses not to adhere to all adult-like warnings. I can sit in any board room and kick it in any hood. I'm grounded in the real.

I take one last look at myself in the mirror, *I'm a boss, baby.*

Briefcase—check. iPhone—check, and I'm glad my truck is clean. Who knows…maybe I'll end up taking her for a drink or dinner after work one day…soon. Off to Penn Station.

There is always something on Sirius satellite radio that seems to play out the soundtrack of my life or captures my current mood. As I arrive at the train station's park and ride, Outkast's *So Fresh and So Clean* is the perfect song to usher in my attitude.

Ain't nobody dope as me, I'm just so fresh and so clean.

Deep Breath…

8:00 am is our moment—the moment that time stops and waits for our initial eye contact before time can proceed. I can clearly see the rest of the world, but nothing is moving. It's as if together we are life, itself, and the world is merely functioning from the power of our connection. Imagining what will happen if our lips were ever to touch makes my heart race. Every morning I surrender to her goddess-like aura. Every morning it's like the first time I've seen her.

Her…

Deliciousness forces my sensitivity to do battle with my self-worth.

I attempt to maintain my cool in her presence. My heart and ego quarrels. One is dumbfounded; the other is confident and says, "this is a piece of cake," and "she's just a woman." Shit, who am I trying to fool? She is a woman, uniquely made up of beauty. Nothing compares to her. Her caramel skin shines closer to the flavor of sweet peanut brittle. I envision licking her skin just below her ear and swallowing her tastes in a hurry. I'm sure I'll want to taste more of her, as fast as I can.

Her hair is in a style that needed to be on the cover of *Essence.* Sun streak highlights her hair with browns and copper layers. I want to wash and rinse her hair, and then for her to feel my hands running through her hair. Later when her hair dries and is wild, I'll hold her hair tight as I make love to her. A savage beast I'd be if I was ever blessed enough to get in between those legs.

I watch her daily and her facial expression is passionate. Her almond eyes have a sprinkle of freckles right under them, and they draw your attention. At some time in her life, I assume she was a beauty queen of some significance. How she walks and sits…it's with pure grace and style.

Judging from the way I've seen her dressed, she must work in upper management in corporate America. Her business attire says, *I'm sexy as hell, but about my business at the same time.* My eyes scan her entire body, undressing her. I let my mind make love in ways many would be ashamed of. The freeness I feel when I think of her! She'd be free to have me any way she wanted me, in every way she wanted me. Whispering in her ear, I would tell her, "Take me; I'm yours." Her skirt encircles every inch of her curvaceous hips; those curves could not be any sexier. Her sculpted ass begs for a deep thrusting and grinding.

It might seem I'm caught up in her physical only. No. Her beauty cannot be denied, but her class…it stands alone. She didn't bite with my nonverbal advances. It's as if she is bigger than that. She is bigger than me. It's as if it didn't matter that I was a New York Assistant District Attorney. Not that she knew. She has to know that I'm someone distinguished from the way I dress. Maybe that doesn't matter to her.

She's my master. I am her everything…one who serves under duress. The moment she discovers this is the same moment I'll be her slave to the rhythm.

Alana Carrington
A Moth to a Flame

Patiently I wait for an invitation.

I don't want to wait another minute, and, if I had my way, because I do believe in love, we'd be in love for life. I'd already know what it feels like to be in his arms and hurrying home to be in his embrace every day. He and love are the absolute same. He's stolen my heart…taken my mind into complete hostage, and I don't know his name.

I beg for the coming of his smile. He adorns a smile that immediately sends me to shame. Anxiously, I yearn for the bounce in his stride. I find myself pleading to the gods for divine intervention that somehow, someway, someday I'll be in the luxury of his arms, and always within a finger-touch of his sweetness.

As my heels protect pretty toes from these filthy halls, I look up and see the hustlers of life again this morning. We're all here for the same reason—to reach intended destinations. Whether by choice or force, the inevitable is upon me on this day, and by the looks on the faces of everyone present, people are displaying a case of the Mondays. I'm enjoying my daily beginnings; I've got love on my mind.

In this game of life, we tend to view those things that we don't like to face or what we despise as hurdles, rather than confronting and tackling the obvious. We all face them. What separates the winners and losers in life are that winners jump the hurdles, break through them, go around and find a way, while losers sit back and complain about a day of the week known as Monday.

I love every day because what comes with it is opportunity. I'm blessed to witness my king in action. My eyes partake in all that's good and glorious about this beautiful, black man. My soul is within reach of his. My spirit is liberated by what I sense to be his freedom. Adoring every ounce of every part of him, I find myself remembering by night his skin—the color of dark grains in walnut. A stranger to me. He makes me hum a tune all to myself in honor of him daily; I sing a righteous song in honor of my king. Nameless to me, I take in his dark beauty and exhale a puff of laughter. Embarrassed about the way my mind continually dances with the devil or my savior, I glance around me, hoping to catch a glimpse of the Almighty.

Patiently, I wait for an invitation....

The barista and the scent of strong java in the morning interrupt my temporary insanity. I make my way to get a cup of liquid heaven. My lips sip flavor onto my taste buds as I want his skin to omit flavor into my mouth. Like java, I imagine his taste is full and thick and lasting. Like my morning brew is hot, he is hot. I want a bottomless cup of his soul.

I thought of that black knight this morning and it made me adorn a dress befitting of a queen. I walk confidently, daily into the direction of my dreams and today is no different. I spin slowly in the mirror looking at all angles of how my form-fitting gray, v-neck dress drapes my stages of curves. The material's unique blend smoothes out any of my imperfections and enhances all that makes me uniquely wonderful.

I run my hands over my backside and my thighs, wishing his hand had the pleasure. In this mirror, I wish I stood naked with him behind me...riding me, loving me in animalistic throws. I see our facial expressions in those push and pulls of lusting passion. Yes, my dress accentuates the curvature of my hips and the fullness of my breasts; it stops at the knee, so my long legs have a chance to shine. My dress and accessories are totally professional and becoming, yet enticing enough to catch the eye of my king.

White Diamonds perfume scent rises from between my breasts and from behind my ears. Body butter and light gloss to my oversized, yet bold and full lips...my look today screams that I'm about my business.

I walk. I search. I look. I walk more. Am I a bit nervous…a little? I yearn. I want. I need. I walk. Anxiously, I await the arrival of my man. I don't see him. I want him. I need him.

Arriving at the place where all meet and greet in the train station, I stand in line, awaiting my turn to be served. The place is packed. Looks like the United Nations of all nationalities grabbing their morning Joe, newspapers, books, breakfast and all other things that make their morning's transition in the good, the bad, and who knows what.

Breaking news covers the flat panel television mounted on the coffee shop's wall. It appears Senator Keith Harvey Hunter from New York is in a world of trouble with the law. The footage is of Mr. Hunter covering his face as he exits his New York City high-rise. A copper-coated woman stands next to him. The scroll at the bottom of the broadcast reads that Mr. Hunter has disappeared after a cleaning crew found a dead prostitute in his New York City office.

The gray-haired news anchor chimes in. "Senator Keith Harvey Hunter, known for his outspoken views and for pushing his liberal agenda, seems to have come under fire. May be one that he created for himself.

Tasha Montgomery, a twenty-four year-old graduate student turned stripper, allegedly turned prostitute, was found dead in Senator Hunter's New York City senate office, according to sources. You may recall that Senator Hunter is up for re-election this year, as this will be the third straight win for the forty year-old politician, should he win this November. Senator Hunter has been a critic of the Republican Party since his inception into politics. The once young and ambitious fresh face highlighted the political landscape when he took the helm at the tender, political age of twenty-eight."

"Oh, my," I say aloud as all of the coffee-getters catch their breath. "I'm sure this is a set-up of epic proportions. Senator

Hunter is a good man…a strong leader. He goes against the grain, and well, time will tell," I speak the words, not fully aware of how loud my voice is while doing so. Onlookers glance. One man's body language and up turned nose signaled for sure that he doesn't feel the same as me, but I don't back down by either voice or my own body language.

The scent of floral enters my bouquet sensory. The kind of flowers that can only come from a man's distinctive cologne and the way it blends into his skin, his pheromones overtakes my senses and places me into brief psychosis. I'm frozen in time…in this space where fantasy meets reality. I smell him…almost taste him.

The brush of his jacket against my back, I want to push back into him. His presence sends me into immediate shame. Feeling as though I want to repent, my eyes peer down to a countertop to the right of me and I see his hand. Mr. Fantasy and Reality all in one big, black, bold, with strong hands of a man who is obviously like black coffee—strong.

His presence draws near me, and I feel the heat of an African sun on the back of my neck. I smell him. Feel him. The coolness of his breath whispers sweet sentiments and brushes across my shoulder. My head bows. I smell my pussy getting hot. I hope the others cannot tell that I'm sending up smoke signals. I'm wet. My nipples are starting to ache; I feel them expanding, firming and exposing me.

He moves closer. I feel him. If he put those huge hands on my hips, I'd get on all fours for him. I look at the television to break this tension, but it's thick, I can cut through it. I exhale and then intake a breath so deep I know I have given myself completely away.

"I'm sure the good Senator is guilty as charged." His voice is smooth, silky and inviting. Damn. I want to cum all over his face.

Wait, did he say the senator was "guilty as charged?" Every ounce of me needs to leave this alone, but every part of me cannot. I won't.

"He hasn't been charged yet, you know?" I respond in a strong, confident tone. I don't want him to feel he had any part of me going. I move up in line as if I'm moving away from him. *You want me; you need to work for me.*

"Yeah, but he will be. And he had something to do with that poor, little, innocent girl being murdered." The smugness in his voice makes me sick, literally. I hate him. Already. I hate him.

He moves in closer to me; I move away. He moves in more. I take a step further.

"Rushing to judgment, I see. I hope in your regular, daily existence you're not so close-minded." I place my hand on my hip and move.

Would this damn line move already!

"You'd be surprised what a part of my regular, daily existence is," he replies. A smile covers my face. I hate him.

"Well, from the words that are parting from your lips that reveal the nonsense floating around in your head, I'd say your daily existences, including its thoughts, need a major overhaul."

Turning around, I want him to see that I am not happy about his assumptions regarding Senator Hunter.

"You're beautiful."

I smile.

"Thank you," I reply, trying not to allow my elation about this moment to be revealed. Poker face takes over.

"You're wrong about Hunter, you know?"

"No, I'm not. *You* are, my darling."

"Are you done?" I'm a bit disgusted.

He smiles. Lips so sweet. Chiseled face. Black skin. This gorgeous man has been blessed with more than his fair share of all that God has to give and hand out in the way of aesthetics. Refined, brilliant and majestic, he permeates a radiant glow—one that speaks of authority. Regal in physical form, he must have been born of blessed seed to appear so righteous by design.

The parting of his sweet mouth once again reminds me of the succulent kiss I've never had. He tells me, "You wear that dress well."

He has a wrong opinion of the Senator, and even though he has spoken badly of the Senator, this man speaks with an education of knowing how to make a comeback. Mixed emotions consume me, drowning me in divine thoughts my tongue dare not speak; striking inside of me a flame, with no mercy for the weak, from my heart to my cheek and I smile all the same.

"I love your smile," he gushes. If skin so dark could turn red, it would.

"Thank you, again."

"I could call you 'Beautiful,' all day but I'm sure there is a name behind all the splendor."

"Alana…Alana Carrington. Nice to meet you."

"Alphonso, but you can call me Al…Alphonso Ibari."

"The pleasure is all mine, Al."

Did I just say that? Oh God, Alana, get it together.

"I can't accept that."

"Why not, Al?"

"Because the pleasure is indeed all mine."

Pleasure is interrupted by the lady at the counter who is ready to take my order. I move up in line, and he trails closely behind.

"I'll have a Hazelnut Latte', extra whipped-cream, please."

He interrupts.

"I'll have what she's having, and it's on me," he says as he hands the lady his credit card.

Looking over my right shoulder, I peer into his eyes, and with a seductive smile, I tell him, "I appreciate that."

"You deserve it," he responds, staring deep into my eyes. Damn, his soft, brown eyes. He has that glaze in his eyes. The glaze, the glow, the gloss covers the windows to his soul…that glaze that indicates that he is craving. I'd kill over those eyes. Have mercy; he is wonderful.

Grabbing my cup, I make my way to the foyer and prepare to get onto my track for the train ride to New York. He follows closely behind. I stop. "Are you following me?"

"Yes, I am."

He moves closer. I can tell he wants to talk, but no…I can't make it that easy. Plus he spoke rudely about the Senator.

I smell him. I smile. I wonder was that a blushing smile. I nod and turn to walk away from him, but I stop and turn back. "You have a nice day. Maybe I'll see you around, of course, when your outlook on life and your viewpoints change." I turn and move swiftly as to remove myself from his sight. The heat between us is palpable; it's real. I need time to process.

He wants to say something, but I move like a cheetah.

I glance to my left and see him. The doors to the train open and I get on. He vanishes…

It's six o'clock on a Monday evening, and the sun hasn't quite set. My office floor-to-ceiling windows overlook the New York skyline glowing against the light chocolate walls. I requested the color and my interior designers complied. They value me. They understand my wants and needs. My office is professionally coordinated to match my copper framed art and bronze figurines of African women—my queens of beauty and power. Deep, dark, wood desk and small meeting table with leather and ultra-suede chairs…it all makes me know I have worked hard and I'll keep working hard. My office is beautiful, but my command of the law sometimes brings in the not so beautiful.

I turn on the evening news and witness State's Attorney Todd Shumaker discussing the case against Senator Hunter. "Senator Hunter abuses his power and pushes his failed agenda on the people of this great state. I suppose karma is very real because he's caught up in this horrific tragedy. I'll certainly pray for that sweet girl's family. God rest her soul."

What a crock of shit.

After this long day of victories, settling cases and making plea-deals, I'm ready to head home. Al, if that's his name, or is it Alton, and he's goes by AL? Maybe Ali is a name…hmm, even Altron. Whatever Al he is, well he has been on my mind all day. When I turn back the hands of time to this morning, I smell him in my mind. I still feel him standing close and controlling the space we shared. I liked that. He damn well knew what he was doing to me. I didn't mind because I know my presence had him almost twisting out of his chic veneer. Yeah, what lies under all his outer-control? It remains to be seen and felt.

Bending over to pack my briefcase, I think of him, remembering the sight of his shoes…impeccable. Matching his blue suit, he had burgundy Stacy Adam's wingtips. A classy, stylish man. That unexpected, unanticipated rush goes through my veins, shoots through my body and lands on my clit. I sit my ass back down and face the New York skyline. I crane my head to see if my door is closed. *I squeeze my thighs tight, and fuck trying to wish away the feelings of desire. Al has awakened the river; he thawed-out the mountain and the flood gates are open to lustful fantasies. I see him standing in front of me, loosening his tie, and it seems so quick after he is naked over my thigh, and his erection is limp, but thick and long. I lick my lips and I see it stirring, and a little clear drip stretches and falls on my thigh. Al has taken complete control over me; I grab my breasts and squeeze my nipples due to him penetrating my yearnings. The sight of his chest, brown sugar in full form, has me crying…yearning for a piece.*

His smell…the deliciousness of his skin inches away and I reach out and fist his hardening. It's strong and makes me adjust my hand as it grows out and up. His length is so fucking pretty. "Shit," I exhale through lust-filled lips.

I scan over my shoulder again to make sure my door is closed, and slowly slide my dress up. One leg lands on part of the window ledge. I'm under the understanding that people cannot look in through the building windows. I flash New York and a fading sunset. I have pulled my panties to the side. I go back to visualizing that Al is standing over me like a king…my master.

I release his hardness, and it points to the ceiling above my head. I lean my cheek against its firmness and breathe him in, and then brush my lips over it. I turn my head to the side, and that thick vein on the underside of his dick fills in between my lips. I slide my lips up so damn slow and his pre-cum runs down faster and coats my lips.

I cannot touch him in the flesh, so my hands run up my own legs. The softness of my own skin turns me on as I imagine Al and those lips becoming familiar with all that is me. His big hands reach down under me, and he lifts me up out of this chair. He steps down to his knees, grabs me firmly and buries his face between my thighs. I feel his tongue curl and slide in me, and then drag up to my clit. He whispers something to me as he is licking me, but I can't hear a damn thing over my own crazy sounds. I feel him licking me like I lick chocolate ice cream from a cone. Slowly, but removing layers of my sweetness, I'm melting.

My right hand pulls my panties to the side and they're saturated. I'm embarrassed about the way I long for him. My fingertips dance with the devil and enter my warm, wet cave. I moan loud and strong as if he penetrates me, but it's my fingers. The sensation and the thought of having him inside of me makes me flow like a fountain. I feel this cum, it's strong, and it's releasing all over my hands.

Undeniable in nature, loving and lustful in intention, it's meant to happen…me being here with him, in my dreams, and him talking imaginary, sweet shit that I love to hear.

Temptingly tested by his touch, I envision him in this office pushing me against the window. I'm totally naked as he has removed my dress. I hear his voice. He said, "You wear that dress well." His hard body is pressing against me as his lips have locked on my neck. I feel him reaching around and teasing my clit while his length is probing…getting to know me, marking his territory and staking his claim. He tries to get that angle. When he finds it, he'll glide because I'm so wet with anticipation of what's to come next. Me...fully undressed, he left me in pumps only, and him.

Damn, him...he tells me, "I want this," as he runs his fingers across my righteousness.

"Damn, you're wet," he moans as he licks my juices from the tips of his fingers. I hear the sounds. It's nasty, and wet, and loud, and he licks. His mouth sounds as sweet and as good as it looks.

I feel his erection. It's long. Oooh, he found that angle. It's good...it so damn good! It's so good as he pushes deeper into me. I'm biting my bottom lip, my head tilts back and I release.

A knock at my door scares the shit out of me. I jump up and pull my skirt down. Immediately, I reach for a napkin from my desk, and as I wipe my hands, *she* enters.

Tall, brown, well-suited woman. Gorgeous ringlets of hair dance around her face. A natural woman. Worried look on her face, like the world is crumbling around her. I recognize this beautiful, brown woman.

"Ms. Carrington?" she questions as she walks toward me.

Hope she can't smell the remnants of lust. Damn, my hands are still sticky.

"Yes, I'm Alana Carrington. How may I help you?"

"I'm Senator Keith Hunter's wife. I need your help."

She reaches out her hand to shake mine. Reluctantly, I reply in kind.

Lord, help me.

"My husband is in a bit of trouble."

"I see."

"What did you see?"

"I saw the news."

"That's not true, how they're portraying my Keith, Ms. Carrington."

"Tell me more."

Alphonso Ibari
Stunned

What would Billy Dee Williams do?
What just happened?
An encounter with the queen I have been dreaming of.
Opportunity knocked on my door.
Being tough on myself?
I need to.

Al, why didn't you ask for her number? It's okay. Why didn't I say nor do quite a few things? That's not okay; I needed to move more smoothly. Damn, she gave me that first time a boy talks to a girl feeling. Too funny. I have to laugh at myself.

My queen might be tripping on me for not stepping up right away from out of the gate. Hell, I'm tripping. Might I need some science? Maybe a law book to pull out some rules of engagement. For sure, I wished I had reached behind her ear and put some magic in front of her eyes. Won't it be something when she opens her purse and finds my card? I do have game, but she's no game, she looks like a woman you take home to Mom. All that butter below her waist, sunshine on her face and beautiful spirit all makes me a bit weak.

Yeah, I'll make this happen—taking baby steps, which is something I'm not use to doing. Usually, when I see a woman that interests me, I go in at full speed ahead, but this woman…there is something different about her. I cannot seem to put my finger on the reason why I'll take my time, but I will. Maybe that's how I maintain control—laying back in the cut. I'll wait a bit and have her mentally raise her hem line and drop her neck line, and make her expose her da-la-soul. Muéstrame cómo te amo, Mama. *Show me how to love ya, Mama.*

Nah, say it isn't so; could it be that I'm playing for keeps?

Shake it off…

I channel everything foolish prideful men think and say. Any other time. My mind tells me to stay strong; don't give into the notions of LOVE. Stay strong, man! You're single and can sleep with almost any chick you want with no strings attached, yet, I'm alone every night. As my mind rambles, my heart is calling my mind all sorts of derogatory names. My heart wants to break free from the shackles of Playasville.

The heart asks, *"What is the reason man is given a heart? Just like anything in life if it's not being used the way it is meant to be, it will wither and die. Listen to your foolish pride if you want to. I'll show just how importantly LOVE is needed in your life in order to survive.*

Rewind thirty minutes earlier.…

After my daily drive from home to the train station, I become a part of a worldly, well-oiled functioning machine called *Monday's Mad rush to New York City.* I avoided three homeless men asking for money, a man declaring the end is near and a sister with a crying baby and one on the way.

I filter out an argument in Chinese. I avoid inhaling a cloud of weed smoke as the Rasta-man attempted to sell me oils and bootlegged movies. I quickly ducked into the coffee shop.

As I prepare to grab a cup of java, lo and behold my goddess was there. It's as if she's waiting on me. The TV's in the shop were blearing with breaking news, but nothing mattered. My queen is drawn to the TV programming. I see my chance to make a move. I crossed the borders of her personal space, breaking the ice by saying,

"I'm sure the good Senator is guilty as charged."

Surprised at my stance, she says, "He hasn't been charged yet."

"Yeah, but he will be. I'm sure he had something to do with murdering that innocent girl."

"I hope you don't always rush to judgment in your daily existence."

I can tell I hit a nerve; I had to pivot out of this mess I just created for myself. We were holding the line up with chatter. The cashier waved for us to keep the line moving. I couldn't help but to zoom in on her curvy frame. She switched legs, and it sent out drum signals back to Africa as her ass gyrated. Her curvaceous hips had a place to hold on to, fitted for my hands only. All her curves makes me dream of finding myself behind her, gently putting my arms around her and burying my lips deep into her hair to find her ear and whisper, *"I want you."*

She turned and made eye contact. We locked up eye to eye. If we had a combination, we lost it for ticks on the train station clock. Her scent had to mingle with mine. The Rasta-man never had anything as strong.

Her almond-shaped eyes and lashes blinked, as if to say, *"Let's try this again."* She was giving me another chance to make an impression on her. No turning back! I smile while my mind buffers.

I love your smile…despite Mr. Man with strong opinions.

I laugh, and I know I'm smiling now. I thanked her and returned a compliment. "You're beautiful like you are everyday." She blinked again, this time in shock. Yes, I want to her to know I have seen her and observed her. We're grown folk here, but two nervous grown folk. At least *I* am. Hard for me to admit. I try not to stutter or show that my nerves are getting the best of me. I continue, "Now, I could call you beautiful all day, but I'm sure there is a name behind the splendor."

"Alana…Alana Carrington."

"I'm Al…well, Alphonso Ibari, but please, call me Al."

"It's a pleasure meeting you, Alphonso."

My *What would Billy Dee Williams do* senses took over and I reply, "I can't accept that."

"And why is that?"

"Because the pleasure is all mine. "

Not much of a fancy coffee drinker, she ordered something with hazelnut in it. "I'll have what she is having."

I put my credit card out front. "Please, it's on me."

"Thank you, Alphonso."

Her beautiful sounding voice sent chills down my spine… cliché yes, but seriously true. That chill, by the time it reached below my waist, had turned hot. I flexed and squirmed and felt my thickness becoming thicker. I attempted to maintain my smooth and cool.

She held my attention at the same time even though she was engaged with the news. Soft, her facial expression was deliberate with each blink or swallow Alana Carrington took. Something in me wanted badly to place two fingers under her chin, tilt her head up and slowly place my lips on Alana. I wanted to kiss this Ms. Carrington…this woman of my dreams. The keeper of my soul. The queen who owns me.

What's going on in her life, I wonder. I want engage with all that is her. *Man, don't let this woman get away.* The dress she was wearing captivated my thoughts. Both my mind and lips were on auto pilot. I hope I wasn't doing that LL Cool J thing of rolling and licking my lips as if I'm salivating over her.

This is a dangerous position. I'm treading lightly in a place of vulnerability. I usually mess it up by saying something stupid; however, I'm trying not to make it obvious that I'm looking at her nipples extending into my sightline.

I'm wondering if she is wet over the fact that I'm nearly hovering in her air space. I'm thinking about walks on a beach, hearing love songs, glasses of wine by a fireplace, and ballroom dancing to Barry White.

Standing next to her, I'm seeing her in vivid, living-colors in the most intense love making, complimented with her screams and moans of pleasure. I'm wondering what she sounds like when she's in the midst of a climax. Would she be almost silent? Would her body tremble and shake as she holds my head in place as I taste her sweet juices? My eyes are wide open, by seeing her curl that magnificent ass into my hips as we spoon and I hear her whimper from the pleasures of us.

Damn, snap out of it....

I quickly move my briefcase in front of my pants in an attempt to cover any potential evidence of the crime of becoming hard from having lusting thoughts. I wouldn't mind being exposed in front of her. I want to get inside her...inside her freakiness. I am treading on a thin sheet of perverted ice.

Look at her, standing like Nefertiti, pure and classy...but I know, I know, I know...I have to kiss inside her mind and heart. Only then will I be able to crawl throughout her body, letting her feel my nakedness, my stiffness, and my openness as she takes me in with her freeness.

Be ready to love her in all the ways a man can. I'm ready to be naked with my soul...ready. Wide open, she's got me.

Upon entering my building, I found it rather odd to see State's Attorney General Todd Shumaker exiting the building in a mad rush. It's not unusual to see the Attorney General in the New York City office, but it's a big difference to have seen him so early and leaving so abruptly. Attorney General Todd Shumaker jumped in an official state town car. He didn't even let the driver get out and open the door for him. Dude is in a hurry.

My goal is to one day to be the AG in the state. My dream is to see my office door with a brass nameplate that reads, "New York State Attorney General Al Ibari." One day. From my lips to God's ears, I suppose.

The moment I stepped off the elevator and turned to go to my office, my legal assistant, Connie, met me. Bright and wide eyed, she almost had panic in those eyes. She bombards me with loads of information as we walk from the elevator to my office, and she doesn't stop as I take off my coat.

"Al, The D.A. is waiting on you in the east wing board room."

"Already?"

"Yes. From the looks of things, you will be heading up The Senator Hunter case."

"Damn it," I think aloud. I'm on the wrong side again…twice in one morning. "I saw the news this morning."

"Yeah, well, the D.A. and others are waiting on you."

I walk toward the east wing board room. It is weird for the D.A. to be here so early, as was State Attorney General Todd Shumaker, but it all makes sense now. My boss, the D.A., he's usually up in Albany rubbing elbows with his right-winged cronies like Todd Shumaker, and kissing multiple asses. Senator Hunter is incredibly liberal, if I can even say that. He is almost a bit of a firecracker that has a very high approval rating. Right-wingers hate him. He is here wanting for me? To head up my first high profile case? Which happens to be…*a black senator*! "Dammit," I say aloud again. I enter the boardroom.

The D.A., with a big overzealous smile, says, "Ahhh yes, gentlemen, this is Al Ibari. Al is one of our rising stars." The new chief of police introduces himself and another fellow, who he says is in charge of the New York state RNC. The D.A. explains how the state has a strong case to prosecute the senator with first-degree murder.

I asked a question that needed to be asked. "We are charging with first-degree murder/premeditated murder?" The look on everyone's faces told I was not to ask, yet. I'm the best face of color to put out there, and the same color of a face they don't want asking questions about their motives.

The chief of police jumps in. "We are gathering information as we speak. They're working on more evidence to officially charge him with murder. The detectives had enough to bring him in for questioning. He refused to answer any questions until he had time to speak with legal representation. We need probable cause to make this stick and right now it's not looking good."

"What do we have so far?"

"We found hairs on her body that we believe to be his, and we have him on camera leaving the scene."

"A warrant to search his office has allowed us to compare hairs from his office and match them with the hairs on the girl's body. We have a positive match," the D.A. chimes in.

"And he is saying nothing so far?" I ask.

"After denying that he had anything to do with her death, my detectives pressured him a little more until he just lawyered up."

I scan the room, looking in all eyes. I want to make sure I'm acting in charge since I'm handpicked. I ask the chief of police, who is new and I know he wants to look good, and he may put his foot on the scale. "So where do we come in without probable cause? We need to have that in our hand for any leverage. This is already a high profile case; a US Senator who's accused of murder means there is a lot at stake. The state and the voters are going to be all over our asses on this one. We have to get this one right. We have to be prepared before the official announcement from this office."

"Atta boy, Al! I know we have the right man for the job."

No, this fat motherfucker didn't just say, "atta boy!" I shuck that bullshit off and concentrated on bringing justice to this innocent, white girl. It wasn't a good hour until the chief called me to say the hairs came back positive.

The D.A. came into my office and said, "With the evidence we have, we can make a public announcement that an arrest warrant for the senator has been issued for first-degree murder. I would like for you to make the announcement before the public. We will have a press conference today at 2 pm. This gives you roughly four hours to prepare."

I replied, "No problem, sir."

"I have faith in you, Al. The world will be watching."

Those words made me feel apprehensive. Talk about piling on the pressure. I have enough confidence in my team and myself that we can handle this task. I called a staff meeting so we could brainstorm the case. I wanted my facts to be straight before I address the public. Any falsities can and will affect the case. There is no room for error. Connie ordered lunch, anticipating a long morning. We went back and forth for two hours. Everyone involved created a solid page of copy and speaking points. I knew we were going to have to answer several uneasy questions.

With the next ninety minutes, we held a mock press conference in the board room. I was not expecting this to be this intense; this is certainly a thrilling experience. I dipped into my office and closed the door in order to go over my notes and have some quiet time. The media has been gathering around the building for a good hour now. Butterflies are increasing in my belly as the minute draws near show time. Nervous is an understatement!

I break the tension with any distraction, and that came easy. I reflected on the best part of my day, which was meeting Alana Carrington. This is unquestionably a beauty and the beast kind of day. I hope she finds my card in her purse…my little magic. My senses tell me she is a good woman. My perception is that she is full of substance. In the test I'm about to take, the trials and tribulations this could cause a man, I'll need a queen to support me. I imagine that sometimes it's not what she might say, but her presence and just being near me and knowing she is there no matter what, will comfort me. This situation tells me I need that more than ever. I need a queen. I need Alana.

I have to contact her and ask her to get to know me, and if she could hang out with me just as my friend while I'm on this journey. If she is what I think she is, it will be as I think. I have to close my eyes for a minute. I think about her.

She's next to me on the train. She smells like the freshest flowers. Her smile is warm. She laughs and giggles softly as I hold her. This train is comfortable, with nice seats holding our bodies close to each other. We have two nearly empty wine glasses…for the second time. The country zooms by and we're humming, Till the Cops Come Knocking. Maxwell's got us rocking in our seats as we share a dual outlet jack of my iPod. On our way to DC for the Presidential Inauguration, I'm her Barack, and she is my Michelle. Our faces are laced with smiles as we nod at each other. Leaning in, we sponge each other's eyelids, noses and cheeks with our lips.

Whatever ensues —we have overnight bags packed…leading to the probabilities of lovemaking for the first time. We know we are. Alana moves her upper body into my space and places her ear to my heart as my hand massages her back. She kisses my chest through my shirt, leaving it wet and I love it.

She lightly bites my chest through my shirt…accidentally, her hand touches my pants where I can hardly contain hardening feelings. She angles her head up, stares at me looking down at her, and she bites her lips to hold back a smile. She's fucking with me. My queen.

I run my hands through her silky, long, flowing hair and tighten my grip, turning her head. I lean down and kiss her hard and deep and then release. We are festive. We order more wine from the porter. We're being prized by the other women. Many of them black, women passengers wishing their Barack rode the rails with them. They see our passion and those other women start living through us, wishing they had our zeal…our romance. Alana stands to stretch. I make sure she knows I'm looking at her up and down, waiting to devour her completely. She leans into my face and whispers something that I really wanted to hear…

A soft knock on the door breaks me out of my trance.

"Al."

"Come in, Connie."

"It's time. They are calling for you."

"Okay, let's do this."

I took a deep breath and headed down to the podium. It could have been my nerves, but the elevator took forever to come up and once on it, took forever to go down. When the doors opened, cameras began to flash. I could see reporters just off to the left talking live on the news. I made it up the podium and began my address.

"At approximately 12 noon today, an arrest warrant for first-degree murder was issued for Senator Hunter, and we expect the senator to turn himself in by close of business tomorrow. We are confident that justice will prevail. We have notified the victim's family. I will now take a few questions."

"Sarah Wallace, channel 7 News. Is there any truth that the victim was an intern and a former mistress of the senator's?"

"This is an ongoing investigation and at this point I cannot speculate on the relationship between the senator and the victim."

"Well, can you at least confirm that she was indeed an intern with the senator's office?"

"Like I said, the investigation is ongoing."

"Larry Glassberg here, Channel 2 News; do we know how she was found and by whom?"

"Yes, a cleanup staffer found her body during her routine house cleaning. Once she noticed the victim's body her screams alerted the rest of the staff. A supervisor then alerted the authorities."

"Has there been bail set yet for the senator?"

"Not as of yet; he will be arraigned later, Thank you, guys."

I grabbed my things and walked off the mock stage. Cameras continued to flash and reporters continued to cover the moment live. After the smoked cleared, I realize that five minutes of fame has just changed my life. Somehow, thoughts of Alana crept into my head. I thought that I could no longer ride the train from fear of someone recognizing me and causing me grief.

After a long day, I took the chance on taking the train home. To my surprise, no one noticed me. Maybe I look like all the black men who wear suits in New York City and can't get a cab. My cell phone was full of voice and text messages, but I was in no mood to check any of them.

Once I arrived at my place of refuge, I immediately took a long shower, replaying the events of the day in my head.

I should feel like the man, but for some reason narcissism wasn't sitting well with my spirit. I took an Ambien so I could get a good night's sleep and turned my TV to ESPN until it was lights out.

Morning...

After hitting the snooze button twice, I eventually got up... slow motion, but I was moving. I had to pick up the pace if I want to get my daily dose of Alana. I rushed to the train station. I didn't see Alana as of yet. I figured she would be in the coffee shop. The TV's blasting as usual, showing clips of my press conference. No Alana in sight.

A raspy voice says behind me, "Finally, someone with the balls to take down these crooked politicians."

Influenced by Alana's statement yesterday, I replied, "Well, we have to let the judicial process run its course."

Looking for my queen, I brushed off the older lady and her political opinions. I asked the cashier if she saw my queen come in here today. She had no idea of whom I was talking about. I went outside and still no Alana. My day was starting out with one in the negative column. Giving up and giving in to the idea that I won't see my queen, my head bows in disappointment and disgust. This is the first time after seeing her that I will have to ride the train without seeing the woman who has moved past being my fantasy. A lonely train ride. Nothing like my daydream train ride of us together. A sad morning...what will my day be like?

Alana Carrington
Dreaming Eyes of Mine

We lust for the very thing which is beyond our grasp.

There's a time to act proud and a time when you don't want to get in the back seat of a nasty cab. I hail a cab, but let Jeremy, my assistant, open the door to inspect first, and then I slide in. We're on our way to a press conference we could watch on TV, but my inside sources tell me Mr. Alphonso Ibari is the assigned assistant D.A. representing the state against my client.

My man of many mornings of wishful wants and desires will oppose me. I can't wait to show I'm the *Big Boss Lady,* and I can't wait to be closer to him…period. Prepared and professional, I will be. What a fine way to prove to a man that you can be that rib he is missing…that queen that needs to be sitting next to him on his throne, being his equal. Any man worthy of being my king will not be threatened, and I do not want to run a man just because I'm his equal in our careers. I want a man, and I want to be the woman. I'm not down with the role reversal thing. Blessed enough to be Al's woman one day, a beautiful wife I'd be in every sense of the word.

"Do you think we'll have trouble with them putting all the evidence on the table or should I start filing motions with the court for full disclosures? …Alana, Alana?"

"Yes, what is it Jeremy?"

"Are you okay? You seem a bit off balance? You're about to be in the spot light."

My assistant Jeremy is gay, and can be a karaoke king. It is king and not…whatever. With all of the flamboyance he can muster with an off-beat Mariah Carey hand wave, he breaks out into song…Jennifer Hudson's *Spotlight.*I laugh. When he's finished, I have a question for him. "So Jeremy, the *spotlight* thing…does that have anything to do with you wearing your Sunday's best suit today?"

"My dear, Alana…back to the questions I asked which are far more important. Now once again, *spotlight* or not, do you think we'll have trouble with them putting all the evidence on the table, or should I start filing motions with the court for full disclosures?"

"Yes, we can assume they will withhold."

"Well, they're done as of 9 am this morning. The filings are prepared." He smiles.

I love my team that I assembled this morning from the firm. They gave me full blessings to defend the senator, and I shall. Walking up the stairs of the D.A.'s office, we stop when we find a good spot near the side. Reporters are scurrying with cameras and microphones.

We are standing near one side and I see Al standing almost hidden behind police and suits worn by lesser men and women. From my vantage point, I see him clearly, but I don't think he can see me. People are talking to him sporadically. He is in full command. His body language has power and control. He's taller than everyone is; even the security walking around don't look as powerful as he stands. Strange, but maybe not, I don't see arrogance in his authority. He talks to everyone with full eye contact but with a soft expression, and end every exchange with a smile.

When it's all said and done, this news conference is just for show. He will say nothing with any bombshell information. I'm here just to see him. He steps to the podium. His voice is strong and powerful as he introduces himself. His mouth—its shape; his lips—how they move…he moves me, as I want him to touch me.

As I dreamed of having him in my office, I want to be in his. I want to be in any room with him alone. Approaching Al as I hike up my skirt, my right leg straddles his and I sit on his lap. My arms embrace him and wrap around his neck. His soft, brown eyes connect with mine, and, as if on cue, our tongues meet in the midst of heavenly bliss. Me, sitting in his lap, tasting his tongue is what I've dreamed of for what seems like forever.

His hands caress my leg and he doesn't miss an ounce of my flesh as he feels every curve of my body. His mouth is so sweet. Exhaling every time he does this magical thing with his tongue… damn, he's making me crazy. My lips part from his and my tongue licks his chin. Moving down, I find my way to his neck and I can smell his cologne; it's strong and powerful and inviting. I kiss his neck. I think I've found his spot. He moans. I kiss more. He grabs my ass…palms it like his life depends on it. He breathes deep and hard. I've got him. Light flickers of my tongue drive him insane. And I don't stop. Biting softly, I whisper in his ear, "I love you," and he moans loudly.

"Baby, please," he implores as he attempts to leave the chair we're both sitting in…me, in his lap, my dress now off.

"I need to be inside of you," he demands as he lifts me.

My legs straddle his waist and he carries me to the bed.

"I need you inside of me, baby, please," I tell him. He lays me down on the bed.

The night is young and love and lust collide between two hearts and two minds…two souls yearning for the chance to become one. A love affair in the making, emotions cloud our vision and thinking, and who we are at the core takes the reins. Longing to be his forever, faithful concubine, I'd do whatever needs to be done to keep him in my life. Unafraid to bare my soul, even if only to satisfy him, to please him in every way imaginable is my life's only goal.

We lust for the very thing which is beyond our grasp. The tables have turned and he is mine and mine alone, in my presence, I've captured his heart, his mind, his soul, his body. Mine, he is and I love him in a way I can't explain.

My legs part and he pulls my panties off. Taking my right leg into his hand, he kisses my feet, gently licking my cherry-red toes. I sigh with anticipation. His tongue travels up my thigh and I already know his desired destination is the inferno that impatiently rests between my thighs. I'm so wet for him.

"This is so wrong, baby," I whisper. He looks up at me. "I love you. That can't be wrong. It feels too fucking good to be wrong."

As he makes his way to my sugar walls, I stop him. His energy tells me how badly he wants to taste me.

"Let me taste you first," I tell him. He struggles to reply. "Please, Alana, your pussy looks so good."

"Baby, not yet. I need to taste you," I reply as if I'm begging.

His fingers enter me uncontrollably. He finger-fucks me long and deep. He pulls them out, tastes my juices all over his fingers and then puts them back in. I moan.

"Al, please…you can't do that. Let me suck your dick."

"Alana, I can't move. Let me just lick it one time. I promise, just once…then you can have your way."

"I need my way, now, Al. Baby, please."

He exhales and we're at a stand-still. He wants his face to be buried in my pussy and I need him there, but I need to taste him. I need to see it. I've dreamed of this moment for so long.

I move away from him. He grabs my hips to keep me in my place. He kisses my pussy lips like he loves them. Tasting them and becoming acquainted with what rightfully belongs to him, he inhales my scent. I want to cum all over his face.

I move more and tell him, "Al, I need to taste you now."

Reluctantly, he gets up and removes his suit pants. I see it. It's bulging through his boxer briefs. Beautiful, dark chocolate staff, hard, firm, long, gorgeous black dick. I rush to it.

"I can't believe you're not going to let me taste your sweet pussy, Alana." He tells me as he caresses my ass.

On my knees, on the bed, I'm within eyesight of my new best friend. Slowly, I kiss it. I taste it. With circular motions, I lick it. Softly, I devour it.

Closing my eyes, I take it in like a champ, like this man, this beautiful man, is my man…my beautiful king, and I love him, adore him, suck him, taste him, like a real woman should.

He smacks it with his strong hand and it gives me a sting, sending shockwaves through my entire being…gets my juices flowing hard.

"Alana. Alana. Alana, did you hear what this pompous asshole just said?" Jeremy, my assistant, interrupts my daydream.

"Uh, no, what did he say, Jeremy?"

"Alana, he is really acting like Hunter is guilty."

I look up at Al, my king. I mean, Al, as he talks to the press about my client's case. He is a bit smug and every part of me knows that my lust for him is both unprofessional and quite stupid. Yet and still, he is wearing the shit, hell and damn out of that suit. My Lord….

Smooth, black, luscious skin. His body seems to have just exquisitely fallen into that navy blue, pinstriped suit. He is sharp as all hell and wow, part of me is proud of this strong, intelligent, articulate black man. He just happens to be on the wrong side of the law. God made us all flawed, so I guess he has to be.

I chuckle to myself, and Jeremy asks, "What's up, Alana?"

"Oh, nothing, Jeremy. I am simply laughing at this clown, Ibari."

"He is a joke, isn't he? You know he's just the D.A.'s token, anyway."

"Right," I say as I lower my head in shame. Damn, I love him, but now I have to play the part, my role as his adversary, and part of that hurts me.

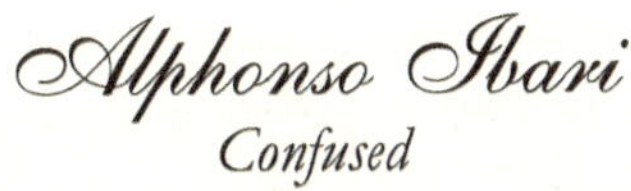

Alphonso Ibari
Confused

The cherry in my chocolate-covered dream.

I couldn't wait to get a moment alone. I found myself avoiding the cameras and reporters. I couldn't risk saying or doing anything that will affect the case. The D.A. rushes by me with other elected colleagues who are for sure on the other side of the political spectrum of the senator I will be taking down.

"Great job, Al."

"Yes, excellent job Al."

My name might as well have been Joe. Game recognizes game; I know what time it is. I did graduate at the top of my class. Something for sure I have an advantage in, I went to Howard and Georgetown, and both schools taught me how to win in the courtroom and behind the scenes. Sometimes, the people you work with are more suspect and scandalous than the suspects you prosecute. I didn't get here by my good looks alone.

I rush behind the D.A. and pass him and face him. "Sir, I need a moment with you." One of the many unethical cronies hanging around since this morning injects into a conversation I don't want with him as if he's playing wingman for the D.A.

"Al, my main-man, you were great in front of the cameras. They loved you!"

I give the jackass a smirk; I'm sure he thought it was a smile. I stare the D.A. down, I'm not playing *the boy* right now, and this case is some serious stuff that I'm heading into, so I demand. "Sir, we need to talk…alone."

He finally responds, "Absolutely, Al…soon as we get back to the office."

I nod, but keep my eyes locked on him. I want him to know I'm not being submissive; I'm just agreeing to meet later. I understand that some conversations are meant for a pay grade above me, yet what confuses me is why so many politicians are hanging around the D.A...It's almost as if these bureaucrats are overjoyed to see the senator in deep shit, as he is in tight...like between a horse's ass.

I head back to my office and have an afternoon snack to hopefully help calm my stomach. One of the reasons my stomach is a bit queasy is becauseI caught a quick view of my dream girl queen at the press conference. I saw Alana and it seemed she was lost in all that was going on. I can assume from our conversation at the train station about the senator that she may be looking at me not in the best of light. But then again, she's a highly intelligent woman who has to know I'm doing my J.O.B. People can—not like, but still love.

My assistant, Connie, pokes her head in my office, "Al, are you ready to meet with us, or did you forget? You did say the team will meet at 3:30 and to have all the information you requested. It's 3:32."

"I'll be there in three minutes."

"Al, are you okay?"

"Yeah."

I enter the room and pinned on the separate boards are articles of information and pictures. My eyes captured one picture and it slapped me into shock—the legal firm and team I will be going up against. At the top of totem pole stands Ms. Alana Carrington. My mouth felt stuck open and numb as if a Novocain shot was in full affect. My stomach rumbled; I had to pinch my butt cheeks tight to keep pressure from escaping. I sat my ass down.

"Okay, tell me what we have." I scan the room strangely, feeling exposed when I'm not. No one here has a clue I have met and have a crush on the enemy, so to speak.

"Al, on the board we have Alana Carrington from the firm of Carrington and Associates, and to put it mildly, she is a rising star somewhat like you." Fortlow Smithe, the new guy in the office chuckles out his out-of-place response. Everyone in the room gives him a shut-the-hell-up look. The brother with a strange name is straight out of the hood—Trenton. He has a high IQ, but lacks professional etiquette and keeps flipping his lips.

"Alana Carrington is skilled as a defense attorney in how she defends black men. The word is she is passionate in how she goes about her work. I know a guy. I saw him at the press conference and, I uhh…well he told me that he met her for drinks a few times, and says she's tight between the ears. I guess he wanted to date her and he got nowhere."

Connie did me a big favor and cut dude off from me whooping his ass. He was closer to a beat down than he could ever imagine, or anyone in the room could know, how I felt listening to dude talk about Alana in such a casual way.

The team took their time informing me of needed information as we discussed all the evidence we had and the next steps. Something annoyed all of team to the core. Why would the D.A. suppress evidence? Why are we in the blind? Apparently many finger prints were found in the room, and we're told they are not significant to our case, but we need to know to explain to a jury. Most importantly, why would he keep that evidence from me? These reasons alone have my mind going haywire. Something just doesn't smell right. It's not adding up. For the first time in my career I feel like an Uncle Tom sell out. Even worse yet, I feel like I am a token. I really hope and pray that my intuition is wrong. I'm sure there is a perfect explanation and I am just over thinking again.

Home…

Turning the news on wasn't the best idea to get today's press conference off my mind. Although, I must admit I did look pretty damn good on T.V. I was even on the national cable channels. MSNBC and Fox news were both covering our politics. This thing was bigger than I thought.

Wanting to get work off of my mind, I began to channel surf.

I came across a black couple having sex. It was a soft porn film on HBO with nothing but black people. This was hot and different. I was fully aroused after fifteen minutes of watching. I found my head slowly rolling as well as my eyes fighting sleep. My head fell back and I started mentally scanning Alana from memory of every aspect of her physical being.

La la land…

We were alone on an empty train. Every car was empty. Alana is standing next to a pole, holding on and wearing a beautiful, red dress that hugged every curve. Her brown eyes were submissive, explaining that she is all mine and to come have her. She glances at me seductively. Her voice echoes in my ear, *"I'm worth everything you must do to have me."* I give in to the voice in my head, *Follow her, slowly sauntering.*

The train cab opens up into my bedroom and my bed. The red dress peels off of her body and drops to the floor. I walk up behind her and hold her close and begin to kiss the back of her neck and all over her shoulders.

We lie down on my bed and I curl in behind her and we spoon. I feel the heat of her ass and she feels my hands cupping breasts. Her hair smells so good and it makes me feel…feel…feel…

Beep…Beep…Beeeep…

My alarm clock woke me up from a deep, yet great dream. Damn, that was the best sleep I've had in a while. Sweet, yet bitter that I went to sleep dreaming of my queen, but I wake this morning without her.…

I make the train in the nick of time. Lo and behold, I see Alana standing at a pole like in my dream. She playfully teases me, raising her eyebrows and smiles. Her sweet lips tell me, *you look good to me but you're the enemy.*

"Good morning, Mr. Ibari."

"Good morning, Ms. Carrington. Well we…"

She puts her pretty finger to my lips.

We say no more, but we stare at each other as we ride the train, feeling the bumps, the surges, and the slow downs.

Alana Carrington
Simply Beautiful

I've allowed a stranger to change my life.

My assistant's voice blends in with the sounds of an eclectic jazz piece that reverberates throughout my office. I hear him, yet I don't hear a word he's saying. He's talking to me. I hear jazz. The music makes my foot tap. He's going on and on about the missing discovery. A few well-placed, cordial replies from me makes Jeremy believe that I'm digesting all of his words. Jazz. Constant solo flowing from his soul to his fingertips. Jazz. Harmony and chaos, united holy, yet lovely. The alto sax has my attention more than he does. I want to rock side to side or snap my fingers, but I can't because that would give me away. My foot taps. I enjoy what I'm hearing. Jazz. It is very much a part of me…fluidly.

All smiles as I read through the discovery that somehow missed the files I was handed regarding Senator Hunter. I motioned the court. Through a tantrum of epic proportion, I cited the Brady doctrine. I screamed and shouted to my ancestors about how unjust the system is and how the ills of justice and the imbalance of her scales have weighed on this case. It is of my expert opinion that the scales, this time around the mountain, will lean forward in the direction of all that is righteous. So, I smile. I'm nothing but smiles…smiles because while I can concede that these texts prove an affair between Hunter and the intern, it proves absolutely nothing else, well, except for a hot and steamy romance that boiled over. Hot, heavy, loving, caring, beautiful if I can even apply that word to something so obviously sinister. It meant something serious to the two of them. That's what I know and that's what the world will know.

"So, we motioned the court. Any ruling yet?" Jeremy asks as he paces the room.

"Nope, nothing yet, Jeremy."

"You can't be this calm, Alana?"

"But I am."

"How?"

"Because if there is something egregious going on, I will simply and vigorously use it as ammunition to proceed however I need to. I'm mad, yes, Jeremy, but senses go to bliss or shit in the heat of moments. I have to remain calm."

"I see. Ah…okay."

"Got it?"

"This is why you're *the* Alana Carrington, huh?"

"So, I've been told."

"I'm watching and learning. Oh, by the way, Alana, you do have that Holiday Gala tonight for the Minority Lawyers Association something or other."

"Damn. Is that tonight?"

"Sure is."

"I pray I have something to wear. Geesh. I don't."

Reaching down in my purse, I pull out my credit card and hand it to Jeremy.

"Listen, please, Jeremy, I need you. Run and pick me up something to wear. Nothing ordinary. Only extraordinary. Nothing basic black. Nothing typical. Size sixteen. I need room for my triple D-cups. Attention to detail. I wear reds, blues and purples really well. Think about all of the skanks that will be there tonight— the brown-nosing women…the high-faluting wannabes. Think about the predictable American standards of beauty that will be in attendance and then think about your boss and make sure I'm going to appear to be the furthest thing away from all of the usual suspects."

Jeremy grabs my card. I interrupt.

"Oh, Jeremy, diamond earrings and necklace, and heels, two-inch, peep-toed heels. Size nine."

"Got it, Boss."

"Good."

As Jeremy heads out of my office, he turns around to ask one more question.

"Hair?"

"I got it covered, Jeremy."

"Makeup, Boss?"

"Calling in the team, Love. Thanks. Now Bye...I have to finish reading through these text messages and, as a matter of fact, call Ruby, tell her I need hair, nails and makeup for tonight's gala. Thanks."

"You got it."

Juicy. Scandalous. The texts.

Senator: "How was your day, beautiful?"

Intern: "Just fine. How about yours?"

Senator: "Better, now that I'm talking to my angel."

Intern: "I'm your angel now? J"

Senator: "You've always been my angel."

Intern: "Hard to tell."

Senator:"Don't do that."

Intern: "Do what, Keith?"

Senator: "Baby, my feelings for you are real. Believe that."

Intern: "If you say so."

Senator: "I do. I do say so. J"

Intern: "You're cute."

Senator: "You're gorgeous."

Intern: "I'm glad you think so."

Senator: "I know so, baby."

Intern: "I love your confidence."

Senator: "I love YOU."

I notice there is a gap in time, from back to back texting. The pause lasts for about three minutes.

Intern: "You know how to get to my heart."

Senator: "That's a beautiful thing."

Intern: "What are you doing now?"

Senator: "Thinking of you."

Intern: "I see."

Senator: "You see what? You see that you need to be with me, don't you?"

Intern: "Ha. Ha. J"

Senator: "Did you think about me today?"

Intern: "Why?"

Senator: "Because I know you did. That's why."

Intern: "Perhaps."

Senator: "You did. Didn't you?"

Intern: "Yes."

Senator: "What were you thinking?"

Intern: "Wonderful thoughts about you. That's all."

Senator: "What are you wearing?"

Intern: "Why?"

Senator: "I need to picture you."

Intern: "A red nighty."

Senator: "I bet you look delicious."

Intern: "Keith."

Senator: "Tell me you look delicious, baby."

Intern: "I look delicious, Keith."

Senator: "Panties?"

Intern: "No."

Senator: "Sounds so good."

Intern: "Right."

Senator: "I miss the taste of your lips."

Intern: "Keith."

Senator: "What, baby? I miss tasting that pretty pink pussy."

Intern: "I miss you, too, baby."

Senator: "Can I just touch you?"

Intern: "Anytime."

Senator: "Lick your fingers for me…slowly…one by one."

Intern: "Okay."

Senator: "Are they wet?"

Intern: "Everything is wet."

Senator: "Good girl. Spread your legs. Take those wet fingers and slide them all over that pretty pussy of mine. Rub that clit for me baby."

Intern: "You're such a fucking tease."

Senator: "Slide those fingers in and out of that pussy."

The sweet sounds of John Coltrane create an alluring backdrop to the mood set in this office from the reading of these text messages. The crescendo at the most pivotal moment, displayed by alto sax takes my spirit to a familiar, yet, uncomfortable place. I think of him. I wonder if his text game is as naughty as Senator Hunter's. I've never engaged in such indulgence.

A phone call further disrupts my pleasurable reading of the discovery. It's Ruby, one of New York's finest hairstylists and makeup artists. She's on her way.

I glance out the window. The world is going by. I can only imagine, in this time and space, why I'm still so lost in him. I gave myself away. Even in those few encounters, I've allowed a stranger to change my life and now it won't change back. I can't forget him. Now, I have to work with him. In opposition to him. It's funny; nothing means anything to me. I'm just lost in him. I wonder why I'm lost in him.

Intern: "You feel so good."

Senator: "Damn, I want you so bad."

Intern: "I'm all yours for the taking."
Senator: "Cum for me, baby."
Intern: "I'm going to bust."
Senator: "Me, too."
Intern: "I need you here with me."
Senator: "I need to be with you."
Intern: "Feels so good, baby."
Senator: "I can taste you right now."
Intern: "Damn, I wanna cry."
Senator: "Hold all that loving for me, baby. I'm on my way."
Intern: "Hurry."
Senator: "I gotta feel myself inside of you."
Intern: "Oooh, what you do to me."
Senator: "You make me crazy."
Intern: "Come to me. Now. Please."
Senator: "Coming, baby."
Intern: "Now."
Senator: "Close your eyes. I'll be right there."
Intern: "I love you, baby."
Senator: "I love you more."

There has to be something I'm missing or more discovery is being withheld. This was the last text, if I'm not mistaken, that the two of them shared prior to the intern's death. What am I missing?

Jeremy did a fabulous job. The purple, long gown in airy chiffon is textured with multidirectional pleating, strategically placed to flatter my figure and all my curves. Languid ruffles top the shoulder, while a side slit lends an alluring finish. It is the one-shoulder piece of perfection for the evening. I feel it. I know it. I walk into the exquisite hall believing every word of confidence

I've uttered to myself in the form of meaningful, encouraging whispers.

Jeremy takes my hand and accompanies me to the beautiful seating area. Crystal, fresh flowers and candles adorn each carefully placed table. Decorated to complete and absolute perfection, the people who put this gala together are certain of their gift and their craft.

Jeremy and I continue to walk through, admiring all that is splendid. Attorneys and their guests and whoever else was invited to this shindig make their way around. Cupped hands cover concealed thoughts as whispers leave the mouths of gossiping attorneys and enter the ears and psyches of willing participants. They look at me. Maybe not gossiping, but they're definitely talking, and about me, that's for sure. My name has grown in this society over time because of my ratio and percentage of wins and also because of the clientele I represent. I serve no attorney-gods, I don't quite conform to the legal norm, I'm not pulled by any legal puppet strings and I march to the beat of my own legal drum. Yes, that's the reason for the display of cupped hands over hushed words.

We walk together behind the waiter who leads us to our table—a corner table overlooking the New York City skyline. The night is dark, the stars are out, the moon is glowing and the hustle of the day is behind us. The evening is here, the gala is on, and life is rich and full in its splendor. If there was something missing it would be my king.

My king.

Jeremy hands me a glass of champagne, one of two that he lifted from the waiter on the way in. I receive in kind, and we toast.

"To winning this case for Senator Hunter and for kicking the District Attorney's ass."

"Touché," I reply with an indifferent look on my face.

"What's the matter, Alana?"

"Oh, nothing. Just trying to figure out what I missed in the text messages."

"Scandalous or psychopath?"

"Juicy, but loving and endearing, if you will. Weird, Jeremy. I'm a bit baffled by this one."

"Alana, you know you'll figure it out. You always do."

"Thank God for small favors." I chuckle.

We laugh in unison until the Master of Ceremony takes the stage to commence with the evening's events.

A live band takes their seats and begins a wonderful offering of sweet soul music. The lead singer is one I remember seeing in the various clubs in and around the Tri-state area and he's something to contend with. It is often those underground artists who possess the most talent and get the least in the way of publicity and true recognition.

Grabbing my hand, Jeremy pulls me out of my chair and off of my feet.

"Come on, Boss. Your hair is flowing so carelessly along your shoulders. You look beautiful. You work so hard. Let's dance."

I pull back.

"No, Jeremy."

"Alana," he pleads with sad puppy eyes.

"Damn you."

Smiling, he leads me to the dance floor.

I commence with a fabulous two-step and I must admit, I'm having a great time. Glancing over to the band, its lead singer keeps eyeing me. I return his smile with one of my own. Praying he understands it's just a gesture of acknowledgement and respect for his craft and not an invitation to anything more.

Jeremy twirls me around. We both laugh.

"See, you needed this, Alana. I know every man in here is wondering why you're dancing with your ultra-fine, gay assistant. Did I mention your assistant is ultra-fine?"

I hit Jeremy on his shoulder.

"You're so silly, Jeremy. And, yes, my assistant and friend *is* ultra-fine and you are breaking all sorts of hearts in here tonight, looking like a black Adonis."

"Your prince is coming. If you stopped working so hard, you could catch him."

"Oh, Jeremy, I have no time for romance. I'm too busy saving the world."

He twirls me again. Something about gay men and twirls go together like a hand in glove.

Lead Singer Man and the band prepare for a rendition of Al Green's *Simply Beautiful.* I can hear it in the first few bars of the instrumental. Adorned in black, tight slacks and a red top, Lead Singer Man is nice to look at, perhaps a bit too flamboyant for my taste and not professionally rugged like that beautiful opposing attorney king of mine, but I suppose that goes well with his line of work.

"Oooh, this is my song, Alana," Jeremy pulls back and does his own version of a two-step.

"May I have this dance?" A deep, delicious voice overwhelms my senses. I recognize it. My heart flutters as I am too ashamed to look to my right to see who that long arm, placed in a well-fitted expensive tuxedo belongs to.

"Sure," Jeremy says and makes his way back to our table, but not before grabbing another glass of champagne. He gives me the *You Okay?* look and I nod slightly to let him know that I am indeed okay.

A smile I'm embarrassed to claim covers my face as Alphonso places his left hand around my waist and takes my left hand into his right. I exhale under my breath. I just look at him and he looks at me and we rock side to side.

"If I gave you my love..." Lead Singer Man croons into the mic and wow, does he sound authentic.

"You look beautiful tonight, Alana," he tells me and I bow my head.

With a delicate hand, he places his index finger and thumb under my chin, lifts my head gently and says, "Look at me."

"Alphonso."

"Yes, Beautiful?"

"This is inappropriate, don't you think?"

"What? Me falling in love with opposing counsel? Maybe, but I don't care."

Bowing my head once again, he forces me to look into his eyes.

"This doesn't make sense to me, Alphonso."

"It doesn't have to."

"It absolutely needs to, Al."

Pulling me closer, his hand treads lightly on the small of my back. I can smell his Versace. It penetrates my senses…makes me crazy. Gazing up to his lips, they look like they taste like a last meal to a dying woman. His goatee is trimmed to perfection and his dark chocolate brown skin makes me want to give praise, jump up in mid-air and give our Lord and Savior, Jesus Christ, a high-five for working his divine magic on a man so supreme.

"There are so many things I've wanted to tell you over the years in that train station. Like, how the very first moment I saw you, I knew I loved you. Like how that day last April in the middle of spring, when you wore that yellow flower in your hair, how beautiful you looked. Like an angel. I remember how you struggled to carry Christmas presents and your briefcase last year. I cheered for you in the State vs. Apollo Childs case."

"Oh, my," I reveal through shocked lips and eyes welling with tears.

I swallow hard. He pulls me closer.

"People are watching us, Al. This is not good."

"To hell with them."

Lead Singer Man sings, *There's a whole lotta things you and I could do.*

"The text messages, Al. They're nothing. Why hide them?"

"I've been trying to figure out why my boss failed to give them to you. I will say no more. Can't break the law, beautiful."

"The texts are just loving, sweet and erotic. It only proves an affair."

"What texts did you read?"

"There are more, Al?"

"Much."

"I don't have those. Something's not right."

"I agree. Alana, I promise, it's not me. We need to get to the bottom of this."

"We're breaking all types of protocols here, Al."

"Right now, at this moment, I don't want to think about anything other than you being in my arms. Damn, I want to kiss you. I've been dreaming about tasting those perfect lips for a long time."

"You can't," I whisper under my breath.

"I can. I will."

"Not here, Al. Oh, God, this is wrong on every level."

"Do you love me, Alana?"

"I don't even know your middle name, Al."

"It's Patrick, Alana. Do you love me? Because I love you. I love you."

I bow my head. Lead Singer Man sings, *Simply beautiful.*

"Look at me."

"I do."

"You do what, Alana?"

The parting of my lips is interrupted by Al placing his thumb in between them. A slight smile crosses them and I exhale.

"I love these pretty lips."

Taking his thumb, he places it to his lips, kisses it, and then places it on mine.

"You love me, don't you?"

Confidence covers him so well.

"I do."

"Tell me."

"I love you."

Alphonso Ibari
Soul Eyes

Feeling the good and slightly indifferent about the day's events, and the new knowledge and developments had me all over the place. I was trying to be positive and keep my dream alive in the all the things that I want and what is important to me. I don't want to lose sight of my goals when it comes to love or my career. I have a desire to be on cloud nine with all I do.

Al Green's *Simply Beautiful* was on repeat all the way home. After listening to the song about twenty times, I've managed to pick up the words and what I didn't know I replaced them with my own words. Once I got home, I became Al Green while I undressed.

What about the way you love me, aww and the way you squeeze me, yeah
Yeah, ya simply beautiful Yeah, yeah, beautiful, yeah
When you get right down to it
Oh, mmh-hmm

Alana had me singing in front of the mirror, imagining I was singing in front of a sold out crowd and she was sitting front and center. I was pouring my heart out to the woman of my desires and she felt no envy of the other women enjoying my performance.

Her style and awareness would sit on a throne of what others want to be. Later, she would meet me backstage and off in a town car for a night to remember. Yeah, that's how she had me feeling. The only thing that would have made the night better is if she would have come home with me. That little thing called reality can be a bitch at times. Once reality finished having her way with me, I managed to fall asleep.

Man up…

Sitting at my desk daydreaming. For some reason I can sense a hypothesis shifting. I'm not sure if it's for the good or not, but this case is the center of my view of everything that is going on with Alana and me.

I can feel life changing before my eyes. This case and my career might not allow me to love the one I want, and at the same time my heart refuses to yield to wanting it all. Calling this a catch 22 is an understatement! I want this case to be over, yet this is what I signed up for. This is what I wanted to be!

Man the fuck up, Al and make it happen!

I need to know more about Alana. I enter her name into www. nylawyers.org. They'll have her profile and other info, and I'm sure she has checked me out from whatever sources she has.

Wow, her photos are pretty, but she's fine in person. Oh, she went to Morehouse and finished her law degree at the top of her class at Seton Hall Law. Shows no children, but that's not a problem for me if she does. Oh, she likes poetry, photography, and working out. She really loves traditional jazz, particularly Miles and Coltrane. It says she loves to sing jazz. Well to her surprise, I play sax and played in every school jazz band. I still sit in here and there.

Maybe her love for jazz is what I'm reading from the paper that dropped out Alana's book or journal when we were getting our coffees. I feel bad because of my attempt to drop my card in her purse when she dropped some papers. I accidently put one in my coat my pocket and I've been carrying it around ever since. It reads like a song.

Before I head to the meeting with the D.A. and Schumaker, I could use some soothing jazz the calm my soul. Let me see comes up when I write Coltrane into my iheart radio favorites.

"Welcome to iHeart radio where we just finished listening to a track from Julian "Cannonball" Adderley and now one of my favorites from John Coltrane, Soul Eyes.

Wow, that's a nice track. I'll have to pick that up and maybe... hopefully...if ever I have a chance to fix dinner for Alana, I'll play *Soul Eyes* for her. Maybe, I can have her read or sing her words. I could learn to play it for her and she'll listen to me living in la-la love land.

Damn what is not to love about this woman? To hear her favorite song and read her words...she is not just any man's conquest. She can lead tribes of men with lesser minds. I wish my fingers were soloing all over her body, changing the pitch of her tenor, making her reach into her baritone, and finally sending her soaring into her soprano.

Fuck! Turned out by her and don't have the slightest idea as of now how things stand or if ever I'll have a chance to accompany her into our own groove. The job...I must do the job.

I gather my things and head downstairs to meet with the D.A. and Attorney General Schumaker in the small board room. Laughter and outbursts were coming from the other side of the doors. A sign of confidence or arrogance awaits me. I opened the door and ....

Hey, there he is—the man of the hour! Come on in. Schumaker and I are just throwing the bull," the D.A. smirks. "The reason why we called a meeting is that we have a couple concerns regarding this particular case."

I throw on my listening yet analyzing cap...

"Concerns? What kind, sir?"

Schumaker opened a folder and looks over his bifocals. "Yes, Al the concerns, we need to be aggressive. We need to attack the senator and his legal team. Ultimately, we want them to show their hand early. We need to know what their defense is going to be." Schumaker smiles and rolls his head around as if his head is screwed on too tight. "They got a pretty little ass...excuse me. I mean a little, feisty mama over there heading up their team. Not to mention she's pretty smart. Her record shows that this would be her biggest case. The word is she thinks like man. I'm sure she could use a nice stiff one up in her to loosen her up."

"Excuse me, Mr. State Attorney. What did you just say?" Both their faces get a little tighter, realizing I'm not letting that slide... his off color, sexual innuendo joke.

"A woman so pretty, single and enjoys toughing it out in a man's game has to have a girlfriend." He liked his joke too much and dribbled his coffee on his tie. The D.A. has now lost his mind.

I'm offended with the shit I'm hearing. I force myself to keep my cool. Poker face is on. I know I can't let on that I have feelings for Alana. They have crossed the line. I give a Denzel Washington type laugh and smile. I am now *a man on fire*. A black man coiled like a cobra, ready to strike. These fools don't understand that I'm a black man who knows his history. They are talking about a black queen, and I will defend her honor as much as I will fight her for what is right when it comes to justice for all.

"This sounds good, but where do I come in at?" I smile another disarming smile knowing my iPhone is recording our conversation...as always, when dealing with people who can destroy me, I respond to their craziness with my mental guns loaded.

"Al, we need you to find out what pretty Miss. Pretty Girly has down her uh...blouse. She has a history of defending and winning when it looked as if she could not." Schumaker's jaw squares when he finished talking.

Reluctantly, I agreed with a nod. But wait! "What are they asking of me?"

Al you're too damn bright. Don't play with me...I mean us. You need to get to this little filly. Throw some of that soul brother charm on her. Take her to a nice restaurant on the upper eastside and to B.B. King's club for of that booty shaking music. I have a state credit card already set up for you to use. Then have a little fun on me, just tell me the dirty details after you checkout of the St.

Regis. I have a room already booked. It's all on me. Do what you need to do to get her brain on a platter. Give a little love, but at the same time, we're at war to win.

Taken aback to say the least!

"What are you talking about?" Schumaker looks at me as if I'm lost. I know what he is saying, but is this shit real?

We've got a lot at stake and you can't allow your dick to have a conscious. Use what you've got, son, to put us in the lead on this case. You're not committing a crime." He laughs an evil laugh. "Well, son, it will be a crime if you perform well enough to make little mama squeal." He's laughing and reaching out with his fist for a fist pump. Really? I don't reciprocate.

I decided to play the game until the cards fall in my favor. With all this pressure and hostility, there is definitely something going on outside of my control. Something isn't right.

Sorting it out.

I couldn't help but to feel like a pawn with them wanting me to sacrifice myself and forget all my beliefs and values for their higher cause. This doesn't sit well with my soul. I have to approach my queen with a winning legal and ethical offensive, and as if there is no love between us. But as of now, if there is love, I don't know, so I will not hurt her with deceit.

Back in my office I have my assistant call Ms. Alana Carrington and see if we can meet. I'm going to approach this as a professional for both of our souls. We are dealing with a situation where a man has been accused of murder.

She agrees to meet in one hour. She is bringing her assistant, and I will have mine. Business! Professional! Nervous! We meet in one of the conference rooms at the law library. I want to avoid others knowing, like the D.A. and Schumaker who want to jerk her and me around. It's a dark, dreary day outside and raining hard against the widows as we are having some preliminary talks. Everyone and everything seem to be moving in slow motion. I don't eye her and she, as far as I can tell, isn't crossing any lines. We talk back and forth for an hour

We get down to the case and she puts it out there that there is no motive, and she knows we are holding back evidence that they will contest in pre-trial hearings and make it public, possibly putting the D.A.'s office in a bad light.

I act like it's not a big deal and we can try the case in the court of public opinion, too. The senator is caught with his pants down having affairs. We do know of others. I let her know those women will be on the stand to testify and to muddy the water for the senator.

I know the D.A., and Schumaker and the conservative agenda ultimately want the senators' seat. I make what is a generous offer that the senator should take a plea deal of first-degree manslaughter or bear the full power of the D.A.'s office to put him away for first degree. He might get a chance to see his grandchildren without bars if he takes the plea. I let Alana know unless she knows something that I don't know. I believe she or anyone representing the senator cannot win. I had to go hard…very hard on my baby. I know I've hurt her. No response from her, but if she is as good as I know she is, she is analyzing options.

The four of us—her assistant, my assistant, and her and I—stand and pick up. We all leave to exit. Alana does look at me and I stare at her. Time stopped before she turned right and I turned left. I want a drink. I want to go to sleep, and wake with her soul eyes looking at me.

Alana Carrington
Equinox

The heavens must feel the need the same as I.

An equinox has been defined as either of the two times during a year when the sun crosses the celestial equator and when the length of day and night are approximately equal. Makes me wonder if time and space and rhyme and reason has its own place today in the scope of my life? Day and night seemed to have met, and my mind ponders whether or not my equal is in the midst.

Opposing counsel tore into my psyche something fierce today. I may be a bit bruised, but never broken. Pierced into my soul, he did. These are the dangers of falling in love with a man who doesn't quite know me, and one who has a job to do first and foremost. And I, a woman to fall for as a complete afterthought, was evidenced today by his behavior.

Coltrane's horn sings a familiar tune by way of staccato and rhythms that only true jazz lovers can appreciate. Ironically, *Equinox* reverberates from my office speakers and my head nods as I commune with the soul-stirring sound. It calms me—jazz that is. Coltrane feeds my spirit and somehow transports me to a place of Zen. I need this place at this moment. Desperately.

I'm searching—attempting to find the place where the fairness of life will meet with my own set of circumstances. I can't conceive that I have no way of out this…that I have no way to demand my client's charges be dropped and that his innocence will sprout from the earth like brand new leaves. The heavens must feel the need the same as I. I only pray. A loss in this case will not only tarnish my reputation, but losing to a man I can't stop thinking about will humble me in a way I have not yet earned. I don't deserve this humility. Not this way. Not right now. Maybe never.

Never let them see you sweat.

I must remember those words. A sense of panic is overcome by a sense of fearlessness as Senator Hunter walks into my office. His face spells defeat in every language under the sun. I cannot allow myself to be defeated along with him.

My suit jacket is making me hot along with other negatives; I remove it and place it on the back of my office chair. "Have a seat, Mr. Hunter."

Senator Hunter takes a seat and pours a glass of water, which I readily have available on my desk for all of my clients.

"So, Alana, what's next?"

Calmly, I walk to the senator. My ass finds a place on the edge of my desk. I sit, slightly. My skirt rises above my knee. I see Senator Hunter's eyes gaze up my legs and to my thighs. This irritates me. I don't say a word. I follow him with my eyes.

"Senator Hunter?"

My voice snaps him out of a trance.

"Yes, Alana." He loosens his navy blue, striped tie.

"Have you told me everything? There has to be something missing. I'm good, Senator. I'm damn good. My record is 120 wins, 0 losses. I don't want for you to be the one to ruin both my record and reputation."

"Ala___"

Interrupting the senator's words, I lean into him and place my finger to his lips.

"You know what I think, Senator?" I lean in to whisper in his ear.

He looks up to me and responds, "Yes."

"I think that you're a selfish, low life, son of a bitch! My job is not to care about you as a person, but I want to let you know that your behavior is disgusting. You disgust me."

"Ala___"

"I'm not done." I face him eye to eye, and place my hand on my hips.

"You have a beautiful wife. She is a lovely woman who loves you…a queen who supports you from your nasty ass to the goodness you do. She loves you! And look what you do. You go and put your life and your reputation and your family on the line for some pussy. That's right, Senator. My career, your wife's happiness, your family, and not to mention you're one of a handful of black senators in congress, and you put all of us on the line for some pussy. Pussy!"

"Listen…"

"No, *you* listen, Senator. Repeat after me. I."

His head jerks and his eyebrows rise, but he repeats "I."

"Put."

"Put." He rolls his eyes.

"My."

"My."

"Life on the line."

"Life on the line."

"For."

"For."

"Some pussy."

"Some pussy."

"Now, Senator, doesn't that feel better? You admitted you're a self-serving, arrogant bastard. Now, while morally you disgust me, I'm still your attorney and I will fight like hell to clear your name. I need your help. None of this makes any sense. What are you not telling me? You're going to jail for life unless you tell me something useful."

Senator Hunter reaches into his jacket pocket and pulls out an envelope and hands it to me. At first I hesitate to take it, but when I try to pry it open he interrupts me.

"No, Alana, don't open it here," he says in a pleading voice. "When you get home, watch it. The person who killed the intern is on here committing the murder."

Now my head jerks, and I stand slowly. My eyes light up like the light of the sun.

"I have a hidden motion-sensitive video camera in my office." He almost smiled, but he stopped himself and it's a good thing. I would have killed the freak, myself.

"I know that's hard for me to say and for you to take seriously. But, please, watch this when you get home. Your reputation will not be ruined. This will prove it. The whole tape will ruin me, though. It will ruin my life, it will ruin my wife, my family and all those who believed in me. I don't deserve anything else after all this commotion. I've caused enough trouble and maybe drove people to come after me because of my arrogance. Here's your evidence. Alana, I know I need to get my life in order. Now…but…now…how will I help my wife after this?

Senator Hunter rises from his seat and walks to the door to my office. I stare at him in disbelief. He turns around.

"Alana, look at this when you get home."

"I will, Senator."

"Thank you."

I'm not sure I want him to give me thanks without being sure what I will see on this tape.

❧

I bypass a chance to see a man who I could love. I opted to take a car service home. The senator's words keep replaying in my mind. "Watch this when you get home." Placing my key into the lock on my front door, I turn the knob in a hurry, enter, and drop my briefcase on the floor. I enter the password on the alarm's keypad in a hurry.

I walk into the kitchen and pull a wine glass out of the china cabinet. My favorite sweet, red wine awaits me in the fridge as it has been on chill for a few days. I pop the cork, pour a glass and head to my bedroom…glass and the senator's envelope in tow.

I kick my heels off and place the envelope on the bed, setting the glass of liquid love on my marble nightstand. Peeling off the layers of clothing that kept me confined in many ways today, I exhale a puff of laughter after I reminisce for a split second about the day's events. From being caught in the middle of an imagined love affair between opposing counsel and myself, to defending one of the most admired and well-known, African American politicians in the country, to everything else in between has me internally conflicted, anxious, mad, and a bit giddy all at the same time.

The remote to my surround sound system sits on my nightstand and I hit the power button. Pre-selected CDs commence and first up is Coltrane. I need him now.

As I slip on my chemise and robe, my pretty red toes slide into soft, pink, fuzzy slippers. I grab the envelope the senator gave me and empty the contents in a hurry.

Placing the DVD into the player, I press play and then stop, immediately.

Damn.

I can't do what Al's office did to me by trying to conceal evidence. It's only fair that Al views this video also. If nothing else, I respect the rule of law and abide by it every time. Conflicted, yet remaining true to my oath, I decide to call Alphonso.

The bastard.

Damn, I love him.

I can feel the butterflies inside me. A smile covers my face. Embarrassed, I look at myself in my bedroom's mirror. Running my fingers through my hair, I feel hot just thinking about hearing his voice. I wondered how it would be if we took a step to see if this was really going to be something. He makes me...so.

I take a seat on my bed, and cross my legs. I watch my toes dangle and my leg sways side to side as I wait for Alphonso to answer the phone.

"Thank you for calling. At the tone, please leave your name and number and I'll get back to you at my earliest convenience."

Damn, I want to cry.

"Uhm, Alphonso, this is Alana…Alana Carrington…"

"Hello?"

"Hi, oh, Alphonso, is that you?"

"Yes, this is Al. Alana, wow, I'm so glad I caught the call. I was just heading to the shower."

Lord, have mercy.

"Alphonso."

"Call me, Al."

"Al, I have some new evidence in the case. I just received it today. Is it possible for to come to my place? It is something I believe you should see. I have not viewed it yet, myself."

"You just got it today, huh?"

"Yes, Al. I don't play dirty tricks like the D.A.'s office."

"Yeah…about that, Alana. I want to apologize about a lot of things that I don't have control of."

"No need, Al. I live on Cambridge Court in the Hills, number 777."

"I'll be there in thirty minutes."

"Thank you. And sorry for the late night call."

"No apology necessary."

❦

Alphonso said he'll be here in thirty minutes, which makes me think I need to shower. I've been working all day and I don't want the poor man to think I'm not serious about my hygiene. Funny, all the nervousness that occupied my soul just moments ago has fled from my psyche. I can't even tap into it if I wanted to. It's amazing how the mind works.

Removing all my clothes, I run the shower. It will be brief. I just want to freshen up a bit. Warm Vanilla and brown sugar body wash covers every part of me as hot beads of water make acquaintance with my flesh. My loofah criss-crosses over honey-coated skin, and then I rinse.

My longing transcends into that galaxy of the unknown, in my sleep, my walking daydream and night fantasy, where my dreams reveal all of my life's fears and desires, and he represents an equal part of both. Thoughts of him travel with me throughout my day, and I often take him to places he shouldn't dare go. I'm ashamed of where's he's been in my world…on my list of life's goals and priorities. In my dreams, he yet remains. He has effortlessly and deliberately become a permanent fixture in my fantasy and reality.

The two of them often collide.

Stepping out of the shower, I quickly dry off with an oversized peach-colored towel. I laid out a pair of leggings and a t-shirt and placed it alongside the back of my chaise lounge that sits in my bedroom. Peach must be the in color for me today. I throw on my peach and black chemise and robe as I exit the bathroom. I tie the belt around my waist and proceed to my bed. My fingers run through my hair and I fluff it just a bit to give it life.

The doorbell rings and the panic that exited my life earlier reappears in full force.

He can't be here already. Oh, my goodness!

Rushing down the stairs, my pink slippers are moving way faster than my body, and I almost lose my way on the last step. My eyes peer down to my legs…my…legs…oh no, I'm still in this robe and nighty. I'll find a way to explain this. I mean, I don't want him to wait outside my door.

I make my way to the front door and peek outside to make sure it's him. It is. Opening the door, I feel a rush of blood go through my body and my heart is racing so fast. I maintain my cool as I open the door.

"Thank you, Al, for coming over."

A wide smile covers his face and he checks me out from head to toe.

"Wow, you look beautiful, Alana."

"Oh, I'm sorry, Al. I…just…got out of the shower. Oh, never mind."

"Ha, ha, ha. It's okay. I understand."

"I'll change into my leggings and t-shirt as soon as I get upstairs. I promise. You got here a few minutes early."

"I know. I tried to pace myself. I was anxious to see you, I suppose."

He moves in closer to me. I smell him. His eyes tell me everything I want to know. I feel his spirit trying to become one with mine. The tension is real. It's powerful. It's undeniable. Oooh, I want to kiss him. I turn around and walk instead. I'm so embarrassed about being undressed. I make my way to the stairs, but before proceeding, I ask him, "Al, would you like something to drink?"

"Sure."

"What would you like, Al?"

"Whatever you want to give me, Alana."

A sly smile crosses my face. "Follow me to the kitchen."

He does. He follows. I lead. I feel him watching me. He's noticing every curve. I try not to bounce as I walk. I'm scared to turn around. I turn around anyway. Looking to my left, my hair runs alongside my shoulder, and I ask him, "How was the drive over?"

He smiles. He's not interested in small talk.

"Good."

We make our way to the kitchen. I pull a glass from the china cabinet.

"Red wine, Al? Milk? Tea? Soda? Water?"

He moves closer to me…almost standing directly behind me. I exhale. I move away. He comes closer behind me. Leans in. Inhales the scent of my hair.

"You smell so good, Alana."

"Thank you, Al."

"Wine?" I ask as I hand him the glass.

"Yes, please."

I pour and he smiles.

"The tape is upstairs in my bedroom. I started to watch and immediately paused it to call you."

"Okay. I'm ready."

"Great, follow me."

"My pleasure."

Carefully, I climb the stairs and we enter my bedroom together. I grab the remote and push play.

"Al, take off your coat; make yourself comfortable. You can sit anywhere you want."

"I'll take the chair."

"Sure."

I sit on the edge of the bed.

The screen is dark, and after a few seconds, we see Senator Hunter in his office. From looking at the windows behind him, it's dark...very dark. It's safe to assume it's night time. The senator is naked and so is...the intern. Wow! She appeared. The senator has her on her back on the desk in his office. Oh, my!

Glancing over to Al, I look for his reaction. He's still. Quiet. Attentive.

Senator Hunter spreads the intern's legs wide open and begins fallacio. She's enjoying every second of it. His head moves into her as his tongue enters her so deeply and her body convulses each time. Her moans get louder and louder with every lick. My heart races.

The intern grabs the senator's head, she pulls him deep into her and her legs shake uncontrollably. He then smacks her thigh. Wow. My peripheral sneaks a peek at Al. I don't want to look at him. He's quiet. Still very calm. Silent. He crosses his leg.

The senator grabs his erection, strokes it slightly with his hand and enters the intern. Long, slow, deep strokes he gives her. She is going wild. There is definite sexual chemistry between these two.

Wrong, dead wrong, but I can see how the two of them would think this is so right.

I must break the tension.

"Al, I had no idea what this tape had on it."

"I, uhm, I understand. Maybe it's something we need to see."

"Right."

The senator ejaculates all over the intern's pussy and the sounds they both make are enough to wake this entire block I live on. I exhale under my breath so Al doesn't notice. He takes a long sip of the wine I poured for him earlier. He has been crossing his legs and uncrossing them. I noticed.

The senator gets dressed, kisses the intern on her lips and leaves his office. Slowly, she makes her way off the senator's desk, and heads for the sofa. She sits and I guess she didn't get enough. She spreads her leg and starts to rub her clit. She is groaning and grinding. I only need a quick second of this going into my eyes. I'm watching Al. He is immersed in the action. I like it. The intern cums again, and after a few minutes she starts to put her clothes on.

The door to the senator's office opens. He must have left something.

Wait.

Wait a damn minute.

Is that?

"Damn, that's Todd Shumaker," Al shouts and rises to his feet.

"Oh, my!" I say aloud and move closer to the TV.

Al walks toward me and moves in close.

I look at Al. "I can't believe this."

"You've got to be fucking kidding me," Al says as he places his hand on his hip. "Got damn Todd Shumaker," he yells. My eyes glance over his body, and although this is not the time, I see up close and personal that he is built like a well-oiled machine. Six-foot-three in height, I'm guessing. He has to be about two hundred and thirty pounds. He's like a god. And, I'm like a worshipper.

I face the TV again.

The intern turns around and is startled by Shumaker.

"What are you doing here and who are you?" she yells in fear.

"Shut up, bitch," Shumaker tells her and pulls a knife out from behind his back.

Shumaker stabs the intern, repeatedly, in her side and her stomach.

The image startles me.

I sit back on the bed. I'm scared. This is horrible. I run into my bathroom and close the door. A certain amount of panic sets in from watching a murder. It's one thing to defend someone and totally different to watch it.

Al knocks on the door and I come out with my head down. He takes my hand and leads me to sit on the bed next to him. He puts his arms around me. I lean into his chest.

"It's okay, Alana."

Holding onto him for dear life, I don't think about letting go.

"It's okay, baby."

I remove myself slightly from his grasp and look up to him. "Al, please believe me. I just got this tape today."

"I believe you, baby."

"Sorry that frightened me so."

"It's scary, Alana. I'm here. Hold me."

I hold him tighter. He grabs me, hard, strong and with force. He makes sure I feel safe in his arms.

"If you were my wife, I would never do this to you. You're too precious, Alana."

With tears in my eyes, I look at Al. I don't say a word. I just look at him.

Taking his right hand, he grabs my chin softly and pulls my face close to his.

"Please let me kiss you, Alana. That's all I need. I promise."

"Al…"

"Please, baby."

"Al…this is not right."

"Baby, this is all that matters."

"Al…"

"Kiss me. Kiss me, now, Alana."

My lips part and Al's tongue enters. It's wet. It's sweet. It's good. I lick it. I suck it. I love it. I bite his bottom lip.

"Mmmm," he moans. He moans loud. It turns me on. My nipples harden.

"You're all I need, Alana."

Grabbing my face, he kisses it. My cheeks. He kisses my nose. My lips again. He licks my lips. Licks my neck. Bites my neck.

"Damn, I've been dreaming about this for so fucking long, girl."

Al gently removes my robe, loosening the belt with one hand while holding onto my body with the other.

"Al, this is moving too fast."

"Baby, let me just look at you. Damn. Please. Let me just look at you."

His tongue enters my mouth once again. Our tongues dance with the devil. His moans get louder and so do mine.

"You're so fucking beautiful, baby."

"Maybe you should go, Al. This is out of our control."

"No, baby. I think I'm going to stay."

"Al."

"Do you want me to leave, Alana?"

"No."

Alphonso Ibari
Forever. For Always. For Love.

Our solaced spirits emanate earth-shattering harmony.

As I sit here, the midnight clear greets me in desperation, yearning for penetration as my right hand presses against the chocolate-coated staff that beats and pulsates in anticipation of her. From her toffee-colored, rich, butter soft, butterscotch skin, to the flowing brown hair that shines and cascades, framing a face that the gods took extra time to create, to her deep-pitted dimple in her right cheek, to her radiant smile, this woman has everything I've ever prayed for. I have scoped, watched and jocked her physical existence for quite some time, but she's been in my soul, in my thoughts and dreams, a part of my nightly talks with God, for as far back as I can remember. I'm almost ashamed of how long I've wanted Alana. Well before I even knew her name.

She walks away and I grab her arm, pulling her near me. There's no way in hell I'm losing her. No way. Alana turns around and faces me. I can see terror in her eyes. Her spirit is full of lust. The smell of her flesh getting hot fuels my desire and rage and love and lust for her. I smell her pussy getting hot. I need to eat it. I need to taste it.

"Al…this doesn't make any sense. This is not how this is supposed to go."

"Do you love me, Alana?"

She hesitates and walks away. She's heated. Mad, happy, confused, attracted, she's delirious; I can see it in her eyes. She's walking like there's a flood, like rain and hail and wind and a tornado are between her legs in that nasty, wet, delicious cave that belongs to me.

I walk up behind her. Her body trembles. She grabs the first thing before her—the arm of her chaise lounge. I pull her body to me. I know she can feel me, feel this staff, this rod. It's harder than the Rock of Gibraltar and has her name written all over it, etched in eternity. It's hers and she doesn't even know it. I belong to her.

"Alana. I know you love me. Because I fucking love you." I kiss the back of her neck. Her body melts in my arms. I kiss it once more and then make my way to the back of her ear, kissing and sucking the lobe before I whisper in her ear, "I love you. I've loved you. I fucking love you. You get that?" Pulling her closer to me, I press my length against her ass. Grabbing her waist, my hand travels to her breasts and I gently run my fingertips over her nipples. They're at attention, needing and wanting my attention.

"You hurt me, Al." She pleads.

Grabbing her forcefully, I plead my own damn case before her. She is my judge and jury and I need her pardon. I need her to forgive me.

"Baby, you know I didn't mean it. I would never, ever, ever hurt you on purpose. You understand that?"

She turns away.

I grab her face and turn her toward me.

"You hear me?"

With tears in her eyes, she replies, "Yes."

She's so sweet and beautiful and angelic as her eyes well with emotion. That emotion is meant for me. She's turning me into mush…into a man I don't even recognize. She's got my heart on lock.

She's angered and then cooled. She's conjured up this fire down in my soul and only she can quench the thirst that she has caused. I'm not thinking straight…not properly. I want what I want, and I have to have what I need, and that's her.

With my left hand, I remove her gown and toss it on the floor. Just as I had assumed, she was naked underneath it. Her silky skin smells so good. My hand travels down to her sweet, wet, cave. I place my hand over it and feel the heat rising.

"Al." She barely has the strength to fight me back. She whispers, "Al, I…"

Biting her bottom lip, I prevent her from saying another word. My pants hit the floor and I remove my sweater.

Sweeping her off her feet, I rapidly carry her to the bed and lay her down. My mouth finds its way to her sugar walls and I take in a mouth full, biting her clit in the process and she yells in ecstasy, "Al, please…"

Big, juicy lips…

Moving up to her face, I taste her lips, tongue kissing her like my life depends on it, and at this moment I feel that it does.

My life depends on this moment.

Taking my fingers, I place them into her love, vigorously, I move them around into her goodness until they become saturated with her luscious liquid; her juices cover them. I bring them to my mouth, taste them, suck them, put them into her mouth and watch as she licks them.

I hear her let out the most tantalizing moan I've ever heard in my life.

I can't take it any longer. With one thrust, I'm inside her. I cry out. She cries out. Damn, my baby is so sultry…searing, scorching and sweltering with lust and love.I can't believe that I am inside of my baby. I thought I'd lost her forever after that grilling over the case. I can see her nipples getting harder right before my eyes. As her body shudders, I go deeper.

Hearing her sensual sounds of pleasure makes me try harder than Avis.

"Tell me I'm not your man, Alana! You can't, can you? You better not ever tell me I'm not your man."

An unfamiliar feeling runs through my being. The magnitude of this moment takes over me. I hold her tight as I somehow climb higher and dig deeper. She's so wet and so soft that I feel her walls of comfort give way to each of my blows. Our solaced spirits emanate earth-shattering harmony—a melodious blend of worship and devotion as I rise to depths unbeknownst to mankind. Having my share of sex in abundance, I've done this plenty of times, but I realize now that this is the first time I've ever truly made love. I'm making love to my baby, my woman, my future, my wife.

"You are my man, baby!" She yells.

Damn, I'm ready to explode. I'm in so deep it's up to my waist.

Kissing her forehead, kissing her nose and her cheek, she grabs me and pulls me into a passionate kiss. She gives me her tongue. Ooooh, it's so wet and hot and juicy and nasty and perfect; it's mine…all mine. I suck it. I love it. We lick one another's tongues until they land in the other's mouth.

Taking my shaft into my hands, the chocolate rod shines from my baby's desire for me. I give it to her again…pull it out…tell her "Look at what you've done to me." I bite my lips. Reaching down, I lick her breasts. Kiss her. Lick her. I pull out again. She cries, "Al, please."

I tell her, "Look at how wet you got me." I thrust harder inside of her. About to lose my goddamn mind. In and out, out and in, my strokes are full of force and rage. I hear her cries. I feel my blood boiling. I suck her breasts.

Coercing me into demanding confirmation, my lust and love is fueled for and by my lady and overwhelms me. It has me struggling with rhyme and reason.

As Alana's warmth turns to heat, her wetness drowns me so good…devours me…takes me to a place that I don't recognize, but I love it. I love her…everything about her. She has her legs wrapped around me so tight, pulling me in deeper and deeper. Taking her mouth into mine, as if on cue and with so much determination, makes my heart race faster. My emotions climb and my feelings for her grow more and more with each stroke.

Unfeigned love empowers me as I stroke her with every inch of my body. Powerful, blunt force impacts take me to deeper plains.

Making love to her face-to–face, mouth-to-mouth and soul-to-soul becomes too much for me.

Alana's so sexy and sweet that I feel myself spiraling into a cosmic free-fall of intoxication. My head spins and the air in the room seems thin. Sweat runs down my head and I'm dizzy. My body jerks.I try to pull out.I can't. I won't. She refuses to let me break free. Sugar walls clutch on to me, grasp me tight, hold me captive, seize the movements and paralyze the moment.

Slowing down with my thrusts and my strokes, I need to rest in all this deliciousness. Needing to love her, I want this to go on for hours. I need to be inside of Alana for as long as I can. Nothing else in my life makes sense anymore, aside from me loving her, making love to her and giving her all the love that she's deserved for so long.

I owe this to her.

She is going to get every piece of this loving that belongs to her.

All of this dick is for her tonight.

Forever. For always. For Love.

Alana Carrington
Damn You

The walls of my righteousness grab hold of him.

The touch of his chocolate hands on my skin makes me quiver, and my body fills with intense anticipation of what's to come. Slow motion sets in, and it is still the touch of his hands that has me dizzy and dying…deliberately desiring all that he wants to offer. Hands glide across my waist. Strong and mighty strokes escape him and massage so deep. His rhythm penetrates deep down into my soul. His fingertips land on the small of my back…forces my walls to clinch and release syrupy sweet juices that flow from my love to his length and then to my sheets. Cosmic waves of lust shoot from my mind, where every erotic adventure begins, and they soar to my hardened nipples and finally land in the valley where want and need will collide and combine. His hands on my skin, I get it. He repeats it softly and gently into my ear as he nibbles on my earlobe. The touch of his hands.

"Right there?"

"Oooh, right there, baby."

"Damn, Alana, I love to give it to you right there."

"Baby, don't stop. Keep it right there. Oooh, baby, right there."

"I swear, I'm gonna keep stroking you right there. Shit."

"Goddamn, you better not stop, Al."

"No way in hell I'm ever leaving this sweet pussy, baby."

"Damn you, Al."

"I love you, too, baby."

So incredibly ashamed about the way I've freaked. Shedding my innocence in such a manner is wrong on every level imaginable, but right now I feel like this is exactly where I'm supposed to be—with the love of my life I never knew existed.

I had only dreamed of being in this time and space where wonder and reason and rhyme would allow me to be so free. And as I enthusiastically enjoy the mighty strength of his power, I anxiously anticipate the next course on this menu of decadence. I remember the time when having his hands on my skin was a distant and far reaching dream.

How we ended up here was inevitable as the chemistry between the two of us was too powerful to ignore. Undeniable in nature and loving in intention, it was meant to happen—me being here with him and him talking that sweet shit I love to hear.

Pulling back, his love escapes me and he withdraws.

I will kill him dead if he doesn't give me that dick.

"I have to eat your pussy. It looks so good," he tells me as he moves closer.

Bending to his knees, he dives head first. His fingers enter me and wiggle inside my slick, hot, wet cave. His tongue lands gently on my clit where he licks light, gentle licks. The teasing of his tongue makes my pussy gush and I'm a hot, wet mess. His strong hands spread my legs far and wide across continents until he gets to the epicenter of his journey—my sugar walls. He inhales me.

"You smell so good," he says as he licks my inner walls.

Tongue fucking me, he inserts on rhythm, which forces orgasmic waves and makes my pelvis flip. I squirt; I didn't mean to, but I had no choice.

"That's right, baby, come all over my face. Don't be shy."

He kisses my lips and continues to lick and now I'm crazy.

"Please, fuck me Al," I beg, grabbing his head.

"How bad do you want it?

"So fucking bad, please, Al. Please fuck me now."

As he rises, I see his manhood is still hard as the rock of Gibraltar. He points straight forward, on a quest to justify my love.

"How do you want it?" he questions.

"Any way you want to give it to me, Al, please."

As he leans over me, his sweet, slick tongue slithers over my ripe, hard Tootsie-roll nipples. He sucks them hard, and fast. And as he lies on top of me, I smell my cave on his lips and it turns me on. With one thrust he's in, and his love fills me up. He's all I want and need.

"Ooooh," we both cry out in passion.

He digs deep and slow, plowing inside as if he's making hip hop beats. He gets deeper…a greedy lover who delves deeper and deeper with each powerful blow.

"You feel so good, Al," I cry out.

"Your pussy is so juicy and sweet. I've wanted this for so fucking long."

"I've wanted to give this to you so bad."

As he rocks and rolls me, he licks my lips. I taste my pussy and the sweetness of his breath. Sweat covers my breasts and if he spreads my legs any further....

"Shit, Al, that's it, baby," I yell as I bust.

"That's a good girl; come all over me. I love it," he whispers in my ear as he goes deeper.

"I've wanted to fuck this pussy. Lick it. love it. I've wanted to spank it and empty myself inside of it for so damn long," he cries out as the walls of my righteousness grab hold of him.

"I can't hold it any longer, Alana."

"Hold it, Al," I pout.

"I can't. It's too good, baby."

"Please, Al," I cry.

The Morning After…

Sunlight is dancing slowly and softly through love's window pane. I blink and blink again and see the sunrise. My bed is unusually warm. I feel secure. Safe. Wait, I'm in his arms…in his embrace. He hugs me. He won't let me go. I think he's still sleeping. I try to get out of bed, but he spoons me more. I lean into his chest. I smile.

"I feel you smiling," he tells me.

"Wow." I smile harder.

"How are you feeling this morning, baby?"

"I feel good, Al. Confused. Embarrassed. Elated. Good," I tell him as he inhales the scent of my hair.

"I feel good, too."

Al releases his embrace and makes his way to my bathroom.

He comes out and smiles. Wow, he is incredibly beautiful. I just stare at him. I simply lay here and stare.

"You're gorgeous, you know that, Alana?"

"No, Al, I didn't know."

"Well, I'm happy to be the one to tell you. What do you want for breakfast?" He walks over to me and gently kisses my lips.

"You," I reply with a coy smile.

"You got it, my love. Listen, Alana, I'm going to take care of this Senator Hunter situation. His image will remain intact and the D.A.'s office will know that Shumaker murdered that poor girl. As a matter of fact, the police should be on their way now to arrest him. I even alerted the news stations."

"Shouldn't you be in New York, then, Al?"

"No, I think I'll lay low for a moment until some of the smoke clears."

"Understood."

"Besides, I need to start this next chapter of my life in the arms of the woman I love."

Tears fill my eyes once again. I swallow hard.

"Al...."

"Alana, don't fight this any longer."

"Okay."

"Besides, they can't get away with messing with my woman." He laughs.

I smile.

"Now bring your sweet ass downstairs and tell me what you want for breakfast, woman."

Learn more about the dynamic storytellers of
Pillow Talk in the Heat of the Night
at www.pillowtalkduets.com

Elissa Gabrielle & Rory D. Sheriff

Lorraine Elzia & K. Roland Williams

Carla Pennington & Kenneth Alan Campbell

Niyah Moore & Stacey L. Moor

LaLaina Knowles & Marc Lacy

Ebonee Monique & Torrian Ferguson

Renee Daniel Flagler & Alvin L.A. Horn

9 780985 076375